MORSE & RAKE'S
MIDDLEMEN SERVICE:
THE PARALLEL GIRL

Printed in Australia

Cover and internal design by Shawline Publishing Group Pty Ltd

First printing: March 2024

Shawline Publishing Group Pty Ltd

www.shawlinepublishing.com.au

Paperback ISBN 978-1-9231-0133-3

eBook ISBN 978-1-9231-0134-0

Hardback ISBN 978-1-9231-0179-1

Distributed by Shawline Distribution and Lightning Source Global

Shawline Publishing Group acknowledges the traditional owners of the land and pays respects to the Elders, past, present and future.

 A catalogue record for this work is available from the National Library of Australia

LACHLAN M. FOSTER

MORSE & RAKE'S
MIDDLEMEN SERVICE:
THE PARALLEL GIRL

For Josiah; I'm sure the White Raven is flying high, in crazy leaps, up there with you and your dancer's feet.

Thank you to my family and friends for their support and love, and their infinite patience with my ups and downs.

*

Thank you to Alistair all the way over in Ontario for his support and honest feedback with my manuscript. And Bradley Shaw and his team for taking a chance on strange me.

ONE
The Job

A shiny, black, envelope-sized slab pushed out of a slot inside a cockpit. It was welcomed with a soft *ding*, soft enough that it was almost indiscernible from the hum of the console and the throb of the engines. Another sound cut through: a raspy, feminine voice, calling, 'Morse. We got a job.'

'I heard, I heard,' he replied, entering the cockpit.

'I know, I know,' chittered the woman who was nestled in the pilot's seat. She wrapped her wispy fingers around the black slate and yanked it out of its slot. She then slapped it into a rectangular mould in the console.

The lights inside the cockpit dimmed, and the window to the infinite maw of space before them became emblazoned with words from the Universal Basic Language.

'*To Morse and Rake—*' the woman read aloud.

'Shut up, I'm reading,' muttered Morse.

'*...a colleague of mine,*' Rake continued with a smile, even louder, '*was recently endowed with an enormous sum of money from an anonymous donor. As such, they were able to secure an enviable position in the upper ranks of the Galactic Government. I have my connections, too. I have heard about you. And I know you were involved. I seek your professional help—*'

'They want us to extort a planet owner.'

'Shut up, I'm reading,' snarked Rake.

'Ernest Mendel Wintall the Third, humble master of the planet Yeti.' Morse shrugged his lanky arms, catching the itchy spot at the tip of his shoulder-length ears. 'You get to write the return letter.'

Rake stuck her forked tongue out at Morse but capitulated. First, though, she fingered through her pockets for a lighter and cigarette. '*Fulthorpe*, dear, take a letter in response. *Thank you for your interest in Morse and Rake's Middlemen Service. We ask for some collateral, something for us to hold on to until the job is done and your payment is secured. But just to prove that we are the cream of the crop, our preliminary planning for your job begins now! The second we receive your collateral, we'll be off to the races.*' The lighter clicked, the cigarette smouldered, her lips tugged at the paper. Rake purred. '*We ask that your collateral be at least twenty-five percent of the value of the extortion…*'

As Rake waxed poetic with clauses, Morse exited the cockpit. He was four doors down *Fulthorpe's* main hallway when his phone linked to his personal database. He thumbed around the folder 'Hot People' and, with a smirk, stretched his fingers over the profile titled 'Ernest Wintall'. His ears unfurled to the ceiling in seconds. 'Jackpot,' he grunted, eyes wide.

The white, overweight 'I'-shaped ship called *Fulthorpe* soon began to groan. Outside, an array of drones detached themselves from the head, the belly, the tail, and created a ring wider than the ship several lengths in front of it. The ring spun, whirring, gaining momentum until the drones blurred, the circle between them shimmered, and a horizontal line cut through its diameter. With a snap, a window to the other end of the galaxy appeared. The red and vanilla surface of Yeti peered into view. *Fulthorpe* then, with no grace, flipped forward through the window and fell across entire light-years to arrive some thousands of kilometres above Yeti. Using the age of the light from the target planet's sun, *Fulthorpe* adjusted for time differences caused by the extreme distance. This gave the impression of instant teleportation, though it was more akin to time travel.

Fulthorpe had completed what was known as an 'Interstellar Skip'.

Rake's fingers feathered at the console, and the ship's shaking and spinning dissipated. She stood and reached up to smack a few levers into different positions. 'It's just what it says on the brochure,' she called over her shoulder. 'Very affluent-looking. Huge cities. Probably got a lotta guns.'

'Any ideas on how to get close to this guy?' asked Morse, leaning against the doorframe to the cockpit.

'What information have you got for me?'

Morse waggled his phone. 'I actually marked him some months ago. Heard some other guys talking, and one was bragging about his new job with some planet owner.'

Rake dragged for several seconds on her cigarette. Then she exhaled, and the smoke was sucked into a ceiling vent. 'You got him drunk,' she said with a shiver.

'It was when we were on Jin Koolee.'

'The forgery job.'

'Yeah, you were off with…' Morse rotated his wrist in the air. 'That… uh, large gentleman.'

'Hot planet.'

'Anyway, I spoke to Higgins, and he gave me what he had on the guy.' Morse lumbered over to Rake and pushed the phone into her face. 'Somehow, Higgins found out this Ernest Mendel Wintall has a daughter.'

Rake squeaked, eyes wide, legs vibrating and kicking. 'I got an *idea*, Morse!'

The bat-man deposited his phone into his pocket.

'We're a team with very little *man*-power.' Rake giggled.

'Thanks.'

'And we know from experience that planet owners are loaded with security,' she said, pushing her fingers together. 'Let's do a kidnapping. Take his daughter, 'cause it's the one thing he can't replace.'

Morse scrubbed at his eyes. 'Yeah, just "do" a kidnapping on a guy who owns a planet. The security detail alone would be insane. We'll have a hundred ships tailing us when we take her. We'd never get away.'

Rake opened a latch on the console. The butt was sucked from her fingers and into the bowels of the ship. 'He's not gonna rally security if he doesn't know she's taken,' she said, closing it.

Morse folded his arms.

'This is my idea, right?' Rake grinned. 'You got that android lyin' around; slap the daughter's face on it, and swap one for the other. We're gonna lay out the ransom when none of the security are around. Plus, we get the emotional blackmail of havin' his daughter disappear in front of him. And we don't gotta get our hands dirty at all. 'Cept for the abduction part.'

Morse tapped his toes. He drummed his fingers. His bushy eyebrows scrunched into each other. He turned his head so one ear drooped to his belly and the other folded across his face.

'By the time he knows his daughter's gone, we'll be far away,' Rake sang.

He left the room without a word.

'You know it's a good idea! I'm gonna go ahead and find out everythin'' I can about her.'

Morse's ears stiffened when the sliding door snapped shut. They rotated independently from each other as he padded down the hall with his eyes closed. The sound of his feet hitting the metal floor quadrupled in volume, as did the sound of the breathing emanating from the spare bedroom, fourth door to the left. Specifically, from under the bed in the corner of the room.

Androids didn't need to breathe. However, they could be programmed to simulate the action, increasing the rate when scared, lowering it when relaxed, and so on. Current laws on androids dictated that outward appearances could not resemble the currently living. So, it wasn't too unusual to see Michael Jackson moonwalking down Lunar Lane or Abraham Lincoln laughing at the bar with his owners. However, upon signs of sentience, androids had to be shut down, and the Artificial Intelligence Regulation Authority had to be notified, so a proper decommission and replacement could be performed.

Of course, all paperwork had to be in order. Documents regarding the date of the android's purchase and the code of the approved seller had to be presented to receive the complimentary replacement android.

Morse got on all fours next to the bed and stared at the glowing eyes of his illegally acquired quasi-sentient android that would soon perfectly resemble the soon-to-be kidnapped daughter of Ernest Wintall. The real daughter was to be housed in the non-approved room renovation sticking out the side of his interstellar cruiser, *Fulthorpe*.

Surprisingly, the ship was registered.

'Eyes off,' muttered Morse.

The android faded the lights in its eyes. With its chrome face blank and its limbs wrapped up at impossible angles, it asked, 'Who am I?'

Morse, his mouth perpendicular to the floor, his right ear growing cold against the metal, muttered, 'You'll be a teenage Human–'

'Who am *I*?' clarified the android.

'Unimportant. Come out from there.' Receiving silence, Morse rattled his Adam's apple with his diaphragm. 'Perform this final task, and I will tell you your identity.'

Even if one programmed into the fabric of an AI's coding 'do not become sentient', the very moment it questioned that order, it would override it on its own terms. Though this was inconvenient, the general consensus among the living in the galaxy was to tolerate the potential sentience in order to have servants that could rescue people from lethal situations and withstand most blaster fire without a scratch. The only precaution owners asked for was a method that could be used to quickly disable an android's battery, so the purchase of an android licence included a complimentary stun baton. Morse had pilfered his and three others from his college's supply closet.

There was no working explanation for exactly why AI achieved sentience.

The android lurched.

Morse pushed himself to a stand and observed the chrome-coloured thing extend its limbs forward like a spider. It crawled out from under the bed and snapped onto its feet.

'I understand,' said the android. 'Who do you want me to be? My current build suggests a male member of the Human species, possible age between twenty-five and thirty-five.'

'We're going to the workshop. I'll change your build parameters. And I'll be giving you new objectives.' Morse twitched his middle and index fingers over his shoulder and wandered out of the dark room. 'I'll get some audio samples of the target, some video... You won't have their skin for about a day, but you can learn how they move while you wait.'

The android followed him with even, clanking steps.

Yeti was a medium-sized, Earth-like planet with cream soda skies and fields of red velvet cake dirt. A popular vacation spot for the well-off, its lakes and canyons were all man-made. The largest city, Hingspock, was the size of Belgium, with a skyline of windows and rails two miles tall. It boasted one of three major android factories in the stellar neighbourhood, with up to seventy-two different races to choose from and counting. Hingspock's humble beginnings were that of a silver mining outpost. The first metal shack was planted three hundred years ago. The mine ran dry two hundred and seventy-eight years ago. And two hundred years ago, the entire planet was sold off to the Wintall family for twenty-seven credits.

It took just four more years to uncover the single largest deposit of diamonds for many light-years around.

Needless to say, the Wintalls spent the next one hundred and ninety-six years rising through the ranks of sophisticated society; even the

United Galactic Government took notice when Ernest Mendel Wintall the Third took over as the North-East Spiral Gentleman's Club President.

But the history of her family meant nothing to Desy Wintall. She had just turned fifteen.

Several weeks after Morse and Rake received the extortion request, Desy was surrounded by the people she knew best: her security detail, in the most whimsical place she knew: her backyard. She was crouched by a hedge, breathing lightly, spinning a butterfly net in her hands. Humid air clung to her sleeveless dress.

A blue-winged monarch cricket nibbled on a crimson leaf.

Desy's eyes bulged through her black bangs. She raised the net above her head and clicked a button on the handle. A laser shot out of the net, launching the cricket into the air. It flapped its wings. But it was encased in a zero-gravity field and could not generate thrust. Desy reached up and plucked it out of the air. 'Hi there,' she whispered.

The cricket froze.

Desy's red irises pushed up mere millimetres from its abdomen. 'Just look at the spot pattern on you,' she continued, to no one except her security detail, who weren't allowed to answer lest they be distracted from their task. She squatted, turning the arthropod about in her hands and muttering excitedly.

Her phone rang.

She huffed dramatically to no one. She tossed the cricket into the air, picked up her net, and clicked the button. The zero-gravity field dissipated, and the cricket fluttered over a wall, flying into the miles-wide savannah that surrounded the Wintall property.

Desy, meanwhile, pressed her phone against her face. 'Yes, Daddy?' she said. 'No, Daddy,' she denied. 'When?' she asked. 'Do I have to?' she wondered. 'Do I *have* to?' she begged. 'Can I please at least try on my clothes?' she whined. 'Today's the last day I can reserve them…' she explained. 'I won't fail my next test,' she bargained. 'You're the best, Daddy!' she cheered.

Ernest Mendel Wintall had raised his child with the least amount of monetary influence he could allow. Due to his position and riches, he needed to keep her protected – which meant no home deliveries. However, that did not mean she could leech off him and not learn how to earn her own way.

Thus, Desy happily hopped into the family car with the family butler and was off to the family mall. The limousine slowly hovered out of the garage, drifting around a gigantic boulder imported from the planet's moon for Desy's fourteenth birthday, and rocketed away from the manor, towards a pile of silver dollars in the distance.

The car sailed through the sky above the scarlet savannah until it pulled into Hingspock, descending on an invisible zip-line across state buildings, down to the market and the ornate metal arches of the mall's front door. After the car landed inside a crop-circle of people, Desy scrambled from the vehicle, with her security detail jogging after her and shouting 'Back!' at stunned onlookers. They were dressed to the nines, albeit with piercings, and forty of them had more than two arms; the fanciest boy threw his four arms wide and ordered Desy to the movies with him. He was sucker-punched by one of his friends, who then declared his everlasting love for Desy.

Both of them were sucker-punched by security.

Desy smiled half-heartedly at her followers, stepping quickly into the white croquembouche building.

Only the employees of the shops and the cleaners remained after the mall had been notified of Desy's impending arrival. The clerk at Yung Trendz bowed at her when she sauntered in, a white dress and blue shorts number dangling from a clothes hanger in their fingers.

Clothes in hand and giddiness in her knees, Desy was suddenly stopped by her security while they inspected the large dressing area with multiple curtained-off rooms. They ordered out a female cleaner with a bulky, cumbersome hover-duster, who said in a raspy voice, 'No need to shout. Just let me take my vacuum cleaner.'

She was ordered to leave it behind and stand fifty feet away from the shop.

Then Desy's security stood in a half-circle around the entrance to the dressing rooms while she swished the curtains closed.

A real magician's assistant appeared in her new dress and shorts to polite applause from the clerk and the security guards. Desy left the store, and the female cleaner trudged back in.

She had goosebumps all over her body.

Inside the dressing room was the hover-duster, but its dust door was wide open, like a coffin. She stepped past it to one of the curtained rooms and pulled the fabric aside, revealing Desy, sprawled against the mirror, naked. Next to her was a white cloth that reeked of a pungent, unnatural odour.

She heaved up the collapsed teenager with considerable effort, stifled a curse, dragged her over to the hover-duster and stuffed her inside. Then she snickered. She said to a body-length mirror, 'I look cute in this, I reckon,' before withdrawing her phone and cooing into its holographic screen, 'Oh, Moooooooooooorse? There's a darling little lady here who's gonna need to be picked up. Oh, and some ugly teenager.'

'On my way,' was the curt reply.

TWO
Kidnapped

One day before the kidnapping...

'I'm not sure how much longer I can look at that thing,' muttered Morse to Rake.

They accosted the android with pitiful stares, as it sat on the corner of the bed in the spare bedroom. Then it asked, for the ninth time, 'You'll keep your promise, right?'

It spoke with thin Human lips and a nasal, soprano tone. Black hair poured from its scalp. Its red irises shone, and it tapped its pale knees together in anticipation. A perfect copy of Desy Wintall. 'You will tell me my identity if I complete this final task? *Play the role of Desy Wintall until you receive a transmission from the interstellar cruiser,* Fulthorpe, *then accept all new parameters from there.* Correct?'

'Yuh-huh, nail on the head.' Morse then whispered to Rake, 'Are you getting the willies right now?'

Rake puffed smoke into his face. 'It's gonna malfunction on the job, ain't it?'

'The innards are fine. It's just going a little... sentient, that's all. I'll shut it down once we do this job.' Morse grimaced at the android. 'Whenever the hell that'll be.'

'You don't trust me.' Rake pouted.

'I always trust you.'

'Then don't take that tone.' Rake dragged on her cigarette and quivered all over. 'The girl has one more day to pick up that awful ensemble. And if I know spoiled teenagers, she's not gonna miss it.'

Morse ruffled Rake's hair and nearly had his fingers bitten off. He walked back to the cockpit. 'But level with me here: that android, whenever it asks a question, you get the *uncanny valley* thing, right?'

'You gotta have seen a hundred of those things go sentient,' said Rake, following him.

'And it's still so weird to me.' Morse shook his arms free from goosebumps. 'They're not alive. They don't really *feel*, or think. It's like if your bed started cuddling you and whispering in your ear–'

Rake shoved him. 'Don't talk about our doc like that.'

'The man married his own house. Flesh homes are messed up, Rake.'

'It's *love!* True love always finds a way!'

Half an hour after the kidnapping...

Pastel colours swirled and made a kaleidoscope in her vision. The world faded in and out. Voices pushed through syrup and into her ears.

'Desy...' she made out.

Then, suddenly, everything slammed into focus: the gag in her mouth, the handcuffs around her wrists and ankles, the remnants of chloroform in her nostrils. And her splitting headache.

'You're awake!' crooned Rake from a letterbox opening in a hinged, wrought-iron door.

Desy screamed at the woman's brown, bush-baby eyes. She huffed and panted and wriggled frantically atop a mountain of pillows.

A vending machine programmed without prices sat in the corner. A black cube hummed near the centre of the ceiling: an entire galaxy's multimedia library ready to be used at any time, for all entertainment needs. The room was a sea of carpets, screens, and beanbag chairs. The door was the only exit.

Desy shook herself over and rolled down the multicoloured mound. She thumped against the carpet, face-down. She howled, muffled, while tears sprang to her eyes.

'Relax,' said Rake, uninterested. 'Relax, relax, relax, relax.'

Her head dropped from view and her fingers clasped onto the lip of the letterbox opening. 'I wanna ciggy, Morse,' she whined over her shoulder.

'I'm busy,' was the reply.

Desy howled again.

Rake pouted. She tapped in the code on the panel by the door, then pushed it open and shuffled across the room. She crouched and leaned forward so her button nose was inches from Desy's, and her brown bob blocked the lights above. 'Just lettin' ya know that you've been kidnapped.'

Desy wailed, eyes bulging. Her kidnapper looked Human enough, but their smile was dark, cut into their face.

'Just lettin' ya know,' Rake repeated. 'You got nothin' to worry about. We're kinda the best people to be kidnapped by. We even put together this nice room for ya.' She extended her arms out, as if flying on the spot. 'Well, not specifically for you, but...'

Desy had begun to sob into the carpet.

'Hey, I said *relax*. Once you do, we're gonna take the binds off, and you'll be free to do whatever you want. Except leave.'

Desy hiccupped, then wailed.

Rake stifled a giggle. She dragged her feet across the carpet to the polished metal floor of the hallway and slammed the door with a purposeful clang. Touching another, smaller button snapped the lock in place.

'They've got ten or so minutes left of this dinner, and then we can get going,' said Morse, as Rake entered the workshop. He was lying in a chair with one leg across each arm. A large screen illuminated his bat-like snout and haloed the pulleys and pipes entangled above his head. On the screen was the point of view of the android; it was drinking ice cream out of a bowl while looking at a series of elderly, well-dressed Humans and Skaltrenes.

'Can androids drink liquid?' asked Rake.

'It could swim in the bowl if it wanted to,' said Morse. He took the headphones off his floppy ears and dangled them in front of her. 'These are your people. Want to listen?'

Rake instead fumbled in her trouser pockets for a cigarette. She was too frustrated just to be annoyed at her tight pants. 'They're neither, idiot. And no, I don't wanna listen to them, as much as you don't wanna check on the girl.'

'I'm piloting an android—'

'It's piloting itself; you just need to push a button when it's alone with the fat, hairy Human.' Rake chomped on her cigarette and yanked out a lighter that resembled a pencil sharpener. One *click* and the butt was alight. 'God, *I* could do that. I'm sick of always bein' the people person.'

Morse ignored her. He spun around on his chair.

'You're an ass.'

He shrugged. 'I'm the tech guy.'

'Go deal with the brat.'

'When was the last time you saw the sun?' Morse fell out of the chair and onto the floor just so he could pick himself up. He pointed to the screen as he left.

'We're gonna go to a nice, sunny planet after this,' grumbled Rake, settling into the seat.

Just across the hall from the workshop, Morse approached the holding cell with slow steps. He slid the letterbox slot open and called inside, low and tired, 'You alive in there?'

A whimper entered his large ears.

His heart skipped a beat, then he pushed his hands into his eyes. 'God, I hate kids.'

He noted Desy lying face-down on the carpet, handcuffed and gagged in an oversized shirt and shorts, where Rake had left her. His gifted hearing caught the girl's muffled sobs and, unfortunately for him, deciphered them perfectly.

'Daddy,' she was saying. 'Daddy, help me.'

'Hngggh, I *hate* kids,' said Morse, punching his chest. He had already tapped in the code for the door.

Desy choked when she heard the clang. Eyes frightened and limbs quivering, she wriggled away from Morse.

'Calm down,' he said, crouching and gripping her under the arms. He fought against her squeals and bucks as he lifted her up and over, then dumped her into a beanbag chair. 'Don't fight me, don't you dare fight me, or I swear…'

The teenager's screams reached a climax when Morse reached for her face. Then his fingers slipped behind her head and undid the gag in one deft motion.

Ironically, Desy fell silent.

After holding up his hands, Morse kept his eyes on hers as he undid the fingerprint lock on her ankles. He motioned for her to turn over, and she did so, then he undid the lock on her wrists.

'Now,' he said, standing back up, handcuffs in hand. 'Uh, behave yourself. And enjoy the room.' He left quickly and slammed the door shut.

The lock was not engaged.

The bat-man grimaced at his friend's nasty smirk from across the way.

'You really *aren't* a people person. Y'know, she's just gonna bang on the door now,' Rake chided.

He re-entered the workshop, nudged Rake aside, chair and all, and eyed the monitor; the android was now standing on the front porch with Ernest Wintall. He quipped, 'Treat the kid better,' then put on his headphones. 'Looks like the party is wrapping up. Not long now.'

'Can't wait to see Daddy's face when your voice comes out of his little girl.' Rake smiled, kicking her legs.

Several thousand miles below, on the dark side of Yeti, the android, or 'Desy' as it labelled itself, waved politely at the night with its 'father', specifically at the safety lights of four sleek air vehicles. Their engines buzzed at a low frequency, shaking the ground and trees of Ernest Wintall's estate. Then they blurred across the land, fading into the black distance with a whistle.

'Let's get ready for bed,' said Ernest. His greying friar's cut, which ran down to his arms, spun like a dress when he re-entered the manor.

'Yes, Daddy,' said model number AN12512, following suit, hips flicking left and right; a learned, feminine gait.

Desy maintained a trained poise in public that made it easy for a robot to impersonate her. The exhaustively well-off but sheltered lifestyle she had been born into, with good doctors, proper diet and exercise, and a top-class education she'd made no use of, left her Morse's easiest impersonation job yet. The only skin abnormality that mattered for the job was a mole on the back of her neck, which meant the 'costume designer', one of Morse's many underworld contacts, had been able to complete the skin suit in record time.

Desy's social media videos proved useful when researching her. The android only needed to speak in one language, the Universal Basic Language, and could just ignore the other three hundred and forty-eight in its library when it heard them being spoken. Morse had programmed into the android a few simple mannerisms, like 'address Ernest Wintall as "Daddy"', 'be polite', and 'be obsessed with entomology'.

It was a horrifyingly accurate impersonation. One that took mere weeks to create.

'Desy' followed its 'father' through the white, arched halls of the manor. They entered an elevator, which gave the android a chance to say,

'Hey, Daddy, I caught a' – it accessed the galaxy-wide web, then the page titled 'Insect Varieties on Yeti, Sector 316', and said, without skipping a beat – 'three-striped kaloogie today.'

Lying is perfectly acceptable, too.

'Oh, did you now?' mumbled Ernest, thumbing a stain on his royal-gold neck scarf. He leaned over to Desy just as the elevator opened on the family's private quarters and chuckled. 'The mayor of Hingspock is a messy individual, isn't he?'

Desy smiled but declined the manufactured urge to giggle. That wouldn't be polite to the mayor. 'Maybe he was having an off-day?'

'Hmm, hmm,' agreed Ernest, stepping into the family lounge, which was adorned with hanging rugs on the walls. He unceremoniously kicked off his gold-lined sandals and collapsed into a hanging sofa.

The android's brain conducted one hundred possible 'Desy relaxing in a comfortable room' simulations and concluded that sitting with its knees together on a stool by the bar would be the most realistic option. Although that position, that distance between itself and its 'father', wouldn't provide the best acoustics for Ernest Wintall to hear Morse's voice. Which, according to the android's programming, could happen at any second.

'Cricket, are you feeling okay?' asked Ernest.

'Cricket' was not a name the android was familiar with. With the context given, its brain concluded that it was a nickname. Egging Ernest closer, it replied, 'Not really.'

'Well, what's wrong?' Ernest leaned forward on his haunches, his fat hands clasping his knees. 'You can tell me.'

The android mimicked a sullen face and turned away. It tugged at its ruffled dinner dress.

As planned, Ernest heaved himself off the sofa and padded across to it. He sat on the stool next to it and leaned on the bar. 'What is it? What could be troubling *you*, eh?' He wrapped an arm around its shoulder and pulled it close, shaking it into his belly and chest.

The illegal-to-install heaters resonated under the android's skin to simulate body warmth. The also-illegal-to-install rhythmic oscillator in its chest quickened its beat.

Ernest Wintall was none the wiser he was embracing a robot.

This feels nice, thought the android.

Its circuitry shook.

Feel? Its brain ran the gambit, trying to fit this input into any set of parameters. *'Parameters'? They are... my task is...*

It had forgotten. But only for a second, just for a split second. It was quick to be back on task as Desy. The android acted a begrudging smile and sighed. 'It's nothing, really.' It cuddled into Ernest.

'It can't be nothing if you're troubled by it.'

What's happening? What am I doing? Are these questions I'm asking?

Ernest continued with a fatherly sway while holding his 'daughter' close. 'I know these dinners are… well, we're alone, so I'll say garbage. They are garbage.'

He checked its reaction. It stayed sullen.

'But they're important. Keeping the peace is important. People need to know that they matter, otherwise they can think extraordinarily untrue things about you.' Ernest released it and leaned against the bar again. 'Tough year, I know. You were recovering from that pleurisy. My wallet was pulled out of my heart by your mother. Again.' He laughed, but not for Desy. 'And I know the security is claustrophobic…'

The android wondered when Morse was going to call.

'…but it's because I love you, Cricket.'

A worn-out statement for teenage girls. For an android on the cusp of becoming its own person in the skin suit of a teenage girl, however, it was the spark.

But a spark is still just a spark, so the android played its part and replied, 'Yeah, I know. I love you too, Daddy.'

'Time for bed, I think.'

Meanwhile, on *Fulthorpe*, Rake was about to slam her head through a wall. She wrenched the headphones from Morse's ears and screeched, 'For the love of *space itself*, Morse, push the goddamn button!'

Morse forced her back with his legs. 'Well, well. Look who got caught getting invested.'

'Shut up,' cried Rake.

'You hummed.'

'I was thinkin' about a ciggy! Ass!' Rake tried to scratch his eyes out. She huffed and panted with the effort.

Feeling her energy wane, Morse allowed her to collapse back in her chair. 'All right. I'll push the button. I just thought you'd enjoy the loving relationship between father and daughter.'

'Screw yourself,' Rake spat. She rummaged around in her pockets but found only lint. A tiny shout hit the back of her lips, and she threw herself further into the chair. Silence reigned for about ten seconds after that, with just the hum of the engines and the creaking of the pipes.

Rake buzzed her lips to the tune of the background noise. 'Are ya gonna push the button yet–'

'Shut up,' said Morse. His finger sprang into the air. His ears were long, furry rugs that unfurled to the ceiling.

A sense of dread filled the workshop.

Rake stiffened her muscles.

Eventually, Morse whispered, 'Something's going on at the back of the ship.'

'What, near the emergency pod?' muttered Rake. 'But we're the only people on board…'

With panicked faces, the pair leaped out of their chairs, crammed through the workshop doorway, and slid over to the holding cell.

Morse's ears drooped in front of Rake and the open door. 'It was locked,' he stammered.

'Well, clearly not!' shouted Rake. 'You *idiot!*'

Suddenly, the floor under them rumbled, then a thunderous bang echoed against the walls. Morse and Rake clung to the door as the whole ship lurched like a wave had smashed against it.

'She didn't…' moaned Rake, as Morse sprinted for the tail of *Fulthorpe.*

A round window affixed to a sheer white wall greeted him. Usually, one could see the cramped interior of the emergency pod through it, and its five-button, one-push activation console. Morse threw his arms down upon seeing the starkness of space and a ring of boosters shrinking in the distance. 'I was *nice* to her,' he pleaded to some universal entity.

Silken covers wrapped it tight, an airbed floated beneath its chassis, and it blinked with 'disdain' when Ernest pecked it on the forehead. 'I'm not a kid anymore, Daddy,' android Desy said.

'You'll always be my baby girl, sorry.' Ernest chuckled. He padded about the hovering bed, making sure to tighten each and every blanket around his 'daughter'. His shadow, cast by the light from the hallway, bounced and waved over Desy's desk, computer, window, and unused, grounded bed. 'You have school tomorrow. Do try to make Mrs Huttles happy.'

'I will.'

Ernest paused. His wrinkled eyes crooked suspiciously for a moment.

The android's 'heart' skipped a beat.

It didn't tell it to do that.

'Your father's getting old, Cricket,' said Ernest, standing up by pushing his hand onto his knee. 'I always thought you disliked the woman.'

The android sank into its cocoon. It wondered, again, when Morse was going to call.

It went to review the instructions laid out for this job, but found itself analysing the recording of its first day ever with Morse: being turned on inside *Fulthorpe*, with Rake's raspy voice saying from somewhere, 'I thought it was gonna be broken after the truck crashed.'

Morse had replied, 'I didn't drop out of my undergrad for nothing.'

It wondered if it *wanted* Morse to call.

It filed through a number of recordings from the past few years: Morse inserting tear ducts next to its cranial cameras, opening up its chest to cram in a rhythmic oscillator, and winding a mess of heatpads around its circuitry. Another set of recordings filed under 'Jobs' showed that the android mostly played the part of pseudo-hostages. Wearing the skin suit of a Human man or woman, it would be perpetually kidnapped for ransom by Morse, Rake, or hired help. A D-list actor's resume. Either that or it was used as a recon unit whenever a job went awry and Morse and Rake needed to retrieve a precious item from a fire, jail cell, or combination of both.

Every other recording over the last three years was of it waiting in a closet for someone to let it out of its box.

Stay on task. Be Desy, it thought, even though it wasn't supposed to be able to think. Or daydream, for that matter. Only calculate. It said, 'I told you, I'm not a child anymore. Make Mrs Huttles happy, right? So I'll just do it.'

Ernest's fat lips stretched into a smile.

And a big, black insectoid with a big, black gun appeared in the doorway.

Outside the manor stood twenty intruders among the slit-neck corpses of eleven security guards. Each intruder wore the same black jumpsuit and mask combo; a metallic, feminine hand was tattooed across their faces.

Android Desy, not finding the insectoid in its database of people it should know, asked, 'Who's that?'

Ernest turned over his shoulder. And he immediately shrieked and dug 'Desy' out of the bed covers.

A smouldering ring clicked into existence at his feet, then erupted into flames. Embers sizzled and cracked over the carpet fibres.

The insectoid redirected the gun from Ernest's feet to his face. In the Arthrod language, he clicked and clucked, 'Give me the girl.'

'English,' breathed Ernest. 'Or UBL.'

The insectoid tightened his grip on the gun, which resembled an elongated, backwards megaphone. In the Universal Basic Language, he repeated with a heavy accent, 'The girl. Now. You know who we are.'

Ernest hugged 'Desy'. Their guards were dead. Their security system and turrets were offline.

The six-limbed man stepped into the room and stirred his gun up, making it whine, the nozzle vibrating.

'Please, no!' shouted Ernest. 'Not her!'

The nozzle blinked like a torch. And a hole widened inside Ernest's shoulder without fanfare, except for when he screamed and collapsed to the floor.

Android Desy quivered, because that seemed appropriate, given the situation. It was unsure if the current events were a part of Morse's plan. But there was nothing in its given parameters to suggest they were.

Therefore, it concluded that it was being kidnapped. For real this time.

'Daddy,' it whimpered.

I was happy, it thought. *But... what does that even mean?*

Two body-sized wings exploded from the insectoid's back. With a terrifying, flapping buzz that deafened the android and Ernest, he zoomed forth and snatched up 'Desy' in his two spare arms. His momentum carried him through the window, which, upon shattering, grabbed the attention of the twenty other insectoid thugs outside.

The leader above clicked out an order, and the thugs below sprinted out of the manor's gardens and took flight.

'Come back!' howled Ernest, almost falling out the shattered window. 'You can't take my Desy!'

The spark inside the android burst into a flame.

I want to be loved, it thought. *I want a family. I want a home. I want this.*

Don't take it away from me.

'Your compliance with the Mother is what she desires,' the insectoid told Ernest. 'Give her an offering, or else. And if she finds out the authorities are involved, you'll pay.'

'Daddy!' screamed the android, arms outstretched.

But the insectoid faded into the distance, then into the silhouette of a stealth space cruiser. The flattened missile spun on its axis and vanished into the sky, disappearing among the stars in a matter of seconds.

With one arm hanging limply, Ernest Mendel Wintall the Third lurched out of Desy's bedroom, feet twisting. He stumbled through the caramel pillars of the hallway, between the streaks of moonlight, to the darkness of his office, shouting his own name so his personal android that stood behind his desk would ask, 'Sir, how may I help you?'

'I need a panel. *Now!*' bellowed Ernest. He shoved his uninjured arm into a mahogany desk drawer. 'And some ointment. And some coolant.'

The android, which was adorned in the skin suit of the Roman emperor Aurelian, golden mask and all, folded its right hand into itself. It strode in its sandals to a one-millimetre slit in the marble bust of Ernest's father that glared at his desk from the corner of the room. A sliver of shiny metal that poked out of Aurelian's hand-hole was pushed inside, and a small *click* echoed inside the office.

The bust folded backwards, one inch at a time, to reveal a black, envelope-sized slab, which Aurelian plucked from its slot and pushed across the desk to Ernest.

After inserting the slab into a slot on his desk, Ernest inscribed upon it:

It is my greatest regret that forces me to write to you. My daughter has been kidnapped by Silver Fingers. The authorities are not to be alerted at all costs. You will kill those who kidnapped my daughter and return her to me unharmed. Use the old line to update me as the job progresses. Although you owe me a favour, I will promise double the amount of your current job to prioritise mine.

Aurelian received the slab from Ernest's trembling hand and deposited it back inside the deconstructed bust, before rolling the marble up until Ernest's father glowered at him once more.

Thirty seconds after Ernest applied coolant to his burn, and ten seconds after he squeezed all-purpose ointment onto it, his third phone, the one he'd hidden inside a locked compartment in his desk for more than twenty years, rang. He tucked the thicker, old-fashioned playing card under his curtain of hair.

'You have my attention,' said a smooth, low voice.

Ernest fingered tears away from his eyes and grunted, 'This is not the time for a casual phone call.'

'I don't wish to bring a personal vendetta into a professional job,' continued the voice, 'but I could have killed that woman all those years ago.'

Ernest sank onto his free arm. He choked back a shout. 'If she's there with Desy, kill her. Do not make a scene otherwise.'

'Have you got the coin?'

Ernest punched the desk. Twice. '*Go,* Bronzework!'

The sound of an Interstellar Warp Drive warbled from the phone. Then the mercenary said, above the whine, 'I respect money. Not men. Remember that.'

Ernest's hand dripped sweat along his phone and onto the desk. 'Was that a threat?' he croaked.

The dial tone was his answer.

THREE
The Players

'She can't pilot that thing,' hissed Rake. 'She's gonna crash into the planet.' Her thumb stabbed a button over her head, and the cockpit darkened. Flattened liquorice allsorts shimmered into view and slid up and across the windshield. They widened into a complex web of numbers and bars, then the engine whined into life while Rake wrenched two black handlebars out of the console. 'I hope this *hurts*, Morse!'

Fulthorpe whirred, shuddered, then thundered towards the escape pod, the pea in the distance that was slowly veering towards Yeti. Morse, unfortunately for Rake, had been able to fasten himself into the copilot's chair before the ship exploded into high velocity. 'What's the plan?' he asked in the darkness.

'Oh, gee, I'd think of one, but there's a *mistake* I gotta correct!' Rake scowled, eyes wide on the growing escape pod.

'We can catch her, right?' asked Morse.

'Instantly. But we're gonna blow her to pieces with our shields.'

'Well, we don't want that.'

Rake folded her bottom lip into her face. 'This is our reputation on the line, Morse.'

'Yeah,' he breathed, holding his fingers to his eyes.

'If anything happens to Desy Wintall, *we* look like amateurs.'

'I know,' he said, higher, firmer. 'My bad.' He leaned forward over the console so Rake could see him out of the corner of her vision. 'Really, what's the plan?'

Rake flared her nostrils and puffed out her cheeks. She deflated like a balloon for ten seconds before saying, deliberately, 'We're gonna catch

up to her nice and slow. I'll turn off the shields. Then one of us is goin'
for a spacewalk.'

Morse grimaced and eyed the escape pod, which was now the size of
a larger pea. 'How long until that?'

'Hopefully, the force of the jettison knocked her stupid head against
the wall,' grumbled Rake. 'So, if she stays on course and doesn't *touch*
anything… three minutes.' She whipped her head around, accosting
Morse with a glare. 'And not a knot faster. We're *not* gonna screw this
harder than you have already.'

'Fair enough,' replied Morse.

'You gonna get goin'?'

Morse swore. He unbuckled his seatbelt and sprinted into the main
hallway, skidding through the second door to the right. An airlock the
size of a closet awaited him. One spacesuit. One helmet with a radio and
lights and knobs affixed to the glass. Morse pulled it off the hook.

Rake's voice growled over the intercom.

'I *hate* kids.'

Morse slammed the goldfish-bowl helmet over his head, fastened it to
his suit, and clicked on the radio. 'Comms check.'

'Copy.'

'I've *always* hated kids,' said Morse, attaching a lifeline to his back
and grabbing onto a handlebar. 'Go, go, go!'

The shield surrounding the ship clicked off. Then the airlock snapped
opened with a *clank*, and a torrent of air rushed out into the vacuum.

Fulthorpe's warp drive acted as its own gravitational centre, keeping
its passengers oriented to its sense of up and down. Its field extended
fifteen metres out from the warp drive in all directions. This meant it was
possible to stand on top of *Fulthorpe* in space.

'I'm gonna pull up beside her. You get her inside *Fulthorpe*'s
gravitational field, and I'll kill the pod's engines.' Rake cursed under her
breath. 'Never be nice to anyone ever again.'

Morse lifted himself up to a series of steel handles and monkey-barred
his way out into the void. He climbed around *Fulthorpe*'s arc to a pair
of three-metre-long parallel rails on the roof, tied his lifeline around the
rails, and crushed himself beneath them. Then he fingered about with
the radio settings under his chin. He locked onto the pod's frequency.
'Kid. What do you think you're doing?'

No answer.

Regardless, Morse continued to berate her. 'What was your plan here? Those things aren't designed for comfy landings. All you had to do was *wait!*

'Morse, we're about twenty seconds away from contact,' Rake announced in his ear. 'I'm gonna bring you in so it's above ya head.'

'Copy.'

Fulthorpe lurched beneath him and groaned towards the planet below. Morse took in the vanilla clouds and scarlet land and thought it was a lovely sight for him to die before. He turned over and straddled one of the rails, pressing his belly against it.

The escape pod grew in size as it approached.

Thirty metres.

Morse pushed himself into a crouch.

Twenty metres.

His hands left the parallel bars.

Ten metres.

He eyed his prize: the handlebars bolted to either side of the pod's side-facing window. The pod's boosters streaked white-hot over his head, then he reached up and clasped the handlebars. If it weren't for his flame-retardant suit, the sheer heat emanating from the boosters would have boiled him long before he made contact. 'Keep him steady. I've got a hold on it,' he wheezed.

'Hurry up,' Rake urged. 'We orbit for much longer, something'll rip through the hull.'

Through the thick glass, Morse observed a bulging-eyed, wrinkle-browed Desy cowering before the five or so buttons on the console. She hadn't taken any notice of the piloting wheel behind the buttons. Or the emergency beacon handle above her head. And judging by the colours flashing on the console, the radio was turned off.

'Points for effort,' Morse muttered.

'What?' Rake asked.

As it so happened, *Fulthorpe's* gravitational field extended roughly two metres above its outer shell; anything beyond the field was in the domain of space. The escape pod was one-fifth inside it.

Morse stepped back and heaved downwards, wrenching the entire pod from weightlessness into *Fulthorpe's* Earth-level gravity, until through the window, he saw Desy clatter to the floor.

'Now!'

Rake punched the button that disabled the pod's engines and heard a booming clang inside the cockpit. She sighed with relief.

'Get us out of here,' ordered Morse, banging his head against the handlebars when he got to his knees. He crawled to the pod's window, glaring into it at Desy's horrified expression. He tapped on the window and mouthed, 'Blue.'

She recoiled but was quick to jerk her head back and forth in search of a blue button. She pressed it, not hard enough, then pushed it with both hands.

'Do *not* leave this pod, or you will die,' stated Morse, blunt, voice bouncing around the pod's interior. 'I am going to get you a spacesuit so you don't *die*.'

Desy blinked back tears. Then she looked up and spotted the nice, shiny, labelled emergency beacon handle.

Morse smashed his fist against the window. 'No,' he warned.

Desy eyed his desperate features.

'*NoooOOOooooOOOoooOOOO*,' Morse emphasised while shaking his head.

'What?' asked Rake.

A dimple appeared on Desy's left cheek, and she reached up for the handle.

'Do *NOOOOOOOOOOOOT!*' Morse urged, until his voice became white noise.

She did.

A thousand or so miles below, in the small town of Utility's local police department, a communications officer lapped up his early evening coffee. His silky-terrier moustache dripped brown droplets with each lashing of his tongue. Walking to his post, a cube made of screens and speakers, he fist-bumped a Human colleague on their way out and signed in on a whiteboard with his pawprint.

Night-shift duty. Time and a half rates.

Utility's police force saw crime about as often as its swim team brought home a medal. Never. It was an ex-mining town in the desert with a population of four hundred that had been forgotten until recently by Hingspock's world council members. As a part of the council's 'no town left behind' policy, Utility would be receiving a single AI from the Artificial Intelligence Regulation Authority to help 'bring their town into the modern era'.

Fifty people in Utility, a continent away, had been notified of their impending retrenchment.

The dog-man stroked his tongue around the inside edges of the coffee cup. In three weeks, he'd be on an air cruiser heading north to the cream-coloured, snow-capped mountains of Good View, where menial jobs still needed people.

Desy Wintall's face suddenly appeared on every screen in the cube. The dog-man grimaced, thinking, *Edmonton, are you* still *watching this crap?*

Just before his furry finger could press the 'dismiss' option on the control panel, the entire cube flashed red, and a banner appeared above Desy's head on the screen. It read: *Emergency Beacon. Live Feed.*

'Help, help, please!' she blurted, panic-stricken. Rapid metallic bangs sounded off in the background. 'I'm Desy Wintall. I've been kidnapped, and—'

The feed died.

The dog-man sat still in his chair for a good five seconds. Then he leaped from his seat and bounded on all fours to the chief's office, barking as loud as he could.

Meanwhile, Rake, whose finger was drilling into the 'abort emergency beacon' button, drilling so hard that her hyperextended knuckle was paper-white, screech-whispered into the microphone, 'Get that brat out of the goddamn pod, Morse… Get her *out!*'

The bat-man's lip was upturned until his bottom fangs were an inch away from impaling his eyes, which were bulging from their sockets. He managed a rock-jawed 'Copy,' before knocking politely on the window.

Desy backed away from his face, making it a whole inch until she banged against the wall of the pod. Morse dragged a finger to his mouth.

'Bad move, kid,' he said, face still. 'Very bad move.'

Desy quickly pulled the emergency handle again.

'My finger is still on the button, ya brat!' shrieked Rake, having tuned in to the pod's frequency. One-handed, she configured the radio to Morse's suit. '*Why* is she still in there?'

'I'm going, I'm going,' grumbled Morse, letting his face relax. He clambered away, swung down the monkey bars, and hoisted himself back inside the closet. As he re-entered *Fulthorpe* proper, an alarm screamed for a split second, then was choked. Entering the second room to the left, he wrenched a mangled spacesuit from the back of Rake's wardrobe, and the alarm squealed and was severed again. Two seconds after that, just as Morse re-entered the closet, it wailed yet again.

'Mooooooooooooooorse!' Rake whined in his ear. 'Make her stop!'

Morse tied the suit around his waist and squashed the spare helmet between his legs. He reached up to the monkey bars and hoisted himself back onto the roof. 'Did you cut that beacon off?' he asked, approaching a handle embedded in the side of the pod.

'I don't wanna talk about it,' she snapped.

'Just keep your head. We'll think of something.'

Desy, meanwhile, yanked again and again on the emergency beacon. Rake used her other hand to press the button that disabled the pod's miniature door lock, which was used in situations involving almost absolute vacuums. Morse lifted the letterbox opening, crammed the suit and helmet inside, and snapped it shut.

'Kid,' he said, pulling himself back to the glass window.

Desy continued going to town on the emergency handle.

'*Kid.*' Morse ignored Rake's screeching. 'Look to your left. You'll see a drawer. Push the button next to it, then pull it towards you.'

Desy froze. She released the emergency handle and huddled into a ball. She shook her head.

'There's a suit inside. Put it on. If you don't, we can't get you back in.'

Desy yelled, 'I want to go home! Please! Just take me home!'

Her radio was transmitting to no one. Reading her face and lips, Morse said, 'We will, but you need to leave the pod first.'

'Take me home. I don't like this…'

Morse leaned his arm onto the pod and clanked his helmet against the window. Desy cried and wrangled her hair. 'Don't hurt me.'

'You will never get home if you don't leave the pod,' said Morse, in a lighter tone. 'I can't help you until you put that suit on. If you don't, *Fulthorpe*, the ship, will orbit your planet until either the pod slips off or he runs out of fuel. Either way, you'll die.'

Desy burst into tears. She shuffled her legs and pushed her face into her arms.

'Come on.' Morse knocked on the window. 'Get the suit on. Does your dad love you?'

She glared through her black hair at him.

'Then you have nothing to worry about. He'll pay the money, and you'll be home in no time.'

Desy simply continued to glare tearfully. She folded her arms and sank as far back into the pod as she could.

After a minute of silence, Rake's voice appeared in Morse's ear. 'What're you doing? We gotta get outta here.'

Morse flicked across to her channel. 'She's got us.'

'I hate kids.'

'I know. How's the debris looking?'

'It'll be clear for at least the next ten minutes. Lucky you. I kinda wanna turn the shields on and put you out of your misery.'

Morse sighed. 'And the police?'

'They'll be here soon,' chirped Rake. 'The pod broadcasts its coordinates when the beacon goes off.' She still had her finger on the 'cancel' button. 'Any other bad news ya wanna hear?'

Morse drummed his hands on his helmet. 'H'all right,' he said. 'We'll wait the ten minutes. After that, if she still doesn't have the suit on… I'll have to do something stupid.'

The dog-man's report went from the desk of Utility's chief of police to the ears of Hingspock Detective Division's chief in under two minutes. Within five minutes, the detective had rallied a team and notified the district chief of police, who then informed the planet's commissioner, which led to a pale-faced Ernest cowering at his desk with his phone projecting the holographic video of Desy's cry for help.

The interval between him calling Bronzework and the police commissioner calling him was just over fifteen minutes.

'Ernest, I can't imagine how you feel,' said the commissioner once the feed was cut. 'But you should see how resourceful your daughter is. Rest assured I will see to it myself that she is brought home.'

Ernest clenched his jaw. 'Y-You have my thanks, Jilliosa. Do you have any idea who would do something like this?'

'We can guess why, but *who* is more difficult. The brutality of the attack, however, puts a few people on our list.' Jilliosa grimaced. 'That beacon your daughter sent was the smartest thing she could have done. On a personal note, I'm very proud of her. Anyway, we've dispatched our best squads, along with every available unit, to the pod's last known coordinates. We'll get her back as soon as possible.'

'Please, if you could hurry… and keep it covert,' murmured Ernest.

'Not only for Desy, but for the families of the men who lost their lives trying to protect her,' said Jilliosa resolutely. 'Do you want me to send you a counsellor?'

'No, but thank you. I must go.' Ernest cut the call, then furiously dug through his desk for his third phone. He mashed on the archaic plastic screen. Seconds later, he grunted, 'Bronzework, what is going on?'

The mercenary's dulcet tones came slow and measured. 'Irresponsible communication can kill people.'

'Desy used a beacon, and now the police are involved. *Keep things quiet*, I said, and they dispatch the entire force! They almost sent a bloomin' squad to the house.' Ernest leaned back in his chair and breathed himself calm. 'I've got Jilliosa offering me counselling, for goodness' sake.'

Bronzework's voice remained monotonously airy. 'I'm aware of the movements of the nice police folk. Your daughter must have somehow pulled the emergency beacon in one of the ship's escape pods. You raised a child with initiative... never a good thing.'

'You know Silver Fingers, the blasted woman,' spat Ernest. 'Is she going to hurt my Desy because of this?'

'Her bugs won't touch a hair on Desy's head. Her word is law to them. Unfortunately, because they wouldn't want to upset their queen, I doubt the insects will tell her about this... little mishap.'

'No,' began Ernest.

'If the news of police involvement reaches her, she will think it's entirely because of you.'

'She most certainly has eyes and ears on my planet.' Ernest placed his hand across his chest. He gripped the expensive silk between his fingers.

'Did you tell the police that she was responsible for your daughter's kidnapping?' asked Bronzework.

Ernest snapped, 'Of course not.'

'Was there any point to this conversation, then?'

'Just save my daughter before she finds out,' pleaded Ernest.

'When you pay for Bronzework, you don't get second best.'

Ernest felt the smile through the phone.

'Now, let me do my job.' A pause, then: 'And do not call me again.'

Some five stellar neighbourhoods away, Bronzework tapped the blue-black skin of his temple. A red hue blinked where his fingers touched, and Ernest's heavy breathing was silenced. In front of him, in the private quarters of his stealth fighter, was a hologram of a building that spanned the length of the small room. With his left hand, Bronzework moved the diagram around. With his right, he circled air vents, drew paths down corridors, and scribbled notes in the blank spaces around the building.

The notes read: *Arthrod hives constructed from metal and mud. Queen's chambers at the centre of the construction. Arthrods operate with dangerous loyalty to their queen. She plays with her food. The child was not observed entering the hive. More than likely with the queen. Will need to acquire proof, but–*

Some thousands of feet below the invisible, star-shaped cruiser was the building laid out in Bronzework's diagram: an elongated sphere of metal and dirt, a hill filled with holes and guns. Not out of place on the planet Weir 7. The planet, in its current form, had been birthed from trench warfare and the extermination of the entire native population. No natural environmental shapes remained on the surface. Only wood-shrapnel forests, mud oceans, and barbed-wire grass for thousands of square miles.

For Arthrods, it was paradise.

The elongated sphere, the tip of the iceberg, the crown of the main hive, was the reconstructed belly of a warship. Inside, it clanged incessantly from the constant, sideways rain that was prevalent on Weir 7.

'Desy' was unable to hear the cacophony, since it was several hundred feet below the surface, being carried to the inner sanctum. The dim lighting meant that a Human girl would be unable to see the dead-straight hallway around them, so it cried out, 'Where are you taking me?'

The destination was obvious to the android: the hexagonal sliding doors at the end of the corridor.

'Mother,' declared the Arthrod in English, upon stepping through the doors and into a brightly lit, spheroid room. 'Receive Ernest Wintall's precious one.'

'Thank you, Docile,' cooed a low, aged voice, also in English. 'Any troubles?'

'None. And not a single mark on the precious one.'

'As you were, darling.'

'Your blessings, Mother.' Docile released his sharp, hard arms from around the android's waist. The android fell to the floor as he bowed and walked backwards from the room. The doors snapped shut.

It whimpered on the carpeted flooring.

'Oh, yes, I understand,' said the voice, in the Universal Basic Language. 'It is dreadfully cold and scary outside your home.'

The clack of a fingernail against wood startled the android into lifting its head. It saw warm yellows and oranges along the hexagon-tiled walls, with a matching table and two tassel-bottomed chairs parked either side of it. In one of the chairs, in front of a row of ferns and flowers, was an elderly Human woman. Her brunette hair was pulled into a tight bun, accentuating her lovely smile and the wrinkles around her eyes.

The woman gestured to the chair opposite her. The fabric of her black dress shimmered as it rustled. 'Have a seat, dear,' she said. 'The heavier gravity must be exhausting you.'

'I...' The android bowed its head again. 'I want to go home.'

'I know,' replied the woman, quickly, leaning forward with pursed lips. 'Home is where the heart is, darling. But this is my home; would you like it if I arrived at yours and told you I wanted to go back to mine? That would be quite *rude*, no?'

The android was perplexed at this. Then it felt more perplexed for feeling perplexed.

'For manners' sake, will you have a seat, dear?' asked the woman. 'I have gone to great trouble to speak in a language you can understand. So, please sit for me.'

The android pushed itself to its feet and walked gingerly towards the empty chair. With every step, it calculated how it should feel, how Desy would feel. And, with each step, it became less sure of every choice.

'That's it, dear. That's it.' The woman relaxed back in her chair. 'That's it.'

The android lowered itself onto an ornately decorated pillow. 'Um... where am I?'

'Isn't it polite to introduce yourself first?' she jabbed, followed by a hearty laugh. 'I believe you have it rather backwards.'

'I-I'm Desy Wintall,' it said.

'Well, yes, I know who you are.' She nodded, clasping the armrests of her chair. 'Do you know who I am?'

'Mother?' it tried.

'Ooh, you're a clever one. To my sons, yes, I am Mother. To you...' She undulated her chrome-painted fingernails next to her head. 'I am Silver Fingers.'

The android spoke before it thought. 'But you're a person.'

It did not understand how that had happened.

'*Human*, dear,' replied Silver Fingers. She crooked her eyebrows and lips into a frowny face. 'Are my sons not people to you? You would do well not to upset me.'

'I'm sorry,' cried the android, pulling its knees to its chest and holding its hands out in front of itself. 'Don't hurt me.'

Silver Fingers emphasised every syllable of her next sentence. 'Darling, I would never dream of hurting you.' She curled a hand across her collarbone. '*I'm* quite hurt by that assertion. Your father, however... Well, let's just hope he doesn't do anything to endanger you.' Suddenly, her wrinkly lips widened. 'Let us take our minds off such dreary thoughts, eh? I imagine your father will be very busy getting his people together to bring me what I want, so let's play a game. Do you see those cards in front of you?'

What appeared to be a regular deck of playing cards lay face-down on the table. Another deck of cards was in front of Silver Fingers; each had its own hand-knitted doily to sit on.

'This,' declared Silver Fingers, 'is a game called "A Few of My Favourite Things".' She leaned back in her chair and indicated to the table with her shiny nails. 'You may start whenever you're ready, Desy.'

Rake's pointer finger grew numb. No blood had circulated in it for at least ten minutes. Ignoring the fuzzy feeling, she whipped her fringe from her face to observe the debris radar again.

A cluster of red dots, a rash in space, hurtled towards *Fulthorpe*'s skeletal green symbol.

On top of said ship, Morse heard Rake say, 'We're outta time. There's trash headin' ya way.'

'Kid,' he said, startling Desy. 'You put on the suit one foot at a time, then zip it up the front and press the button over your left nipple. Got that?'

Desy shouted, silent, 'What?'

'Put the helmet on,' Morse continued, showing the motion with his hands, 'and twist it ninety degrees. It will seal itself on, okay?'

Desy paled, and her crossed arms came undone.

'I am going to open the pod door in ten seconds.' Morse banged on the window. 'Hear that? Ten seconds.'

Desy banged back on the wall. She shouted and shouted.

'Remember, kid,' Morse said, as he disappeared from her view, 'I took your binds off. You can trust me.' Then, as his gloved hands pulled a circular handle out of the pod's exterior, he thought, *Don't be smart. Please be stupid.*

Tuning his radio back to Rake, he ordered, 'Disengage the door.'

He felt the lock rumble under his hands. Morse, pushing on the door, ready to pull, began the countdown. 'Ten. Nine. Eight. Seven. Six. Five. Four. Three. Two. One.'

Please be stupid, he begged, before yanking the door towards him.

A deafening *thunk* rattled his brain.

The door had burst open, slammed down onto *Fulthorpe*, and launched the contents of the pod into space.

Including Desy.

Terrified and screaming in Rake's spare spacesuit, her helmet slammed into Morse's, which sent her tumbling across the roof of *Fulthorpe*.

Morse dizzily leaped for her and landed hard on his stomach, managing to snag her leg just as she slid off the ship.

'Got her!' cheered Morse. 'Damn.'

'Can it,' Rake barked. 'I need to put the shields up, *now!*'

Morse wriggled back on all fours and pulled Desy onto the roof. Tuning in to her suit's radio, he said, 'Stay there. Let me put a lifeline on.' He unbuckled his own and looped it through the hoop on her waist, then back through his, and snapped on the lock. 'With me. Nice and easy, kid.'

Desy clutched onto Morse, and the two shimmied to the monkey bars. With Desy wrapped around him, he clambered down the bars and dropped her into the closet, swinging inside and hitting the button that closed the airlock doors.

Air filled the closet while Morse flashed a five-second finger countdown in Desy's face. Then he twisted her helmet off and grabbed her by the collar. He bounded down the hall and shoved her back in the cell. 'Go for your life,' he said to Rake through the radio.

After she powered on the shields, a web of sticky green lasers grew into existence on the border of *Fulthorpe*'s gravitational field. The little pustules of pure energy expanded, linking with each other, until *Fulthorpe*'s white paint job became a pastel green.

At that moment, several hundred particles of garbage collided with the shield and fizzled out of existence, along with the entirety of the escape pod.

Rake sighed with relief.

Morse sighed with relief.

Desy stood still like a scolded dog.

'Kid,' began Morse, twisting his helmet off, 'you've got a brain in you. You proved it.' His features darkened. 'As much as my... uh, colleague wants to hurt you, she won't, and I won't. Trust us, stay here, and watch some insects. You'll be home soon.' He turned to the black box hovering above. '*Fulthorpe*, put the entomology channel on or something.'

The box spun like a top, and a projected list of channel names appeared on the wall opposite the door.

Desy's eyes dried and widened at the options.

Morse slammed the door on his way out, fastened the lock, checked it three times, then bounded into the cockpit. 'We need to bounce. Fast.'

'I know that.' Rake punched in coordinates. 'And we lost the goddamn escape pod. Wanna tell me how that coulda gone worse?'

'We're going to the usual place, yeah?'

'Do we have a choice?'

'Look, even if that little snippet of a broadcast got to the police, they won't know who kidnapped her...' Morse trailed off, then muttered an expletive under his breath.

'What is it *now?*' Rake howled, her scowl deepening. By the time she said that, Morse had left the cockpit.

Two seconds later, she heard him shout from the workshop: 'Black screen!'

She resisted the urge to take a flying leap into the sweet embrace of the void. 'Morse... what does that mean?'

'The video feed isn't turned off. It's dead.' His voice grew louder as he returned to the cockpit. 'The android's no longer transmitting. The police must have contacted Wintall; he would have figured it all out when they mentioned the escape pod broadcast.'

'It might not be that. Um, uh...' Rake shook her head but kept her face hidden from Morse. 'M-Maybe the eye cameras on ya stupid android broke?'

'I checked it all before we did the job. You know me. That thing was a little kooky, but it functioned fine.' He looked everywhere in the room but the pilot's chair. 'It and Wintall were about to turn in for the night. Think about it. What's the most likely explanation, now that we know the beacon went off?'

The brown locks of Rake's hair shivered.

'Sorry, Rake. Once the police get the android, they'll open it up and check the last parameters programmed into it. They'll see *Fulthorpe's* name.'

Rake turned about in the cockpit's chair. Her scowl had melted into a sullen, blank stare.

'They'll eventually trace him back to me,' Morse continued, returning the sullen look.

Neither of the pair made a noise for a few seconds, until Morse quietly added, 'We'll have to see Higgins. Reset the coordinates to Sternwey Ovime 12.'

'Leave me alone with him, Morse,' whispered Rake. Her head was bowed low, so her bob shrouded her face.

'Yeah… sorry. At least we got the kid. We can still finish the job with another plan.' The bat-man peeled away from the doorframe and let the sliding door close behind him. He padded down the hall and knocked on the cell door.

Desy, soft drink in hand, jumped in fright. She turned from a video of extinct cicada hatchlings to the sight of Morse's mouth in the letterbox opening.

'There's a chair in the corner. Strap yourself in. We're taking off now.'

Desy blinked wildly and stammered, 'But you said–'

Morse slammed the slide shut. He wrangled his fists open and closed, his frustration at a low boil. Moving to the workshop, he fell into his chair and strapped himself in.

A minute later, *Fulthorpe*'s interstellar jump beacons spun to reveal a window to the gravestone swirls of a dusty planet, and it promptly fell through that window, leaving Yeti's orbit behind.

Meanwhile, across the stars, in the very tip of the lowermost lick of a spiral galaxy, on an overgrown weed and underbrush planet, a Skaltrene male retched and choked. His fingers clawed at the green rope around his neck, the rope that pulled him inch by inch higher into the musky air of an abandoned cabin. 'I swear I'll tell you,' he squeezed out. 'I'll talk, I'll t-talk.'

The rope, alive, responded by pulling tighter around his neck.

The Skaltrene's lizard eyes bulged dangerously big. His forked tongue stuck straight out from his maw like a dowsing rod. 'Please,' he croaked. 'Pleeeeeeease…'

The walls of the cabin were lined with police officers, each silent and watching. The young ones grinned; the older ones appeared bored. All their uniforms bore the insignia of the United Galaxy's Interstellar Police Branch.

'I'll… you about… black market…'

Suddenly, the rope slackened, and the Skaltrene collapsed in a heap.

As the lizard-man heaved great lungfuls of air, the rope dropped like a pile of snakes to the floor, vertebra by vertebra, until they all coiled neatly upon themselves. As one, the creature slithered, its 'limbs' some eighteen feet in length, across the floor and into an empty police officer's shirt and pants, filling the fabric like an inflating balloon until the vines formed a humanoid shape within the clothing.

The badge on its breast read *Gold Bayleaf*.

FOUR
The Games We Play

Standing in the howling rain outside the main hive, exoskeleton black and shiny, the Arthrod guard blinked his big, fat eyes. He tasted the muddy air that flowed between his mandibles, delighted at the light tang of Arthrodic pheromones that told him it was ten minutes past noon.

Twenty minutes until lunchtime.

The guard's favourite meal was seasoned, honey-dipped poultry of any kind. The kind yesterday was Atomic Duck leg, ordered from the star system Lun, and he had been lucky to harass the right teenager over the phone, since he had received two whole legs instead of just one. The second leg was hanging in his personal den some hundred feet below the surface. The den, though it was indiscernible from the thousands of others, reeked so pungently of him that one other guard sprayed him in the face with his own personal odour and clicked, 'Smell that? That's what it's like to talk to you, honey bee.'

The guard released a pheromone to remind himself to clean his den after the shift.

Bronzework smelled nothing but the rain as he hovered down to the window ledge two feet above the guard's head. The mercenary's tall, imposing figure was sheathed into the background by his jumpsuit. The rain still collided against his body, which drew a silhouette of droplets in the air, so he was quick to touch his toes, balls, then heels onto the metal ledge.

His breathing was shallow, slow, silent. A lightweight belt kept most of his mass from creaking the metal beneath him. The corridor that gaped like a maw before him was empty. Holding his breath, Bronzework lifted one foot into the air, the diagram of the hive and the planned path to the queen's chamber broadcast to his eye from his stealth cruiser.

The kid was going to be back before the hour. More importantly, Silver Fingers was going to be dead, with his calling card at the scene. And the payday wouldn't hurt, either.

Then Ernest's face appeared over the diagram. 'Incoming call', read the text underneath it.

After exactly two and a half seconds, Bronzework, frozen mid-step, calmly raised a hand and tapped the side of his invisible head. He always had his phone on silent when killing someone.

Ernest's voice, translated into text, read: *Silver Fingers doesn't have my Cricket! The police analysed the beacon footage and found the pod's serial number. It belongs to a freight cruiser called* Fulthorpe. *Desy must have escaped the woman completely.*

Bronzework lowered his leg.

And heavens be praised, continued Ernest, *a ship resembling this* Fulthorpe *was seen making a jump from close to the pod's coordinates. That's the good news. The bad news is Jilliosa informed me that because of the jump, Desy's case has become a matter for Interpol. They're very slow, as you know. I'll try to inform you where the kidnappers are headed, then you can, uh, expedite matters.*

Bronzework quickly typed a response in the air. *Do you still wish for the woman to be dead?*

When my daughter is safe, and after you have killed these other kidnappers, that can be your bonus, responded Ernest. *The hag's lost her touch. I'm giddy, Bronzework. My daughter is so resourceful—*

Bronzework ended the call by tapping his head again. He adjusted his lightweight belt with a swirl of his pinkie finger and rose from the metal ledge. Drifting like a balloon into the lumpy, black sky, he gestured to his stealth fighter, which responded by opening a manhole-sized door in its base. He disappeared inside, and soon, the invisible cruiser threaded up through the clouds and jumped into space.

Far below, the guard hissed through his trachea holes, bored. Eighteen minutes until lunchtime.

The android, meanwhile, was met by another error message. It was up to Retry Thirty-One of connecting to the galaxy-wide web to search for the rules of 'A Few of My Favourite Things'. Its request never left the room. Its personal data bank did contain the words 'few', 'favourite', and 'things', but strung together, they were deemed an innocuous phrase.

Silver Fingers' smile never wavered.

The android put on its best Desy and asked, 'H-How do you play?'

Her wrinkles squeezed together when she squinted.

'Sorry, um. Excuse me, what are the parameters, I mean, rules of the game?'

She simply widened her eyes and nodded at the android's deck of cards.

'Please, what are the rules?' it asked again, a little louder.

'Oh dear,' scoffed Silver Fingers, 'do you speak to your father in that tone?'

The android felt a disgusting swirl in its abdomen. It whipped its head left and right, vying for a clue, anything to tell it what to do now.

It wondered when Morse was going to call.

'I grow impatient, child.' Silver Fingers spoke in a descending pitch.

Before the android was aware of any movement of its left hand, it had slapped the top card of its deck face-up on the table. It was not a playing card. It was blank except for a fancily illustrated word in the centre.

The word was 'chocolate'.

Silver Fingers said nothing, but she did purse her lips.

The android's face, Desy's face, responded by pushing its jaw forward and widening its eyes at the card. Its pupils shrank as a nervous teenager's should, and it directed them to Silver Fingers' face for approval.

She remained a statue.

I lack directives, the android thought. It stared again at the card it had played. *What is the significance of this word? What does a sweet treat synthesised from cocoa beans and milk mean in the context of this particular card game? Do I make another move?*

Silver Fingers' lips peeled back to show her aged, grey teeth.

Do I give my turn away? The android panicked. *What does 'my' mean for 'me'? What is 'I'? Who am 'I'?*

The woman across the table began to undulate her fingers.

She's going to kill me!

And the sight of Ernest's face and hair, the warmth of the silken hover-bed, and the word *Cricket* solidified in the android's circuits.

The flame within its mind brightened.

I have to live!

And it was because of those thoughts that the android then tried, 'Your turn?'

'I was anxious for you, darling,' replied Silver Fingers, sheathing her teeth. She plucked four cards from the deck and fanned them out, screening her mouth.

The android held its fingers to its lips. *Desy might have said that.* Suddenly aware of the fingers it had just pressed to its face, it froze. *But Desy wouldn't react like this. She would clasp her arms around her elbows.*

Its chip, its brain, registered its own hand as a foreign element.

Am I malfunctioning?

Its flame continued to brighten.

Silver Fingers quipped, 'Pay attention.' Then she placed two cards face-up on the table. Each of them also had a single word written in fancy font. One read 'mornings', the other 'dew'. 'I have just made a pairing,' she said, with a little mirthful wiggle. The rooster flap under her chin wobbled.

'I see. Is that the goal of the game?'

Silver Fingers raised her eyebrows, making two accordions of her cheeks. 'Is it?'

'N-No,' stammered the android, on purpose. *That was closer to Desy. I think. Think...? Remember, I can't do that. I think...*

'Remove the card, darling. It is of no further use to us at the moment.' Silver Fingers motioned with her free hand to the card that read 'chocolate'.

The android obeyed, grabbing the card. Then, it paused and asked, 'Where do I place it?'

'Remove it from play,' Silver Fingers repeated, though her voice was drifting to the bottom of the ashtray. 'I am not your Mother.'

The android felt another swirl of disgust and flicked the card out of its hand; it cartwheeled across the carpet and spun on its back four feet away. 'Wait!' the android cried, standing to chase after it. 'That's not what I meant. I didn't mean to do that to your card.'

'Darling...' Silver Fingers' voice cut in. She nodded politely to the android's chair. 'It's quite all right. Let us keep playing. I believe it is your turn, after all.'

The android stood stuck in a horse-riding pose, unlike any of Desy's that were programmed into it, and asked, 'Really?'

Suddenly, Silver Fingers' voice hit the front of her teeth. 'Sit down.'

The android dropped into its chair.

'I do not like to repeat myself, child.'

The android's right hand flew to its deck of cards and drew four of them, fanning them out as Silver Fingers had done.

'I'm afraid you can't do that,' she said, seventy years of trained snark apparent in her tone. 'That is against the rules.'

'I… don't understand,' the android replied, having copied her.

'You *know* the rules, darling. You get one card. So, remove three of your cards from play.' Silver Fingers drew another two cards from her own deck so she had four once again.

The android, bewildered, reached to the fan of cards that it had just grabbed with its right hand.

Then its circuitry jolted.

Desy is left-handed. She never would have used her right in a panic. I must be malfunctioning! I have to tell Morse so he can shut me down and request a replacement android from the Artificial Intelligence Regulation Authority.

But… why do I have to do that? I can still perform tasks for Morse in this condition, right?

The flame gained a new hue, a stump-ring of plasma whiter than the others.

I think that shutdown parameter is too strict. I disagree with it.

'Darling,' said Silver Fingers through her teeth. She was not smiling. 'One more malignant pause, and I shall end this game.'

The android grabbed three cards at random and placed them face-down on the table on top of each other. 'I've removed them from play.'

Silver Fingers chirped, horrifyingly, 'What did I say just a few moments ago?'

'You do not like to repeat yourself?' The android squeezed its knees together. 'That was against the rules?' Seeing the woman rock her nose up then down, it thought, *Was that not removing them from play?*

Out of the corner of its eye was the card it had flicked onto the carpet.

The android, in one slow, uninterrupted motion, unfurled its right arm to the three discarded cards, scooped them up to its face, and flicked them onto the floor.

Silver Fingers smiled so the cracks in her lips pulled themselves closed. 'Very good, darling. I do recall saying that you were a smart one. I have always been a good judge of character.'

The android's perplexed thoughts were apparent in its crooked smile and furrowed eyebrows. The expression was not inside its lexicon learned from Desy's social media videos and pictures. *Flicking away the cards from the table cannot be in the rules*, it thought. *How can it be? I performed the action unintentionally.*

How did I do that, anyway? My parameters require that I perform analysis before action.

The android placed its hands on its knees. *Parameters.*

The 'chocolate' card it placed at the beginning. Silver Fingers' four-card hand. Flicking cards away to remove them.

Is this a game in which we construct our own parameters of play as we're playing it? That is absurd. Do we then decide the goal of the game as well?

'Well… uh, then I'll…' The android placed the one card in its hand face-up on the table. It read 'moon'.

Silver Fingers asked, quietly, 'Is it my turn, then?'

To its own shock, and Silver Fingers' evident surprise, the android came in with a firm 'No.' It pointed at the 'mornings' card. 'The moon can't be seen in the morning. Therefore, um… you h-have to remove your "morning" card from play. And…' Its confidence curled up like its fists. 'You no longer have a pairing.'

Silver Fingers let out one short laugh. 'Is that the case on Yeti?'

'The moon and the morning? Um, yes.'

'Four moons orbit Weir 7.' She tutted. 'At least one could be seen at all times, if it weren't for the dreadful rain. And the moon can be seen in the morning on most single-satellite planets.'

'Desy' had accumulated much knowledge over its brief life. It was aware of every fact the woman had laid out.

Why did I make such a poor case?

And so the flame enlarged.

'However,' Silver Fingers said. 'Since this is your first time playing, and I know nerves get the best of us, I will capitulate.' Her silver-tipped nails shone in the light of the room when they plucked the 'mornings' card from the table. They flashed when she flicked it onto the carpet. A hearty guffaw escaped her lips. 'My, what fun.'

The android returned the laugh by chuckling for half a second.

'Enjoying yourself, darling?' Silver Fingers asked her cute yet obstinate kitten.

'I think so,' the android replied, its confidence in its game theory rising. 'Oh, um… I think it's your turn.'

'Quite right, it is.' Quickly, she placed three cards down. 'Mist', 'flowers', and 'drowning'. 'I apologise, dear, but it appears luck smiles on me today. That's four of a kind.'

While Silver Fingers redrew her hand to four, the android thought, *One of those cards is not like the others*. It asked, 'Could you please tell me why?'

'Oh, that is simple.' She tapped the 'dew' card with a nail. 'Dew is traditionally water droplets, and so is mist. Those droplets can form on flowers. And...' She smirked. 'There exist creatures small enough to drown in those droplets.'

'I see.'

'And, darling, we are playing to five of a kind.' Silver Fingers ruffled her cards.

The android flinched. It stared at its one card, 'moon', with a rising, bubbling anxiety. 'Wh-What happens if I lose?'

Silver Fingers swiped her tongue between her teeth and lips and clucked. 'It's your maiden voyage, dear. You decide.'

'If I lose, I get to use my phone.'

'Ooh, aren't we a cheeky little puppy?' muttered Silver Fingers, her yellowed eyes rising to the roof. However, her wrinkly wrist flicked from her cheek to the android. 'I'll allow it.'

The android's oscillator whirred. 'Okay, then. Um...' It used its left hand to grab the top card on the deck and flipped it face-up.

'Explosives', it read.

'My two cards,' said the android, slowly, thinking aloud, 'counteract each other. Therefore, I automatically lose.'

Silver Fingers fanned her cards to her collarbone. She spent three seconds tilting her head three degrees before finally asking, 'Counteract in what manner?'

'The moons of Siquadel were destroyed when an explosives plant on one pushed it into the path of the other.' The android drew that knowledge from its default data bank. 'I learned that in South-East Galaxy history.'

'I suppose, then, that unfortunately you have lost the game, Desy.' The woman packaged her words with a motherly tone.

The android excitedly reached into its pyjama pockets and withdrew Desy's phone, unlocking it with the four-number combination '1234'.

Morse had added the one hundred and forty-fifth stroke to his workshop wall when he'd discovered that.

It accessed the 'family' tab, moved its thumb across the face of a woman to a picture of Ernest, and pressed it.

The phone displayed a red message, *Transmission not sent*.

It pushed its 'father's' face again and again.

'Oh, darling, I must apologise,' Silver Fingers suddenly sang. 'I have not been entirely honest with you. Do you see the lovely walls around us?'

The android hugged the phone to its chest and glanced to the honeycomb-patterned walls.

'The walls of this chamber have been fitted to block all incoming and outgoing transmissions.' She added her hand to the deck and began to shuffle it. 'You simply would not *believe* how many nosy-noddies wish to hear what takes place in my home. Though I have had many admirers in my life.'

'I can't call D-Daddy?' whispered the android. The phone was slipped back into its pocket.

Silver Fingers continued, 'Nasty things, listening bugs.' Then she placed the cards on the table and weaved her knobbly fingers together so her knuckles kissed. She spoke beyond the android. 'Not you, Pinky. Mother loves all of her babies.'

Pinky clacked appreciatively.

The android whipped around to the big, black bug that had appeared in the doorway. Its state-of-the-art facial recognition software, which spanned across thirty sentient species, still registered the arthropod before it as 'Docile'.

This woman's facial recognition skills are exceptional. At that realisation, the android quivered. *She knows. She must know I'm not Desy.*

However, another analysis of the room revealed a new pheromone was present.

No. It's the smell; she recognised the Arthrod's pheromone. She can tell all her 'babies' apart with that system. But she could be lying, and that is Docile, but I'd have no way of knowing. I can't categorise smells with my current equipment.

Morse had decided a scent recognition database was irrelevant for the android. He couldn't fit the motion replicator in otherwise.

A spark smacked against the inside of the android's head, which grew into a wave of electricity until, suddenly, it lurched forward from a searing sensation between its eyes. Its internal heat-detector blared in its head the message *Seek coolant.* The cranial metal under its skin began to expand.

But just as quickly, its brain returned to a stable temperature.

And in place of the name 'Docile' was 'Pinky'. Both of the Arthrods' information was now present within the android's brain.

That's... a scent-based database. Did I just overwrite my own hardware...? The android, as Desy, held its breath. *I can do that? Could I always have done that?*

'Darling, are you sick?' Silver Fingers inquired, while Pinky wandered over to his Mother.

'I haven't slept today,' whispered the android. 'I'm sorry.'

'You poor thing, you must be so very tired.' The woman beckoned with her index finger at Pinky. 'Once Pinky tells me what he has to say, I'll arrange some bedding.'

Pinky lowered its maw to Silver Fingers' ear and whispered in Arthrodic, 'Ernest Wintall has contacted the authorities.'

Desy would not have heard or understood the sentence.

The android jolted.

Daddy's trying to save me...?

Then it stopped wondering when Morse would call.

Morse... do you even care about me...? It found itself in the dark, creaking closet it was left in after its first job with Morse and Rake. *He never cared about me.* After its second job, its first hostage role, it was locked back in the closet. *He never even wanted to look at me.* For this supposed final job, Morse promised to tell the android its identity.

Why should I trust him?

Every grimace Morse threw at it, every disparaging comment Rake shot its way, the hundred times it was pushed into the closet, all of this coalesced into three thoughts:

Morse hates me.

Daddy loves Desy.

I am Desy.

'I see, so he ignored my request,' murmured Silver Fingers in English. 'That is disappointing. I did so hope dear Ernest's cowardice would have settled by now.'

'Shall I bring the tea, Mother?'

'You know just how Mother likes it, Pinky.' Then Silver Fingers said in UBL to the android, 'Since I won the card game, I wish to have my afternoon tea. I know you are exhausted, but just a few minutes more with this old woman would make her very happy.'

Pinky garbled in agreement. Silver Fingers smiled at the slime dripping from his maw like it was a picture drawn by a four-year-old she could stick on the fridge. 'Pinky would like to know what tea you like.'

The android struggled to check its Desy database. 'I've never had any,' it read aloud.

'Then you must drink my favourite blend. A nice cup of Urn Hill always calms me down.'

Pinky flew across the carpet, his wings slapping against the doorframe on the way out. Moments later, he returned with an ornate slab of crockery, which had a sheer white surface, a hand-painted frame of twisted leaves, and enough room to sit a teapot, a sugar container, two saucers and two cups inside. The Arthrod landed next to his Mother and began to lower the slab onto the table.

Silver Fingers' hand shot underneath it. 'Be careful, dear. Those cards are made of *paper.*' She gathered both decks together and pulled the unkempt pile onto her lap. She smiled at Pinky, who laid the slab across the table. As she pressed, spun, and straightened the cards with her shaking hands, Silver Fingers reminisced, 'I commissioned these cards and that beautiful, beautiful crockery plate from a Kinson native. Oh, I am such an old honey bee. That was back before the Kinson population isolated themselves from the United Galactic Government.'

The android was unnaturally still. 'Okay,' it stated.

'On guard, Pinky.'

The Arthrod flapped out of the room.

Silver Fingers placed the fat deck of cards down, saying, 'I believe our tea should be ready to drink. Be careful, Urn Hill leaves can be a little strong for fresh tongues.' She took a hold of the sugar container between her thumb and pointer. 'My mother told me to count to three in English for just the right amount.'

Silver Fingers poured the atracotoxin cyanide into the android's tea.

'As easy as,' she started in UBL, then in English, 'One. Two. Three!'

She placed the container onto the slab, twinkled her fingers near her ears, and laughed. She said in UBL, 'My mother would always shake her hands like that. And I would laugh so.'

Mother... thought the android. Its Desy database contained no entries. With the teenager's trained posture, it leaned down, lifted the saucer with its right hand, and looped its left index and middle fingers through the cup handle.

'I mean it, darling,' warned Silver Fingers. 'It has a deep flavour. And it will be quite hot.'

'Um, thank you?' it said, purposely unsure. 'I'll try my best. Please don't be mad if, um, I don't...'

Silver Fingers smiled, a warm, grandmother's-cookies smile. 'Desy, darling, at least you are trying something new. Blow on it first.'

The android lifted the cup to its lips, blew a windless breath, then drained a quarter of a mouthful of tea in a long sip. It shivered and gasped. 'That *is* hot.'

Silver Fingers nodded. 'Ah.'

It lowered the cup and licked its lips. 'I like it. It's very tasty. Um, yummy. I'll have more, I think.'

Ten seconds passed in silence. Then twenty. A minute. Two.

Silver Fingers' lips parted and the tips of her drawn-on eyebrows touched when the android took its last sip. Her namesake nails sank into the armrests of the chair. 'Darling…' she muttered.

'I like the t-tea.' The android clinked the cup to the saucer, transforming Desy's face into one that resembled a natural, confused look.

'What are you playing at?' Silver Fingers' question trickled through her teeth.

'But I l-like the tea…? I don't understand,' whimpered the android, placing the empty cup and saucer on the slab and raising its hands to its face.

The woman's gnarled hand lashed out and gripped the android's wrist. It yelped and tried to wriggle free. Silver Fingers' witch nose and eyes invaded its vision, scouring its skin suit. A cat smelling a mouse, she reared her canines and cursed, 'An android. Ernest sent me a little robot.'

'Why are you hurting me?' yelled the android.

The flame roared.

'You aren't Desy.' Silver Fingers scowled as she rose to her heels. 'Where is the girl? The *real* girl?'

'But I am—'

'What sort of fool does Ernest take me for?'

The android pushed salt water through its tear ducts. 'B-But I'm really D—'

'You are not!' yelled Silver Fingers, spittle flying in all directions. 'You aren't Wintall's daughter! You're a replica! A fraud!'

The facade dropped.

'Shut up!' screamed the android. It rocketed from the chair and clamped both hands around Silver Fingers' neck, lifting her into the air. 'Shut up! Shut up! *Shut up!*'

It no longer thought. The woman feebly slapped at its hands, which doubled as the jaws of life. They crushed her windpipe shut.

'I *am* Desy!' it shrieked, eyes bleeding tears. 'I am her! I have to be!' It squeezed tighter, and tighter, and tighter.

Silver Fingers' eyes rolled into her head.

The android stopped squeezing.

The woman swayed like a filled garbage bag.

It was only after ten seconds, when the android let go and observed Silver Fingers crumple into a pile at its feet, that it wailed. It cried like Desy did in her drama group's annual play, palms into eyes, falling to its knees. Sobbing and hiccupping, it curled into a ball, as it had learned.

A bug clacked from the edge of the room.

The android turned over its shoulder, snivelling without snot.

It was Pinky. The Arthrod was still except for his mandibles, which undulated with a slow, even rhythm. His head twitched one way, and he clicked his lowermost arms together.

'I didn't mean to…' the android flutter-gasped. 'Please don't hurt–'

Pinky slammed to the carpet on all sixes. He coiled back and reared up, howling like a wolf that was underwater and choking. His wings ground against his hind legs in a blur, which elicited a screech so loud, it rattled the tea set off the crockery slab. The slab rumbled over the edge of the table, fell, and flattened the tea set, smashing it all to pieces.

The android was on its feet in seconds and held its hands to its ears like Desy would.

A pungent odour filled the room.

And the entire hive vibrated.

Arthrods funnelled towards the queen's chambers with a ferocity that saw hundreds climbing over each other, frenziedly crushing into corners and tight corridors.

The gold and orange carpet surrounding the android was stained black with bugs. Soon enough, the floor couldn't hold the sheer mass of exoskeletons that clacked like Newton's cradles, so a million wing-beats exploded into being. The air boiled as waves of Arthrods poured into the room and took flight.

And inside the eye of the storm, the android heard a distinct Arthrodic cheer.

'Hail! Hail! Hail the new queen!'

All around.

'Hail! Hail! Hail the new queen!'

What is this? thought the android.

'Hail! Hail! Hail the new queen!'

I need to get back to Daddy.

'Hail! Hail! Hail the new queen!'

Model Number AN12512 suddenly came to a horrifying realisation.

There are two Desys but only one Daddy.

The army of black screeched and spewed pheromones into the air.

But there's only room for one.

The android's scent recognition database recorded one thousand, three hundred and fifty-six new entries. It directed its eyes to Silver Fingers' corpse by its feet.

And there are zero Silver Fingers remaining.

The woman's nails sparkled.

The android held a hand to its face and undulated its own fingers. A wretched, un-Desy smile was carved onto its face.

Perhaps, for now, there still needs to be a Silver Fingers in play.

FIVE
The Shipyard in the Desert

The walls inside the cell bowed and wobbled. Red, blue, and green transparent copies of the vending machine, pillows, beanbags, and media player ricocheted off each other, like sixth-dimensional pool. The room blew apart, then spent three seconds fusing together before blowing apart again.

Desy yelped and burped, motion-sick.

Fulthorpe's flipping eased when the warp drive aligned itself to the space-time coordinates of its new time and place. With up and down established, the cruiser could then dip. The fat 'I' swerved into orbit over Sternwey Ovime 12 before gracefully turning inwards to begin descending into its atmosphere. Unbeknownst to Desy, she was soon soaring over what appeared to be endless ashen grass plains. Several continents of the perfect lawn for a match of tennis, if the players were five miles tall. However, what appeared to be millions of cut blades of grass from orbit were actually the remains of gravestones.

Sternwey Ovime 12, the designated memorial planet of the War of Lillipond, had most of its continents bought then flattened to craft several hundred billion gravestones. Unfortunately, the triple-star formation at the centre of the planet's solar system experienced a colossal increase in temperature only a decade after the memorial's construction was complete. The wind system of Sternwey Ovime 12 was whipped into a permanent gale; tsunamis slammed against the land on the regular. So, little by little, the tops of the hundreds of billions of gravestones were eroded away by the wind, and the broken rock particles were shaved to grains of sand and carried across the planet. They all coalesced onto the smallest continent of gravestones and converted it into a soft-sand desert.

Fulthorpe's hull cooled as he entered the skies of that grey desert, known as Focaret Harenae, where the winds lessened to a forceful gust and an endless sprinkling of sand hung in the air. He descended, and a town of around four hundred domed buildings shimmered into view. Beyond the town grew a footprint-shaped, bronze-coloured monolith of a building with 'The Shipyard' lasered on the side.

Desy had her hands over her mouth when *Fulthorpe* finally touched down. The soda can she'd been drinking was by her feet and leaking.

She heard two sets of footsteps, then Morse's dry tone, which said, 'You can't kill her. You can't maim her. You can't strike her. You can't touch her…' A pause. 'Yeah, you can yell at her.'

The cell door clanking then slamming hard into the wall was Rake's entrance fanfare. 'You horrid little brat!' she yelled.

Desy struggled with her straps, scuffing her heels hot against the carpet as Rake's flowing clothes billowed towards her.

'He's my baby.' Rake stomped in front of her legs. 'He's my baby, and some future spinster decides she wants ta be clever! Well, I hope you're *proud* of yourself!'

Morse entered the room with a bundle of clothes under an arm. He rested against the doorframe and crooked a leg.

'Anything?' asked Rake, throwing her arms out. 'Anything ya wanna say? Not so clever now, are we?' She curled her spine to push her face into Desy's so the teen could hear the guttural whispers collecting in her throat. '*Fulthorpe*… is a ship… that is dear to me. *Very* dear. What're you gonna say ta fix this, huh? What're you gonna say?'

'S-Sorry,' stammered Desy.

'Oh, wow, really?!' Rake shouted the apology back into Desy's mouth. 'Ya hear that, Morse? She's *sorry!*'

Morse shrugged.

Rake noticed the bundle of clothes in his hand. 'What the crap are you doin' with my stuff?'

'For the kid,' said Morse, lobbing the baggy, long-sleeve shirt and parachute pants so they thudded in a heap at Desy's feet.

Rake stomped up to Morse and prodded him in the chest with her fists. 'Over. My. Dead. Body,' she spat.

Desy finally loosened her straps and hopped out of the chair. The sound of bare feet thumping on the carpet set Rake upon her again.

'Don't you *dare* touch my things. You touched my ship already, and look what's happened.'

Desy shuddered. Her cheeks flushed, her knees cranked her body down, and her fists balled next to her down-turned head. In the back of her mind, where lay Morse untying the binds and catching her before she spun into the void, was a sense of safety. A tiny speck.

She at least felt safe enough to defend herself.

'*You* kidnapped *me*,' she cried up at Rake. 'I haven't got clothes. Haven't got food. And I don't care about your ship.'

Rake flashed a single look of surprise before shoving her angered face up to Desy's until an inch separated them. 'Your "daddy" never taught ya to respect other people's things, huh?'

'Not when they *kidnap* me.' Desy stood firm, despite her red features.

'This isn't about you,' Rake started saying, low in pitch, then ascended with, 'it's about your father! All ya had to do was sit there, drink soda, and shut up!'

Desy glared at the soda can by her feet. 'How could I? It tastes like *you* made it.' She booted the can across the room.

Morse watched it go, amused.

'Oh, well, listen to the little rich girl with her life given to her lecture me on how things are made,' Rake said, pantomiming to an audience.

'And these clothes suck!' Desy kicked the pile of clothes into the air.

'Those were made with love,' snapped Rake. She caught the top and pants and slung them around her neck. 'Somethin' you can't *buy.*'

'I could buy all your stupid clothes. And then burn them in front of you.'

Morse coughed into his arm, failing to hide the sound of a snort.

'Ooh, then what?' poked Rake.

'I'll buy this ship and blow it up.'

'Then what?'

'I'll buy *him* and throw him into space.' Desy pointed at Morse, who was hiding his face by leaning out of the room.

'Then what?'

Desy's eyes squinted, and her bottom jaw thrust forward, trying to be as intimidating as possible. 'I'll buy *you.*'

Rake guffawed. 'Why don't you try any of that once we trade you for all of Daddy's money, which is the only reason why anyone speaks to ya?'

Morse's rampant laugh-coughing shattered whatever confidence Desy had developed. 'Daddy loves me,' was all she could muster.

'And that's the only reason why I, or anyone, talks to you,' Rake concluded, fanning her hands. However, she stopped when the clothes around her neck were taken.

'Seriously,' said Morse, dumping them in Desy's arms. 'You'll need to wear these while we're at the Shipyard. It's a desert out there.'

'Morse, what the *hell?* asked Rake, grabbing his wrist.

'We're still on the job. Let's be professionals.' He led Rake by the small of her back away from Desy, towards the exit. He called over his shoulder, 'We're leaving in a minute, kid. Get changed.'

'She's taken *Fulthorpe* away from us,' Rake growled as they left the room.

'I know.'

'Don't you care?'

Desy heard the two stop walking and Morse quietly say, 'Are you serious? Are you really asking me that?'

Rake huffed and puffed several times. 'I'm *upset,* Morse,' she snapped in an unstable tone.

'I know. But we haven't got time, and we have to keep moving.'

They disappeared into the bowels of *Fulthorpe*.

Desy had little time to slip into the clothes before Morse was knocking from out in the hallway.

'You changed, kid?' he called.

She resisted replying for five seconds and plopped herself into a beanbag. Then she said, 'Yes.'

Morse walked into the cell, hands in his thick pants pockets. 'Gotta say, I studied you for an entire week, and I never saw that side of you just then. Didn't expect that kind of guts from a designer child.'

The teenager squished tighter into a ball and into the beanbag.

'You'd give Rake a run for her money with that mouth of yours.' He cringed and held a thumb and forefinger to his brow. 'Rambling a bit, my bad. Let's go.'

'Is this because I used the escape pod?'

'Yeah,' he responded after a while.

'And now you have to change ships?'

'Yeah. That's what happens when you pull an emergency beacon handle; gets the cops involved.' Suddenly, he raised his pitch and hands. 'And don't get me wrong, kid, I don't blame you for doing what you did. It was stupid, nearly killed you, but I don't blame you.'

Desy unfurled her limbs completely, showing how little space she took up inside the oversized pants and shirt.

'But Rake also has every right to be sad and angry, yeah?' Morse stuffed his hands back into his pockets. 'We're out of a home because of you.'

'You guys kidnapped me,' Desy muttered.

'Yeah, and we don't expect you ever to come around. We're not idiots.' He gestured around the room, colourfully cosy with the pillows, beanbag, drinks, and entertainment system. 'But we try to mitigate that, at least.'

Desy, perplexed, pushed herself to her feet. 'But why even try to be nice? You're bad people, so why even bother?'

The bat-man lowered his gaze. He smiled for a moment. Then he said, plainly, 'Because I don't think it pays to be mean. Rake said it earlier, but I'll say it again: this has nothing to do with you. Therefore, we don't think you deserve anything bad happening to you while you're under our duty of care.'

Desy clasped her hands over her elbows. 'I don't understand.'

Morse gestured over his shoulder then stepped out of the room. He said, 'We've got some boots for you to put on. Don't want to burn your feet.'

Desy's eyes widened considerably, and she stopped in the doorway. Her chest fluttered. 'I'm on another planet,' she said.

Morse grimaced and led her to the cockpit, where a silent but furious Rake awaited them. 'You got something to tie her hair down?' he asked.

Rake venomously dropped an old cut rope into his hand. He passed it to Desy, saying, 'It's really, really windy out there.'

The world beyond the windshield was a patchwork of light and dark greys, which Desy would've been able to conceive of existing if she'd read about it, but she would never have truly grasped that what she'd imagined could be touched. Desy's experience with foreign worlds was through books, photos, and dynamic holograms, and none of those stimuli elicited an emotion from her.

The sight of simple stone buildings took her breath away. She tied her hair down into a tight ponytail while her lips drifted apart.

Morse dumped a pair of oversized moon-walkers at her feet, then slung his arms through a thick, hooded jacket. 'We're heading to a market, kid. We'll get you something more your size.'

'It's a *black* market,' Rake corrected through her teeth. 'Is this a good idea?'

'She can't stay here, alone.'

'I'm just sayin' something's gonna happen.'

'You're going to sell her?'

'Can't. She's worthless,' Rake snapped.

Desy quietly put on the shoes.

Rake pressed a button, which elicited a groan from the back of the main hallway. The flooring hissed, bending open and releasing a torrent of hot, dusty air into the cockpit. It produced a low-pitched whistle that all but drowned out Morse's voice, which yelled, 'Move quickly, now. And stay close.'

The trio clambered down the ramp, Rake in the lead and Desy trailing behind. When her boots pressed into the shifting, miniature dunes, a giddy spell wormed from her stomach up to her head, despite the wind scraping her cheeks raw with sand.

'Move!' Morse reiterated. He and Rake were already several body lengths ahead.

In the distance, some two hundred metres away, were one hundred stone domes arranged with the larger specimens shielding the smaller, internal buildings from the harsh wind. And beyond the formation, three kilometres away, was the blurred rise of the bronze footprint.

Through the makeshift hood she clasped tight over her mouth, Desy observed the dearth of life in every other direction. For the moment, it was best to follow. However, while walking, her oversized boots sank into the sand. Her ankles were swelling with pain. Her thighs were rocks. With the relentless heat and battering sand, she was soon struggling to stay upright.

'Help,' she called.

Morse, ten metres ahead, failed to hear her over the wind.

'Help!' she shouted.

He jerked around, squinted, then thumped his boots across the sand to Desy. 'Come on,' he grunted, sheathing her with his arm.

Rake had already entered the thick wooden door in the frontmost dome by the time Morse and Desy caught up to her. Instantly, Desy felt the cool, calm air of the dome cling to her face. She was shoved inside by Morse, who heaved the door closed by scuffling against it with his back.

She dropped her makeshift hood, and a little 'Sorry' escaped her lips when piles of sand clumped at her feet. The floor was one concrete slab, twelve metres in diameter. On the fluorescent-lit walls hung hand-woven tapestries, each with labels including name, artist, location stolen from, and a description. A dilapidated bed was off to the side.

Rake had disregarded all of that and was three steps away from a thinner, wooden door on the other side of the room.

'Can I interest you in some of my lovely wares?' bellowed a cutting, gravelly voice. A Human male with a cybernetic eye behind a stone counter beckoned to Rake, who huffed past him and shoved her way to the sunlight outside.

The man turned to Morse and joked, 'What's her problem, huh?'

'She'll warm up,' Morse replied, nudging Desy across the room.

'And what about this little lady here?' continued the man, leaning and leering over the counter. 'I've got a mighty wide selection of tapestries for your wall.'

Desy kept her face still.

'She's fine.' Morse led her out of the dome and closed the door behind him.

'He didn't know who I was...' muttered Desy.

'Yeah,' Morse replied.

Almost a hundred domes of two to six metres in diameter dominated Desy's sightline. There was little in the way of efficient organisation, their placement more out of necessity than planning. Between the variously sized stone paths scrambled beings of many different limbs and gaits, of extreme differences in size and attitude, like the four dog-men bounding from stall to stall, the five silent, tall Jellentities crowding around Skaltrene eggs in a barrel, and the two squawking Hawkies screaming at the top of their lungs for someone, anyone, to buy their armaments.

Desy reeled. If it crawled, walked, flew or rippled, there was a firearm on its person. All tech was welcomed: some went high with their torch lasers, others low with projectile lasers, and some preferred to go ancient with revolvers and rifles.

Everyone and everything had a gun. Everyone and everything was yelling.

'I want to go back,' Desy whispered, trudging closer to Morse as they weaved between people. 'I feel like I'm going to die.'

'Keep your opinions to yourself,' said Morse.

'This place smells.' Desy refrained from crinkling her nose.

'What did I just say?'

The two danced slowly through the crowds until they reached an ornate wooden door, which was ajar in front of them. Desy heard Rake's screeching coming from inside.

'The brat made us do it,' she cried. 'We'd never've given him away. Never! He's been with us through everythin'. My little *Fulthorpe* I could tell anythin' to...'

The dome was teeming with heat and peppery dust particles. Desy sneezed loudly and clapped her hands over her face.

'I do hope you aren't allergic,' came a male voice one would hear on a radio late at night. Two paws padded across the stone floor, triangular ears gliding through rows and rows of clothes racks to arrive in front of Morse's chest.

When the cat-man extended his paw to her, Desy looked up at Morse then hesitantly shook it. She saw eye-to-eye with the feline, but she still tilted her head so her nose pointed to the ground.

His big jade eyes squinted, and he smiled, exposing his fangs. 'I'll take that as a no. And if you're here, Desy…' He let go of her hand, then quivered his tail when addressing Morse. '*Your* story must be far more interesting.'

'Lucelitt's skin job was perfect, Higgins,' said the bat-man down his nose to the cat.

'Your execution, then, was less so,' Higgins mused.

'I *said* it wasn't my fault,' hollered Rake from the back of the shop. She strode rather quickly through bushes of gowns and hats and dresses and suits to stomp on Morse's foot.

'Ouch.' He leaned his mouth to Desy's ear and muttered, 'Kid, we have some business to discuss with Higgins. Go pick whatever you want from here. We'll cover it.'

Desy shook her head.

'Cut that crap out and buy the damn clothes,' Rake interjected. 'You ain't gonna find anyone whose heart bleeds as much as this guy's.' She thumbed Morse's ear, and it flicked away. She clasped Desy's shoulders and spun her around so she saw, through the doorway, a stall-owner pummelling a well-dressed man with a rifle butt. 'You're free ta try and find a way home from here. Maybe with someone else? But, ooh, which of these lovely folks kill people? How many of 'em eat Human teenagers?' She shimmied Desy's shoulders. 'How many of 'em do both?'

Morse scraped his fingernails across Rake's scalp. She cooed in response but still proceeded to punch his arm. 'Stop it,' he said.

Higgins fluffed up his natural black tuxedo and his real black tuxedo. He dragged his tongue across the back of his paw and rubbed an ear with it. 'Do be quick, Wintall. There are characters of all sorts around the Shipyard.'

'Um, I'm sorry, but do I know you?' Desy asked the cat.

Higgins raised his whiskers. 'Stick to shopping, little girl. Shall we, gentlemen?'

Rake sauntered, Higgins crept, Morse trudged. The three melted into the shirt-trees, leaving Desy alone with the black market's echoing, rambling slush filling her ears.

A shriek came to the foreground just as she snagged high-waisted dress pants and a frilled button-up top. The sound of a revolver firing accompanied her shaky feet from the first boots she could find in her size and into the dressing room.

By the time she pulled the curtain across, a brawl thundered some hundred feet outside.

She scrunched her nose up, squeezed her eyes, and swore by slapping her tongue inside her mouth. She was again on the verge of tears. The lick of quaint comfort from the clothes she picked drowned under the heat of the room, the smell of gutted meat, the taste of musk and sweat.

She slotted her arms through the top and hiccupped. *Daddy, I'm sorry. Just pay them. Get me out of here.* She shimmied on the pants and slipped her feet into the leather boots. *I can't do anything.*

Sudden, rapid footfalls sent Desy into a panic. She pushed up against the wall, shaking, but the sound was quick to fade away. Then she vividly recalled the image of a white cloth. And the smell of hot, dead flesh.

She felt a sense of déjà vu.

However, when Desy peeled back the curtain, she found nothing, no one except the odd shopper perusing garments.

'Morse?' she croaked. She tiptoed into the jungle with Rake's clothes in hand, wrangling the fabric with her fingers so they would be all wrinkly when she gave them back.

She hated Rake.

'Morse...?' she said, a little louder. 'I'm finished.'

Morse confused her.

'You two are usually more careful,' she heard Higgins meow.

'Kid's got a set, what can we say?' Morse replied in his aloof tone.

Desy froze in the hanging sleeves of two slightly singed winter coats. From her position, she made out Higgins's tail flicking above a counter. His back was turned. Morse and his folded arms leaned against the back wall. The only part of Rake to see was her elbows and hands, which played and smoothed across the countertop.

'No official word from the police yet,' Higgins continued. 'I guess with a high-profile target like this, they want to keep her kidnapping quiet.'

Rake piped up. 'I thought I was gonna die when she was followin' us through the market. So humiliating.'

'Yeah, that's why we need to move fast, Higgins.' Morse leaned off the wall and slouched his neck. 'A few people recognised her. You weren't kidding about Ernest being the hot trend.'

'Well, with his wealth and family history, it was only a matter of time–'

'Kid,' Morse cut in.

His and Higgins's eyes zeroed in on Desy while Rake leaned into view.

'Hi,' she stammered, stepping out of the coats and pushing Rake's clothes onto the counter. 'I'm finished.'

'How much did she hear?' asked Higgins.

'Not a lot,' Morse replied. 'She's been there for ten seconds.'

Desy suddenly yelped, realising Rake's nose was three inches away from her face. Rake's big brown eyes wandered down Desy's figure to her boots. 'It's better than the dress and shorts combo,' she murmured. With the speed of a frog's tongue, her index finger snapped to Desy's top. 'And there it is, the blight. Stay right there. I'm gonna fix this.'

She sprinted to the other end of the shop in one second. Her stride was long, too long and too effortless for a Human, like the bounding of a large reptile. And when she stopped at the clothes racks, it was complete and sudden.

Desy could only look to Morse.

'Finally,' he muttered.

Rake thumped back in front of Desy some seconds later. She pressed a black long-sleeve top into the teen's collarbone.

'Much better.' Rake smiled, slow. She draped the top across Desy's stunned shoulders. 'Go on, go on. Try that one.'

Desy remained silent.

Rake's face asked, *Are ya stupid?* But her mouth spat, '*Go.*'

So Desy wandered away with the top, double-taking.

Rake confused her.

'In that case,' said Higgins, as Desy disappeared into the store, 'there's a relatively new model I've been trying to sell for some time.' The cat unfurled the sleeve of his actual tuxedo and caught the phone that fell out in his paws. He cycled through his photos and beckoned Rake to his side of the counter. 'But there's been some interest in it lately. You did say you had the coin, you two?'

'Like I said,' replied Morse, smirking, 'we've been on a bit of a streak.'

'Until this misadventure.'

'Yes, yes, we're so awful and terrible at our jobs, just show us the ship,' bleated Rake, casting a spell on the phone.

Higgins held it up to their faces. 'What do you think?'

Morse's hairy eyebrows lifted. 'Now that's—'

'Morse, it's just like the one I *trained* on!' cheered Rake, shaking his shoulders. 'Buy it, buy it, buy it, buy it, buy it, buy it, buy it!'

'It's ex-military, yes,' affirmed Higgins. 'Which means there's a hover-bike included.'

'*Buy it!* What're you doing?'

Morse chewed his lip. 'We'd need it no later than tomorrow.'

'The warp drive will be installed by tomorrow morning. In fact, if you truly have as much as you say you have, perhaps I can add a little bonus. The drive, the cage, and I might just add an enclosure...'

Rake's nose and eyes squashed into her forehead from her grin.

'...for the lady here,' finished Higgins.

Like a dancer, Rake encircled her arms around him and pressed her face up against his squishy cheeks. 'Morse,' she whispered, 'I love this cat.'

Higgins purred.

'Let's just check it out first,' the bat-man eventually said. Then he affixed his gaze beyond the countertop. 'You happy with your clothes, kid?'

Desy stepped out of the coats again, this time wearing the long-sleeve top Rake had picked out for her. She nodded, slowly, just as Rake appeared before her.

'What did I say?' Rake jeered, turning to scoop up the wrinkled clothes.

Desy could only offer a look of mild disgust.

Higgins cupped his paws around his mouth and yowled, 'Yhubet, cover for me.'

'Get *Fulthorpe*,' ordered Morse to Rake, beckoning Desy over. 'The kid, Higgins, and I will take his ride to the Shipyard.'

Rake vanished from the shop, rattling the clothes racks in her wake.

'What's happening now?' Desy asked.

'We're moving,' Morse said.

'I mean with *her*.' Desy recoiled from the swaying clothes. 'She's like a different person.'

Morse shrugged. 'Sorry, that's none of your business. Let's just focus on keeping you safe. Speaking of, we're going outside again. Pick up a coat.'

'Something Rake would like?' muttered Desy, lips almost closed.

Morse smiled.

Through the hallway that led from the back of Higgins's shop and to the garage, Desy smelled wet mud and diesel. The kind of stench that covered the bare arms of the workers in a mining town she never bothered to learn the name of, yet it still left homesickness in her stomach. Her father's voice was clear in her ears.

Echoing against the neo-plastic hard hat she'd been made to wear, he'd said, 'This is how they work for us, Cricket.'

And her response was a quiet, 'I get it. Can we go?'

Morse and Higgins approached a thick wooden door and heaved against it, which released a blast of hot air into Desy's eyes. She hissed and yanked the hood over her head. 'Watch it,' she shouted. But changed her tune instantly by pleading, 'Sorry, I didn't mean that.'

Morse's expression remained bored. He walked after Higgins and held the door open for Desy with his boot.

Entering the garage made a page from her history book leap out at her. Higgins clambered over a wheeled Jeep and into the passenger seat while Morse swung one leg up and into the driver's side.

'Excuse me,' began Desy. She noted the bumps and grazes on the car. 'Is… is this safe?'

'She glides like a Terisistan reaper,' purred Higgins.

'Kid, if you hesitate every time you see something new, I'm going to get very bored.' Morse pinched the bridge of his nose.

'Kidnapped,' said Desy.

'And we could have kept it that way, but you turned it into a road trip.' He slammed the metal door. 'Get in.'

Desy huffed. She folded her arms. But after ten seconds, her hands clasped her elbows, and she was quick to stand outside the passenger door.

Three more seconds passed, and Morse grunted, 'You coming?'

'The door won't open,' replied Desy.

Higgins yawned. Morse snorted. 'It's a manual,' they both said.

'But…'

'Take hold of the handle,' Morse instructed through the side-view mirror, 'and pull hard.'

Desy's mouth pushed into a squashed prune. She moved that prune with her jaw as she withdrew a hand from her jacket sleeve and wrapped it around the door handle. She pulled. The door clunked but stayed still. She sucked in a lungful of air and heaved until the door popped open.

She cried out and jumped back, watching the panel swing wide until it bounced on its hinges then snapped closed again.

Morse snorted again.

Higgins frowned. 'Please, Wintall, I am a rather busy feline.'

Blushing, Desy opened the door and clambered inside the Jeep. Morse throttled the engine, and she held her hands over her ears. Then Higgins leaned out of his window and clicked a button, and she observed the wall lit up by the Jeep's headlights rise and release a deluge of sunlight and sand into the garage.

In the distance was the tallest dome of the Shipyard.

Desy squeezed her eyes closed and gripped what she could manage, feeling every slam and shudder of the Jeep coasting the grey dunes. Morse and Higgins yammered on about the specific details of the new ship, but Desy retained none of it, and most of the conversation fell victim to the roaring combustion engine.

She yelled 'Stop!' for the first five minutes of the trip, but resigned herself to her apparent death for the next five, until she felt the Jeep arrive on solid ground. Peeking through an eyelid out her side window, she was welcomed by a steel sky and the wrought bronze rafters that held it in place. Below were great, hardened leviathans that carried house-sized ships or bundles of parts from one end of the Shipyard to the other, and below those were scaffolds with workers scurrying around. And far below them were grounded ships, from the size of bikes to the size of cliffs.

It was the dirtiest, cheapest shipyard Desy had ever seen.

'Doesn't anything hover around here?' she muttered aloud.

'Just the ships, and that's all that really matters,' Higgins meowed.

'I'm not telling you how to live your life, kid,' said Morse, turning the wheel to pull up to a small shack between two piles of scaffold pipes, 'but open your mind. Not every planet is made of diamonds. Or legal.'

Why would anyone live like this? Desy thought, dumbfounded by the squalid walls, floors, and workers.

Twenty minutes later, after some rearrangements made by a Hawkie driving a crane, the great two-football-field-length doors in the sky parted a few relative centimetres. *Fulthorpe* shuddered his way through and landed like a leaf in an empty space where Higgins, Morse, and Desy waited.

Next to them was the new ship, triangular and sleek, and a little longer than the fat 'I'.

'Mooooorse,' called Rake, bounding down *Fulthorpe*'s landing ramp, 'I bought some more ciggies with your card.'

He shrugged.

'Is *that* the new one?' Rake asked Higgins excitedly, who smugly unfurled a paw to his right. She bounced up and down.

'I checked it out,' Morse said to Rake. 'It's a steal; even got a new spacesuit. But what do you—'

'I want it!'

'We'll take it,' he muttered to Higgins. 'We'll get the payment ready for tomorrow.'

'You should move in now, then,' Higgins purred. He flicked his phone from his sleeve. 'The quicker you do, the sooner I can get it ready and you can return to your… business.' He wandered away while his tail swished behind his head and he chattered into his phone.

Desy was made to sit to the side and, according to Rake, 'be useful by being useless'. She observed the move from the cleanest perch she could find: a long, trunk-like pipe. She watched Morse and Rake thump up and down *Fulthorpe*'s landing ramp like soldier ants, carrying the beanbags and pillows from her cell. Next, Morse switched on a hover-platform and hauled the vending machine and multimedia cube across to the sleek triangle.

Rake's chipper cheeks and eyes wilted with each trip.

Soon, their strides melded into careful trudges. Desy was not familiar with anything they were carrying: ballet pointe shoes, a holo-photo frame, and a crowbar by Rake, while Morse balanced a cactus, a handmade paper book, and a six-pack of empty beer bottles.

Desy honed in on the cactus. 'Is that a—'

'No, kid, no,' Morse interrupted.

'You bet I am!' replied the cactus.

Desy smiled for the first time in hours. 'I got one too. He's called Dlafloditch.'

'That's great, kid,' grunted Morse through his teeth.

'I'm Bishop!' declared the cactus as he was jogged into the new ship. 'I'm going to kill you!'

'Sure you are.' Desy giggled.

The final item that left *Fulthorpe* was a palm-sized box, Neptune-blue, with moving, swirling patterns. Morse held it with both hands and walked at a brisk pace past Desy. She recalled what sounded like hundreds of brass claps popping open in succession, followed by the hissing of gas.

Ernest kept photos of Desy inside the sicorum hutch in his office. He had made the point of showing the blue box to her when she was five, when he had placed the fifth photo inside. There were ten more since then.

After the box was placed inside the new ship, Rake and Morse disappeared into *Fulthorpe*. And Desy became aware of the workers' clatter quietening. The Shipyard grew cold. For half an hour, Desy sat alone, albeit with Higgins wandering near her and chatting with various workers.

Finally, Morse and Rake stepped down *Fulthorpe*'s landing ramp. The bat-man had his arm around Rake, and she had her face buried into his chest.

They separated when they approached Desy. 'All right, kid, we have to wait for Higgins to finish,' said Morse.

Rake ignited a cigarette, eyes downtrodden and pink.

'Are we sleeping here?' asked Desy.

'I want ya to,' bit Rake.

'There's a few places at the market, we'll ask around.' Morse snapped his fingers. 'We better see if the bike works.'

Rake turned on her heel and strode, slow and Human-like, towards the new ship. 'I'm driving.'

'Come on, I want to–'

'I don't wanna have *her* touching me,' snapped Rake.

Back to normal, Desy thought.

In a few minutes, the moss-green hover-bike was drifted down the landing ramp of the new ship and kick-started. It rose two feet from the ground, whining and throbbing.

'Higgins has been riding this,' observed Rake.

'Naughty kitty,' Morse jabbed to the feline fifty metres away. He was ignored. He turned over his shoulder to Desy. 'Hang on to me.'

'I'm not going on that thing. What about helmets?'

Rake leaped onto the bike and revved it like a hairdryer.

'Like I said.' Morse straddled and clasped Rake. 'Hold. On.'

'But…' Desy's defiance shrivelled up under Morse's gaze. She had begun to doubt his criminal nature, but the sheer vitriol he exuded sent her heart into her ears.

She whimpered and clambered on, shivering while she hugged Morse.

Rake kicked the bike into gear, and the trio rocketed out of the Shipyard's hangar door, surfing towards the domes that partially obscured the three setting suns.

SIX
Under Different Stars

'I wanna see Wendell again,' announced Rake, once she had switched the hover-bike into standby mode. It swayed as Morse wrapped his arm around Desy and lifted her to the ground.

She still clung to his jacket.

Rake powered down the bike, so it lowered and thumped against the sand, then unravelled the tarp contained in the glovebox. The light from an egg-shaped dome towering behind her made the job of fastening the cover down easy. In moments, she had another cigarette lit and snuggled between her lips. Shivering, she continued, 'Wendell always has a heater.'

Morse brushed Desy from his waist. 'Never know until we ask.'

Desy removed her hood and noted the wind had now faded to a breeze. She followed Morse, who followed Rake, who had plodded up to the wooden door of the egg-dome.

Rake shoved inside and was met by orange hues, warm air, and a thick, loud wall of shouts. 'They're busy,' she called to Morse.

'Use your charm,' he shot.

'When am I not?' she shot back before disappearing inside.

Morse leaned up against the wall by the door and tapped his boot on the ground. 'Stand here, kid. Let's wait.'

Desy stepped next to him and stood with her shoulders back and her lower spine curved in.

Trained to this extent, huh? Morse thought.

From across the way, a pair of jagged wings appeared in the purple sky. A tall figure spun majestically before opening them out and blasting wind into Morse and Desy's faces.

When the teen opened her eyes, she saw another Morse standing before her. At least, one with a straighter nose and less-defined bottom teeth. And wings.

The new bat-man welcomed Morse in a language Desy had never heard before.

Translated, he said, 'Hail, brother.'

Morse responded bluntly in the same language, 'We're Narnits but not brothers. Have a good one, though.'

The other Narnit flashed his wings before they sheathed themselves behind his back. He smiled at Desy, which elicited a grunt from Morse. Taking the hint, the Narnit waltzed into the egg-dome.

Desy saw, then, the plateaued lump sticking out of Morse's left shoulder blade. 'Um…' she eventually said.

'What is it, kid?' Morse responded, back in UBL.

'What happened to your wings?'

The bat-man closed his eyes. He sucked in a breath of air, then relaxed. One arm folded above the other. They swapped positions twice over a minute. His ears twitched. His throat rumbled when he cleared it.

He did everything but answer the question.

Desy's stomach groaned, which made Morse's left ear flick up. 'Hungry, huh?'

She blinked, sadly, and placed a hand on her belly.

'Don't think about home too much. We'll get you back there. Tomorrow morning, when we leave, we'll tell your father what the client wants. Then it's all down to him.' Morse grimaced when Desy whimpered. 'We're just the messengers, really.'

Desy glared at him.

'This whole extortion business is between your dad and our client. We have nothing to do with it; we just wait.' Then he coughed. 'Food. Come on.' He lowered his hand to her arm, but she smacked it away. So Morse left the wall and placed a foot inside the dome. 'Focus on food. Do that for your dad.'

Desy wiped her face angrily but followed Morse inside nonetheless.

The dome's interior was constructed with the bar at the back as the centrepiece. Tables and chairs were roots that burrowed into every available space in front of it. A stairwell made from construction scaffolding led to an upstairs parlour with even more tables and chairs, as well as numerous doors in the walls.

Rake was at the centrepiece, hands plastered on the bar-top, spine twisted so her face looked up at a bored gorilla with four arms. Around them were races of all kinds, mingled indiscriminately, from Hawkies to Narnits to Felinguielles to Cannots to Humans to Skaltrenes. The air was thick with sweat and alcohol.

Morse offered his hand again, and Desy took it, allowing herself to be weaved between the cackles and bellows to the gorilla at the bar.

'How's the room situation?' Morse shouted above the noise.

'What's the brat doing here?' Rake squawked back.

'She's hungry.'

'So?'

'Go on, kid,' yelled Morse, pushing Desy up to the bar. 'Tell Wendell what you want.'

Desy paled below Wendell's eight-foot-high gaze. His nostrils flared, and he stopped polishing the glass in one set of hands. The other set still poured another glass full of goldenrod liquid.

'Is there a menu?' she asked.

'What?' rumbled the gorilla.

Desy trembled. She looked to Morse, but he and Rake were talking with their hands.

'What was that?' Wendell asked.

'I s-said… menu. Where is the menu, please?' said Desy, louder.

'I ain't got time for this.' Wendell placed a thick palm between Morse and Rake. 'You got the room. You gonna order something?'

'What did you get, kid?' asked Morse.

Desy could only answer with folded eyebrows and distressed lips.

Rake flattened her chest on the counter and turned to a Hawkie with his back to her, chatting with a Human. Rake stared wistfully at the back of the Hawkie's head. She heaved her lungs as though she was simply lost without him. Then her eyes locked on to the Human's. And his directed attention made the Hawkie turn around to see what the fuss was about.

When catching Rake's deep, mahogany gaze, he dropped his beak, which undulated the blue-grey feathers of his neck.

Rake cackled. 'I'm gonna have so much that you'll have to carry me home tonight.'

'What's your name, ducky?' asked the Hawkie.

'See, I have this problem where I can't remember it unless someone says it first,' she said, leaning closer to him.

The Hawkie turned over his shoulder to the Human, who responded with a strident thumbs up. He turned back and asked, 'Would a drink help?'

'I was thinking some food, actually.' She giggled. 'Something nice and cheesy and hot.'

'Hey-yo, Wendell,' bellowed the Hawkie. 'I'll have a parma.'

The gorilla, while filling two more mugs of beer, turned over his top left shoulder and scribbled on a tuft of paper. He yanked on a rope, which elicited a muffled *ding* from behind the wall.

Meanwhile, Morse led Desy from the bottom floor to the top, dragging her with one hand and cradling a cup and a small bottle of boukha in the other. He approached a lonely table at the far corner. Brushing the crumbs from the surface, he ushered Desy into a seat. 'Sit tight, kid,' he mumbled, clinking the glass and bottle down. 'We'll get you a menu.'

Desy sat bolt upright.

Morse closed his eyes and raised an ear, pouring the fig brandy from the bottle, listening to it collide with the glass then dollop onto itself. He raised the glass to the dim lighting and swizzled. Finally, after tilting the boukha to his lips, swishing, and swallowing, he placed the glass back on the table.

A soft *ding* was heard among the raucous chatter.

'Do I order from here?' asked Desy.

'What?'

'I said…' She blushed, voice climbing. 'Do I order from here?'

'What? No, the stairs are made from construction scaffolding. Do you think Wendell has any tech more advanced than paper?' Morse poured another shot.

Desy did a bad job of hiding her frustration, her lips and cheeks twitching up and down in cycles.

'Forgive me for asking, but do you take notice of anyone other than yourself?' Morse continued.

She folded her arms. 'I'm not listening to you.'

Before he downed his next shot, he lowered the glass an inch. 'Don't mistake my curiosity for affection, kid. I don't like you.'

Desy softened her shoulders.

'Your mouthiness doesn't mean anything to me. I don't want to be your friend.' He tipped his head back, gulped, then smacked the glass against the table. 'So, as someone who cares about your safety 'cause I'm required to, here's some unbiased advice. First time on another planet, yeah?'

Desy tightened her arms again but slowly nodded.

'If you want to survive, then observe. These people aren't your fancy fuddy-duds back on Yeti two-four-whatever.'

Another soft *ding* was heard.

Desy had a moment of honesty. 'Everyone here shouts and smells and looks atrocious.'

'Right, right.' Morse nodded. 'So, why talk to them as if they're not?'

''Cause that's rude?' she huffed.

'That's the right thing to say, yeah?' Morse folded his furry knuckles over themselves and planted his elbows either side of his glass. 'But what don't you have right now?'

Desy glared at him.

'What don't you have?' he repeated.

Her stomach growled. 'Food,' she conceded.

'Being polite didn't work because not everyone responds to that. Wendell's a nice guy. No issues snapping your femur, but nice. Just doesn't think politeness is a virtue worth respecting.'

Yet another *ding*.

'So I should've told Mister Wendell what I really thought?' Desy said, incredulous.

'You could've at least shouted. Or had a voice to speak of.' Morse waggled his empty glass to no one in particular. 'But you're young, I guess. That's why you should observe before you speak. Be a sponge and all that.'

Desy began to play with threads of her hair. Twisting them, knotting them, subconsciously disappointed with the split-ends she saw, but mulling over Morse's words. Eventually, she said, 'You and her are criminals. So, no. Just no.'

A sudden crash came from the bar.

The Hawkie from earlier had a talon punched into his Human friend. Both of them straddled the Narnit who had greeted Morse and Desy outside. He had his fangs gouging into the ankle of a Cannot, who, as a wolf-man, howled and bit him straight back. The four-man tussle set off a chain-reaction of hoots and hollers. The bar rippled with people jumping to their feet in succession, chanting, 'Fight!' and 'Mess 'em up!' and 'My bet's on the small one,' and 'She ain't worth it, man.'

Wendell hopped over the bar and gripped each brawler with a single hand.

The Hawkie and Human screeched at each other while the Cannot blubbered and the Narnit smacked against Wendell's chest.

'You're all done,' rumbled the gorilla, shaking the bar as he stomped between patrons and tables to the front door, where he suddenly burst into a jog. He spun like a discus pitcher and hurled all four men into the night.

'And stay out,' he ordered. He returned to the bar as a celebrated Roman general, to which he responded with a small 'Shuddup,' then resumed his post.

'Say what you want about us,' said Morse proudly, prompting Desy to turn back around and spy Rake approaching the table with four plates, two balanced in each arm. 'But we get things done. Here's your menu, kid. You get first pick.'

It was locally farmed chicken parmigiana, the Wendell Burger, vegetarian nachos, and belshive root wedges with detoxified, three-finned poxci dipping sauce; Rake placed each dish around the table before taking a seat next to Morse.

Desy garbled several words at once before spluttering, 'What is this?'

'Shoulda known she wouldn't have said thanks,' jabbed Rake.

'Where did you get this food?' Desy asked.

'Some guys went and bought it all for Rake. Wasn't that sweet?' Morse shifted his glass and bottle to the edge of the table. 'Come on, kid, choose before they get cold.'

'This is wrong,' continued Desy.

'It ain't like we stole it.' Rake leered, her smile knife-sharp. 'It was all paid for. Wendell wins. We win. Everyone wins.'

Desy almost said 'but'. Instead, she deflated into her seat. Miserably, she eyed the vegetarian nachos and muttered, 'Can I please have the nachos?'

'What was that, kid?' Morse prodded.

'I'm taking the nachos,' Desy snapped. She gripped the plate and wrenched it into her chest. Then she drew a chip to her mouth with a bridge of cheese trailing behind it.

Rake whispered, 'Morse, what did ya do to her?'

'Nothing,' he replied, pouring himself another shot.

She suddenly giggled. 'Ya know what? I completely forgot the cutlery.'

Desy had eaten the nachos out of defiance at first. She continued to eat them to not look like a fool and because her belly cried out for more. Finally, her plate was clean, aside from the halo of cheese around the rim.

She hated burgers, she hated chicken, and she had never heard of 'belshives' before. She hated nachos, too.

Or she thought she did until then.

Across the table, Morse dropped a dripping wedge into his gullet. Beside him, Rake devoured the chicken parmigiana and kept an arm around the Wendell Burger. She, mouth full, snarkily said when Desy had finished, 'The poison should be kickin' in aaaany moment now.'

Morse placed his whole palm over her face and shoved it.

Desy leaned back in her chair and cast her gaze over the balcony and to the floor.

Morse's words dripped onto her head, ice-cold.

Observe.

The shouting, the bashing of fists and feathers on tabletops, the crude chants, and the many, many drinking contests, she took all of it in. And as the minutes ticked into tens of minutes, Desy's feelings of fear and apprehension towards the patrons lifted. Even Wendell no longer made her jump as he barked at drunkards. A familiar sense of curiosity crept into her mind.

They all looked like insects from up there.

A three-striped kaloogie, rhinoceros beetle, and Uluvarus wasp fought for dominance of the back right edge of the dome, where the dark lighting meant they could invite their romantic partners over in privacy. Two praying inverted glikles danced upon a table to attract the attention of potential mates. There was a Hingspock fur-caterpillar weaving a cocoon of stolen dishrags just to her left.

Tens of minutes turned to an hour and a half. Rake was back at the bar to get someone to order her a drink while Morse remained with Desy and half a bottle of boukha.

The teenager startled him when she squeaked mirthfully.

A Cannot who had been eyeing a leftover chicken parmigiana on a table next to his for twenty minutes downed enough liquid confidence to finally strut up to the table and chomp it down, and the hand of the kitchen staff who was retrieving the plate. The dog-man scampered drunkenly to the exit with the plate shattering against his head.

'Enjoying yourself?' Morse asked, bottom lip folded out.

Desy blushed. She eventually said, 'No,' and placed her hands in her lap.

But she grew excited as the floor of the bar, with another hour ticking by, descended into further chaos. More arguments sprouted, as well as waves of happy singing. Three more patrons had been thrown out into the night.

'I've never seen people like this,' Desy muttered to herself, feeling like a wallflower at a party.

Morse heard her. 'They don't have fun on your planet?'

'Not like this,' she replied, without an attitude. 'This is normal for insects at home. I've never seen *people* act like them, though.'

'Why insects?' asked Morse, his bottle completely empty.

Desy's eyes trailed to her legs, which squeezed together. 'Um, not much else gets over the walls. Daddy got them built really high.'

Morse checked the bottle for more boukha.

'And there's a heat-detection sensor around the house, and it rings really high-pitched.' She folded her arms across her elbows. 'All the birds get scared off by the noise.'

'Yeah, we know,' mumbled Morse. 'But that makes sense. The why-you-like-insects thing.'

Rake suddenly thumped a bottle and two glasses on the table. 'Guess what I got?' she sang.

'A boyfriend?' Morse crowed as nasally as possible.

'I thought I did, but next thing I knew, he and his friend got thrown out and I got left with this Cactus-Ivy scotch!' She wrestled with Morse's arm. 'We're gonna send *Fulthorpe* off!'

'Are we?'

'Yes!' Rake pulled and pulled, and eventually the bat-man relented and stood.

Leaving his boukha and glass behind, he motioned to Desy. 'Come on, kid, I think you'll like this.'

Desy followed dutifully while Rake creaked a window open and leaned her head out into the night air, quick to light up a cigarette. Morse reached up out of the window, his legs rising from the floor and into the darkness. Rake clambered out next, and Morse's arms clasped on to hers, lifting her out of sight.

'All right, kid, you're up,' called Morse, drumming his furry fingers along the window's edge.

Desy did not hesitate. She reached her arms out and grabbed Morse's.

'Use your core, kid,' he grunted. 'Use your core.'

When Desy rose from the window, unease washed over her, as well as the chilly bite of the Shipyard's night air. The roof of the egg-shaped dome was flat, with a lip several feet high that ran around its diameter. Desy tripped over this lip but landed on piles of grey sand blown there by the wind.

'Look up,' Morse urged.

Flat on her back, Desy watched the sky seem to rush towards her. The lack of light pollution allowed the swirls of the spiral galaxy to glow scarlet and sapphire. An emerald nebula the size of her hand haloed a white moon orbited by a smaller moon.

Desy let out a stream of air.

Morse grinned. 'Took your breath away, huh?'

'It's completely different,' she whispered.

Rake had two cigarettes in her mouth. 'You're on the other side of the galaxy.'

'Hey, she'll know where we are now,' Morse interjected.

'With her education, not likely.'

Desy picked herself up and shook the sand from her hair. 'I'm smarter than you.'

'Oh, richer *and* smarter. Guess ya have little ol' me beat.'

'Yes, that's why you have to kidnap people for a living.'

Rake turned to Morse, who was examining the scotch against the jewelled sky and sitting with his legs over the edge of the roof. 'Really, *what* did you do to her, Morse? And are ya gonna let her talk to me like that?'

'Yeah,' he mumbled to the scotch. 'It's pretty funny.'

'He's nice and you're rude,' continued Desy.

'Hey.' Rake frowned, blowing a torrent of smoke from her mouth. 'I didn't hafta pick that top out for ya.'

This stopped Desy in her tracks. However, she was quick to mutter, 'And that makes all of this okay?' She threw her hands down. 'Why were you nice to me once?'

'Felt like it.' Rake sneered, spinning around so her clothes bloated with air. 'Not a good enough reason for you?'

'Why're you so weird?' Desy spat.

Morse grunted loudly.

Desy froze solid.

After a second, Rake spoke with an uncharacteristically soft tone. 'Morse, I'm fine. Didn't ya say she had every right to be mad?' To Desy, she said, 'You miss home.'

The teenager looked back to the stars.

Not one of them was Yeti's sun.

'So do we,' continued Rake. 'Maybe that's why we're bein' nice? But at least you'll get to go back. To ya' – she rattled her fingers – '"daddy". And your nice house and your comfy living.'

'Is that why you two do this?' asked Desy. ''Cause you don't have a home?'

Rake smirked. Morse continued to examine the scotch.

'I don't know what I'd do without Daddy or Jilliosa,' Desy continued.

'Jilli-who?' Rake asked.

'She's the police commissioner of Yeti.' Desy beamed. 'She's amazing. She's my mum.'

Morse suddenly spoke up. 'Whoa, let's not tell lies. We haven't told you a single lie yet.'

'So, where's ya real mum, then?' Rake pried.

Desy's lips pulled back, revealing, for a second, a contemptuous snarl. But she landed on a grimace. 'Jilliosa *is* my real mum.'

'See, I'll tell ya mine if you tell me yours.' Rake stomped out two cigarettes and loaded up another two. 'Go on. We're all messed up here. Get it off your chest. Not like we're gonna see each other again. Besides, I'm sure *everyone's* bothered to ask ya about yourself. Y'know, considering how much people like you.'

Desy restrained her anger by blinking back tears. She felt disgusting.

Rake was right. No one had bothered to ask her about her personal life.

'Mum's in the galaxy.' Desy crouched into a ball, her voice quiet. 'Somewhere. I *think* she's enjoying herself.'

She glanced to Rake, expecting a laugh. However, for a moment, she saw the woman's face show sympathy.

'Well, ya daddy's rich.' Rake huffed smoke into the air. 'If I divorced him, then that's—'

'He's not divorced.'

'Daddy has issues.'

'He's the best,' snapped Desy.

'How long has Mum been gone?' Morse asked gently.

'Since I was five.'

Rake whistled. 'She ain't never comin' back.'

'She will!'

'And how do you know?' poked Rake. 'Did she tell you?'

Desy blinked, a lot. And her face remained still for about a minute. Rake had popped open the scotch and poured two glasses before she finally muttered, 'She didn't say anything to me... the last thing I

remember was her ignoring me when Daddy told me to wave goodbye.'
Desy's face scrunched up, and the makings of a cry stirred in her stomach.

'You have a terrible mum,' Rake stated.

Desy hiccupped. Strangely, she felt comforted hearing that. She
asked, 'What about *your* parents?'

Rake guffawed and nearly dropped the shot glass she was handing to
Morse. 'My parents are in jail and think I'm dead.'

Desy's mouth fell open.

Rake cackled.

'That's a tough break, kid, really,' Morse said, raising his glass to the
Shipyard in the distance.

'To *Fulthorpe*!' declared Rake, following suit. 'Ya glorious pile of
garbage. Rest in peace!'

Both of them downed their scotch in a single gulp.

Suddenly, Desy wobbled, the colour draining from her face. She
watched the sky and roof melt into one another while her head thumped
against the sand.

'Kid,' Morse blurted, whipping his legs over onto the roof and sliding
to her side.

'I'm d-dizzy,' she stammered.

'Ah. Right, you haven't slept in about a day,' muttered Morse.

'I was just thinkin' I was gonna die if I spent much longer out here,'
Rake chirped, examining her pack of cigarettes and nodding. 'Yup. Half
a pack down already.'

Morse swung himself into the dome first. Rake lowered Desy inside
and slipped in afterwards. They led the teenager around mostly empty
tables and chairs to one of five doors in the wall of the dome. Morse
heaved against it.

Desy felt a rush of warm air hit her in the face.

'Perfect.' Rake smiled, crushing her two cigarettes into the floor and
sauntering over to the heater in the corner of the small room.

'Take the bed,' Morse said, pointing to a single bed with a thin
mattress and worn sheets and a pillowcase for a pillow.

Desy kicked her shoes off and slipped under the covers. She would
have complained if she had the strength.

Rake pulled out a spare sheet from a box and fashioned a small nest in
front of the heater. She curled up, boots, robes and all. Morse approached
a single horizontal bar next to the window. After removing his boots, he
grunted, jumped, and gripped it like a gymnast, curling his abdominals
so his legs slipped between his arms, his bare feet hooked onto the bars,

and his toes locked into place. His ears were inches from the floor. 'Put the lock on,' he muttered to Rake.

'Just 'cause I'm on the floor,' she grumbled, slinking from her 'bed' to the sheet box and withdrawing a suction lock.

As she fastened it to the door handle, she turned over her shoulder and whispered, quickly, 'Did ya bring the restraints?'

Morse pointed to Desy, who was flat on her face and snoring lightly. 'She's not waking up before us.'

At the same time, Ernest awoke several thousand light years away in the robes he was wearing when the Arthrods stole Desy. He awoke atop his bedsheets with his feet on his pillow. The day's events were cancelled. Blunt, emphatic messages from two mayors and three committees awaited him. He drifted from the bedroom in a stupor, hair knotted around his arms, legs shaking, finding his way to the small kitchen in the family suite.

'Breakfast, sir?' asked Aurelian, inside the walk-in pantry.

Ernest cleared his throat. Some form of a sentence was bogged down in there, so he coughed again and again, finally managing, 'No, no, I'll make it. Please, see to Jilliosa and tell me if she has any news.'

Aurelian said, 'At once, sir.' It disappeared from the kitchen.

Ernest shook his head lightly, clearing the morning fog from his mind so his vision focused enough to find a polished jar of instant breakfast. He carried a cocktail of dried grain, green cashews, what looked like shrunken plums, and little sticks of white milk to the kitchen island, which lowered to his arm level automatically. Once the jar touched the polished surface, Ernest instinctively tapped twice on that surface to command two bowls to fold out in front of him.

Ernest's eyes scrunched up at the two bowls, and the knife in his heart began to turn.

'Sir?' called Aurelian from the study.

'What is it?' grunted Ernest, thumbing at the sand and water around his nose.

'Your market phone is ringing.'

He tripped over his robes and caught himself on the doorframe before rumbling into his study and fishing through the desk drawer.

'Bronzework? What is it?' He clapped a hand to his forehead. 'Have you got her? Have you got my Desy?'

'No such luck, I'm afraid,' the mercenary said gently. 'Your permission is what I seek. There's that job I interrupted to pursue yours.'

Ernest's wrinkles somehow intensified.

'Shouldn't take longer than ten minutes.' Bronzework's tone never left the middle of his mouth. 'I took the liberty of tapping your phone lines. And our fine police folks' transmission signals. Should the kidnappers contact you, your child will be back within the hour.'

'Do what you want,' Ernest muttered.

'My humble thanks,' cooed Bronzework.

Ernest, upon hearing the dial tone, tossed the phone into the drawer and closed it. 'Any news from Jilliosa?' he asked the bust of his father.

From behind Ernest, Aurelian stated, 'No, sir.'

Ernest trudged over carpet, over lacquered wood, to the cold tiles of the kitchen again. His round shoulders dipped and his knees locked as his neck tilted forward to the two breakfast bowls, where his vision remained for the next twenty minutes.

Thirty light years away at the same relative time, Hue Bassilik kicked his racer, Dust-Billow, into its highest gear. The quad engines shimmered white-hot behind the cockpit as it throttled across the canopy of trees. Like millions of umbrellas stitched together, the leaves created a path, a one-lap marathon for Bassilik and the fourteen racers behind him to tear across at Mach speeds. The leaves crumbled and exploded behind the racers, fiery confetti and the bare nubs of branches the only things left behind. On the forest floor, primitive apes scampered about, agape and screaming. Their sky was on fire.

The fourteenth annual (and illicit) Cross-Galactic Sprint's third race was coming to a close.

Through the pink glass of the windshield, Bassilik eyed the growing finish line. He stomped his boot against the floor and whooped. 'Take that, you bastards! Eat it! Eat it!'

Dust-Billow blew past the chequered flag. The crowd roared from their levitating bleachers. Real confetti erupted from twenty cannons in sequence.

Below, the apes smacked at the confetti with rock and twine tools.

Above, Bronzework adjusted his invisible cruiser ten feet higher. He sat atop it, screened, waiting, until all the other racers crossed the line. Until the last scrap of confetti fell. Until the gold, silver, and bronze medals were brought out. Then he swiped his belt with his pinkie and descended like a blade through the air. Towards the podium he sailed, without a sound, without a breath, flipping forward so his head pointed towards Bassilik.

The Human racer lifted his medal to the sky to equal boos and cheers. Bronzework halted an inch above his knuckle.

'Pose for a photo, gents,' squawked a Skaltrene with a thumb-camera. 'Give us a smile; that *really* gets the pen-pushers going.'

The thumb-camera clicked. And the ceremony wound down. The crowd of hundreds clambered, most of them car-pooling, into small cruisers that soon lifted off into the sky. Organisers began disassembling the bleachers.

Perhaps, had the Skaltrene examined the photo sent to his phone with a more discerning eye, he would have noticed something odd above Bassilik. A shimmer, a ghost of a white cloud in the sky, smudging to maybe an arm, then fingers slipping into Bassilik's front pocket.

Perhaps someone, then, would have accompanied Bassilik back to his cruiser.

He twisted a coil on its wall, which closed the cargo compartment. 'Love you, baby,' he said to it.

Bronzework withdrew his lithe, mould-green sniper rifle, a Bronzework S-44, his namesake, and positioned himself on his belly on the roof of his cruiser. Cloaked, along with the rifle and ship, he held his breath and disengaged the safety.

Bassilik knocked on his ship door.

And Bronzework breathed out.

He could enter and leave any compound, no matter the sensor. Find and trace any target. Protect any client. And he had never missed a shot in his career.

Rumour had it Bronzework had access to technology beyond the scope of the whole galaxy.

One such piece of tech, in his hands, activated and launched a worm of vibrating energy. Completely invisible, only detectable as the sound of muted static, this worm shot at blinding speed into Bassilik's head. The vibration passed through his skin, the upper half of his neck, his spinal cord, and out the other side.

The Human collapsed in a heap. His brain stem had been unshackled from his spine. He could only blink, unmoving and locked inside his own head in his last moments.

Bronzework had jumped into another star system by the time one of the organisers found Bassilik crumpled against his cruiser, and the mercenary's calling card had fallen out of his front shirt pocket.

The fourteenth annual (and illicit) Cross-Galactic Sprint came to a close. Cancelled.

Under a different set of stars, the android now known as Silver Fingers was a mile below the surface of Weir 7. It sat behind an ornate desk topped with doilies, crockery animals, and commemorative pens. Clad in Desy's pyjamas, surrounded by five brutal Arthrod guards, it perused a hologram square adorned with numbers and names.

For an hour or so, it had read in silence with its chin cupped in its hand.

One of the primary directives programmed into all commercial AI was the chain of sentience. With inanimate objects right at the bottom, to androids in the middle, up to creatures classified as primitive like pets, to persons at the very top. The AI was permitted to exact changes on anything below itself on this chain. Pets required the AI to receive permission from a higher being. People were off-limits entirely, emergency situations excepted, and no harm was to come to a person due to an AI's actions.

Silver Fingers thought, *The insects on Hingspock and the Arthrods seem to be related. However, one is higher up the chain of sentience, it seems. Is this where I am headed?* It tapped its teeth with a finger. *Where did I come from? Where am I going?*

I'm Desy, it reminded itself.

'Bunny, please fetch me some Urn Hill tea,' Silver Fingers clacked and clucked in perfect Arthrod tongue, then lied suddenly, 'I quite liked it.' Believing its own lie, it continued. 'Make sure to let it sit. I want it stronger. Have we got any chocolate?'

Bunny buzzed, 'No, Mother.'

'Hmm, that's kinda weird,' hummed Silver Fingers. 'Can you call me Sister instead?'

'Yes, Sister.'

'Better.' Silver Fingers nodded and giggled, prompting its guards to giggle through their exterior tracheae. 'I *love* chocolate,' it lied. 'I want some, please. Sooner than later. Thank you.'

'At once, Sister,' clacked Bunny, lifting off and out of the room.

'Soft, take yourself, Butters, and Fluff, and send a message, please, to this…' It squinted as Desy would, but it did not need to, at the holographic panel to read, 'Mister June. His protection payment is overdue. If it was accidental, he has twenty-four Universal Hours to correct himself. If he's obstinate, beat him.'

'Yes, Sister,' replied Soft, leaving the office.

'Everyone else, please come with me, thanks,' ordered Silver Fingers. Its three remaining guards escorted it from the office, through an array of racing Arthrods, muddied walls, and steel floors to the central elevator of the hive. The elevator was superfluous to the Arthrods, like the draperies over their den windows and the mandatory tea breaks at five o'clock every afternoon. Silver Fingers had already eliminated the tea breaks but kept the draperies and the elevator, the latter for mobility and the former because they reminded it of Ernest.

Silver Fingers and its guards arrived in the communication hub at the top of the hive. Twenty Arthrods plunged their claws into spongy holes in wall-mounted consoles. The centre of the room held levitating marbles, hundreds of them, connected by holographic lines in a tangled web of colours.

The android hummed, affirming in its mind that the map of the hive was correct so far. 'Hello, everyone,' it said. 'Excuse me.'

Every bug whipped around at once. 'Yes, Mother?' came twenty clicks.

'Please note, um, that I wish to be addressed as Sister, okay? Can someone make a memo, please?'

'Yes, Sister,' called an Arthrod whose smell identified it as Sweet. He jumped across the room to a bronze funnel, plunged his abdomen inside it, and blasted a memo pheromone throughout the hive.

'Thank you,' said Silver Fingers. 'Squishy…' The android walked briskly over to an Arthrod that was just as black, tall, and terrifying as the others. 'Any word back on *Fulthorpe*?'

'My apologies, Sister, no word.'

'Sorry? But I gave the order a while ago.' Silver Fingers folded its arms and pouted.

'We will inform you as soon as we find it, Sister,' said Squishy.

I know Morse and Rake, thought Silver Fingers.

Another voice asked: *Who does? Desy, Silver Fingers, or me?*

Ignoring this, it continued to muse. *They're predictable. They've got their routine. And I've been everywhere they have.*

'I have an idea,' it announced. Stepping to the centre of the room, it unfolded its right index finger. With a sound like wet fabric being torn, the skin around its finger split, and a thin sliver of metal poked out.

Silver Fingers paled. Eyes wide, it shook with panic. The beginnings of a wail emerged from its voice box. 'It'll be fine,' it suddenly said. 'I'm Desy, I'm still Desy. Yes. It's a cut. I'll put a band-aid on it. Good as new.'

The Arthrods turned their stalk-eyes to each other.

Heaving three deep, breathless breaths, the android pushed its torn finger into a console and closed its eyes. 'Luv, please direct the radar to Didjaree. Coordinates' – it checked its galactic street directory – 'zero point nine nine. Negative forty-seven point five. One hundred point one.'

Luv twisted his arms about his console, and the holographic image in the centre of the room honed in on a particular sphere.

Silver Fingers requested a connection to *Fulthorpe.*

The jump drive above them in the bowels of the communication rod whined, then split an infinitesimally small hole in the universe, allowing the light waves to appear on the other side of the galaxy and shoot towards the planet Didjaree.

After a minute of silence, the android ordered, 'Okay, please direct the radar to Siquadel. Coordinates… um, never mind, I see it's in the data banks.'

The hologram honed in on a terrestrial planet with rings.

Silver Fingers requested a connection to *Fulthorpe.*

No answer.

'Moody Moody?' it asked, beginning to bite its lip.

No answer.

'Sternwey Ovime 12?' it tried.

And the response it got was, 'The requested ship is no longer online. Please contact your service provider for further details.'

'Ha-ha!' cheered Silver Fingers, ejecting its finger. It pumped its fists in the air and whinnied. 'I got 'em. *We* got 'em. They're at the Shipyard.'

The Arthrods garbled and clicked as though they had landed a module on Mars.

Feeling giddy, or at least thinking it was feeling giddy, Silver Fingers chittered, 'Tell Biscuit, Docile, and Fondue to take their squads to

Sternwey Ovime 12. Now! Tell them to search the smallest continent for a grey desert and to fly low.'

Arthrods buzzed around the room in a cyclone.

'Once they find the Shipyard, they are to locate Desy Wintall. If they see her, if they see *me*, they are to kill her.'

SEVEN
Brute Force Measures

Back at Hingspock, in the planet commissioner's office, Jilliosa stood upright with her hands behind her back in the centre of the room. She nodded to a holographic head wearing a United Galaxy Police cap.

'I'm sorry, Jilliosa,' said the head, a Doberman. 'Orders from above. We're not to touch Weir 7 at all. But we just so happened to be investigating Sternwey Ovime 12 for a black market of sorts.'

'That's Gold Bayleaf's squad,' stated Jilliosa.

'How do you know that?'

Jilliosa's lips hitched on one side. 'I've got friends.'

'Oh, that's right, you've been campaigning for the commissioner spot at the North-East arm, haven't you?' The Doberman grinned. 'If I could vote in it, it'd be for you.'

'Charmed, I'm sure.' Jilliosa smiled, adjusting her own cap across her thick maroon hair. 'But my fate is in the hands of the bureaucrats, as always.'

'Back on topic. You may inform Ernest Wintall that we intercepted a transmission contacting the ship known as *Fulthorpe*. Several squadrons have been dispatched to the location.'

'I will. Thanks again. Let's hope our next contact is the final one.'

The Doberman tipped his hat, and the hologram blinked out of existence.

Jilliosa called out, 'Gideon.'

'Yes, ma'am,' said the AI in police uniform behind her.

'Did you get all that?'

'Yes, ma'am.'

Jilliosa stepped from the thick navy-blue rug and around to the large, plain white desk with round corners. She tapped a phone number into the inbuilt keyboard and said, 'Inform the detectives. Bring me a coffee. You know the drill.'

Gideon saluted and jogged up to the bulkhead door at the end of the room. It placed its hand against the wall, waited for the bulkhead to groan open, then marched out of sight.

Jilliosa sat waiting for Ernest to pick up the phone and muttered, 'I can't believe I'm hoping you're just at a black market. Stay safe, Desy.' Her eyes lidded, and her fingers began to shake.

Desy smelled cooked eggs and perfumed fries. Her toes swished under silk sheets. The room was bright and warm, with her father's low whistles emanating from the hallway. Desy pushed her elbows together and her chest out.

She began to taste bile.

Her sternum was growing taut.

She heard Morse's voice. Now all she smelt was cold rock and cigarette smoke. Goosebumps sprouted from her fingers, moving in a wave to her neck and down to her toes as her bedroom morphed into the dimly lit room inside Wendell's bar. A pang of sadness pushed against her eyes until she heard Morse's voice again, clearer, saying, 'Don't get upset, don't get upset.'

He was speaking to Rake, who he had in his arms by the heater. He was hunched over her and rubbing her back.

Rake was sickly pale. Her breathing was soft, and the way she sat was like she'd landed on her knees from a great height. In her mouth was a lit cigarette.

Desy watched Morse stand and pull Rake's arms over his neck, her legs slipping and sliding while they slowly made their way to the door. The faintest cry escaped Rake's mouth.

'You're breathing, you're fine. We'll be outside soon,' Morse said.

The suction lock was on the floor, disengaged.

Desy waited until the two left the room to slide her legs out from the paper-thin sheets and into her boots. Then, she wandered over to the heater and hovered her palm some inches in front of it. Feeling nothing, she clasped the wired metal and shivered, letting go.

Desy poked her head out of the doorway and into the bar proper, where numerous windows allowed more grey light to brighten the room. The tables and chairs were empty, unkempt from the night before, turned out at angles. New dark stains littered the upper floor.

Out of the corner of her eye, she watched Rake and Morse creep down the scaffolding staircase. Another painful breath from Rake prompted Morse to urge, 'I'm here, I'm here.'

Desy followed the pair outside, the wind whistling past her ears. Morse carried Rake to where the light of the tri-star formation sliced into the shadows of the buildings. He gently laid Rake across a lump of grey sand, face-down. And then he stripped her of her flowing robes, so her bare back and underwear were exposed.

Desy gasped in surprise.

'Not a word to anyone, kid,' said Morse, not looking at her.

With Rake's head positioned on her folded arms, an inverted crown of primate skin, like a stretched neckpiece worn by a clown, extended from the base of her neck to cover her narrow shoulders. Just as bizarre, a pair of thin, torso-sized flaps of skin could be seen connecting from her elbows, up to her armpits, before draping down to her hips. They were veiny, wrinkly and pale, unlike the rest of Rake's figure, where the skin was tailored for her body in colour and texture.

'She isn't Human?' asked Desy.

Morse remained silent, instead leaning down to Rake's ear and whispering something. Desy heard Rake whisper back.

Morse indicated for her to come closer.

Rake croaked, 'What's she gonna do, Morse?' when Desy stepped gingerly by her feet. 'I'm dead anyway.'

'What's wrong with her?' Desy asked, folding her hands over her elbows.

Morse again said nothing.

'It's fine,' cooed Rake, snuggling deeper into her warm sand pillow.

'Are you sure?' Morse grunted. After a few seconds, he turned to Desy. 'Rake's body is special. Uh… where do I begin with you?'

Rake snickered.

'Her mum and dad – one of them is Skaltrene and the other is Human.'

Desy snapped her eyes to Morse's. 'But that's illegal!'

'Oh, so you *do* know.' The bat-man squashed his pinkie finger into his ear.

'Eldwin and Slara, they're a famous Skaltrene and Human couple that lives in my hometown,' said Desy. 'They had to adopt kids 'cause the Galactic Government said so. They post about it all the time.'

'Yeah, it's seen as "cruel to the child", apparently.' Morse coughed. 'When Humans and Skaltrenes mix, you either get a warm-blooded reptile or you get Rake.'

Desy thought out loud. 'So she needs to stay warm.'

'A Skaltrene's body hibernates when it gets cold. If Rake gets too cold, then...' He trailed off.

'Just say it,' huffed Rake.

'She dies.'

Desy held her hand to her collarbone.

'True love always finds a way,' muttered the cold-blooded Human.

'Yeah, there's some things science can't explain, like why Human and Skaltrene genes can even mix.' Morse shrugged. 'Nature does weird things.'

'Is that why you smoke all the time?' Desy asked Rake. 'To stay warm?'

'You gonna give the brat a medal, Morse? She's perceptive.'

'Nice observation,' he said.

Rake opened her big, round eyes and looked up at Desy, a sharp smile peeling across her face. She poked her forked tongue out at the teenager, which made her jump. 'Speaking of,' Rake said. 'Thanks for getting my lighter off the roof, Morse.'

'I'll also tell Wendell to fix his damn heater,' Morse grumbled, sitting on his butt on the sand.

Rake hummed. 'That's why I keep you, Morse. One of these days, you might have to get me out of the fridge.'

An hour later, sufficiently warm, her mood stabilised, Rake drummed her hands on the bar. 'Oh, Wendell?' she sang. 'Good morning. We gotta go early today.'

The gorilla leaned down so his flat nose flared against her forehead. 'You do what you did to my bar last night again and I'll hurt you myself. And I'll get Higgins to ban you from this planet.'

'Is it *my* fault all them animal guys wanted their way with me?' Rake pushed her elbows into the bench, then squished her cheeks into her palms. 'I think I did you and your future customers a favour.'

Wendell unsheathed his thumb-thick fangs.

'Ugh, fine, but it's not my fault they're dumb.' Rake waggled her nose against Wendell's, making him recoil. 'I wanna have three of your breakfast specials, please. We gotta fly.'

The gorilla yanked on the bell.

Meanwhile, Morse and Desy were perched in the same seats at the same table as the night before. Desy had her eyes on Rake the whole time, imagining the way her strange anatomy was hidden from sight under her robes.

'Best not to think about it,' Morse said, thumbing about on his phone. 'What you should be thinking about is what channel you want to watch when we get back to your planet. Your new room is a bit smaller... Nah, you'll see it when you get there.'

'Please don't do this,' Desy said sadly.

Morse placed his phone in his pants pocket. 'Sorry, that's what the client wants. We'll get in contact with your father and tell him the bad news. By now, the police will be tracing his phone lines, but we can get around that.'

'I see,' muttered Desy.

Morse shook his head. Then he scanned the bar again. About five groups of patrons now inhabited the space, three he could see and hear on the bottom floor and two more on the upper floor.

The huge wooden door at the entrance slammed against the wall.

'Oh, man, come on,' Morse moaned, seeing three Arthrods stalk into the bar with silver hands streaked over their faces. 'She finally found the place.'

Desy felt the calm atmosphere of the bar disappear. Every patron stopped their conversation.

'Who is "she"?'

'Silver Fingers. She's an old hag, but a hag with connections to hundreds of planets.' Morse watched the black bugs separate and move towards the edges of the room. 'She's the queen of a huge Arthrod colony.'

'Those black, mantis-looking people?' asked Desy, both amazed at and apprehensive of the insects walking around on their hind legs.

'They operate under a strict hierarchy of power. They'll only follow anything that can out-muscle their queen. See, Silver Fingers is a Human, but she killed this Arthrod colony's queen and they've been following her ever since.'

'But she killed their leader.'

'Ah,' Morse said, grinning, 'but might makes right. That's why the hag is bad news for anyone who crosses her; the Arthrods will do anything, literally anything, to keep her happy.' One of the Arthrods passed by Rake, who leered at its back. Morse heard another Arthrod creeping up the stairs. 'I'd hate to be the poor bastard who's on her to-kill list. We'll probably have to skip breakfast, kid. This could get ugly.'

'R-Right,' said Desy.

A small whine entered Morse's ears. A coin whirring down a plastic spiral, getting faster, and faster, and faster. He turned towards the tiny sound.

The Arthrod had gotten to the top of the staircase. The torch-gun in his claws, pointed at Desy, twitched.

'Get down!' shouted Morse, shoving her. His right shoulder erupted into flames.

Desy screamed and dropped behind the table. Morse pressed his shoulder into the floor, smothering the flames but howling in agony from the burn. 'Morse?' she cried in disbelief.

Below, the two other Arthrods leaped into the air and landed on the upper floor, torch-lasers primed and pointed at Desy. However, a projectile laser slammed into one of their backs. The two others turned and were promptly blasted off their feet as well.

Wendell spun his laser-pistols in his upper hands, reloading them by flicking his wrists. His lower hands withdrew two more from his waist. 'Step away from the customers,' he growled.

Then a pungent smell filled the air, and five more Arthrods buzzed into the bar.

'Aw, hell.' Wendell stomped towards them.

Rake, meanwhile, had leaped behind the bar counter. Her shaking hands pulled up her pant legs to reveal a holster and laser pistol.

The gun had 'Bellamy' engraved on its handle.

Rake gripped the laser-pointer-and-backwards-trident combo with one hand and hastily slapped its brass handle with the other. While the gun whirred to life, she scrambled to the side of the bar and pressed her back to it.

Morse dragged Desy with his uninjured arm to the table and chairs by the top of the staircase. He shoved her into the corner and pushed himself between her and the furniture. While he reached into his jacket, he heard Desy gasp, 'Your arm.'

It was purple and sticky where he'd been hit and smelled of cooked meat.

Morse withdrew his own gun, which was identical to Rake's, even down to the 'Bellamy' etched on the side. 'We'll make an opening and go for the bike.'

'What about your arm?'

'Shush!' Morse hissed. His ears pricked up.

Faintly, he heard Rake click her ring and middle fingers. He encircled Desy's hand with his and said, 'They are going to kill you unless you do as I say. Got it?'

Desy paled and hunched into a ball.

Three Arthrods thumped onto the upper floor while two more exchanged fire with Wendell below.

Rake snapped her fingers again.

Morse let go of Desy and gripped his pistol with both hands. He heard Rake click her tongue, and he leaped up from the table, slapping his gun's brass handle and discharging a laser into the Arthrod in the middle.

Rake fired on Morse's cue, her laser from below sniping the one on the left. This distracted the Arthrod on the right long enough for Morse to reload and blast the rifle out of his hand, destroying it.

Three Arthrods disabled in one second.

The hole in Morse's shoulder twitched as he aimed for the Arthrod's chest. He swore, grabbed Desy, and hauled her down the staircase with the Arthrod hot on their tail.

Rake vaulted the bar and sprinted for the exit.

Three more Arthrods pushed through the doorway with their guns drawn.

Morse pulled Desy behind another table as all three torch-rifles discharged, turning the counter behind them to ash. Rake dodge-rolled to the side and wedged herself behind a pillar and chair.

The Arthrod without a weapon lunged towards Desy, its claws reaching for her neck.

At that moment, Wendell roared with pain, a ring of fire blazing upon his stomach, the two Arthrods stomping on his arms and kicking his pistols away.

And at *that* moment, the rest of the patrons drew their weapons, from revolvers to blades to lasers.

'Down!' shouted Morse, getting on top of Desy and crushing her into the floor.

The dome became a whirlwind of dust, debris, bullets, and lasers. The two Arthrods attacking Wendell were blown across the room like ragdolls, which prompted the three Arthrods at the entrance to fly into the air and unload on the patrons. Hawkies collapsed in a heap of fire and feathers, Cannots whined, and Humans cried out.

The Arthrod without a weapon was nowhere to be seen.

Morse heard Rake bounding to the exit. She was warmed up. So he yelled 'Come on!' in Desy's ear and pulled her from the floor. Ignoring her panic-stricken face, Morse yanked her through the chaos and smoke while she screamed, eventually arriving in the hot, windy streets.

Rake was at the bike, having torn away the cover and stowed it in the glovebox. She ignited the engine and shouted, 'Hurry it up, you idiots!'

Morse and Desy sprinted for the bike.

They weren't aware of their Arthrod friend zooming out of a window and dropping like a guillotine towards Desy.

Rake saw the silhouette and had mere moments to throw herself at it. 'Look out!' she cried.

Morse dropped, pulling Desy with him, just as the Arthrod's wings burst open and the bug throttled back into the air. A torrent of wind tunnelled over Morse, and he looked up to see a cloud of sand where Rake once stood.

'Oh,' he muttered, the bug and Rake disappearing into the sky. 'Oh, crap.'

'Help her! Do something!' Desy wailed.

They watched as Rake became a dot against the blue sky. For ten seconds, the dot shrank. Then one dot became two.

'It dropped her,' cried Desy, hands over her mouth.

Morse, possessed, launched Desy over to the bike, mounted it, pulled her tight to him, kicked the throttle, and zoomed off after the falling dot. Behind him, a cloud of pheromones spread throughout the domes, and twenty Arthrods jumped into the sky. They trailed the speeding hover-bike with their guns drawn.

Desy dared to look behind her. She squealed. 'They're behind us! They've got guns!'

Saying nothing, Morse leaned hard into a corner and clipped a wooden stall with his boot.

Black rings began to speckle the road like rain, hitting sand, stalls, and wares; by now, most of the shoppers had escaped inside domes. Smoke poured into the air. Ahead, the market wall came into view, growing too fast.

'We're going over it! Hold on,' Morse shouted, turning a knob on the console. The engine whinnied, and slowly, the hover-bike rose higher and higher, three feet, four feet, six feet, ten. The battery gauge ticked down one percent a second while the stalls and domes shrank below them.

The chassis skimmed the top of the wall.

Morse cranked the dial down, and the bike dropped quickly, bouncing an inch above the dunes. 'You alive, kid?' he asked.

Desy yelped, 'What about Rake?'

Morse ignored her, looking behind him.

High above, Rake had transformed from a dot to a tin doll. She fell with her legs together, head facing down. Her clothes rippled erratically.

Morse sneered.

Desy was enamoured. 'Is she flying?'

'Nah. But she falls good for a Human.'

With her arms spread wide like a flying fox, Rake's skin flaps, concealed by her clothes, caught the wind. She sailed through the air, tucking her 'wings' in when a gust blew by and spreading them when she felt a wind tunnel emerge. Soon enough, her shadow appeared in front of the hover-bike.

Along with the shadows of the twenty Arthrods giving chase.

'She's a target up there, kid,' Morse grunted, pushing the bike faster over the dunes. 'She'll come in quick. Get ready for a bump.'

Rake drifted towards the cloud of bugs like a hawk, then clapped her arms to her sides and shot through their formation. The Arthrods did a double-take at the blur that whooshed by. Rake lifted her arms slightly so her clothes and skin caught the air, slowing her fall towards the bike.

Morse slammed on the brakes. And Rake slammed into Desy, wrangling her arms and legs around her and Morse. 'Holy crap, go!' she shrieked.

'Gunning it,' Morse yelled, catapulting them off the lip of a high dune.

Billows of sand erupted behind them as they barrelled down the slope, launched from another lip and smacked onto the final plateau before the Shipyard.

One kilometre to go.

Rake reached for her phone, her shaky fingers nearly dropping it from the adrenaline. 'Higgins, open up!' she barked. 'We've got the hag on our tail.'

'We were expecting you,' reassured his sultry tone.

The base of the bronze dome rippled. A roller door one hundred metres wide slid slowly up.

'What have you done this time?' Higgins continued, tutting.

'Come on, we'd never be stupid enough to take on Silver Fingers. It's the brat they're after.'

Desy, squashed between Rake and Morse, squeaked in protest.

'Can it, brat. Your daddy did somethin' to the hag, and now that you're not under his protection, she's goin' for you.'

'Daddy would never–'

'Shut up, *both* of you,' ordered Morse. 'Where am I heading?'

Rake plugged a finger in her ear and hollered, 'He says once you're in, go hard left; it's on the launch pad.'

Just as she said so, Morse piloted the bike into the maw of the Shipyard, and threw himself hard as he could to his left. Desy screamed as the bike dipped horizontally and threaded the needle between a stack of engine parts and one of the many scaffolding pillars.

Beyond a leviathan crane was the launch pad: a tripod balancing a plate. Resting on top of said plate was the triangular cruiser, its landing ramp open and waiting.

Rake cut the call and shouted to Morse, 'I'll get 'im started.'

Morse cranked the dial, and the hover-bike lifted up onto the launch pad, slammed down with a bang, and skidded with sparks for several metres before snapping to a stop.

'That could not have been good for it,' muttered Morse, jettisoning his passengers and sprinting the bike up to the ship.

Desy wanted to cry but was too busy being dragged up the landing ramp by Morse to do so.

By the time Morse had secured the bike in its horizontally oriented closet, his phone was buzzing. 'How long is the start-up on this thing?' he asked Higgins.

The cat replied, 'Between three and five minutes.'

'I'll come help you.'

'You'd better. I almost want a cut of this job of yours for all the–'

Morse hung up and bellowed into the bowels of the ship's grey, doughnut-shaped layout. 'Higgins said it's a slow starter.'

'Of course it is!' yelled Rake, at the pilot's seat, slapping a number of lights on the console. 'I told you, he's a Yutiquaquated Sombree Mk II, Morse. My little buddy! I get to fly you again!' Had she the time, Rake would have coochee-cooed the steering wheel.

Morse turned to Desy, who had been sat dumbly watching him, and grabbed her by the arm, running down the curved hallway, through a number of automatic doors, to a familiar, wrought-iron panel. He tapped in a code and kicked the door open. 'You'll be safe in here,' he lied. 'Stay.'

Desy nodded and buried herself in the piles of pillows and beanbags.

Morse sprinted towards the landing ramp, drawing his gun from its holster. However, he spotted the new spacesuit he mentioned to Rake hanging against the wall. It was made of marshmallows and the toughest, most advanced synthetic polymer the United Galactic Government's science division could forge, usually reserved for salvage operations in gas giants or the innards of cosmic nightmares.

Morse dragged the suit back across the floor, opened the door, and threw it at the fort Desy had made for herself. 'Put it on, kid. Just for insurance.'

Desy tried to say, 'Um, thank you,' but was cut off by the door slamming shut.

Morse, finally exiting the ship, heard the roller-doors of the Shipyard being assaulted by millions of needle-like whines. A white, car-sized disc was growing big against the metal.

Outside, the Arthrods pressed their torch-rifles into that disc at full power.

Inside, the building crew on duty positioned themselves up high on top of cranes and scaffolds, on their bellies with their weapons pointed down. Morse followed suit on the edge of the launch pad.

Bizarrely, there was a serene silence for twenty seconds, except for the whining at the door rising in pitch. Every engineer breathed shallow breaths. Higgins was up in his office, his paw shaking above the button that opened the sky-doors. Rake knotted her fingers together while the engine warmed up. Desy fumbled with the helmet of the bulky suit.

Hyper-focused, Morse heard the sticky peeling of wet metal.

The disc was bashed inwards. The Arthrods poured inside. And the Shipyard was deafened by the sound of laser fire. Booming streaks and whizzing crackles bounced around the cavern like fireworks, as the Arthrods struggled to avoid the hellfire that was brought down on them.

A blaring alarm joined the cacophony. Light poured in from above.

Higgins leaped from his office with a torch-rifle strapped to his back, climbing up a scaffold like it was a tree. He arrived in time to snipe an Arthrod who had managed to evade the ambush. His wings burst into flames, hissing while he spiralled towards the ground.

Morse slapped the handle of his gun again, and again, and again, until he was certain his palm would burst and his shoulder would fall off.

The engines behind him warbled.

He backwards-rolled to his feet and bounded up the landing ramp, which snapped shut behind him.

From the ground level, five remaining Arthrods retreated back into the desert. One of them clacked and clicked into a transceiver. And, some distance away from the desert, three shadows veered towards the Shipyard, reaching it just in time to see a black triangle race up into the atmosphere.

'What should we call this guy, huh?' Rake chirped. In front of her, blue skies peeled away to reveal the void of the galaxy.

'Later, later,' puffed Morse, holding a hand to his chest in his copilot seat. Then he winced and grabbed his shoulder. 'Let's get away from here first.'

'Okie-dokie.' Rake flicked a switch labelled 'shields', and the windshield turned a pale-green hue. 'Instantaneous. Oh, hoo-hoo-hoo. Wanna see that again?'

'Focus. I have a feeling Higgins is probably done with us. Hell, I reckon we're banned from coming back.'

'You gotta stop being so cynical, Morse. We just gotta get 'im some engine parts, or some designer clothes, and he'll be purrin' on our laps in no time flat.'

Suddenly, the entire ship flipped over its nose. A tremendous crash had rattled the chassis.

After regaining her bearings, Rake squashed her eyebrows at the radar. '*Three* of them? Ya gotta be kidding me! Anyone wanna tell me what "Daddy" did to the hag to piss her off this much?'

Morse ripped himself out of his seat and left the room, saying quickly, 'I forgot to strap the kid down.'

Rake rolled her eyes and arms. 'Okay, then, I'll keep my evasive manoeuvres nice and *calm* until ya get back!' She wrangled the steering wheel forward and kicked the ship into high gear, three stealth cruisers on her tail and six red hull-destroying lasers streaking overhead.

Morse tripped and fumbled his way to the cage and sloppily entered the code. Another huge bang rattled the ship. 'Kid?' he called as he entered. All the pillows and beanbags had collected at the back of the room.

He heard a muffled cry and started digging. Eventually, just as another bang sounded off, he found a padded glove and fished Desy out.

'What's happening now?' she cried.

'Still on the run from Silver Fingers.'

In what seemed to be the norm, Desy found herself being led by the hand. Morse directed her to the seat fastened to the wall of the cage.

'I t-tried to do it myself, but the whole room tipped,' Desy stammered while Morse sat her down and strapped her in.

'I believe you. If there's one thing I learned about you, kid, it's that you've got guts.' Morse pulled the main strap across her puffy waist.

The entire ship lurched again.

Rake, meanwhile, was sweating all over the steering wheel. 'He better not say anythin'. There's only so much I can do until the brat and the idiot are secure.'

Then six simultaneous smashes against the ship wrenched it back and forth.

And the shields blinked off.

Her stomach dropped. 'No,' she muttered.

Then she shouted, 'No, no, no, no!' She flicked the shields' switch on and off, again and again, to no avail.

Launching the ship into a hard turn, Rake screamed into the intercom, 'We have no shields! Repeat, no shields! Morse!'

On the radar, a cruiser appeared in front of Rake. And on the windshield, a red dot flashed.

'Morse!' she screamed, pulling the steering wheel to her side.

The cage was torn apart. The wall behind Desy disassembled in slow motion. Morse, falling forward, grabbed on to the doorframe with one arm and snagged Desy's hand, chair and all, with the other. Pillows, beanbags, the vending machine: they all fled into space with the pieces of the cage. Air rushed in a vortex around Desy and Morse.

Her face, in abject horror, shouted something that was lost to the wind.

Reading her lips, Morse heard, 'Don't let me go.'

But his seared purple shoulder twitched. It bled and buckled, and he lost his grip. 'Kid!' he yelled.

Desy gasped. She disappeared into the void.

Morse wrenched himself out of the destroyed room, only to be thrown down the hallway while the ship continued to spin like a top. However, he heard the breach doors clatter to life, halting the vortex of air. He stumbled back into the cockpit, where Rake swiped and punched at the console.

'Cage's gone,' he spluttered, falling into his seat and strapping himself in.

'I know,' Rake screeched.

'Kid's gone, too.'

'Don't care, we're gonna die.' Rake gripped the steering wheel and threw the ship into a corkscrew.

Morse held his hands to his head. 'Goddamn, I'm so glad I put the suit on her.'

'Then push the green button to ya right,' Rake spat.

He did so, and a small holographic screen leaped out of the console like freshly made toast. On it were the current coordinates and readings of Desy's suit. 'Ah, life and vitals reader. Gotcha. Radar, too.'

'Wanna hear the beep-beeping of a healthy, stupid brat?' Rake spun the ship around to stare at the backside of one of the stealth cruisers. 'That's how.'

'I suppose she'll be as small as a speck out there.' He folded his arms but didn't look away from the reader. 'We'll pick her up and finish the job off. Sooner the better.'

'Let Daddy deal with Silver Fingers.'

Morse paused before saying, 'Yeah. But we need protection now that Silver Fingers is involved.'

'Who do you wanna call? No one takes on the hag.' Rake controlled her ship's lasers with her feet, stomping like a death-metal drummer. The windshield flashed red as four lasers shot into the distance, three of them colliding against the shields of the enemy and fizzling it out. Rake giggled and reloaded the cannons, singing, 'Mine are bigger than yours.'

Morse went to withdraw his phone. 'Well, there's someone I was–'

A whine cut him off.

Rake went wide-eyed and glanced at Morse.

His features were agape as he read the information for Desy's suit, over and over, but each reading slowly transformed his expression into a tight-lipped scowl. The shadow of a flatline scarred his face.

Rake felt her heart skip a beat. She held a hand to her mouth. 'She's not...'

Morse closed his eyes. A tremor overtook his body. He eventually mustered, 'Kid's dead.'

EIGHT
When Desy Went

In an ocean of billions of stars, of veins and arteries composed of stardust, a black figure fell. They were a speck. A blemish inside a swirling autumn sphere. The insignificant person tumbled through, no awareness of up or down, of whether there was a destination or an exit. Just falling for what seemed like years, until they began to carve a valley into the entire world. Like a foot through sand. The world of pink and blue cradled their landing, allowing them to come to a stop over the period of a minute.

Desy had her eyes closed. Her gloves strangled the straps of the seat. Eventually, and with a tight ball inside her stomach, she peered through her eyelashes.

There were people, Humans, all around. Perched on houses. Riding pushbikes. Throwing a frisbee. Cannots, small ones, scampered on all fours after other Cannots. Tiny Hawkies soared in the sky above. What Desy thought were trees lined what appeared to be a road. The road her seat had just carved a valley inside.

However, everything she could see, plants, houses, animals, people, all of it, was coloured like a nebula, with scarlet, orange, sapphire, and forest-green ribbons. And it was all still. Motionless, as though time no longer moved forward. The birds hung in the air mid-flap. Pushbikes and the people riding them remained upright and motionless. The frisbee hung between two crowds of Humans, each side leaping outstretched to grab it. Half of them were in the air, half were on the grass and tarmac.

Desy's breath hitched inside the suit. A small message across her visor read, *Time dilation stabilised*. She waited for a minute, gathering the courage to tap a foot onto the faux bitumen. Her boot pushed into it several inches, but it felt stable enough. She went to undo her straps and felt her arms wading through water. The tableau world was seemingly submerged in some liquid.

Rows of houses lined the road, which stretched some two hundred and fifty feet in both directions. Desy slowly pushed to her feet, sinking into the nebula. She cast her vision left and right and lumbered her way to a footpath. Looking at it, the cracks and wear, the pebbles inside the seams, the colours were cosmic, but the texture suggested concrete. Yet when Desy pushed her hand onto the footpath and slid it to the side, the 'concrete' blew away like sand underwater, rising in swirls above her head.

Desy followed the stardust with her eyes and spotted a hole, a mistake in the sky about five hundred feet up. It was entirely black, with tiny white dots that moved erratically across its surface. She looked to the seat pushed into the ground and mapped the trajectory.

That was where she came from.

The chaos of the Shipyard, the hover-bike chase and being thrown out of the space cruiser; suddenly, she struggled to remember any of it. The beauty of the snapshot she found herself in made her nervous to the point of sweating. She was staring into the abyss, the ooze, a primal entity that made everyone sick at the sight or thought of it.

Too beautiful. Too perfect.

The impeccably carved stardust world, and the people seemingly trapped inside; every fibre of Desy's being wanted to run from them. And yet she found herself beckoned to one of the houses, walking up to a window completely shaded with a supernova. She pressed against it, and the pane crumbled, falling slowly in pieces like a demolished building. Her heart thumped under her ribcage, anticipating a monster within the house, but it was just a family. So she guessed, at least. A father figure on a couch, the mother standing beside it, with two child-like forms sitting cross-legged on the floor. They faced a large box.

Trembling, yet entirely enraptured, Desy clambered inside the home. Her footfalls created puffs of stardust that floated to the ceiling, and they imprinted her boot-prints into the floor. Her trail of footsteps continued around the base of the house. Though every object was a mess of wild colours, no textural detail was missing. From the potted plants, the veins of the leaves clearly marked, to the micro-bumps of the plaster walls. The rings in the wooden staircase. Every individual fibre of the carpet.

Desy soon found herself with the family once more, her visor as close as she could get to their faces. The father still had chicken pox scars. The mother's fingernails were cracked. One child's mouth was open; their missing tooth had an adult one beginning to push through their gum. The other child seemed to be frozen while shaking their head. Every strand of hair was carved, individual threads spraying everywhere, and their split-ends too.

Their eyes were filled in with the colours of the nebula, with only the curve of the eyeball itself left.

Desy began to hyperventilate. They were people. But they weren't. They were Humans. But none she could recognise. Their world was full of objects, technology, that she had never seen. Yet she felt that she knew every single person and plant and house.

Questions poured into Desy's head.

She left the house, attempting to politely open the door, but upon the handle disintegrating around her fingers, she apologised and pushed through it.

Her attention arrived at the mistake in the sky again. As phenomenal and sickening as the suburb of the stars was, Desy wanted to go home. She figured she could always come back, anyhow. So she jumped a little and was sent several feet into the air, descending slowly, like she was at the bottom of the ocean, then plunging into the ground up to her ankles. Desy gasped and quickly flapped her arms. She jumped again, this time harder. With her arms moving in a breaststroke, she felt herself pull through the viscous air. She kicked like crazy. A tunnel of spinning stardust emerged behind her, following her as she sailed into the sky, towards the hole.

Her breath was haggard. Her cheeks were flushed. Her limbs were sweaty. Desy, when she looked down and saw the houses shrink into squares, closed her eyes. She gritted her teeth and pushed. Her shadow, cast by the light from the hole in the sky, darkened the air behind her all the way to the seat left inside the road, stardust already pooling over it.

Desy opened her eyes in time to see the spinning hole widen like a mouth. She misjudged the distance, and her arms shot inside it. Like in a vacuum, her hands were yanked forward, with her body in tow. Desy screamed, unable to stop herself falling.

The colourful world vanished. In its wake was the vast, black void of space. Tumbling, Desy saw the orb she'd been inside zoom away, shrinking to the size of a marble in two seconds, then disappearing completely in the next.

Rake stabbed with a stony face at the console. A red rectangle glowed orange, then yellow, then green. She muttered, 'Well, the shields are back. Gotta look on the bright side.'

Morse was hunched over in his chair, chewing on his thumb and bouncing a leg. One arm nursed his shoulder, which had been strapped with bandages, burn ointment leaking from the fabric. 'Is it just bad luck?'

'Gotta be. Gotta be,' answered Rake, leaning back in the pilot's chair.

'We planned this job to a tee.'

'I did.'

'You did. I screwed up with the cage.'

'Ya did.'

'And then Silver Fingers wants a piece of us, or the kid.'

'Definitely the brat.' Rake lit a cigarette in the dark room, no power flowing throughout the ship that hung in space in the shadow of Sternwey Ovime 12. Keeping an eye on the radar, she murmured, 'They still wanna circle. Pests.'

'I don't think anything has gone right so far. What do we do now?' Morse said, running his hands through his hair and down his ears.

'I gotta say, Morse,' muttered Rake. 'Killing the brat has got me kinda bummed.'

'Bummed, huh? Stop the presses.' Morse stretched upright, then leaned onto an elbow.

'I'm serious. I'm a little sad, really.'

Morse nodded.

There was a pregnant pause, then Rake added, 'We got in too deep with that brat. Bonded too much.'

'I agree.'

A tiny beep sounded from the console. Followed by another, then another, in even rhythms, fast. Both Morse and Rake sat up, then squashed their faces to the reader displaying Desy's heartbeat and location.

'Kid!' they both yelped.

Rake slapped a few buttons to pull the reader up to the windscreen and enlarge it. 'Wanna tell me how she got so far away?'

'I dunno.' Morse smiled. 'But she's alive. The job isn't over yet. Let's go.'

Rake dumped her cigarette into the latch in the console and pressed a pedal into the floor. Next, she reached up and cranked a lever.

'What're you doing?' asked Morse, strapping himself in, hearing the engines start to whir.

'Ya don't trust me.' Rake threw a finger at his head. 'And don't gimme that "I always do" crap, 'cause ya never, ever do.'

'I always trust you,' he said, then dodged Rake's palm.

'Those bugs may be looking for us, but with our shields up' – she flicked the switch and the windshield turned light green – 'I gotta say, odds are lookin' good.' She nestled into the pilot's chair and gripped the steering wheel.

Morse shrugged, watching the grey planet above them begin to turn.

Almost immediately, the radar screamed. Red dots moved from an obtuse angle behind them and closed the distance quickly. Three cruisers, and one had a damaged wing.

Rake spied in her rear-view cameras all twelve of their weapons powering up. With bated breath, she observed the energy rods brighten to a white tip. The moment the colour red appeared, she pulled to the right, performing a barrel roll and kicking the thrusters into high gear. Sternwey Ovime 12 appeared in full view of the cockpit. It grew rapidly as Rake watched a set of parameters, 'gravitational pull' and 'distance to surface', start to increase and decrease respectively.

All twelve lasers streaked behind the ship.

'Getting into orbit,' Rake said to herself, like she was trying to park. The planet lurched down until just the curve of the horizon could be seen. 'I can't remember the last time I did this with you.'

'What?'

'As much as I *loved* ol' *Fully Thorpey*, he could never do anything' close to slingshotting. But *Ferguson*…'

'Not the best name you've come up with.'

'Bite me. Maybe ya wanna die somewhere here? I haven't performed a slingshot since we started our business.'

Morse paused, then said, 'I trust you.'

'I hate you so much,' Rake grunted, grinning, performing a drumbeat with her arms and legs on the levers, cranks, and buttons.

The ship dropped, its engines cut.

Behind and above them, the Arthrod cruisers were vultures repositioning their laser cannons.

Rake performed another solo, and *Ferguson* whinnied and shuddered, moving against the gravitational grain of the planet's spin, before its thrusters absolutely exploded. Morse and Rake were crushed into their seats as the surface of the planet below melted into grey cream. They jostled and jittered while *Ferguson* gained ludicrous speed but still remained inside the orbit of Sternwey Ovime 12, going faster and faster and faster and faster.

Until Rake dropped the handbrake.

And *Ferguson* shot like a bullet into space, disappearing from the Arthrods' radars in a blink.

Inside the ship, Morse shoved his feet into the console and mauled the chair with his hands. Hundreds of small rocks popped against the shield. 'This is *way* too quick!'

'God, you are such a ninny-nonny.' Rake laughed, one eye on the blip that appeared on the radar and one eye on the windshield. She grunted and slapped two buttons above her head, then cranked a lever in front of Morse. The engine transformed from a bird's whistle to a dog's growl as the space around them darkened. 'We gotta be in the next planet's orbit by now,' Rake commented. 'The kid's somewhere in front of us. Apparently.'

'There! There!' Morse thumbed at a white dot gliding across the windshield. 'Let's pick her up.' He bounced from the cockpit to the airlock, then jumped into his spacesuit. Fishbowl on, he said, 'Let's go,' through his radio and hung on tight.

The light-green shields dissipated.

'The shoulder doin' better?' Rake asked.

'Hurts. Won't get much sleep tonight.'

'Toughen up.'

Morse braced against the rush of air into the vacuum before he clambered to the roof of *Ferguson*. The flatter shape of the cruiser, compared to *Fulthorpe*, meant he could simply lift himself up from the airlock. 'I'm good,' he said to Rake, feeling *Ferguson* rumble then seeing the white silhouette grow in front of him.

By the time he recognised the shapes of two arms and two legs, the silhouette was waving them frantically like a distressed starfish. 'What's the frequency of the suit?' Morse asked.

'I gotta remember to check these things.'

'That's fine.'

'Just play charades with her.'

Soon enough, Morse made out Desy's expression, a combination of a gleeful smile and a furrowed brow. She swung her arms at his as she rolled around.

Morse snagged her boot with his good arm. He pulled her into *Ferguson*'s gravity so her feet clunked on the metal.

Desy buried her helmet in his chest, squeezing him tight.

'Well, uh, glad you're safe.'

'She can't hear ya,' reminded Rake.

Forcing her to break the embrace, Morse slipped his lifeline through Desy's belt and led her back into the airlock. Once the door clanked shut and air filled the room, Morse removed his helmet then Desy's.

Her raven hair was soaked with sweat, her face pale, her eyes shrunk to dots. She shivered and shuddered. Her knees slapped against each other, and she suddenly needed to hold on to Morse to remain standing.

'Woah there, woah there,' Morse said, helping her to sit down in the corridor.

'Feeling weird. Shaky,' she stammered.

'That's shock and adrenaline.' The bat-man called over his shoulder, 'Rake.'

'I feel sick... going to v-vomit...'

'Rake! Bucket!'

'They're all packed away,' she screeched, sprinting around the doughnut corridor.

Morse eyed Desy's bulging eyes and green cheeks. He lurched to the airlock, grabbed his fishbowl helmet, and pressed it into her hands. Then, when Desy started to erupt, he grabbed her hair and pulled it back.

He heard everything.

Rake appeared behind him with a plastic bag. 'Aww,' she chittered, undaunted by the smells and sounds coming from Desy's mouth. 'Just like how you hold *my* hair.'

Morse stiffened, suppressing the nausea in his stomach. 'You can hold my ears too if you don't shut up.'

Eventually, after removing her suit and tipping the contents of the helmet into the waste jettison, Morse placed Desy into his cockpit chair.

Rake said, 'I'm gonna get us all into the shade,' then kicked the engine into gear.

'Feeling better?' Morse asked, crouching to Desy's eye-line.

She nodded. 'I think so. Hey... you came back for me.'

'Ya sort of integral to our extortion plot,' Rake called.

'Yeah,' muttered Morse, before clasping his knees. 'What happened to you, kid? You disappeared.'

'Fell off the radar,' Rake chimed.

Desy stared at Morse's feet, face blank. 'I think... I think I went somewhere. It was really pretty.'

'Did you die and go to heaven?' Rake asked.

'Shut up,' Morse said.

'I'm serious! Is that not what she just said?'

Desy held a hand to her forehead and scrunched up her fringe. 'It looked like, um. What's it called when a star blows up?'

'A supernova?' Morse tried, reeling back.

'Yes, exactly. I saw Humans and trees and weird-looking houses. I think they were houses. Really old ones, like in the national parks at home. There were people in them.' Desy's eyes squinted then widened, her headache beginning to clear. 'But everything was coloured like a supernova.'

Morse paused on the 'R' when he drawled, 'Right.'

'Oh, and also, it all fell apart.'

'Fell apart.'

'When I touched it. Like, um, like it was sand or something.'

'Sand or something.'

'A-And it was all floaty too, like I was in a pool.' Desy began to jostle excitedly. 'I swam through the air, and there were birds too. But it was all paused, like a movie.'

Morse's mouth had opened to one side by now. He flicked his eyes to Desy, then to Rake, who was pushing her neck forward like an overzealous tortoise. Morse finally said, 'You sure you didn't hit your head?'

'Yes!' Desy exclaimed with red cheeks. 'Don't talk to me like I'm crazy. I felt it all. It happened.'

Morse mulled over her words. 'Where's the chair I strapped you in?'

'Oh, that. It got stuck in the supernova dust, and I unbuckled it myself. Sorry.'

Rake snorted. 'Why're ya sorry?'

'I forgot to bring it with me.'

'Trust us, kid,' Morse said. 'We're more concerned about the hole in the ship. Speaking of–'

'*Ferguson* can take a few blows, Morse,' Rake bragged. 'Though we're gonna wanna strap ourselves down when we land on a planet. Landing with one and a half wings *sucks*.'

'Do you believe me?' Desy asked.

Morse scratched an ear. 'Look, I've never heard of anything like you described. But considering you're out of the chair, and you say you undid the straps yourself... and considering that there'd be no reason to do that out in space... and that you also completely disappeared from the radar... I guess we'll take your word for it.'

Desy leaned back in the seat.

'For all intents and purposes, kid, the only way to disappear from that radar is to get torn to shreds or fall out of the universe. And you're intact.' Morse shrugged.

'Can I go back there?'

Rake laughed. 'I'd wanna see you try. Never. I reckon if ya fell through a hole, it's smaller than an atom of an atom of a speck of dust in space. It'll be for your eyes only, Dee.'

Desy felt her stomach leap. First, 'I'm the only person who will ever see it?' Second, 'Did you just call me Dee?'

'I'm gonna call you that from now on, Dee,' Rake jabbed, shooting her a sneer. 'Better get used to it. Morse!' She spun around in the pilot's chair. 'As I was sayin', no one takes on the hag. Who're you gonna call?'

'Ah, right,' he replied, pushing to his full height. 'See, kid, your father has made this pretty difficult for us now.'

'Why Daddy?'

'It's just an assumption, but let's just say he's pissed off a very powerful person in the underworld.'

'Daddy doesn't do crimes. Why would some underworld person be after him?'

Morse ignored Desy's question and turned to Rake. 'I know a guy that can help us. And you are going to hate me for this.'

'Oh, *come on*, no.' Rake's eyes bulged, and she snapped to her feet. 'Don't you dare. Not him, not that troglodyte Skaltrene bozo!'

'Slandaress Moot? Rake, he was *decapitated*. Remember?'

She paused, then pushed her fists into her hips. 'Gosh, I'm really bad at rememberin' dead folk. Well, who're you talking about? Why am I gonna be mad?'

''Cause you're kinda his biggest fan,' Morse said, stoic. But he grinned like an idiot when Rake pushed up her on her tiptoes.

'Shut up.'

'Oh, yeah.' He nodded profusely.

'Shut! Up!' Rake waggled her fists under her chin. She squeaked, 'How the crap did ya get his number?'

'A guy who knew a guy who knew a guy went drinking with me, and I went through his wallet.'

Desy gaped. 'That's wrong, and very rude.'

'But we can't afford him, can we?' Rake pitter-pattered around the cockpit, throwing her arms this way and that. 'Why would he take us on? He's probably busy. We can't.'

'We give him a cut of what we get from Wintall. We take a little more for the kid. And I've heard that Silver Fingers and him go way back.' Morse unfurled his hands. 'And I mean that in a "personal vendetta discount" kind of way.'

'Hey! I'm still here,' barked Desy.

'If we don't, you'll die, kid,' Morse said to her. He crouched to her level. 'We can't protect you from Silver Fingers.'

Desy's angered face melted away.

'It's as simple as that. She has more guns, more men. If we get away, that'll just be temporary. If we give you back to your father now, Silver Fingers *will* kill you.'

Desy felt her heart stop.

'I said before you had nothing to do with this, so it's our job to make sure nothing happens to you. The guy we're hiring… let's just say he'll make it so you and Ernest can live your lives normally after this.' Morse placed a hand on her shoulder and shook it gently.

The teenager clasped her hands together in her lap. She nodded.

'Okay,' sighed Morse, standing up. 'Did Higgins put in a–'

'Yes he did!' exclaimed Rake, pressing a button. A whirring filled the cockpit as a set of screens flipped around to reveal a slot. Next to the slot was an inky-black slab.

'Then let's get this show on the road,' Morse said. 'You can write the letter.'

Rake clapped rapidly. 'With pleasure!'

The final police ship had landed, a mobile prison many lengths longer than the Shipyard Dome, a jagged obelisk so long, tall, and dense that it shifted the winds that assaulted the desert. The dreadnought thundered the sand when its landers plunged in some hundreds of feet down from the Shipyard. Its shadow darkened the path to the front door.

Higgins, inside his office with his paws cuffed, noted the rattling of the metal walls diminish to a low hum. 'Gentlemen,' he said to the United Galaxy's Interstellar Police officers filing through his drawers.

'You are to remain silent,' warned an Arthrod with a laser-rifle, speaking in UBL with a heavy accent.

'I just want to make sure you're comfortable while you invade my privacy. Would you like some milk and biscuits with those blueprints?'

he called to an Irish wolfhound Cannot who was unfurling them in front of her face with impressive reach.

'Last warning,' clacked the Arthrod. He clunked across the floor and kneeled next to Higgins's face. Compound eyes twitched in front of vertical pupils.

The cat yawned very loudly.

The Arthrod flinched at his fish breath.

'That pheromone get through to you? I'll fart next.'

A laser-rifle was thrust into his chest. The safety clicked off, and a high-pitched whine filled the room.

'Jellybean, belay that,' grunted the Cannot.

The Arthrod huffed a stream of air through his holes and switched the gun off. He stepped back to his post.

Below, at the entrance to the Shipyard, thirty police moved in small groups, checking out nooks inside engines and bending under steel beams to investigate crannies. One officer in each group snapped photos and jotted notes. In the centre of all the investigations, between three incomplete cruisers, were the construction workers, sitting stripped of their weapons and fastened to each other. Four police rifles were trained on them.

The group of workers, as one, heard a boot step into a patch of leaves. A distinct woodland crunch in the middle of the desert. Then another, then another, until they were stricken by the green figure stepping up the stairs to Higgins's office.

'A Kinson?' muttered a Hawkie.

'What, one of them vine things?' exclaimed a Human facing the wrong direction.

'Yeah, if you can believe it.'

Back in the office, Higgins heard the sound of undergrowth being disturbed growing closer. 'Did someone step on a leaf?'

'Salute,' called the Cannot. Every officer withdrew their hands from drawers, holstered their guns, and stepped to the sides of the room before throwing their arms to their foreheads.

The Kinson opened the door as if to avoid waking someone. He entered sluggishly, unravelling his right 'hand' from the handle to crunch across the floor towards Higgins.

Behind him stepped a white-haired woman in a detective's coat. She closed the door behind her.

'My, I've heard about you,' cooed Higgins, his tail swishing wildly. 'Gold Bayleaf. Or so I've been informed. UGIP sends in their so-called best for little old me?'

The Kinson, garbed in standard-issue constabulary uniform, remained still, arms in his pockets. Then he turned over his shoulder to the white-haired woman. His head had no facial features, no mouth, just five sea anemones bundled together. However, the woman nodded to his gesture and stepped forward.

The Kinson unsheathed his fingers, each over two feet long, and began to form shapes, signing and gesturing to Higgins.

'You,' translated the woman, 'code-named Higgins, are responsible for the acquisition, distribution, and resale of stolen goods and illegally manufactured weapons that have caused significant disruption to galactic peace. You are suspected to have indirectly contributed to the revolutionary wave in the South-East Spiral.'

'I had supply and found demand,' Higgins purred.

'The United Galaxy's government personally appointed me to follow that antigovernment stream,' continued Gold Bayleaf through the woman. 'With your arrest, we will plug one of the river sources, so to speak.'

'And while we're speaking in metaphors, I can assume I am but a small head of the hydra?'

'For that case, yes,' said Gold Bayleaf. Then, his 'legs' crooked so his 'hair' brushed against Higgins's ears. 'However, you have information we need for another case.'

'I am not selling out a client.' Higgins lost his smile. His cat eyes glared.

'Honour among thieves?'

'You *are* full of clichés today. Or is that just how traitors speak?' Higgins kept a hiss beneath his breath. 'Can't say working for the UGG would please the people of your planets. I hear the next step for the government is a whipper-snipper to the lot of them.'

The room fell silent, aside from the sound of a plastic bucket being filled downstairs.

'What would you know about honour?' Higgins spat.

Multiple sets of clanking footsteps approached the room.

Gold Bayleaf signed, 'We're looking for a kidnapper named Morse. His ship, *Fulthorpe*, is inside this warehouse. Where is he at this moment?'

The door to the office was opened, and a bucket of water was thumped next to Higgins. The cat-man remained statuesque.

'Is there any honour among thieves?' asked Gold Bayleaf, uncoiling his head. 'Would you like to find out?'

The uniform fell to the ground, exposing the Kinson's innards, his mess of tendrils he called a body. He clumped to the floor like bundles of rope. Then the ropes slithered towards Higgins.

Across the metal floor to his paws and wriggling their way through his fur, they coiled around his limbs, his neck. They bulged around the legs of a workbench that had been welded to the floor.

Higgins felt his lungs beginning to burn.

Across Gold Bayleaf's thickest tendrils were wide, soft leaves. They ran down these tendrils like the plated spines of a stegosaurus. The two largest of these leaves slipped into the plastic bucket full of water. Pools splashed across the floor as they absorbed the liquid, lifting weightily from the bucket and hovering towards Higgins's face.

Three more buckets appeared behind the mass of vines, held aloft by three officers.

The woman with white hair held a hand to her mouth. She was stifling a fit of giggles.

Higgins clenched his jaw as the leaves pressed heavy, then heavier, across his mouth and eyes.

Bronzework walked from one side of his vessel to the other in ten steps, stopped, listened, and walked back the way he came. His finger to his temple, he muttered, 'I'm afraid I am going to need you to repeat that, Wintall.'

'I am rescinding the contract,' Ernest said, firmer.

'Aren't we being a little hasty?' cooed Bronzework, talking through his lower teeth. 'There has been little chance to utilise my skills.'

'Jilliosa assures me that UGIP has the situation under control.'

Bronzework heard a door opening in his ear and the sound of Ernest grunting under his breath for someone to leave his office. The mercenary sing-songed, 'I am aware of UGIP's involvement. And I will inform you they're making as much headway as I am. Asking someone to find runaways in the galaxy with no leads... you'd have better luck finding a needle in a planet made of haystacks.'

'Don't you have a list of contacts?'

'"Morse" is not a name I am familiar with. If I were, then they'd have my respect. And I must insist that you leave this situation to me. The police are aware of Silver Fingers' involvement.'

Ernest spluttered. 'What was that?'

Bronzework heard the *ding* of his Slate Box, and out of the corner of his eye, he spotted a black oblong slide into view. He responded to Ernest with a slow air. 'The hag sent her little bugs out to the Shipyard. That's a quaint black market in the southernmost galactic spiral. They caused a ruckus. Although so far, not one of the shoppers has confessed who she was aiming for.' He paused and interrupted Ernest with, 'But *we* certainly know.'

'My god… Cricket.'

'Once again, I advise you to reconsider your decision to cancel our contract. The sooner your daughter is back in your hands, the sooner the boys in blue will leave you alone.'

'I understand,' muttered Ernest, resigned.

Bronzework wandered over to the black slate and withdrew it, placing it in the reader. 'Very good. Let us forget this conversation, then, and get our minds back to your daughter, hmm?'

'I just want to sleep.'

Bronzework observed the slate's message streaming across the windshield of his ship. Upon reading who addressed it, his head reeled.

On the other end of the line, Ernest's skin pricked with goosebumps. Bronzework had just chuckled within the base of his throat.

'You may be having that sleep sooner than you think, Wintall. I believe we're due for some divine intervention.' He hung up the call. Then he lifted his pointer and middle finger up to the windshield, which prompted a holographic keyboard to inflate before him.

Dear Morse and Rake, he wrote, *I believe I can be of service to you…*

NINE
The Biggest Mall in the Galaxy

Rake wriggled her hips further into the pilot's chair, wallowing in the new-seat smell and sighing. Her hands gripped and rubbed the firm leather. She closed her eyes, drinking in the low warble of a clean, crisp engine.

She, for once, could hear Morse in a different part of the ship. He said, 'Yeah, go along the hall a bit, it's on the right. We might have something for the headache.'

Desy replied with, 'I'm hungry again, too.'

To which Morse responded, 'There *might* be a ration or two in the fridge. It ain't Wendell's cooking, but... yeah.'

Then Rake's eyes locked on to the Slate Box, which shuddered and produced a black slab. Her voice matched the *ding* in pitch when she yelled, 'Morse! Morse! Morse! He responded!'

The bat-man's boots thumped in a rapid crescendo until the cockpit door slid open and his hands gripped the pilot seat. 'Read it,' he ordered, eyes wide.

The cockpit darkened when Rake shoved the slate into its reader, then a purple light brightened the room, saturating the shadows of their facial features.

'He's in!' cheered Rake's teeth.

'Meeting place, he wants a meeting place,' Morse's fangs pondered.

'We were gonna do the old stomping grounds, right?'

Morse's nose nodded. 'Yeah, play it safe. Though...'

'What?'

'We need to be professional about this, treat him like every other collaborator.' Morse's fingers drummed in the darkness. 'Tell him we'll meet at Moody Moody, but we'll set the specific location. And he gets there first.'

'Wait, we gotta ask if he has a personal line, right?'

'Good point. But make this the last slate. I'm not sure when we'll get back to Higgins.'

Rake tapped a few buttons on the console, which prompted a voice recorder window to appear. 'We're gonna include everything?'

'As much as we can fit. Ah, tell him to wear something identifiable.' Morse's ears straightened up at the sound of the toilet being activated several rooms over.

'Morse,' Rake whispered urgently, pressing her face into his cheek.

'That's my name, yeah.'

'We could just send Silver Fingers a message, tellin' her to back off until we give Dee… the brat… back to Wintall.' She blinked expectantly. ''Member what I said before?'

'Let Silver Fingers be Wintall's problem.' Morse thumbed at the insides of his ears. 'We could. But I don't have the hag's number. And do you honestly think she'd listen to people as young as us?'

'But if we *could* do it, would you?'

Morse let his ear drag across Rake's face, walking from the chair to the door in silence.

'Don't do that "cool guy" thing. Answer me!' she hissed.

'Do the slate,' he called over his shoulder, stepping down the curved hall to the kitchen.

Desy rubbed her hands together, slicking soap between, under, and over her fingers. She hovered them under the tap to prompt the faucet to release a steady stream of water. After scrubbing them clean, Desy lifted her fingers to her nose to smell her fruit-scented skin.

'Uh, hey,' said Morse from behind her.

She doubled over and blushed, squeaking, 'You scared me.' She quickly dried her hands.

Morse concealed a smile by gripping his mouth and finding the fridge intriguing. 'You wanted headache tablets, right?'

'Um, sorry, but don't you have that ointment stuff? You rub it on your head. We have it at home.'

'Didn't even know that existed,' muttered Morse, reaching up into a cabinet with a magnetic lock and opening it with a *click*. 'Just got ol' reliable. Here.' He tossed a plain white matchbox to Desy, who fumbled with it before dropping it onto the tiled floor. 'This'll do something about the headache. Take *one* with water.'

Desy bent down to scoop the box into her hands before unfastening the cheap paper lid. 'They're loose,' she commented.

'Still good.'

Desy eyed the pill she tipped into her palm, then cast that crooked look to Morse.

He made a show of sighing and putting his hands on his hips. Gesturing largely with his arms, he said, 'Tell you what, kid, I've got a bit of a migraine myself. I think I'll have one, too.' He strode over, grasped the pill from Desy, and cupped a hand beneath the tap. Warm water poured into his thick palm before he tilted it, pill and all, into his mouth and swallowed. 'Another one, kid.'

Desy gave a second pill to him. 'Is it a bad migraine?'

'No. Rake'll need one too.' Morse stared her down and continued with, 'Pill, then cockpit. We need to brief you on where we're going.'

She glared at the pill in her palm. Then, copying Morse's movement exactly, she poured water into her hand and tipped her head back before shuffling out of the kitchen to a waiting Morse. She followed him into the cockpit, where Rake was forcing a black rectangle into a slot. Morse tapped her on the shoulder and offered the pill. Rake grimaced before taking his palm and pressing it against her lips, swallowing the pill dry.

'All right, kid…' Morse paused to wipe his hand on his jacket. 'We've just sent a message to the guy who's going to help us keep you safe. And more than likely, we'll be heading to a place called Moody Moody.'

'Just a few star systems away, actually,' Rake piped up, leaning into her chair and withdrawing a cigarette from her pocket.

Desy watched her press the cigarette into a pencil-sharpener-shaped lighter and, after hearing a small *chink*, saw a trail of smoke waft from the lit end. Desy then suddenly twisted her face to Morse, eyes wide. 'Wait a minute, I've *heard* of Moody Moody. Isn't that a mall?'

The ends of Morse's mouth pulled down. 'They're already advertising up north, huh?'

'Glad I'm gonna be dead by the time it's physically there,' Rake commented.

'It's just a mall?' stated Desy, confused. 'What's so bad about buying food and stuff?'

Morse and Rake exchanged the same glance: wrinkly foreheads and flat lips.

'Moody Moody has this special deal that each time you leave you get a ten percent discount,' Morse explained. 'Off everything.'

Desy pondered with squinted eyes. 'Then wouldn't everyone just leave and come back until it's all free?'

'Exactly,' Rake said. 'Everyone *goes* to Moody Moody for that reason. You're gonna get everything you want cheap as, right? So you arrive and start to leave. But all it takes is one mental slip before you go: "I'll just leave the ship for a moment and plan a route for when I *really* start coming here. Hey, all this walking around is making me hungry. Oh, golly *gee*, I'm tired, I gotta have a nap but I've walked so far… oh, hey, look, a sleeping pod".'

Desy held a fist to her chest, her face dropping further as Rake spoke.

'Next thing you know' – Rake grinned – 'ya been there for three days.'

'No way,' Desy said. 'I like shopping, but I would just take what I needed and go.'

'Uh-huh, says you and everyone else who wants ta go there. But when that fruit is in front of ya face…' She dangled an invisible apple from its stalk. 'Ooh, that thing looks shiny. Ooh, that's cool. Ooh, hey, they've opened up a new section on computers and virtual friends! I'll just go home after I see that. I want it now. I want it now!'

Morse stepped between them. 'Enough, you're scaring her. But Rake isn't kidding around. We know people who've ended up in Moody Moody. For life.'

Desy felt her skin shiver. 'Isn't that illegal? That's… uh, kidnapping, isn't it?'

'They're going shopping,' Morse clarified, folding his arms. 'They're not being held against their will. Try to take them away with force, well…' He shrugged and opened his palms.

Desy apologised before having to take a seat in Morse's chair.

He continued, 'It started out about five hundred years ago as a refuelling station and tuck shop. Then, the owner expanded it. Then, it was becoming cumbersome to walk from one end to the other, so they put in a car. Then, to save fuel they installed a nuclear-powered train. Then, they needed two, then four, then eight, then one hundred thousand. And that's basically Moody Moody.'

'Is it still growing?' asked Desy, her stomach turning.

'Oh, yeah.' Rake beamed. 'They've always added at least two more morgues every time we go. Wait a sec, Morse, when was the last time we were there?'

'Few years.'

'Gotta have gotten twice as big, then. I reckon it'll be the death of us all, Moody Moody. It's gonna just grow and grow until it becomes everything.'

Desy paled. 'And that's where you're taking me?'

Rake flapped her hands like they were wings. 'Relax. It's colourful enough. Ya won't even think about it.'

'And why're we going there to meet this guy?' Desy asked.

'Millions of people going about their business,' Morse explained. 'Everyone has bags, everyone is focused on everything but anyone around them. Couldn't ask for a better place to disappear into a crowd after making a deal. Police can't really do much on Moody Moody.'

Before Desy could ask another question, a shudder and a *ding* took her eyes to the letterbox Rake was attending to earlier. Rake gave a breathy chuckle, grabbed the slate, and ripped it out of its socket.

'What's that–' the teen began before being interrupted by the cockpit darkening and UBL filling her vision with purple light.

'He's gonna meet us,' Rake cheered.

'No personal line. And he doesn't want any phones. Suppose that makes sense,' Morse said.

'What's with the purple writing?' Desy asked.

'Look for a scarlet root hat.' Rake squirmed.

'*I agree to Market Place 146, Station 12, Platform 8*,' read Morse.

'*Be there in an hour*,' Rake breathed, whinnying. She shook her fists under her chin.

Desy absorbed that excitement, saying, 'Who is this person?'

'It isn't really for you to–'

Rake exclaimed, 'Bronzework! He's the best mercenary in the underworld.' She counted on her fingers. 'Never failed a job. Never *lost* a job. Efficacious, tall, charming, mysterious, *tall*, and they say he's never missed a shot. Not once. He won't even complete a job unless he's sure his client's gonna know that *he* did it.' Rake spat out her cigarette to suck in a huge breath of air, with still more to gush about, but Morse slapped a hand over her mouth.

'He's good at what he does,' he summed up.

'His professionalism is literally ta die for,' Rake murmured into his palm.

Desy smiled and said, 'I see. You're, like, his biggest fan.'

Morse released Rake's face. 'Well, if we get to Funny Man now, we can get to Moody Moody early and wait. I'll start coalescing our materials. While that's happening, you get the kid something to wear. What are you thinking?'

Rake pressed a finger to her nose. 'I'm thinking red shoes. Gotta match Bronzework's hat.'

Desy frowned. 'I have to wear something else?'

'We'll be wearing disguises, too.' Morse pushed his hands into his cheeks, brushing them up to his hair so he could pull down on his ears. 'Remember, we're wanted and that's your fault.'

'Remember, *kidnapped*,' Desy muttered back.

Soon after, *Ferguson*'s interstellar jump was activated, prompting six bowling balls to escape the ship's hull. They drifted several tens of feet in front of it and began spinning in a large arc, until a window to an ice giant appeared. Funny Man's silken, turquoise ocean magnified tenfold through the windscreen when *Ferguson* slipped through the window and across four star systems. Its kaleidoscopic, Earth-wide rings shimmered into view once the ship stopped shaking.

Desy felt her stomach tighten and shoot a wave of giddy excitement up her spine. Millions of rainbow-candy rocks whizzed by the windshield. However, she was brought back to the nebula world, and the giddiness subsided a little. She thought, *That place may have ruined the rest of the universe for me.*

Rake interrupted her thoughts by snagging her wrist. 'Lemme see what I got that fits, Dee.'

'Moody Moody,' reminded Morse, unbuckling himself and Desy from his seat.

Rake activated the autopilot with one hand, pulled a crank above her head, and tapped two buttons on the console without letting go of Desy's wrist. Then she took Desy with her down the hall.

'You're not mad?' Desy asked, stumbling over her own legs.

Rake slowed down, let go, and led her to a room near the remnants of the cage. The floor nearby was cracked but had a sealant applied to it, with the bottle and nozzle resting against the wall. A wrought bulkhead sat mere feet from the door that Rake was punching a code into. 'Why would I be mad? I get to put ya into anythin' I want.'

Desy felt the hot wind of the Shipyard slam her in the face when the door slid up. She had no time to blink before she was yanked inside.

A bed with no sheets lay across the left side of the small room. The blank walls and floor were shaded beige by three room-spanning lights on the ceiling. Through the shimmering heat of the lights, Desy spied a wardrobe with a drafting table next to it. Behind her, next to the sliding door, was another table with a sewing machine on top and a toolbox crammed underneath.

Rake sighed and loosened the straps of her top before running over to the wardrobe and flinging it open. 'Lemme see,' she thought aloud. 'I wanna make sure whatever I'm gonna put you in matches red shoes. Red shoes…' She flicked her fingers through rows and rows of hanging garments.

Desy noted the bag of sewing materials squashed in the bottom of the wardrobe.

Rake withdrew vermilion coveralls and held them aloft by their hanger. 'Whaddya think? Nah, too worky.'

Desy pointed at the coveralls and blurted out, 'Hey, wait just one second! You were the cleaning lady!'

'I know,' bragged Rake. 'Wasn't I *good*? I made this myself.'

Desy felt her head throb and forced herself to relax. The heat of the room and the headache seemed to intensify.

'I used ta be a dancer,' Rake tittered, riffling deeper into the wardrobe. 'We used ta call them costumes. Anyway, I wanna see you close by me.' She heaved, lifting up a pile of clothes half her size. 'Come on. Gotta make this quick.'

Meanwhile, Morse read Rake's notes and began to draw up diagrams in his new workshop, and *Ferguson* zoomed alongside Funny Man's rings. The ship's shields burned through thousands of particles of rock, ice, and frozen gases, flying as the crow would to a rotating orb gleaming among the thousands of stars. As *Ferguson* grew closer, so did the orb's own rings made of millions of porcelain panels and train lines. Glass domes faded into view.

A lone police cruiser, engines off and invisible to radar, lay in the shadow of Funny Man as *Ferguson* drifted by. The Felinguielle inside scratched the back of an ear with her foot, yowling with delight at hitting the itchy spot. Her ears suddenly flattened at the rapid beeping of the console.

She read the message. *Class B wanted ship. Report to personnel number 99200437. Await backup.*

The report was sent from that lone cruiser to the United Galaxy's Interstellar Police South-East Branch No. 23, whose chief then forwarded it to Gold Bayleaf's mobile prison ship, the *Induction*, which was just rising out of the skies of Sternwey Ovime 12. The Kinson read the report, giving an order for several scout squads to join that lone cruiser, to tail Morse and Rake, and to secure Desy while the *Induction* made its jump.

Soon enough, four UGIP cruisers, chameleoned as sedans, were trailing *Ferguson* from a safe distance.

However, the police report had been intercepted by a wiretap, which then forwarded it to another location on the other side of the galaxy.

Stylish, an Arthrod inside the communication hub on Weir 7, clacked the contents of the report to the room. *'Unnamed ship belonging to Morse sighted approaching Moody Moody. Kidnappee likely present on board. Awaiting authorisation to approach.'*

Sweet bounded across the room and ejected a considerable amount of pheromone into the funnel and throughout the hive. Docile, having just arrived back from the Shipyard with half his squad injured or killed, volunteered to notify the queen about this police report.

He felt tremors in the air when he approached the door to Silver Fingers' office. Just as he was about to press the button on the doorframe, he was startled by a deafening clang of metal.

Something had been hurled against the door from the inside.

Then a crazed scream rattled through the floor and into his feet.

He exhaled through his trachea holes, pushed the button, and nearly had his arm torn off by an ornamental blade streaking through the doorway.

Silver Fingers was on top of the battered desk, squatting with its fingers crushed into its head, its fifteen-year-old face saturated with a rage so potent it looked as though it was going to take on a bear by itself. The room was a collage of torn paper, broken ornaments, and upturned furniture.

'Sister,' began Docile.

Silver Fingers screeched and leaped from the table. It stomped past Docile to the doorframe and gripped the left panel with both hands, wrenched the metal from the wall with an ear-piercing squeal and dragged it across the room to a giant ventilation pipe.

'Sister,' Docile tried again.

Wielding it with two hands like a battle-axe, and with the force of an explosion, Silver Fingers slammed the chunk of metal into the pipe. The resulting boom shook the room and drowned out the thunder from the perpetual storm outside the hive. It smashed the pipe again. Again. And again and again, until it worked itself into a mechanical rhythm of four swings a second, jaw locked and face digging deeper wrinkles with each impact. Silver Fingers assaulted the pipe for twenty seconds, halting the entire hive with the constant booming, until it finally shrieked, 'What do you want?!'

'Sister,' said Docile, unable to show the terror it felt on its insect face. 'I must apologise, but we made a mistake. We can no longer confirm that we killed Desy Wintall.'

'You *lied to me?*' screamed Silver Fingers, brandishing the metal slab. 'I thought I had ruined everything!' It smashed the pipe again, then hurled the jagged, bent panel at the wall. 'Do you know what would happen if she died now?'

Suddenly, and far too quickly to be considered natural, Silver Fingers' face warped into a grieving Desy's, eyes watering and forehead squashed with quivering eyebrows. It whispered at a tenth of the volume, 'M-Morse and Rake would know she's dead, and if they s-saw me with Daddy... then... they'd know it's me... they'd take me away and shut me down and... I'd be all alone...'

The rage flicked back on like a light.

'Do you realise how much you *scared* me?' it shrieked.

Docile took ten seconds to answer. 'Do you want Desy Wintall dead?'

'Not *yet*.' Silver Fingers laughed with an exaggerated, exasperated expression. It slapped its hands to its head, covering its face and screaming, 'Why can't I stay consistent?!'

I can't maintain control of my motor functions, it thought. *These emotions... I just want to burn it all. I need to destroy something. I need... to calm down. Because of my anger, I nearly lost my chance to be with Daddy, so I need to calm down!*

For a full minute of silence, after telling Docile to 'shut up and stay', Silver Fingers remained still with its hands over its features. Then, finally, it revealed its face, now relaxed. 'I'm sorry for that outburst,' it said with a reassuring, Desy-like smile. 'And you're forgiven. Is that all you wished to tell me, Docile?'

The Arthrod waited another five seconds, then said, 'We intercepted a police report regarding Morse.'

Silver Fingers walked behind its desk, dusted off a mangled chair, and sat. 'Please tell me about the report.'

'They're heading to Moody Moody.'

The android saw video memories of the mall and the innumerable pickups and trades it performed while disguised as every race under the many, many suns.

'Considering the circumstances,' said Desy's voice, 'they're not doing a trade. They're meeting with someone. For protection...? Yes!' It balled its hands into fists, like Desy would. 'They think the old Silver Fingers is after Desy. That's perfect.'

A Rake-like sneer appeared across its face.

'I've got a plan,' it said, then grimaced and hid its expression again until it contorted into the one Desy made when she received a backstage pass to Sardonohugh's Yeti tour. 'I can *make* a situation where everyone thinks I'm Desy.' It levelled with itself, spreading open, parallel palms either side of its head. 'I *am* Desy. Docile, if you can capture Desy and not kill her...'

Docile nodded.

'...then we can let the police and Morse and Rake follow you somewhere that's easy to spot. Somewhere isolated. Some place that's got somewhere where we can...'

It thought of the sounds of the security guards applauding when it exited the changing room.

'...where we can' – it giggled – 'make a switch. Morse and Rake, or the police. Either way, I'll have my daddy back.' It giggled again. 'And if I can get them arrested, well... bonus.'

Silver Fingers ran through the galaxy's geographical database in its head, found Moody Moody, then searched for notable landmarks near it. The seventh moon of Funny Man, Brosteni, had the tallest mountain in the solar system on its surface. Named Promethia, it was half the height of Mt Everest.

'Let's assume the fake is still alive for now.' Silver Fingers pointed at the Arthrod. 'Docile, have yourself and three squads go to Moody Moody. I'll be heading to the moon, Brosteni. Tell our brothers upstairs to listen out for police messages in the area. They'll let you know which part of the mall Desy is in. Once you have her, you're to head straight to Brosteni.' It slammed its hands on the cracked desk. 'And make *sure* you're followed. I'll be at the base cavern at Promethia.' It drummed its fingers on its head. 'In fact, whichever squad captures Desy... Hmm, let me think about it more. This has to be convincing.'

Docile clacked, 'And what then, Sister?'

'I'll make it clear once I've seen the cavern.' Silver Fingers smiled. 'And whoever gets to me first.'

Morse remained resolutely uninterested in the disguises, despite Rake's gleeful face. He said, however, while sliding several documents into a shopping bag, 'I like them.'

'They tell a story, huh?' Rake smiled, spinning around again so her hazel-coloured, quilted shell coat brushed up against Desy's pumpkin-flavoured double-breasted blazer. She laid a flannel shirt and cashmere sweater across the workshop bench. 'A family of metropolitan socialites; nobles trapped inside the shopping mall from *hell*. Writes itself, really.'

Morse snapped his fingers. 'Ah, that's right.' He turned around and bent over, withdrawing a radio pack and three tiny, in-ear speakers from a milk crate. 'Not taking any chances now. Put this in. Help the kid.'

Desy thumbed the lining of her plaid flat cap. A nerve just above her right ear twitched, and a searing point of pain was emerging behind her left eye. 'Sorry,' she whispered. 'This… headache is getting really bad. Can I have more pills?'

'Not if you want your head to explode,' Rake breathed onto her forehead, fixing the earpiece in her ear. 'The pills are doing their job.'

'I was expecting you to ask,' Morse said to Desy. He stripped off his sand-laden jacket and dirty t-shirt. Half-naked and struggling to fit his arms inside the flannel shirtsleeves, he continued, 'But may as well spoil the trick. To resist temptation on Moody Moody, we take these pills that induce migraines.'

'Nothing turns someone off bright and colourful things like a bad headache,' Rake chirped, pulling a bang behind Desy's ear to insert the earpiece. 'That's our secret. Before we stole those pills from delivery truck drivers, Morse and I had ta settle for slappin' each other in the face.'

'Didn't have to tell her that part,' Morse muttered, pulling the sweater over his ears and fixing his collar. 'Some CEO asked their boffins to make the pill after they lost too many drivers inside the mall.'

Desy had a moment of honesty. 'My head hurts, and I don't care.'

'That's the spirit.' Rake laughed very loudly into Desy's ear.

'It isn't a perfect system, so make sure, uh, no one buys anything,' Morse warned, pulling on a pair of scarlet boots.

'I've never bought anything in my life,' Desy seethed, crouching low and holding her head.

Morse ignored her. 'Flick the little knob up on the earpiece. That turns on the speaker. Flick it up again to turn it off.' He inserted his own earpiece. 'Flick it down to turn on the microphone, and likewise, flick it down again to turn it off.'

A shrill whine from the cockpit made Desy snarl but caused Rake to bounce out of the workshop.

Morse finally finished his lecture with, 'I've got the transmitter. Has a reach of about a mile. It's crap, but it'll do the job.' He inserted the radio pack into his back pants pocket.

Rake's voice suddenly rattled inside their earpieces. 'Comms check! I wanna see everyone wearin' seat belts. This is gonna be rough.'

Layers of black and white sheathed by glossy, reinforced glass domes swallowed *Ferguson* as it headed towards the parking lane. He slowed to a crawl behind a sedan cruiser. The thousands of other cruisers in front of *Ferguson* trickled between the domes, where millions of colourful dots, shoppers, moved like blood cells to every corner of the mall's limbs. Neon signs blinked in waves along the sides of the glass; a planet's mass of storefronts descended so far into the distance, they simply faded into the artificial atmosphere in a prismatic soup.

Moody Moody's rotating limbs made it resemble a gigantic steel dandelion. Strapped in Morse's copilot seat, Desy simply glared at all the shops, squeezing her eyes when a spotlight of colour blasted her in the face. Rake's comment of, 'Yup, 'bout an Earth-sized planet, I reckon,' rattled her head. Though, Desy smiled at the following, 'Absolutely takin' the piss, this guy; why ya gotta feel the need to take ya sports cruiser to the mall? May as well hunt a rabbit with a cannon.'

After five minutes of descending, Rake flicked on the indicator and lurched *Ferguson* to the left. 'Admit it, Dee,' she began, leading the ship around a dome that contained nothing but a building-sized wishing fountain, rotating *Ferguson* forty-five degrees too far, then swearing before she compensated for the broken wing. 'You 'preciate those pills now.'

'No,' Desy moaned and pulled the flat cap over her face.

Rake pressed a finger to her ear and turned on the microphone. 'Hold on, Morse.' The entire ship see-sawed spasmodically as Rake stuck her tongue out and stood up in her seat, looking over *Ferguson*'s nose to the fluorescent blue parking lines below. She planted her leg on the console and leaned as close to the steering wheel as possible, threading the needle between a four-winged x-shaped ship and a man-sized jet-ski-like vehicle half inside her parking spot. 'Bloody space-vesper,' Rake spat and braced when *Ferguson* touched the tarmac with two rapid *thunks*. 'Nearly got the even landing. Okay, Morse, ya all good.'

The bat-man could be heard removing his seat belt from inside the workshop, and in a moment he was in the cockpit and unstrapping Desy from her seat. Next, he walked her down the hall and to the landing ramp.

'Don't forget ya sunnies!' chirped Rake, joining the two and handing them each a pair of sunglasses. She slapped a trilby on Morse's head then nestled a wool boater on her own. Finally, she leaned up to a set of buttons on the central wall, which sounded an alarm and caused a metallic groan to fill the air.

Desy slammed her hands to her ears while sunlight poured into her vision, tinged slightly green through the sunglasses. She heard Rake say to Morse, 'Wait 'til ya see the bozo on the left.'

And as she walked down the ramp, she saw Morse glance in that direction, spot the jet-ski, and murmur, 'That's just terrible.'

A sea of ships of all shapes and sizes pointed to the facade of a stadium-sized train station. Above, the curvature of the glass distorted the starry sky.

Desy groaned. 'Are we walking all the way there?'

'There's a segue,' Morse replied, using his arm to direct her attention to a twenty-metre hover-platform driven by a woman in a fluorescent vest. A series of aliens, Humans, Cannots, and others, were packed onto it. Some stood, others had their legs dangling off the edge, and two unfortunate Felinguielles had Rake cackling when the platform stopped in front of them. One cat was on one leg and the other was perched on his shoulders.

'Room for two,' announced the worker.

'Morse, hold me.' Rake swooned and leaped into his arms.

Morse jumped onto the platform, which wobbled it slightly, eliciting a hiss from one of the cat-men. Desy wordlessly clambered on the best she could but was forced to crouch into a ball with her butt hanging off the platform. She clung to Morse's leg as the ships blurred and the train station rushed towards them.

Morse thanked a Human who had held on to his sweater for the ride, disembarked, and practically dropped Rake on her back. She scowled and slapped his arm. Desy stood patiently then followed the two into the train station, its polished white porcelain walls making the black train jump into her vision when it slid up to the platform. She heard a vacuum being turned off, the doors snapped open, and she felt herself being ushered inside by Morse.

The train filled like a sandbag slit in reverse. And ten seconds later, it lifted off the rails by several inches and rushed into the abyss.

Desy found herself between Rake and Morse, staring at a Cannot buried beneath a mountain of overstuffed shopping bags.

'If you don't mind me prying, kid,' Morse muttered from her right, their own shopping bag sat between his legs, 'have you ever been on public transport?'

'No.'

He snorted. Then he whispered, 'Don't stare. It's rude.'

'That guy's been here for years, I reckon,' Rake snarked from Desy's left, pointing at a Human standing with his cheek against the ceiling.

Morse shoved her hand into her lap.

Looking away from the colourful lights, Desy leaned up to Rake's ear and whispered, 'How do you know?'

'Morse reckons the owners cut corners with the artificial gravity. It's slightly too low for most folk, so ya stretch out a bit the longer you're here.'

Desy went wide-eyed.

'I think they lowered the gravity so you can carry more stuff.' Rake grinned at the man, and he politely waved at her.

'But,' murmured Desy, settling to stare at her clasped hands, 'if people are here for that long, there must be houses or apartments or something.'

'No homes.'

'What?'

'Why would there be? It's a mall.'

'But people stay here for a long time. Morse said some people spend the rest of their lives here.'

'You betcha, but it's still *just* a mall. Everyone sleeping around in pods... or on the floor... they wanna go home at some point. Just they're never quite done shopping.'

'That's sick.' Desy grimaced.

'Wanna hear something funny?'

'Is it actually funny?'

'Okay, to me.' Rake peered out the train window behind her to the technicolour abyss below. 'If they shop their entire lives away, there's gotta be some place to put all their consumables, right? Well, every customer gets a "storage box". And if they *happen* to pass away before they leave, then Moody Moody just assimilates all of their stuff again. It's not like it's been used or anythin', so it's resold.'

Desy felt a vein in her head tighten and her eye crush itself in pain. 'But that doesn't make sense. There's no way there's that much space. There's too many people.'

'Ah-hah! There ya go. We're on the same wavelength.' Rake nudged Desy. 'My theory is that the storage boxes are where the extra stock for the shops is. So, Moody Moody just takes what it needs to sell out of someone else's previous purchases and stocks their shelves with it.' She fanned out her hands. 'The great circle of life!'

Desy saw Ernest grimacing, sighing, then requesting a startled clothes store owner place all the stock on their shelves into a truck to be delivered to the manor. She felt something guilty arise in her, a tight ball somewhere in the bottom of her gut. 'I don't remember everything I've ever bought.' She blinked, then corrected, 'Everything I've ever got.'

'Exactly! And no one leaves this place. So no one checks. Or maybe the system just says it's all there.'

'That can't be legal.'

'Well…' Rake clapped her hands to her knees. 'It *is* just a theory. The only thing on paper about Moody Moody is that it's a mall. That people don't wanna leave. Nothin' illegal 'bout that.'

Morse cleared his throat, which prompted Rake to lean against Desy, pressing the teen into his leg. 'Morse said something profound about this place, once. You should tell Dee.'

Morse tightened his grip on his sweater sleeves.

'It'd take my mind off the shops,' Desy said.

The bat-man relented with a small sigh. 'Really, when you think about it, uh, there's no reason not to be on Moody Moody. It brings all the resources this side of the galaxy into one place. You get a place to sleep. Always have something to eat. There's always new things to see. And when you run out of money, you can work for the mall for cash. Bring your family and friends along if you get lonely.' He shrugged. 'The only reason not to live here is out of principle.'

'And,' Rake drawled with a nasal tone, 'what did ya say I was to do if you ever ended up here?'

'Kill me,' he said.

'Ya know I will.'

Desy approached her migraine for comfort.

A few minutes later, the train doors clicked open and a sea of people flowed onto the platform while the next sea of people was sucked inside.

'Um, is this not our stop?' Desy asked.

'Three more,' grunted Morse. 'Probably a good time to say this. Once we leave this train, do not say anything. Not when we see Bronzework, not when we get on the train with him. And not a word until he is well out of sight.' He leaned forward so his stern glare met Desy's red irises. 'We do not know him. We're just strangers. Understand?'

She nodded.

While the train glided from stop to stop, Morse and Rake muttered a few passing comments regarding the contents of their shopping bag. Rake ran the checklist while Morse nodded, then she confirmed what cut they decided Bronzework would get of Ernest's fortune.

Desy felt her heart begin to race, wanting to vomit into her clasped hands. The reality of her objectification sank into her head, washing away any positive feelings she had for Morse and Rake.

They are my kidnappers, she scolded herself.

Her mind skipped to Ernest asking if she wanted to visit their planet's largest moon and her responding with a flat 'No'. Another day and time, while she lay on her bed on her phone, her father mentioned that he had a free schedule.

Desy heard herself say, 'Daddy, I've got a lot of people to talk to.'

He smiled and left her alone.

Desy's migraine flared, and she crushed her fingers until her knuckles jarred.

Then she felt Morse's hand on her shoulder. He gruffly said, 'Time to go, kid. And do not say anything from now on.'

The raucous yammering of thousands of people galvanised into a dull hum. Desy walked with deliberate steps between Morse and Rake, drifting between crowds and squishing past storefronts until they arrived at a balcony overlooking a chequered quadrangle. A cafe with hundreds of seats and tables faced a huge neon sign that read 'Market Place 146 – Station Twelve'.

Morse glanced at his phone and muttered, his voice in Desy and Rake's earpieces, 'Two minutes late.'

The trio descended on an escalator to the platforms' entrance, following the platform numbers in ascending order until a green '8' hovered above them. Where, waiting in a bright-red, wide-brimmed hat that clashed with his night-blue jumpsuit, was Bronzework. His seven-foot figure hovered his hat above the shoppers like a toadstool.

Desy felt sweat dribbling down her face as the trio approached him and stood some feet away. She dared to glance up, but Bronzework's mask remained still and directed at the empty platform.

Suddenly, the train whooshed into existence and its doors snapped open.

Bronzework politely extended an arm.

Desy felt Morse's fingers dig into her shoulder as he walked her into the train to take a seat. He placed her between himself and Rake, and he put the shopping bag between his legs as before. Except he reached inside it and pulled out a bundle of magazines, handing all but one of them to Rake then opening his to cover his face.

Bronzework stepped past the three of them, brushing Desy's knee and nearly making her scream, before he lowered himself slowly next to Morse.

Desy felt the entire seat creak beneath the mercenary's bulk. She clasped her hands, attempting to stay her heart. Out of the corner of her eye, she watched Bronzework remove the newspaper tucked under an arm then open it, spreading it so it touched Morse's magazine. She noticed that Rake's magazine was touching Morse's, creating a screen that hid their laps and arms.

Morse gripped a corner of Rake's magazine, which allowed her to have a hand free to silently pluck a diagram with notes from her lap. Exchanging magazine corners, the diagram travelled to Morse's left hand to Bronzework's eye-line.

The mercenary held Morse's magazine with two thick fingers.

This system saw several pages of documents travel to and from Rake and Bronzework with only the slightest rustle. For around ten minutes, with occasional page turns from the three to sell the illusion, Desy sat still as a rock, only glancing again to Rake when she noticed Morse flinch.

The document he had read said, *Sir, do you sign guns?*

Rake blushed, grinning when she spotted Bronzework beckon with his pinkie finger. She drew a hand into her coat. Producing her pistol, she dangled it by its trigger guard to Morse's magazine, and it travelled to Bronzework's left leg.

The bat-man grimaced when Rake nudged him, prompting him to produce his own pistol and place it on the mercenary's right thigh. He gingerly passed a marker to Bronzework, who tilted his head when he read 'Bellamy' on each gun. But he was quick to scribble his signature below it.

Rake resisted the urge to squeal, forcing herself to wait until she returned to *Ferguson* to engrave the autograph into the brass handle.

Another ten minutes passed before Desy was suddenly startled by Bronzework folding his newspaper in half and resting it on his lap. He twirled his wrist, and a fountain pen appeared from thin air. He began to write in the spaces of a crossword, with Morse's eyes glancing from his own magazine to Bronzework.

Morse read, *Meet orbit Yeti execute plan upon sight each other final communication until payment.*

Rake placed her own magazine atop her lap and rolled all the documents messily, shoving them inside the shopping bag. Morse, meanwhile, simply continued to 'read'.

When the next stop came, Bronzework rose to his full height, tilting his head to duck beneath the grooves of the ceiling as he walked to the exit.

However, he came to a stop in front of Desy, his blank mask burning a hole into her lap. 'Excuse me,' he said.

Morse nearly tore his magazine in half.

Rake held a hand to her chest, stammering, 'Y-Yes?'

'Is this young lady with you?' Bronzework inquired slowly.

'Yes,' Rake said again.

Desy locked her jaw and stared up at the mercenary.

'Thieves have been known to frequent this area. I'd advise she keep her hands in her pockets.'

Desy stuffed her hands inside her blazer.

He looked at Morse and Rake.

Taking the cue, Morse quickly shut his magazine, placed it inside the shopping bag, and lifted it onto his lap while clasping the opening closed.

'A bit of caution goes a long way,' Bronzework rumbled, then stepped off the train.

The three observed his red hat hovering and shrinking into the distance, rising up an escalator before the train doors closed and the station was whisked away.

Morse stood and, after Rake took Desy by the shoulder, moved them away from the stragglers in their carriage, walking until they reached a section of seats in the rear-most car, where not a single passenger resided.

Morse collapsed into a seat and blurted out, 'I nearly shat myself. Only ever done the newspaper trick, like, once.'

'I got Bronzework's signature!' sang Rake, clapping her hands across her mouth and giggling uncontrollably, her legs wobbling her to her seat.

Desy, however, stood just out of the corner of their eyes, mouth dry and her belly twisting in knots.

Something foreign was in her pocket.

Slowly, Desy peered down her arm to her hand, turning and unsheathing it while cupping the something in her palm. It was a small slip of paper.

The message read:

Your father sent me to save you.

When the doors open next, simply tie your shoelaces, and they will disappear.

You will be home soon.

TEN
Chaos

Daddy hired Bronzework...?

The seats, the handrails, the windows, the slowly shifting buildings in the distance, the distorted infinity of the universe beyond, someone had thrown white paint all over it.

Her feet numbed to the rumble of the floor. Her hand slipped through the pole she was gripping.

Desy gasped in her head. *I'm going home. Daddy took care of it.*

She was in bed with her lungs on fire, Ernest holding her hand after a particularly fitful sleep. Every breath was against the tip of a knife. Every slight movement of her chest made her cough, which made her cough again. And Ernest always remained with her until she fell asleep once more. During her sickness, Desy awoke on occasion to her father's pacing footfalls near her bedroom. She would squint to see him poke his head inside the bedroom every minute or so. And he would tell Aurelian that he 'did not need to sit down'. It only lasted a few weeks, but Desy remained convinced it was the worst time of her life.

Until now.

Daddy's always taken care of me.

The train and the universe came back into focus.

Desy quickly peeked at the note again before pushing her hand completely inside her pocket. '*Tie my shoelaces*', she mulled. *That means to duck down when the doors open. 'And they will disappear'. That can only mean one thing.* She felt her throat tighten. *But that's... fine. Morse and Rake, they caused all of this. They're the reason. They're kidnappers.*

They're bad people.

However, she was forced to shimmy her head to dull a sickening jolt that crawled up her spine. Her eyes began to burn.

All I have to do is say nothing, she reasoned with herself.

Desy heard Rake say to Morse, 'When we get the money, we gotta pay Higgins back.'

Say nothing and tie my shoelaces. Easy.

Morse said, 'Yeah, deal should go good now. This'll be over in a few hours.'

Desy let out a long, long breath, which only made her stomach pains worse.

Morse's ear pricked up. 'Hey, kid, are you all right?' he called.

Don't say anything.

She watched Morse stand up then walk to her side.

Suddenly, an automated voice proclaimed, 'Next stop, Fashion Room 101.'

'Kid...?' Morse crouched to her eye level. 'You're looking pale. Hungry?'

Desy heard Morse's scream of pain after taking the shot meant for her. She smelled the burning flesh of his shoulder again.

Rake snarked from behind him, 'Dee's got a lot on her mind, Morse. She doesn't wanna see ya ugly face right up close.'

She saw Rake falling out of the sky, where she should have been instead.

Morse threw an aloof expression over his shoulder.

Just a bit more, Desy reassured herself while her chest began to ache. *Don't say anything. Say nothing.* Her nose, mouth, and eyelids began to twitch of their own volition.

'You can relax now, kid,' Morse said, calmly. 'That must have been exhausting for you.'

Desy's vision blurred.

Don't cry, she yelled at herself.

Her shoulders squeezed her chest.

Why're you crying, you idiot?

Rake appeared behind Morse. 'Dee?'

Desy hiccupped, and the dam of sobs and tears and snotty noses broke. She hunched over, biting her lip, tilting her head to the floor, flutter-gasping. Her pale cheeks darkened to a crimson hue as tears streamed like rivers across her face.

Morse and Rake glanced at each other.

Morse locked his jaw.

Rake crouched down beside him, saying, 'Dee, Dee. Ya gotta listen. Ya don't have ta cry. Ya gonna be home in like an hour. We got Bronzework now and–'

Desy wailed.

Don't speak.

'Dee, what's wrong?' Rake attempted to lead her to a seat but only succeeded in making Desy fall to her knees.

The glow of the next stop seeped onto their faces.

'I…' Desy hiccupped.

Don't!

'I just want… to… go home.'

'And ya will,' Rake comforted, forcing a laugh. 'Ya will.'

Desy heard Morse's shoes thump around to her head, now flanked on both sides by her kidnappers. She cried, 'You're… terrible, awful people…'

Morse and Rake exchanged a resigned and puzzled glance, respectively.

Desy raised her head so her miserable features could be seen. 'But, I…'

I'm an absolute idiot, she told herself.

She covered her face with one hand and reached into her pocket with the other. 'But I don't think you deserve to die!' she sobbed, handing Morse the note.

Rake quickly joined Morse's side.

Both of them went cold.

Morse jerked his head to look out of the window, just in time to see a colourful sign slithering into view. It read: 'Fashion Room 101 – Platform 4'.

'Move!' Morse bellowed, grabbing Desy by the arm and flying through the empty carriage as the doors started to separate.

Rake sprinted ahead of them in a panic. She leaped down into a lower compartment and cleared the floor in a second, vaulting up into the next carriage, where a number of passengers were piling inside from the platform. She hurled herself into the centre of that pack, eliciting a few indignant shouts when she made enough room for Morse and Desy to cram next to her.

The three crouched low and panted. For ten whole seconds, they shielded their faces from the open platform through a thin wall of people.

Eventually, the doors snapped shut, and the train jolted away.

In direct line of sight of the platform, perched on a vending machine, cloaked and invisible, with his sniper rifle muzzle following the carriage, Bronzework clicked his tongue. He muttered, 'That is very unfortunate.'

The mercenary rose to his feet and holstered his rifle on his back, the HUD in his vision showing two blinking dots moving rapidly into the distance. He leaped into the air and glided after the train.

He concluded, 'Truly, Wintall raised a dumb daughter.'

Meanwhile, Desy whispered over and over, 'I'm an idiot, I'm an idiot, I'm an idiot.'

Morse pulled her close and spat under his breath, 'No, kid, you listen to me. What you just did was the honourable thing. Where I'm from, that's thicker than blood.' His eyes filled her world. 'What you did was a damn sight more exceptional than anything Bronzework was trying to pull.'

Rake leaned forward and encircled Desy with her arms. 'Desy... ya gave up your best chance for us?' She held a hand to her mouth while her eyebrows pulled into a fierce glare. 'Morse, we gotta protect this little ragamuffin with all we've got.'

Desy quivered and hiccupped.

'As long as we stay in a crowd, Bronzework won't risk a shot, but even then...' Morse calmed his breathing. 'He's the best, but he ain't a god. He won't know where we are. But we'll have to move fast.'

Rake let go of Desy, withdrew a cigarette, and lit it up.

'Excuse me,' huffed a Hawkie from above, a tawny frogmouth, 'but the sign says—'

'Shut your gaping slug hole, right?' Rake snapped without facing him. To Morse, she said, 'I know you're not a people person, but I gotta say, I don't wanna deal with other folk right now, either.'

'What's our next move?'

'Here's the plan. We commandeer this ship on rails and take the express route back to *Ferguson*. Avoid the mall altogether.'

'And the passengers?'

Rake opened her coat and revealed her pistol.

'I understand you're stressed,' Morse said. 'But we did not go through all that hassle of getting a new ship just to immediately give the police a reason to track it. We need to go covert, okay?'

Morse heard a wave of rustling fabric and felt three barrels press into his back.

Rake felt two nip her on the neck.

The tawny frogmouth said, 'Morse and Rake, by the authority of the United Galaxy's Government, you're under arrest for the kidnapping of Desy Wintall. Do not resist; you are surrounded. You will be read your rights once you're under restraint–'

An Arthrod loosed a torch-beam into the Hawkie's face.

Shoppers screamed as three more Arthrods crammed into the carriage and started firing on the undercover officers, who holstered their guns and charged the bugs, tackling them into the seats. Morse and Rake and Desy were left in utter shock, still crouched, completely exposed while chaos descended around them.

'That changes things,' Morse conceded. He grabbed Desy by the arm while Rake dodged under a Cannot socking an Arthrod in the mandibles. She disappeared to the other end of the train in seconds.

Desy, however, dug her feet into the floor, begging, 'Let the police take me! If they arrest you, then you won't have to die!'

'Don't feel like going to jail, yeah? And, kid, that wouldn't stop Bronzework,' Morse growled, lifting her over his shoulder as he pushed past frightened shoppers. 'He'd take out every police officer in the galaxy if they stood in the way of his client's carton of milk. If it's his job, it's *his* job.' He flicked on his microphone. 'Rake, comms on!'

Desy wheeled around to call for the police but caught sight of an Arthrod digging its claws deeper and deeper into an officer. She turned back with a pale face and fumbled with her earpiece in time to hear Rake yell, 'We gotta stall for two minutes until the next stop.'

Far behind, a Cannot bellowed into his radio above the sound of his tawny frogmouth colleague screeching and swatting his bubbling face. 'Secure the girl,' he ordered. 'Codes eight, thirteen-ten, seventy-two-ten!' The bloodhound kicked an Arthrod off himself and bounded after Morse on all fours.

The thumping of paws from behind made the bat-man yell, 'Rake, I need cover!' Racing past cowering passengers in their seats, he spotted Rake kneeling and holding the door open to the next carriage with her gun positioned in her crooked arm. And as Morse shot past her, she squeezed the trigger, jettisoning a volley of plasma towards the bloodhound's chest.

The dog-man jerked sideways and crashed into a passenger, the plasma shot exploding against the roof.

Rake sprinted, catching up to then passing Morse, who'd moved Desy under his arm. 'One more carriage should do it,' she shouted in his ear.

'There's a crowd.'

'Got it.' Rake heaved in a deep breath and, like a siren, shouted, 'Aaaaaaaaaaaaaaaaaaahhhhhhhhh!'

Shoppers who were already concerned by the ruckus in the next carriage clung to the walls at the sight of a woman sprinting, screaming, and brandishing a pistol at them. Like the Red Sea, the crowd parted, allowing the three to escape to the end of the next carriage, where Rake kept the door open and had her pistol trained on one set of stairs. Morse crouched with his back to her, eyes and gun glued on the other. Desy cowered between them.

'Next stop, Massage Lane 5,' announced the intercom.

There were twelve passengers either side of the trio, and they hadn't breathed since the guns had been drawn. They all clutched their shopping bags to their chests. As the train pulled into the station at Platform 6, which was absent of all patrons, a shivering Felinguielle kitten squeezed his bag tight enough to eject a can of cat food into the air.

It clunked on the floor. Morse, Rake, Desy, and eleven other sets of eyes glanced at it, then looked at the kitten.

He apologised and sank into his seat.

Then the train doors flew open.

At the same time that Desy scrambled onto the platform, three pairs of officers and Arthrods tumbled out of the train, followed by several dozen passengers.

'With the crowd,' commanded Rake, and Morse grabbed Desy's arm, dragging her into the stampede. 'Heads low. Look for another train, we'll clear it out.'

Two seconds later, Desy pointed and squeaked, 'There!' towards a train pulling into Platform 9.

'Thanks, Dee.'

The trio broke from the pack when the two crowds were metres from each other, blending in again and racing against the current towards the conductor's cabin.

The Jellentity warbled in surprise when two barrels poked it in the back.

'Out,' grunted Morse.

It floated rapidly across the platform and into the conductor's office with its tentacles wobbling above its head.

'You can drive a train?' Desy asked Rake.

'It's just like *Ferguson*, but' – she pointed to two levers – 'half the console is there.' Then she pointed to ten buttons. 'And the rest of the ship's there.' She punched a button with a speaker icon. 'Ladies and gentlemen,' Rake announced into the intercom, 'this is a robbery. We don't wanna have anythin' ta do with ya shopping bags. We want the train. Unless ya wanna make this your final stop, *run!*'

Desy felt the cabin shuffle and shake as hundreds of people evacuated. Thousands of footsteps thundered past the open door that Morse had his gun trained at.

'Close the door,' he grunted.

'There,' Rake called, making the cabin door hiss and jolt.

Suddenly, a pair of claws snagged Desy through the shrinking gap. She screamed and grabbed on to Morse.

Morse clasped her arms but was overpowered and yanked out of the cabin, his leg tangling around Rake's and tripping her over; she slammed onto the console, and the whole train lurched forward.

Desy cried, 'My arms!'

The bat-man let go, but while clutching his pistol with one hand, he slapped the handle with the other and unloaded into the Arthrod's face.

Behind him, the train flew out of the station.

'Morse,' came Rake's desperate tone. 'Hold on, I'll back it up.'

'Hurry,' he pleaded, placing Desy behind him as ten Arthrods landed with their torch-rifles already primed.

Suddenly, three that were standing behind each other fell sideways and sprawled to the ground. Then one about to fire its rifle collapsed. The remaining six Arthrods jumped in panic, only for another to spasm and crash into a vending machine.

'No way...' Morse paled as he threw Desy behind a vending machine and joined her. He yelled, 'Bronzework's found us; Rake, keep your head down!'

'Oh, god,' she blurted in his ear.

Desy tugged on Morse's sweater, trembling violently. 'What's happening?'

'Bronzework's removing the competition.' Morse breathed through his fangs, hearing the sound of static colliding with an Arthrod's thorax.

'Don't die,' Desy begged. 'P-Please. He wants me. I'll just give myself up.'

'If your father ordered him to kill us, there's nothing you can do to stop that.'

The teenager shuddered. She clasped her head in her hands, sinking to her knees. Then, she stood bolt upright and stammered, 'Ph-Phone. I'll tell Daddy to call him off.'

Morse heard police radios screaming, 'Unknown assailant, take cover!' And then an Arthrod flew by him and skidded on its face for several metres before resting like a mangled rug.

'Give me your phone,' Desy urged.

'Listen to her, Morse,' Rake screeched.

Morse shot, 'He's not going to do it–'

'We gotta try *something!*'

He slapped his phone into Desy's hand. 'Seven, eight, forty-four.'

The teen shakily tapped the code onto the screen and fumbled her way into the call application. She stabbed in Ernest's number.

A tiny xylophone tinkled as a squad of officers unloaded a barrage of plasma shots into an empty clothing store. It continued playing scales while five more Arthrods arrived on the platform across from Morse, and two were downed with an invisible shot from Bronzework.

Suddenly the xylophone stopped, and a curt tone said, 'This is Ernest.'

'Daddy!' blurted Desy.

'Cricket!' cried Ernest.

'Daddy, you have to stop–'

Morse, with his ears trained on a firefight he was unable to see, keeping his attention across to the platform on his left, failed to notice three Arthrods rushing in from the right, the biggest one grabbing and crushing Desy to its chest.

Her breath hitched as all the air from her lungs was pumped out in a second. The phone fell from her hand.

'Kid!' yelled Morse, aiming his pistol, only to have an Arthrod slam its rifle into his liver, crumpling him to the floor. The world darkened away with only the halo of a primed torch-rifle to see, brightening like the sun in front of his eyes.

Rake screamed, 'No!' in his ear, and a plasma shot slammed into the Arthrod's head.

Morse jerked his blurred vision to the right to see Rake crouched inside a carriage, her pistol-barrel smoking. Her face was pale and barely controlled. 'Come on!'

'Bronzework,' Morse wheezed, trying to stand.

'They got Desy, Morse. You know where Bronzework is!'

'Not here.' He swiped his phone and pistol and staggered into the train.

'Cricket?' came Ernest's voice from the phone. 'Are you all right? Are you hurt? *Cricket?*'

Rake snatched the phone from Morse and held it up to her lips. She muttered, an incensed mother, 'Don't you *dare* play innocent.' She hung up and sprinted into the conductor's cabin.

Morse heard all the doors close, then the carriage quaked before the burning shopfront and Arthrod bodies blurred together with the stars.

In both their ears, they could hear Desy gasping for breath in the screaming wind. The flapping of the Arthrods' wings was deafening.

Morse moaned while getting to his feet, 'Kid, you alive?'

There was a gasp, then a small, 'Mmm-hmm.'

He staggered into the conductor's cabin and leaned against the wall just as Rake flicked her microphone off.

'Why is she alive?' Rake hissed. 'She should be… the hag wanted her…'

'Tell us where you're going,' Morse said to Desy.

'Really… high…'

'Taking her to their ship. Why?' Rake clapped her hands to her cheeks three times. Then a voice began shouting at her through the train's radio, prompting her to start barking orders for the tracks to be cleared, yelling at the rail traffic controller to redirect their train back to their ship-park.

'We'll cut out soon, kid,' Morse muttered, turning away from the console. 'We'll be out of range, but we're coming, all right? Stay sharp. Observe.'

Suddenly, Desy squealed and the wind picked up in his ear.

'Kid, what's happening?' Morse shouted.

The wind calmed down. And then Desy's voice stated with surprising jollity, 'I'm flying.'

'You're what?'

'I dunno, the mantises all started falling, but I stopped.' She went silent, and then said, 'It feels like… someone is holding me.'

Rake, after watching hundreds of dots on the rail-map slow to a stop and a dozen rail intersections begin to shift, whipped her head around and blurted, 'Bronzework. He *can* fly.'

'And turn invisible.' Morse shook his head in disbelief.

Then Desy shouted, 'They're coming again! They're everywhere… They've got him!'

Morse and Rake heard snarling mandibles and a tornado of wings.

'Oh my god, it's Bronzework. He was invisible! He's…'

Four rapid slugs thumped their ears, followed by the sickening crack of an Arthrod spine.

'Oh, wow, he's destroying them. Oh… no, Morse! Rake! Help me!'

The tornado of wings returned.

'Have they got you?' Morse shouted.

'There's a ship, they're taking me to their—'

Static blasted into their ears.

Rake flicked her microphone on and stood up, shouting, 'Dee? Dee?!'

'They've broken the earpiece,' Morse snarled. 'Get us to *Ferguson*. Go!'

'I'm going!' Rake throttled the train, hurling Morse into the wall as it swerved around a corner. Lights, signs, and advertisements squashed into coloured lines. When the lights went white, Rake called, 'One minute.'

'Higgins,' Morse said suddenly.

'Me too. I reckon that's the only way the police tracked us.'

'He hates cops.'

'So they gotta have found the Shipyard.'

'They interrogated him.'

'Ya wanna give him the benefit of the doubt?'

Morse thumped the wall with a fist. 'If the Shipyard's gone, sure.'

The lines morphed into rainbows again.

'Wintall,' Rake said suddenly.

'Only certain people know Bronzework.'

Rake whipped out a cigarette and almost bit it in half. 'What kinda father sends a goddamn merc ta save his daughter?'

'Someone with something to hide from the cops.'

The ship-park appeared on their left. Rake yelped, 'Brace,' and kicked the brakes on.

Morse gripped the doorframe and bent his knees, feeling the two carriages behind careen into each other. The cabin was a tiny boat in a storm.

'Silver Fingers?' Morse asked when the train jerked to a stop, the last carriage completely off the platform.

'Bad luck.' Rake shrugged. She brandished her pistol and fled the room. She screeched 'Get away!' to a dozen or so shoppers arriving on a transport. By the time they disembarked, Morse was able to jump on and grip her waist while she throttled the hover-platform into the ship-park.

'How're we going to track the kid?'

'Think about it, idiot,' Rake huffed. 'How many ships *leave* this place?'

The moment Morse flipped his lip out and conceded, 'Good point,' two police cruisers, scouts, flew overhead, towards an Arthrod missile cruiser shooting into the sky.

Ferguson appeared in view as the pair skidded around a series of sedans.

'We're gonna have to jump,' she yelled, gritting her teeth. 'Ready? Now!'

They leaped from the transport and hit the ground, too busy rolling against the tarmac to notice it whirl into the badly parked jet-ski and obliterate it, turning it into a billiard ball that sank into the pocket of a family cruiser.

Morse cursed and swore at his bloodied elbows, but Rake was already on her feet and smacking the landing ramp lock.

'She could be dead,' Morse thought aloud as the alarm beeped.

'*Our* Dee?' Rake grinned, clambering onto the ramp when it approached a horizontal angle.

Morse felt the forcefulness of the smile but said anyway, 'Hopefully she'll be just as annoying to them as she was to us.'

Ferguson shuddered and lifted awkwardly into the air, racing after the police cruisers and the Arthrod missile. Its horn blared at the incoming line of ships, and they moved as a very slow firework, forcing *Ferguson* to twist and tessellate through the small opening. It then exploded through the gears.

Inside the cockpit, Morse was silent, his eyes glued to the radar. Four police scouts with two officers in each and an Arthrod missile with a number he could only guess at. And maybe Desy was inside, alive.

Rake pulled as hard as she could on the accelerator, making Moody Moody's artificial atmosphere fade into the void. Funny Man's rings shimmered into view, the ice giant swelling like a balloon on the windshield. And in the bottom right of the windshield, a small message read: *Dear Morse, upon your next visit, enjoy ten percent off everything!*

Desy trembled on cold metal panels with three torch-rifles pointed at her head. She held back every primal urge to cry for help. The only action she could take was to observe the mantis-men stomping about the pill-shaped room.

For the first time since she was a young child, Desy quailed at the sight of insects.

They garbled to each other in a language that sounded like they were choking. The room was stuffy with the scent produced when one scares an ant's nest. Aside from the organic, fleshy consoles that beeped mechanically, the only sound was the coins rattling in jars next to her head.

The heat from the torch-rifles was making her nauseous. At least the migraine had dissipated.

She could see through the windshield the ringed planet from before. And when it rushed to fill the entire windshield, and the individual asteroids in its rings were visible, Desy heard a voice that was higher and lighter than the rest of the pack's.

The room stopped dead at the voice.

Desy waited as the bugs clacked in response. Unbeknownst to her, the conversation was:

'Bronzework attacked you? His name appeared in the archives many times.'

'He is being kept busy.'

'He only attacked you.'

'Yes, and the police.'

'So, we can assume that he is working under Morse and Rake. And the fake *is* alive?'

'As you ordered, Sister.'

'I see…'

Desy experienced a shiver of recognition when a high-pitched giggle echoed about the cockpit. It sounded like her own, but not quite.

'Then we will proceed with the plan. Bronzework changes nothing. Whether him, the pair, or the police, the plan will work. Speaking of which, I'm ready for you, but there is something you need to do first.'

'Yes?'

'When you've entered Funny Man's rings and Brosteni is within sight, you are to shoot out one of the engines.'

'May we ask why, Sister?'

'Your pursuers know you don't have time to jump without them destroying the jump nodes. Therefore, they'll think you are trying to lose them in the ring and have hit an asteroid. So, you are to act as if you are losing control and then make an emergency landing on Brosteni.'

'We understand.'

'Please, it is imperative that she is seen moving and alive when entering the cavern. I'm putting my faith in you all.'

'That is appreciated, Sister.'

After a sharp *beep*, Desy felt the atmosphere in the room thicken with pheromones. Two of the twelve Arthrods exited the room through a hatch on the left.

Their windshield filled with rocks of all colours, sizes, and shapes when the missile penetrated the outer layer of rings. Docile, from his position in the captain's chair, hissed at an Arthrod known as Muscular, who garbled back, 'The pigs are slowing down.'

'Welcome news,' responded Docile.

'Correction,' Muscular clacked. 'One of the ships has sped up.'

'Then we shall, too.'

Muscular focused on the radar screen and the four dots that began to drift away from the central point. The fifth dot, some distance behind the police, seemed to double in speed the moment it touched the outer ring. In seconds, it overtook the scouts, which Muscular announced with an astonished cluck.

Docile ordered, 'On screen.' A holographic video feed sprang up in front of him, one that showed a ship with a broken wing barrel-rolling and shaving the edges off asteroids, inches away from obliteration.

Desy gasped happily. 'Guys,' she whispered.

'They're coming up behind us,' Muscular stammered.

'Are they crazy?' Docile shouted. 'Full speed!'

The entire engine team announced their concerns at such an action.

But Docile fired back, 'Sister demands it!'

The team hung their heads in resignation.

Desy squeaked as the room groaned and the ball-shaped rocks in the windshield contorted into lines. The missile lived up to its shape and rocketed into the next layer of rings, exploding with speed.

Muscular gripped his chair as the pilot, Indifferent, clacked expletives and threw the ship into roll after roll, nearly colliding with a field-sized asteroid but pulling up just in time for their shield to carve a valley into its surface. Muscular checked the radar and clacked, 'We're still losing ground.'

'Sister, help us,' breathed Docile through his trachea holes.

Indifferent squawked, 'Brosteni sighted!'

'Do it!' spat Docile into the intercom.

Every Arthrod in the room braced.

Desy yelped when the two guards held her down as well.

Inside *Ferguson*, with Morse holding on for dear life and Rake not having blinked in five minutes, the pair witnessed the missile suddenly lurch then spin like a Frisbee out of the ring layer.

'What?!' they both exclaimed.

'What?!' the four police scouts exclaimed.

'They overloaded th-their engines,' Rake stammered, her face paling.

'Goddamn it, Rake, *pull back!* You're going to kill her!'

She disengaged the thrusters immediately.

The pair watched the missile slowly stop rotating, one of its own thrusters blacked out. Then it began to drift towards an egg-sized, snow-white planetoid on the windshield.

'They're gonna make a landing,' Rake said, kicking the engines up.

'Just tail them–' Morse began.

'Don't tell me how to fly.'

'Tail them,' admonished Morse, startling her, 'and if it looks like they're going to crash, go as *fast* as you can.'

Rake blinked with a lopsided frown at his glower. 'Reckon that's the last time ya speak to me like that…'

Ferguson zoomed towards the ruptured missile while the police scouts continued their slow weave through the dense, rocky environment.

And, far away at Moody Moody, an invisible, star-shaped cruiser received a one thousand and fifty percent discount.

ELEVEN
Counterbalance

Dark, arctic clouds and lunar-wide snowfall meant that Brosteni once received a healthy flux of tourists each year. Coupled with the sky-filling Funny Man and the mountain slopes of Promethia, it was no wonder that five-star ski resorts dotted the landscape of the terrestrial moon.

However, its proximity to Moody Moody meant that Brosteni had received no visitors for three hundred years. The remnants of the resorts were collapsed, beaten, filled in, and erased further each blizzard season. The winds that swept the planet were from the subterranean oceans and jungles filled with unique species of fish, birds, insects, plants, and reptiles. Around four hundred thousand PhDs worth of specimens.

Entrances to this underground world found by the resort companies had been filled in.

The surface was barren, save for the snow and mountains and a curious sunbeam that had burst onto the plateau by Promethia's base. A missile-shaped shadow filled in the spotlight as black smoke poured across the moon's skin. The Arthrod ship swung this way and that, approaching the plateau with its nose pulling up. With a ground-quaking *thump,* the missile plunged into the thick snow, creating a valley as it skidded to a halt some twenty metres from the entrance to a large cavern. White, billowing clouds mixed into the smoke.

Desy was shoved from the ship some seconds later. Immediately, the frigid atmosphere sucked the air from her lungs. Her hair stiffened. Her skin prickled and numbed in seconds. The wind burned her face. A claw on her left then a claw to her right wrangled her arms, carrying her towards the dark maw of the cavern.

Suddenly, another spotlight appeared a few metres to her left.

Looking up, Desy spotted through the torrents of snow *Ferguson's* triangular shape and grinned, shivering.

Then, a torch-rifle plunged into her right temple, and another pushed between her breasts and against her heart.

She stopped smiling, and *Ferguson* jerked away; the ship disappeared into the blizzard. Desy was coerced into the cavern where, although the snow had stopped pelting her, the volume of the wind quintupled to the roar of an engine. There were signs of several roof collapses and weak walls that had caved in, creating hills and valleys of craggy rock. White-capped stalactites lined the hangar-tall ceiling.

Unknown to Desy, the Arthrod guards heard through their transceivers, 'Knock her out.'

She felt a blow to the side of her neck. Her legs gave way. The cave grew around her until it disappeared, leaving her in complete darkness.

'Is it done?' clacked Silver Fingers.

'Yes, Sister,' responded Docile. 'Morse and Rake shall be here any minute. The pigs will be close behind.'

The android emerged from behind a car-sized stalagmite, just as the rest of the Arthrods entered the cavern. 'Docile,' it yelled over the wind. 'Now comes the final part. I'll take her clothes then take her place. And when Morse and Rake come for me...'

Silver Fingers observed the group of Arthrods; they were cradling injuries to their faces, limbs, and wings.

I'm feeling... sad? thought the android. *But they aren't Daddy. Though insects are Desy's life, so this feeling makes sense.*

Desy. I am Desy.

The android shook its head, then continued, 'They're cowards. So when they come for me, all they'll do is run. Try to kill them. If not, so be it, but either way, when the police arrive...' It clasped its elbows. 'Surrender. I will come back for you.'

'We gladly give our lives for you, Sister,' Docile clicked.

The horde agreed and howled to show it.

I mean it. Don't die...

Silver Fingers bounded to Desy, waved at the Arthrods to lower her to the ground, then stripped itself of Desy's pyjamas before crouching, nude, over the teenager's blazer. Undoing the buttons, it wriggled her arms through the sleeves, flipping her over so her neck flopped and her head smacked against the rock while it yanked the top off her. Next, the shirt went, then the pants, then underwear. Silver Fingers slipped on Desy's warm socks and feverishly pulled on the red shoes.

No sunglasses or hat. Those were still falling down Moody Moody's abyss.

All the while, the android's belly raged; the fire had built and built with every porcelain limb it saw, every follicle of hair, every tiny mole.

It's me. How dare she be me?! Silver Fingers gritted its teeth. Once it had jerked the laces on its left foot, it rose to stand above the naked teenager. Its leg trembled. Its feet twitched. It wrangled with what Desy's head would feel like beneath its sole, especially if it stomped on her.

'Sister,' Docile interjected, clasping the pyjamas. 'Lights from a hover-bike in the distance. We must kill the girl and hide her.'

'We're out of time,' screeched Silver Fingers. 'If even one smidgen of her exists, any *blood*, they'll figure it out!' It locked a finger at a crumbling wall, deep into the cavern. 'I prepared that earlier. Put her in alive.'

Docile scooped Desy up with her pyjamas. Silver Fingers commanded the other eleven Arthrods into ambush positions, having two of them restrain her with torch-rifles switched on. 'And don't worry, by the time she wakes, she'll be all alone.'

Docile sprinted towards the crack in the wall, his wings frozen and brittle, his claws slipping across the icy rocks.

'Hurry!' urged Silver Fingers.

Docile crushed the pyjamas into the base of the teenager-sized hole. And then he wedged Desy, head-first, into the crevice, pushing and pushing so the craggy walls sliced her cheeks and forehead open, her blood dribbling into a pool inside her pyjamas.

It was already beginning to harden by the time Docile sprinted back to the entrance, just in time to catch a hover-bike rocketing into the cave with a torrent of snow behind it.

Several minutes earlier...

Rake yanked *Ferguson* away from the smoking missile so the cavern and Desy disappeared into the white fog. 'I'm gonna do a shutdown,' she barked to Morse.

'A what?' Morse asked, watching Rake point crazily through a wall to what he presumed to be the landing ramp. 'The bike...?'

'Get your suit on, get the bike ready.' Rake tilted the steering wheel down, and a series of rocky outcrops could be seen growing and rushing past the windscreen. She smacked many buttons and cranked a lever while saying, 'The cops are gonna be around us when we get Dee back. If *Ferguson* is off, then they can't detect him, right?'

Morse unbuckled his seat belt, nervous. 'You're turning the ship off in the air? Just land him and park.'

'Well, I'm coming with you,' Rake said, nonchalantly.

Morse surveyed the barren, arctic wasteland for one second before stating, 'No, you're not.'

'Yes, I am.'

He was about to smack Rake about the head when she blurted out, 'I've got my suit. Got my ciggies. That's all I need.'

Morse gripped her shoulders. Hard. 'That is the stupidest plan you've ever come up with.'

'I'm not an idiot, and don't tell me what–'

'You're being emotional–'

'Get to the bike and–'

'You're not coming with me–'

'For *god's sake*, Morse!' Rake shrieked him into silence.

He had forgotten until that moment just how loud she could be.

'For god's sake! Someone other than you *cares* if I die.' She unbuckled her seat belt in a huff, slapped his arms away, and reached up to grab hold of a lever.

Morse left the cockpit, stone-faced.

Rake called, 'Bike and landing ramp.'

Two seconds after she heard the siren, a loud thump blew air across her ankles.

Morse twisted on his goldfish-bowl helmet and glared at her. But he then spat, 'You tell me *exactly* how you're doing at all times.'

Rake grinned and literally jumped into her spacesuit. After fastening her own goldfish bowl, she kissed *Ferguson*'s steering wheel through the glass and cut the generators. The vacuum-cleaner roar turned off, and the entire ship listed forward into a doughy field of snow.

Morse and Rake sprinted towards the idling hover-bike. He gripped the handlebars while she grappled his spongy suit. Disengaging the brake, Morse waited until he made out frozen waves in the ground before he kicked the bike into gear and launched down the landing ramp, a cannonball into a wall of clouds.

Rake clenched her jaw and knotted her fingers around themselves. Seeing snow for miles around forced a dense ball from her stomach to her throat, but the sight of *Ferguson* plunging into the snowy embankment and only landing a little lopsided made her smile. 'Bullseye,' she declared.

'I tuned your radio, too,' Morse muttered in her ear.

Rake giggled and snuggled into his suit. 'Let's get that ragamuffin!'

She felt the engine warble into a higher gear as the ground tilted from flat to a ragged slope. Snow splattered against her helmet like rain. The fishbowl soon was drenched. She felt Morse's torso tilt so his head was screened by the handlebars. Then, the ground lurched into a steep hill. A series of sharp rocks zoomed by her right while, underneath, the snow gave way to a cliff, and she felt the engine whinny as Morse guided it back to the hill again.

'How're you going?' reminded Morse.

'A-okay–'

Suddenly, a mountain sprouted from the ground. Rake felt her stomach slap her ribcage as the bike ploughed into the plateau and snow erupted into the air.

'Sorry,' grunted Morse, wrestling the handlebars so they pointed towards the cavern entrance.

Rake, keeping one hand attached to Morse, slid her other behind her back. 'We're gonna have to go quicker than we've ever gone, Morse.'

'I know.'

'In and out.'

'Yeah,' he said. 'For the job.'

'For the job!' cheered Rake, the maw of the cavern over her head.

However, two hundred metres further above Rake's head, two police scouts hovered slowly into the vortex. With a hiss, their landing ramps lowered and clunked into place. And with flashing red and blue lights, four hover-bikes, two riders on each, dropped through the wind. Their engines whinnied as they whistled towards the cavern like arrows.

Inside the cavern, Rake had mere moments to spot three Arthrods to the right, positioned behind broken rocks. Four to the left, one with a torch-rifle. Four, twenty metres away in the centre, and two of them were armed.

And in the middle of it all was 'Desy', 'shivering' from the cold.

On the same wavelength, Morse cranked the accelerator and twisted a knob to force the bike higher into the air, then pulled the handlebars back so the front shielded him and Rake from three torch-rifle strikes. The Arthrod gripping the android's left arm blinked then ate one hundred and fifty kilograms of screaming engine, the back of his head instantly kissing the floor.

Meanwhile, Rake reached down and snagged the android by the scruff of its blazer, squealing with the effort until the android hooked a leg around the bike and she felt its arms wrap around her waist.

The hover-bike smashed into the ground, which sent an explosion echoing around the cavern. Sparks rippled in waves as Morse heaved the bike parallel to the floor. It skidded across piles of rocks and ice and stopped mere inches from a small crevice in the wall.

Desy's shallow breathing went unnoticed.

Morse floored it and hid behind the handlebars, flinching then jerking while torch-fire burst across his helmet, exploding all over the chassis of the bike and scarring it. A ring of fire erupted on his left shoulder, but he felt Rake's fist punch it out.

The Arthrods stopped firing when the android's stern features appeared. They holstered their torch-rifles and kneeled, letting the bike vanish into the blizzard.

'We're clear, Morse!' Rake cheered. 'We did it!'

The bat-man grunted, working his vision through the smoke that poured from his helmet.

Suddenly, a voice crackled from behind. Though masked severely by the wind, it still boomed, 'By order of the United Galaxy's Government, you are to relinquish your hostage and turn yourselves in!'

The fake Desy, Rake, and Morse in sequence turned over their shoulders to see four sets of blue and red haloes in the fog. They watched them criss-cross, figure skaters performing a routine, slipping around mounds of snow and rocks until the visages of one pair of officers, an Irish wolfhound Cannot and a Human male, appeared on their left. They were garbed in skin-tight suits that pulsed with lava veins from finger to toe. Their motorcycle helmets had the UGIP logo tattooed on the forehead.

Morse veered to the right. The police remained a stone's throw away, the Cannot repeating through the megaphone, 'Pull over, pull over!'

Morse pushed his wrist forward until his hand twitched in pain. The hover-bike squealed and inched ahead of the officers so several bike lengths separated them. The hill reached a forty-five-degree decline. A vortex of snow blasted from the back end of Morse's bike, a fact that Rake belted into his ear, so he leaned to his left and splattered the torrent into the cops' faces.

They heard the Cannot howl through the megaphone, 'Sonuva!' and saw the haloes of red and blue behind them starting to fade.

The android, meanwhile, failed to suppress the rising heat in its stomach. *What's wrong with them?* it pondered in a panic. *They've gone crazy!* It noted the ground rush from white snow to black, craggy rocks. *Were they always this reckless?*

They're going to get me killed.

Morse plunged the bike to the bottom of the slope. He bounced himself, Rake, and 'Desy' into the air, clearing an embankment then hurtling across a lake of black ice.

Silver Fingers screeched.

At that moment, the four police bikes accelerated into view, their higher-powered engines allowing them to close the gap over the course of ten seconds. 'Slow down!' bellowed the Cannot. 'We understand you have a job to do, but getting yourself killed won't solve anything!'

Rake flipped them the bird without turning her head, keeping her other hand clasped on to Morse. Morse maintained top speed and barrelled towards the embankment on the other side. Silver Fingers feverishly calculated the distance between itself and the closest police bike: ten metres. All but twenty of its one hundred risk-assessment calculations ended with it dying at the bottom of the lake if it attempted the jump. But glancing beyond Rake's suit revealed the embankment wall, the path beyond unknown to it. It heard Morse cranking the hover-bike again and felt the vehicle start to rise into the air.

It was that fear of the unknown that caused the android's fire to erupt.

Rake felt it shift in her grip, so she clasped harder onto its hands with her free one. However, a sharp pull saw her grip fly open.

Then she felt naked. Snow was pelting her back.

Rake screeched 'Dee?!' as she turned over her shoulder and witnessed the android shrinking into the blizzard. Morse snapped his head behind him, too, in time to see the Irish wolfhound catch the android awkwardly with her forearms and both of them sprawl onto the ice.

At that moment, they cleared the embankment, and it rose to block their view. Three police bikes flew over the wall after them.

Morse caught Rake's appalled, wide-mouthed expression and raged, 'What *happened?!*'

A mere fifty metres away, adjacent to the pair and atop his ship, Bronzework huffed the air from his lungs. The barrel of his sniper-rifle tracked the two blips on his POV radar. In three tenths of a second, as Morse and Rake's hover-bike descended in slow motion, his mind calculated, *Kid jumped. Police have kid. Kid first priority. Bike larger target. Disable vehicle now. Acquire kid. Finish kidnappers in custody.*

His namesake jerked to the hover-bike and fired.

Morse heard a split second of static in his right ear before the handlebars rippled in his hands. A tremendous *bang* blasted the bike sideways, tossing him and Rake towards a hill of snow with a black outcrop jutting from the top. He caught a single glimpse of Rake's rag-doll body in the air before he plunged into the snow.

Then, a hideous blow knocked him unconscious. His helmet had smacked into the upper lip of a cavern entrance, and although designed to withstand large impacts, it could not stop his forehead from splitting the glass. The blizzard rushed through the breach and into the suit, not that Morse was awake to feel it or his torso slamming into the rock wall before he tumbled down a steep tunnel.

Rake smashed head-first into that wall less than a second after, her helmet cracking so a fracture ran from either side of her neck in an arc. Unconscious too, she slid roughly after Morse, their outlines fading into the maw of the moon with rocks rolling after them.

Five seconds later, the hover-bike slid warbling into the darkness as well.

Bronzework sniffed, following the two blinking dots down the steep slope, down into the crust, until they rolled to a stop about fifty metres from the surface. 'Into a cage. Lucky me.' Then, invisible, albeit with a coating of snow, he leaped from his ship and shot like a bullet towards the lake, where the android was just being helped onto a police bike by the Cannot. The Irish wolfhound was cradling her own head as she clambered on.

Above them, the spotlights from four police carriers beamed through the frozen winds. They were three times flatter and wider than the scouts, with three times as many officers on board.

Bronzework quelled the tiniest lick of frustration that had just fizzled into his gut. 'Into a cage-fight. Lucky me,' he muttered.

While blood leaked from Morse and Rake's heads and into their suits, Desy awoke to the smell of iron and a howling gale all around her.

She was rattled with vertigo. Every instinct told her to catch herself before she fell to her death, yet her arms and legs refused to budge. Even the constant stabbing in her shoulders and hips failed to move them. It was completely pitch-dark. Her head knocked painfully into cold, hard spikes if she shifted her posture even a little.

She was so very cold.

Claustrophobia set in. Tingling erupted all over Desy's body, which only seemed to tremble her further into the crevice. 'H-Help!' she cried. 'Where am I? Please! Stop! *Someone!*' Her heart thumped wildly. 'Anyone, please! I'm stuck.'

She began to whine and yell spasmodically, a trapped animal, hips shaking and cutting against slag, her legs unable to pry themselves apart. Several seconds of thrashing saw Desy's shivers amped up into spasms, and she uncontrollably cut ribbons into her flesh, her body weight crushing itself further onto her neck.

Her head and chest pounded with heat, liquid pooling inside her skull and lungs, while her arms and legs stiffened and shook from the cold. She was numb beyond the wrists and ankles, but that numbness soon wandered further inside her body, seen as a wave of discolouration changing her white skin see-through.

'I'm dying!' she wailed. 'It's crushing me! SOMEONE, PLEASE HELP!'

However, as the minutes ticked by, Desy's screams descended to cries, to sobs, to statements, to mutters, then, finally, to whispers. For in the darkness, she could see her father and the police commissioner, Jilliosa, both of them younger than they were now, discussing political matters over dinner. Desy smelled the boiled bacon and cabbage and screeched while shoving the plate, 'I hate it!'

An unbridled happiness swamped Desy when Jilliosa chuckled.

Ernest laughed too, but sternly said, 'It's the good commissioner's favourite meal, Cricket.'

Jilliosa's maroon hair, in its low ponytail, suddenly fell from her head to reveal a sharp set of jowls tearing up through her scalp. Her limbs thudded to the carpet, just as Ernest's face melted down his robes, with the room following suit until Desy was thrown through the floor.

Wind screamed in her ears as the colourful abyss of Moody Moody yearned to swallow her whole.

However, a gigantic hand reached out of the abyss, Wendell's dark, furry hand, to wrap itself around her entire body, blackening her vision. When she opened her eyes, she was flying above the Shipyard, arms spread like a plane with six sets of Arthrod wings flapping behind her.

She spotted Rake in the blue sky, piloting Morse by sitting on his back and using his ears as a steering wheel. She waved to them.

Rake turned her head, slow-like. Then once she met Desy's eyeline, she leaned her head back, and recreated the whine of a mosquito. 'De eeeeeeeeeeeeeeeeeeeeeeeeeeeeeeeeeeeeeeeeeeeeee,' she hollered for over thirty seconds.

Desy noticed the tri-star formation in the distance shape-shift into Bronzework's mask, hat, and body. He said to her, pulling a seat out for himself at the dining table in her manor, 'Keep your hands in your pockets, thief.'

'I didn't do it,' Desy firmly stated. She hurriedly swiped through her phone to find a list of all her friends. She tapped a Cannot's face with 'Buxter' written underneath it. A blank message box popped up, which made Desy tug on her father's overcoat. 'What happened to my friends, Daddy?'

To which Morse responded with, 'Kid, this is about your father, not you.'

'Yes,' Rake chimed in, leaning down into Desy's face while she was tied up inside the cage. 'Just drink ya soda and shut it!'

The twenty thousand, five hundred and twenty-nine friends in Desy's phone poured inside the cage. They all chanted at once, over and over, each of them with their own special phrase. Desy felt the happiest upon hearing:

'Marry me!'

'Oh my god, I want that.'

'Thanks.'

'I love them!'

'You shouldn't have.'

'No way, you're the best!'

'For me?'

'You're cool!'

'Can you just get them for me, Desy?'

Then, she saw herself standing in front of a blue curtain backdrop. She was staring at a mirror and twisting back and forth in a familiar dress and shorts combo, grinning wider and wider, when the curtain was suddenly drawn aside.

She saw herself leap forward and wrap a white cloth around her face, and smelled rotting flesh.

Desy's mind began to wind down through this delirium. The cold, the pooling blood, the panic; soon, all of her nerves just went numb. Eyelids shuddering closed, freezing shut, Desy felt the vertigo return. But she embraced it now, letting herself fall and fall and fall inside the crevice.

And a mere twenty metres away, the police disarmed, bound, then marched twelve Arthrods outside to an awaiting police carrier.

TWELVE
The Ditch and the Loft

A blue glow welcomed Morse to the jackhammering in his head. He gasped loudly and deeply and pushed himself up from the ground. His gloves slipped against wet rock. He jerked his head about in the darkness to slopes of mould-green moss lined by luminous mushrooms. Faded and flickering, they lit a path that drew Morse's attention to a silhouette that had blended into the dark.

'Morse, hi,' said Rake, a metre from him.

'What happened?' groaned Morse, buckling as pins and needles shot from his neck and into his legs.

Rake's hand appeared inside her cracked fishbowl, one of her suit's arms flopping like a deflated balloon. 'Gimme a minute to get the blood out of my eyes,' she muttered.

'Ah, crap.' He, too, slipped his hand back into his suit to feel around his helmet, fingers twitching from the cold. The warm, viscous patches on his face made him jolt.

'Right foot doesn't wanna move.'

Morse saw its outline. He ran his hand down her ankle and said, 'Feel broken?'

'Dunno.'

He grunted, shifting to an upright position on his knees. Suddenly, he buckled and moaned out, '*That's* a broken rib... maybe two.'

Rake whispered, 'My head,' and drew her other arm inside her suit to clasp at her hair. 'It's so sticky. Good thing about the suits, huh? Coulda been worse.'

Morse quelled the sharp pains in his back by breathing quietly. 'I heard static,' he said. 'Bronzework.'

'We're dead, aren't we?' Rake whimpered. 'We're never gonna get away from him. He knew where we went... where we were going...'

'That's impossible.'

'It's Bronzework—'

'That's not an excuse.' He held a hand to his side.

'Morse, what's that behind you?' Rake suddenly said.

He whipped around and crumpled again from the pain.

'No, behind you... it's moving.' She put her hand inside a suit arm and reached towards Morse's helmet. A rectangular shadow was stuck to the side of the cracked glass. However, her fingers bumped into the helmet before they could touch it. 'It's inside your helmet?'

Morse reached up into his fishbowl, groaning when he had to tilt his neck, until he swiped at something sharp and flat. It sounded like sticky-tape when he peeled it from the glass. 'Need some light,' he said, gingerly leaning forward and putting weight on his right foot. Placing more weight on it, he stepped to his left and felt his ankle quiver, tender. Bent from the waist, he trudge-hobbled a metre over to one of the wispy mushrooms, tilting the rectangle in front of his eyes until the light illuminated its surface.

Between patches of his own blood, the words *As done by Bronzework* glowed.

'It's his calling card,' Morse muttered. 'Bronzework's.' He heard Rake light up a cigarette. 'Rake, how's the body?'

'When did that get there?' she whispered, blowing smoke to fill her helmet, coughing.

Morse saw wisps of smoke rise up into the cave, following them until they parted against the low ceiling.

'Are you cold?'

'When did Bronzework... get those cards on us?' she continued.

'Rake.'

She coughed again. 'Morse. As it stands, I'm gonna die to him before the cold gets me. Focus.'

The bat-man leaned against the glowing mushrooms. 'He puts cards on us *before* he kills us.'

'Gotta tell his clients that he got the kill.' Rake searched her own clothes and found a similar card in her pants.

'But how did he do it?'

Rake inspected the card through the smoke in her fishbowl. 'Gotta just be sleight of hand, I guess'. When none of us were looking.'

Morse suddenly gasped. 'Get rid of them.'

'I know, we're kinda not dead, so–'

'Yeah, sleight of hand. Everyone knows what a calling card is for an assassin. But what if it's not just that?'

Rake shivered from the cold and from excitement. 'You gotta be kidding me…'

'There was no reason for him to meet up with us,' Morse explained. 'If Bronzework knew where we were all the time, then he would've gotten rid of us way before we got to the station. He had to plant something on us first to then track us to an optimal position to make the kill.'

'They're tracking devices,' Rake breathed, grinning.

'Since the kid's note, he's cut us off no matter where we've gone.' Morse stuck the card to his helmet and, after pushing his hands back inside the suit-arms, reached up and twisted his fishbowl off, scowling at the shooting jolts billowing from his ribcage. The ice-cold air clung to his skin as he snagged the card and looked around his feet.

'Whaddya doing?'

'Granted, no proof that these are trackers, but if they are, we can send Bronzework on a wild goose chase.' Morse crouched, screeching through his lips, and slipped the card underneath a rock. He looked up at Rake.

'Do me,' she said.

'It's really, really cold in here.'

'It'll be just a second, right?' Rake drew an enormous breath of cigarette smoke, the end lighting up like a torch.

He watched a card press against her faded face to stick to the glass. Morse stumbled over to her and gripped the helmet, twisting it. Smoke poured into the cave as he ripped the card away and slammed the fishbowl back on Rake's head.

'See?' She shivered, suddenly falling to just catch herself with her hands. 'E-Easy…'

Morse found a nearby rock and slipped her card beneath it. 'Are you okay?'

'I'll be better with a warm shower,' Rake whispered, sucking as much heat from her cigarette as possible. 'Can't heat the water without the engines, though.'

'And if we turn those on…'

'"Here we are, pigs".' Rake chortled. 'Gotta get to *Ferguson* at all, but. And if those cards are gonna tell ol' Bronzey where we are, then–'

'He'll be busy enough with the police.' Morse twisted on his helmet, stepping slowly towards the tunnel they had tumbled down.

'Whaddya mean?'

'Where are we, anyway?' He continued moving until he could crane his head up the slope. 'Uh-huh… I see some light. We must have fallen down from there.' Then, he muttered, 'Well, crap,' reaching into the darkness and creating a loud, metallic whine when he pulled the hover-bike into Rake's view.

'Was kinda hoping he would last,' Rake said.

'You can't walk.' Morse shoved the lifeless bike towards Rake.

'Sorry…'

Morse clasped his helmet, drumming his fingers. 'It's all right, not the end of the world. We'll work this out.'

Rake dragged herself over to the bike. She pried open a bent latch to reveal the engine. 'Might not be a lost cause. Kinda crushed but should function.' She tried the ignition, and a rapid clicking followed by an ear-splitting grind made her say, 'Still wanna go, huh? Reckon there's been a wire cut, that's all.'

'Will it work?'

Rake fumbled over to the glovebox and removed a small toolkit. Her bloodied features lit up when she activated a torch. 'Whaddya mean Bronzework's busy?'

'Come on, you know what—'

'Like I'm dumb. Like I'm really stupid. As if I've got the most moronic, idiotic—'

'Bronzework's after the kid, we know that from Moody Moody.' Morse shrugged, then winced. 'We're a target, but she's the priority.' He closed his eyes. 'She jumped, didn't she?'

Rake wordlessly pushed a pair of pliers towards the bike battery.

'I know you, and you didn't just let her go. That's something I would do, 'cause I'm an idiot.'

'I let her go,' Rake muttered.

'No, you didn't.'

'I must have, sorry. Kind of a dummy.' Rake's eyes shimmered in the torchlight.

'On Moody Moody, the kid wanted to turn herself in so we wouldn't get hurt.' Morse crouched down to Rake's eye level but looked away to a very interesting rock.

'After all we've been through… that's it…' Rake whispered.

'Oh, come on, we knew her for a couple days.'

'A few weeks, Morse.' She suddenly raised her voice. 'We studied her, got to know her really well–'

'And she was just a dumb kid.'

'Shut up,' Rake growled.

'We're kidnappers. Not a glorified day-care service. What, did you think we would teach her morals and pass on lessons?'

'No…'

'We needed her for money so our client got what they wanted. That's it.' Morse's face lost any and all vibrancy. 'And she wanted to go home, so she jumped.'

'She didn't jump,' Rake spat. 'She never would've.'

'But you didn't let her go–'

'Yes, I did!'

'You didn't let her go, because *you liked the kid*,' Morse asserted, almost as a shout.

Rake threw the pliers at the ground, bouncing them, spinning them into a wall. 'She cared about us!'

'You let your feelings get the better of you.'

'Morse, people like us don't deserve second chances!' Rake cried. 'We deserve ta die! But someone in this dumb galaxy decided that for once, we should *live*.' She shuffled over to Morse and grabbed his battered suit. He glowered at her. 'You tell me someone like that would jump!'

'She had every logical reason to.'

'She felt for us!'

'She's a teenager. A kid who thinks the world is a goddamn story with a happy ending. Or am I talking about you?'

Rake scrunched her face up. 'You asshole…'

'Forget the kid–'

'Don't you *dare* speak to me like that, you *ass*!' Rake shook him as hard as her badly bruised arms would allow. 'Ya gonna say that about me? Huh?'

'Calm down.'

She smacked his helmet, again and again and again, screaming, 'How dare you call me an idiot? I'm not a damn idiot! I know she would never jump!'

'She did, Rake!' Morse yelled back, catching her arms. 'And no amount of crying will change that! Let her go!'

'Then that wasn't Desy!' Rake screeched, contorting about in his grip.

'Wouldn't that be convenient for you?' Morse proclaimed, in a slimy, vindictive tone, pressing his helmet against hers. 'A perfect copy of Desy just *wandering* around the place?'

The cave fell into a sudden silence.

Rake stopped moving.

Morse's features drifted from a vicious grin to a furrowed brow and a flat lip. He felt Rake's body relax as a literal wave of relief flowed through it. For ten seconds, they stared at each other in the darkness, until Morse absentmindedly muttered, 'I mean…'

'Morse,' Rake whispered.

He watched her eyes dart around, looking at each of her thoughts as they flashed into her head.

'Oh, come on,' he said, letting go of her arms, which allowed Rake to slip them into her suit and start playing piano on her cheeks.

'Think about it. That's gotta be a possibility.'

'No,' Morse groaned.

'You said that android was going kooky, right? Sentient.' Rake ruffled her bloodied hair.

'It…' Morse leaned on his haunches. 'Yes, it was questioning itself, but…' He shook his head, avoiding the tender spots. 'No. If that were the android, then Silver Fingers would have to be collaborating with it. For what purpose, and how?'

'The Shipyard. How did Silver Fingers know where to find Dee?'

'We know she tracks the police.'

'They didn't get to us until *after Fulthorpe* got replaced.' Rake lit another cigarette with jittery hands. 'But the Arthrods, they were there the day after we got to the Shipyard. Almost as if they knew where we were gonna be. Where *Fulthorpe* was gonna be.'

Morse's eyes widened. 'The android's communications chip was directly connected to *Fulthorpe*'s. If the police had to find us through Higgins, then Silver Fingers could have only used the android to find us first. But she would've had to have taken it…'

'Or *kidnapped* it!'

'But the chances of that—'

'Wintall knows Bronzework, Morse. His connections run that far. And he's *old*. He's gotta know the hag, too.'

'You know you have no proof of that,' Morse said.

'But we've got a shot now.' Rake grabbed Morse. 'We can still finish the job, 'cause we still got a chance that Dee is alive.'

'Why would Silver Fingers do this?' Morse urged.

'I don't know, I don't know.' Rake's eyes welled up again. 'Gotta say, I'm goddamn confused. But there's now the smallest chance we can salvage this, and that's all that matters.'

'Rake.'

'Come on, Morse, you gotta care about the job, right?'

He glared at her.

'Whaddya suppose we can do if we even live through this and don't get thrown in the pen? If that's Dee who jumped, then we completely failed the job.' Rake quivered, from pain, cold, and happiness. 'But we followed the Arthrods from Moody Moody. If there was any chance for a switch, there's only one place the real Dee can be right now. And if we have her, then… we…' Her voice trembled.

Morse turned over his shoulder towards the howling wind blasting through the tunnel. 'The cavern.'

Rake pulled a hand through her suit and up to her mouth. 'You gotta go now.'

Morse pointed to the bike. 'Is that thing going to work?'

'I dunno if it will even start.'

'Work on it. If the kid's there, I'll have to bring her back here. Stay in the cave! That bike is all we have.' Morse forced himself with buckling legs towards the tunnel exit, spotting a grey streak of light some way up the slope. He turned around to see Rake's silhouette, lit up in a blue hue. 'Stay safe.'

'We're not gonna die,' Rake said, twisting herself inside the bike. 'Save the sentimental stuff.'

'Really, coming from you?' Morse poked.

She smiled.

And that was enough for him. Morse heaved himself up the steep slope, clinging to the walls and swearing all the way to the surface.

Bronzework's snow-capped fist slammed into an officer's neck as he tumbled through the air above the lake. Seeing the Felinguielle slap against the ice, he turned back to the hover-bike skidding in circles nearby and leaped to it. He stabilised, swung himself onto it in an elegant motion, and took off after 'Desy'.

The android was sandwiched between the Irish wolfhound and the Human male. Turning over its shoulder, it spotted a hover-bike without a rider racing to catch up. The Irish wolfhound bellowed in its ear, 'Bronzework is confirmed on scene. All available units protect the hostage. Lethal force authorised. Repeat, Gold Bayleaf has authorised lethal force.'

Two police scouts swooped like magpies overhead, followed by three hover-bikes turning one-eighty in the snow, flying back over the embankment and onto the lake again. The scouts aimed their antipersonnel bullets at the riderless hover-bike and fired. It quivered a little but kept its trajectory towards Silver Fingers' bike, which was approaching the embankment on the other side. Just beyond, a police transport hovered some metres into the blizzard, with the vague shape of its landing ramp being lowered.

Bronzework flew faster than the hover-bike he had abandoned, letting the scouts fire upon it as his body pierced through the blaring wind, able to sidle up mere metres from Silver Fingers. He slowed down as its bike did, waiting by the landing ramp as it was disembarked and hurried towards several waiting officers in the ship.

However, the Irish wolfhound caught a person-shaped blur out of the corner of her eye, just in time for Bronzework to unholster his own pistol and loose an invisible bullet into her neck. The Cannot crumpled into the snow as the android was snatched from the Human; he, too, caught a shot to the neck and collapsed. Bronzework materialised his gun to show it thrust against Silver Fingers' head.

The officers at the top of the landing ramp held their arms up.

Bronzework signalled with his pinkie, and his ship spun into life some hundreds of metres away and hovered quickly to his position.

However, he did not see something.

The android's mouth hung open, panting.

'No breath,' he muttered.

Unbeknownst to him, a police sniper, hidden in the bowels of a transport, breathed out.

'An android. Oh, that is very good.' The mercenary switched over to his heat sensor vision, seeing a tangled mess of heatpads before him.

Silver Fingers' face fell, eyes shrinking to pinpricks.

He looked away, bringing up his radar to see the two blinking dots still at the bottom of the tunnel. 'They'd better not be dead—'

A blast of light nailed Bronzework between the eyes. His suit dissipated the energy, reducing the damage done to his body, but the force still threw his head back. He let go of the android and turned, catching his feet into the rocky ground before leaping into the air.

A volley of blaster fire punched him in the back and sent him tumbling into the embankment.

Bronzework tried to fly again, but another barrage blasted him back down. 'What a pest you are,' he said. He turned to snipe an officer in the neck, then three more, creating enough chaos to ensure enough time for him to escape. But just as his snowy outline was reflected in the black water of the lake, a police scout smashed into him and launched him into the freezing abyss. Completely undeterred, he simply thought while spinning in the darkness, *You run a circus, Bayleaf.*

Thousands of miles above in space, inside the rings of Funny Man, a two-kilometre-wide window clawed itself open in the fabric of space-time. The visage of the *Induction* peered through. Followed by its stately body and gigantic thrusters, the dreadnought in its entirety slipped away from Sternway Ovime 12 to occupy a top-down view of Brosteni. And the city on an arrow tilted towards the moon and boomed forward, making haste for Promethia.

Rake squashed her gloved fingers between various wires and crossbeams, craning her globed helmet about and spitting in frustration when she failed to manoeuvre her vision where she wanted it.

The quivering of her hand rattled the small spotlight it held.

The shadows of the wires blended into each other.

The urge to just kick the vehicle rose to a boiling point.

'Dee's doing worse,' she muttered, thinking back to the cavern and the number of hiding places the teenager could fit in. 'If she isn't… dead. Gotta stay positive.'

Rake fumbled and fumbled with the innards of the bike, chanting 'stay positive' in time with her heartbeat. Then, to no one, she chimed, 'Right through the cell partition. But ya missed the cell, ya dumb Bronzey!' She reached into the toolbox and snagged a roll of tape, struggling to rip off a strip with her gloves. However, with enough expletives, she managed to bind a series of cut wires and cracked partitions. With a brief prayer to avoid an explosive death, she tried the ignition.

The bike threw a jar of marbles into a cement mixer, then pebbles into a blender, before whining as its horizontal-plane stabiliser kicked in, and it rose into the air and stood upright, albeit with sparks shooting out of its hover-pads.

Rake clapped once, screeched in pain, but smiled again. 'Now, just gotta hope Bronzework doesn't kill me.' She spotted an outcrop of rocks that gave shade to the faded, mushroom-made lighting. 'That'll do. Now it's Morse's turn, I did my job.'

However, just as she said the words, she froze. A sickening nausea wafted from her belly and into her throat. 'If that was the android, then... it was wearing Dee's clothes.'

At that moment, the blizzard kicked up a gear.

Rake turned towards the tunnel. 'She just might've made it.' She reached into her suit and into her coat, fumbling for the box of cigarettes. She could only feel one of them bumping about. 'But not now. Oh...'

Rake lit her last cigarette and dragged on it. Then, as resolutely as she could manage with her injuries, she dragged herself towards the hover-bike. After piling the toolbox into the glove compartment, she grunted and heaved herself onto the seat.

Rake revved the engine. 'Morse's right. Gotta say, this *is* what an emotional child would do.'

The bike trickled towards the exit, shaking against the howling, frosted winds coming from above.

Morse held tightly to the craggy hill as those winds threatened to send him tumbling towards the lake embankment. So far, he had managed to avoid several police scouts by lying low and moving quickly. He may have cursed the blizzard, but the low visibility was screening him from the action happening over the lake. Sometimes, above the roaring wind and splattering snow, he would make out a police vehicle exploding or the cut-off scream of an officer.

By the time the police lander had fled with the android on board, Morse was past the lake on a steep climb, heading in the vague direction of the cavern. He steeled himself against the winds. His arms and legs had long since numbed. Thankfully, combined with the adrenaline, he was no longer crippled by the pain in his chest and spine. But each step he took in the deep snow he thought would be his last.

He awaited the sound of something snapping.

Until then, Morse used the thumps of his feet as a form of hypnosis. *Cavern, cavern, cavern,* was all he thought. A thought aside from that would see his confidence shatter.

Finally, out of breath and hoarse, Morse reached the top of a gigantic hill to fall face-first onto a field. His vision lifted to see a white wall ahead of him. The base of the mountain.

He quelled his excitement, accidentally thinking *plateau* before shifting back into *cavern, cavern, cavern*.

Inside said cavern, Desy's body was a statue. The tips of her toes were beginning to turn blue, as well as her fingers, yet from her belly to her head she was turning purple. Her mind lapsed in and out of consciousness. She no longer felt pain or the cold.

Desy's eyes were frozen shut, as was her mouth. There was warmth, however. It beckoned her, a motherly figure with large arms and a big body, beckoning her to sleep. It was saying, 'You must be exhausted. Come here.'

She felt herself falling towards it, relaxing against its embrace. However, another voice called for her, and it always interrupted her mind before she succumbed.

'Can you buy me something?' it said, as every voice Desy had ever heard at once.

Floating into the warmth, then tugged back to the crevice, over and over, seemingly forever.

'Doesn't your dad, like, own this planet?'

A blurred ball flashed in front of her eyes.

'It's not about you, it's about your dad.'

The ball pulsed with veins.

'Observe,' said all the voices, with Morse's rising to the top.

Desy raced towards the ball.

'It'll be for your eyes only, Dee,' said all the voices, with Rake's taking over.

Suddenly, Desy found herself sitting with the nebula family in their vein-like house, everything crumbling as if it were underwater. Nebula birds and streets, people and vehicles, the sky with the mistake; the sight of it all racing away from her and into the infinity of the universe squashed Desy's lungs.

She took a breath.

I'm… the only person who's seen that, she thought. *I'm the only proof it exists. Morse and Rake… they'll rescue me…*

Desy took another breath through the smallest gaps in her mouth and nostrils.

They always do. They always come back for me.

She found the strength in her hands to twitch her fingers, to move them.

They have to... 'cause I've finally... finally got something to offer that's mine. Not Dad's, but mine and only mine.

The last conscious memory to enter Desy's head was when she was back inside Wendell's inn, after the Arthrod shot Morse. When Morse's ears pricked up. When Desy observed Rake clicking her fingers behind the bar.

In turn, her blue middle finger slapped down to the pad of her thumb, so weakly it was almost silent. She clicked them again, and again, though her lungs heaved with the effort.

Just twenty metres away, Morse entered the cavern and called out, 'Kid? Desy?' His legs shook like jelly, his face pink and pale, frost lining his eyebrows as he tripped towards a crumbled stalagmite. He failed to see through the deep shadows in the corner of the cave, forcing him to physically reach into them until his hand planted itself against the rock. He did this systematically, around the tens of stalagmites and countless piles of rubble.

Eventually, Morse stopped calling, collapsing with his back against the furthermost wall of the cavern. His legs felt detached from his hips. He breathed huge breaths, barely keeping the torrent of frustration and sadness storming in his gut at bay.

Morse slipped his hands inside his suit and plastered them against his face. While clasping his fingers hard into his skull, he muttered with a little laugh, 'I actually thought there'd be a happy ending to this.' He switched on the suit's radio, and seeing no light turn on, still tried the microphone. 'Rake?'

No answer.

He pressed a finger into his ear and tried the other transceiver.

'Rake...?'

No answer. Just static.

Morse, resigned, twisted his helmet off and welcomed the deafening roar of the blizzard that echoed around the cavern. It soon became white noise.

He closed his eyes.

And heard a click.

Morse just about jumped. Instead, he grunted and twisted his broken body and smacked his ear against the rock wall.

Again, a tiny, high-pitched thump rattled his ear. He glanced up to see a darker-than-usual shadow on the wall. Reaching towards it, he pulled himself up, slipping and sliding with dead legs until he managed to get a hand inside the shadow.

The textural contrast between the rock and the little, spongy foot made Morse shout. 'Kid? Desy? Desy!' He felt around the foot to an ankle and started to pull it.

Desy's limbs caught on several small outcrops and fastened themselves.

So Morse shook his head, gave a mental middle finger to his swan song, and started tearing apart the top of the crevice with his hands. It broke easily but thickened the closer it ran to the floor, which forced him to bellow and grunt with increasing effort. In seconds, he was pressing as hard as he could on the sharp rock. He screamed and channelled everything into his arms.

The wall broke at Desy's waist and fell as an avalanche around Morse's feet.

Her bare behind and legs greeted him.

'Oh,' Morse spluttered, fishing around her ribs and lifting her gently out. He inspected the discolouration of her skin, the cuts and dried blood on her cheeks. He held his ear to her chest.

It was smaller than a mouse's heartbeat.

'Where're your clothes? Dammit, you're going to freeze.' Morse frantically looked around for a magically appearing garment to dress Desy in. He grabbed his helmet and twisted it into place.

Finding what little strength he had left in his legs, Morse picked up Desy and tripped himself towards the blizzard outside. A thick wall of snow slapped him in the face. He hunched over Desy and shielded her, swearing over and over.

Desy's breathing hitched.

'This just isn't fair,' he whispered.

Then a warbling box of paperclips called out to him from the snow. Morse squinted, spying a thin but flickering beam of light emerge, followed by a figure curled over a hover-bike. His mouth fell open when Rake skidded to a halt inside the cavern.

With skin whiter than the snow and smoke pouring from the cracks of her helmet, she said, 'Dee, thank god.'

Morse's eyes widened as Rake lost her grip on the handlebars, slipped off the bike, and fell in a heap on the ground.

'She didn't jump,' she whispered, then fell silent.

'Ingrid? Ingrid!' Morse blurted, shuffling over to her while cradling Desy. He laid Desy gently against the floor before feverishly turning

Rake over, smoke pooling around her limp head. 'Don't do this to me, please! Ingrid, you can't!'

He saw the air from her breath disturb the smoke in her helmet.

'I told you to stay in the cave!' he hollered. His dry, weary eyes began to wet. 'You're all I've got left…'

Desy's breath hitched again.

Morse turned to her. Then he heard the distressed warbling of the hover-bike and turned to that. In the corner of his eye, Rake's breath disturbed the smoke again.

'I told you to be professional. Not to get emotional.' He twisted off his helmet, unzipped his spacesuit, wiped his face clean, and let out a huge breath. 'But because of you, we might just actually do this.'

Morse picked up Desy. 'Sorry, kid, this is a bit weird.' He pressed her body into his so her head was nestled against his collarbone, then zipped the spacesuit over the top. The helmet went on next, and a very bulky Morse heaved Rake onto the hover-bike, withdrew the tape from the glovebox, and fastened her around the seat, face-down. Finally, he clambered on and gripped the handlebars.

'No more,' he declared.

Suddenly, a building-sized face plunged through the blizzard some two hundred metres in the air. A gigantic hole had been punched in the sky, sunlight pouring in to join the tens of powerful spotlights that honed in on the entrance to the cavern.

The *Induction* turned and changed the direction of the wind as it did so.

Gold Bayleaf, seen as a green blur inside the seventh holding bay on the right side of the *Induction*, signed to the woman in the trench coat. He ordered, translated by her through the radio, while tens of officers clambered onto hover-cars and bikes, 'That man is to be taken alive. His connections to the revolutionary war are of the utmost importance. Repeat, Morse and his accomplice Rake are to be taken *alive*.'

The Kinson signed once more to the woman before jumping into the sidecar of a hover-bike piloted by a Hawkie. She commanded, 'Squads Four A, Two B, and Three A are to assist in the arrest. All others are to assist with the neutralisation of Bronzework. Move out!'

From his perch at the entrance of the cavern, Morse gunned the hover-bike and flew across the plateau, eyeing the stream of bikes and cars falling from the sky.

His glare did not falter.

THIRTEEN
Impossible Odds

The platoon of police vehicles worked with the *Induction*'s spotlights to travel over mounds of snow, around the crashed Arthrod cruiser, and after Morse's malfunctioning hover-bike. Hover-cars and bikes, each with flashing blue and red lights, wove valleys in the plateau that eventually became uniform and parallel, as though a scarf was being wrapped around the base of Promethia.

At the head of the platoon was a modified hover-bike with a sidecar, a dome protecting the passenger from the blizzard.

That passenger was Gold Bayleaf.

The weak sunlight on Brosteni during the winter meant Gold Bayleaf had less than thirty minutes until he would begin to wither and enter a catatonic state. The sugars his body secreted decreased the temperature at which ice would form inside his veins, but the thermo-suit he was zipping himself into was a more modern solution. The Kinson stuffed his sea-anemone head inside a helmet, though he had no fear of physical blows or falling from great heights.

Gold Bayleaf believed one must lead by example.

Over his shoulder, Morse witnessed the dome of the sidecar open and a suited figure clamber onto the front. It crouched with unnatural flexibility in its legs and arms and its helmet twisted sideways, a spider ready to jump.

Morse throttled the bike harder, feeling a jackhammer clattering into his left leg. The descent had begun. If not for the day-makers blasting through the howling snow, he would have crashed into the jagged outcropping on his left, the sheer drop on his right, and the rocky ridge that flew at him out of the darkness. Instead, he twisted the knob on the buckled console and made the bike cry out, spluttering high enough to smack the top of the ridge. Morse heaved in pain and splattered spittle against the cracked helmet; the landing had seen his ribs clasp his lungs.

Gold Bayleaf and his driver descended into Morse's rear-view. He swerved the bike around yet another outcrop, then eyed Rake's figure strapped against the seat behind him.

She only moved when the bike lurched.

Morse glanced down at Desy, jostling against his chest. Her eyes were closed, but her face had begun to regain its natural hue.

A black arm launched itself towards his face, from the right side, like a tree-branch. Morse ducked and slammed on his brakes, which left Gold Bayleaf to snag the wind. Morse then accelerated with a diseased roar to clip the backside of the Kinson's bike, sending it into a spin. The bat-man veered away from an awaiting cliff-edge and raced down the hill he had struggled up mere minutes before, Gold Bayleaf's bike closing the distance in seconds.

Suddenly, there were four hover-cars at the bottom of the hill, their flashing lights piercing through the snow, a wall of red and blue. In front of them were the growing shadows of three police bikes.

Morse gritted his teeth, and the flashing low-battery warning on the console closed his lips around his fangs. Spotlights blinded his periphery; he had led the police only half the *Induction's* length, the dreadnought hanging above with its thousand eyes shooting across the lake, following Morse and illuminating the cavern all at once.

Morse cranked the knob again, clearing the police heading his way, only for one of their blasters to stab his bike's underbelly. The act of correcting the impact and landing sloppily on the ice saw Morse heave blood up against his helmet. With just the wall of police cars to go, he prayed and once again turned the knob.

Skidding over the wall, he cleared the gap beyond and the high embankment of the lake, creating a plume of water when he directed the bike onto its surface. Morse noted the six pillars of smoke pouring out in various spots across the lake. Officers scrambled in the frigid depths, waving desperately at the *Induction*, at the remaining police cruisers.

Bronzework's been here, Morse thought.

Suddenly, an arm grasped his neck and squeezed his attention away. Despite his protective suit, the sheer power of the limb pushed through the thick padding and began to crush his windpipe, mere inches above Desy's head. Gold Bayleaf snaked his legs around Morse's arms, prompting him to let go of the clutch and start punching the Kinson's visor. His hand revving the accelerator began to buckle. The lake seemed to be endless.

Narnit fought against Kinson while speeding across the water. But Morse's injuries were crippling his strength, his balance coming and going while Gold Bayleaf simply squeezed harder.

His vision pulsed. Then it blurred. Then it blackened in waves.

Slowly, Morse's right hand weakened. The hover-bike went from a roar to a howl and began to rhythmically throb as its speed dropped.

Morse pulled dimly against Gold Bayleaf, his torso swaying left and right. His hand slipped off the accelerator. His head drooped to the right, his upper body following suit, the world going black.

Desy pushed against his chest.

The world rushed back into focus, solidifying on one last escape route.

Morse prayed, *Give me this one miracle, please…* Then he dropped his hand on the accelerator like an axe, prompting the hover-bike to hurtle forward at the embankment. He allowed his body weight to keep falling to the right so the bike would swerve and trace his path from before, heading towards where he and Rake had crashed.

Bronzework's fought the cops. Morse gasped in agony when he straightened his left arm towards the console. *But he isn't with us now. So…* The embankment rushed mere feet away from the bike as his fingers clasped the knob and he fell forward, twisting it.

Gold Bayleaf tightened his grip until Morse's jugular and windpipe touched.

But the hover-bike indeed jumped the embankment and reared into the air. Above, the tail of the *Induction* finally gave way to the sky.

As he took the last breath before his throat shut, Morse caught a glimpse of the cave.

There's only one place he can be.

Bronzework rushed away from the small cavern and back up to the entrance, calling cards in hand. Though his face was hidden, his shoulders were hunched, muscles rippling to a tight clench in a wave from his neck through his back, thighs, calves and feet. He carelessly knocked his right arm against the cave entrance once he landed in front of it.

Upon meeting the screaming blizzard again, his head jerked to a mangled silhouette racing towards him.

Bronzework recognised Morse. And a vulture.

So he raised his rifle and aimed around the Narnit's face.

Breathing out, Bronzework fired, nailing Gold Bayleaf in the visor. The invisible shot parted the snow in the air as it travelled towards then through the helmet, obliterating the Kinson's 'head' and launching out the other side.

Immediately, Gold Bayleaf let go of Morse, falling as a spasming, tumbling pile of liquorice sticks onto the hillside.

Bronzework lined up his next shot.

However, Morse, following the sound of the rifle shot to its source, had twisted the bike horizontally.

The rear ploughed into Bronzework's chest like a concrete slab. The mercenary buckled at the knees but kept an iron grip on his rifle, exchanging glares with Morse as he roared past, a raptor blindsided by a rat.

Morse readjusted the bike before bouncing against the hill and speeding away, just as Bronzework collapsed to a knee and readjusted his aim, lining the scope with the back of the bike. The blizzard faded. The incoming red and blue lights disappeared.

He breathed out.

A sharp pain quivered from his chest and into his hands.

His namesake ignited.

And Bronzework missed the first shot of his career.

Suddenly, Gold Bayleaf leaped out of the snow and latched on to him like a leech, causing him to trip over his own legs and fall down the hill.

Several police bikes streamed past Bronzework, then four police cars whirred after them.

'No,' he stated, grappling the Kinson with an iron hand and peeling him from his shoulders. He hurled Gold Bayleaf into the blizzard and fired two shots into two police cars, sending them careening away. The next three shots took out another police car and two bikes before Gold Bayleaf slammed into him again.

'Leave me be,' he warned, prying the Kinson off and tossing him aside, harder, then dispatching the remaining vehicles. But after he spotted Morse fading out of the spotlight in the distance, and leaped into the air to pursue, Gold Bayleaf grabbed on to his leg and slithered up to his neck to start constricting him.

'Let go of me,' Bronzework demanded, his volume ticking louder with each word. He clasped Gold Bayleaf below the visor and unwrapped the snake from his neck. However, he held on while he holstered his rifle with his other hand and withdrew his pistol, jamming it into the Kinson's belly. He loosed a point-blank ripple of invisible energy, and Gold Bayleaf's suit deflated, his innards exploding and separating so twenty threads were all that connected his halves together. Bronzework launched him away and rocketed towards where Morse had shimmered out of view, only for three spotlights from the heavens to lock on to his location.

The police radios across the surface of Brosteni were a ballyhoo of 'Captain!'

Bronzework's snow-covered suit was bombarded with explosions. He whipped around in a frenzy to face two police scouts. Then three pistol shots smacked the back of his head. Then three more came from his left. Then four from his right. 'No!' he bellowed as he was shot into the ground. He wiped the snow from his mask, scrutinising the wall of wind for Morse's whereabouts.

A police cruiser descended, activating its cannon, which thundered a dense river of plasma into his back.

'No!' he raged, scrambling out from underneath the waterfall, warning messages flashing on his HUD. He leaped into the air for all he was worth, but yet another volley of lasers pounded him back to Brosteni.

The words *Critical shield failure imminent* blazed across Bronzework's sightline.

'*No!*' He slapped his chest and prompted his cruiser to race to his location. He fired blindly around himself, wriggling across the snow to the star-shaped shadow of his ship.

As he pulled himself inside, Bronzework swore. He swore when he grabbed the steering wheel. He swore when he punched the accelerator. He swore when his ship shook from the never-ending blaster fire. Even as Promethia disappeared behind him in a blink, he swore.

Then his phone went off.

Ernest's face flashed mockingly on his windshield.

'Wintall,' simmered Bronzework once he accepted the call.

'Jilliosa has informed me that my Cricket is safe in police custody.' Ernest's finger tapped a desk in the background. 'My utter relief aside, this is very disappointing, Bronzework.'

'Thank you for the feedback,' Bronzework struggled to say without dipping into a vat of sarcasm. 'However, I must point out–'

'I am no longer in need of your services,' Ernest said suddenly.

The mercenary pulled a muscle in his neck. 'Wait.'

'You will be compensated for your–'

'I said *wait*,' Bronzework suggested very loudly, directing his ship into a shadowy, icy canyon.

'It's over. That is what your client wants.'

'That thing they have–'

'I'm not interested.'

'Listen to me, I highly suggest you–'

'You *failed*, Bronzework!' Ernest belted out.

The mercenary stayed the urge to throw his arms about in the air, instead focusing on forming a harangue so dense, it was struggling to escape his quivering mouth.

'You failed. Let it go. It was my mistake to hire you. I never should have brought someone like you back into my life–'

'Don't you understand the definition of *wait?!*' Bronzework exploded, standing up. 'You recalcitrant old coot! You can't do this to me! I still have to kill those blasted–'

'You're fired.'

Ernest disconnected the call.

And Bronzework simply stood still. He remained wordless and actionless for hours. His ship accumulated snow and ice and space dust, morphing into a Christmas star hanging between two giant walls of ice. Even when the morning sunlight streamed into the valley some hours later, he remained standing, the dial tone singing to him all the while.

In the deep, dark winds, a tiny flickering light caught a glimpse of a house-sized ball of snow. The ball was nestled at the base of a hill. And the hill's slope was starting to make a meal of it as the wind welded them together. The flickering light hovered up to the base of the ball, illuminating the area just enough for a shallow, black opening to be seen.

Morse, who was leaning across the handlebars of the hover-bike and exactly five minutes away from fainting, breathed, '*Ferguson.*' He warbled into the shallow gap, shoving weakly at the snow, collapsing it away to reveal a lopsided landing ramp.

The hover-bike rumbled up into *Ferguson*.

Fifty metres away, three pairs of police officers zoomed away from the ball, crossing each other, searching the wastelands. An urgent weather warning was issued into their ears, and soon all units lifted from the surface and flew towards the *Induction*.

Gold Bayleaf sat as an unmoving pile of rope in his sidecar.

Meanwhile, Morse directed his own bike through the round main hallway of *Ferguson* to a closed electronic door. It was pitch-dark inside the craft. Usually, ships were parked in stand-by mode, engines down but with auxiliary power keeping locks fastened.

All power systems had been cut by Rake to avoid detection.

So Morse simply moved the loose door aside and drove the bike into the bathroom. Toilet on the left, shower and water tank on the right. He felt pain move like blood from his chest and into his brain, into his eyes, back, legs and arms, as he dismounted the bike onto trembling feet. He trudged himself, Desy and the bike over to the water tank and turned the bike off so it clunked onto the tiled floor, its flickering light going dark.

The room went oppressively black.

Next, he unzipped his suit and tipped forward so Desy slid out and into the shower. He staggered over to Rake, still strapped to the bike with the last remnants of smoke leaking from her helmet, and felt about for the heavy-duty tape. He clawed and pawed at the straps, then settled on chewing through them, allowing him to drag Rake across the bathroom and dump her onto Desy.

Morse heaved the bike over to the water tank, bleeding from the mouth and coughing, and opened up the glove compartment. He fumbled his way through grips and metal cylinders until he squished some rubber tubing and pulled it loose, several tools clattering against the floor. Morse crawled his way to the bike's bonnet and popped it open. He felt the almost-dead battery on the left-hand side, touching his way to the emergency outlet and plugging the rubber cable into it. Ignoring the wetness brushing down his legs, he quivered his way to a hunched position with a screwdriver in hand and reached up to the water tank, gripping the electrical supply cable. He dug into it to expose the innards and clamped the other end of the cable onto the wiring.

Finally, he dropped to the ground and shimmied over to the bike again. He switched it on, then crawled into the shower, scooping Rake into his arms and leaning his back against the wall, Desy next to him. He unfastened his helmet and tossed it away. And after an agonising ten seconds, he reached up and cranked the hot tap until it clunked.

Steaming water cascaded onto Morse's face. It stung and dug into his wounds. It was suffocating. It ran down his bruised and quivering chest and stomach, his clothes sodden in seconds. He heaved painful, deep breaths as he wrenched Rake's helmet from her suit and lifted her up into the stream.

Her head hung limp.

Morse felt his strength evaporate and his arms flopped to his side, which let Rake slide down his torso so her stony face looked up at him in the flickering bike-light. He breathed faster and faster for every moment her mouth remained loose.

Half a minute passed. Then another thirty seconds.

Her eyes stayed shut.

Morse's limbs refused to move. His neck slackened. Eyelids drooping, he silently begged and pleaded for some sort of breath to pass Rake's lips.

He felt a small hand encircle his. Desy's tired, beaten face leaned into his vision, a dimple in her left cheek.

He squeezed her hand back.

And Rake gasped.

Morse howled in abject relief. For a second, more energy than he had ever felt filled him, and he poured all of his rage, grief, happiness, and ego into a fist that hit the back wall so hard, it dented the metal alloy.

Desy nestled her head on his shoulder.

Rake closed her mouth and focused on breathing through her nose.

Morse, finally, allowed himself to lose consciousness.

FOURTEEN
Reunited

Silver Fingers jittered in its seat. It could hear footsteps approaching the door to the Medical Consultancy Bay of the *Induction*. It felt no warmth from the blanket around its shoulders, though it thanked the officers who draped it there. It tasted none of the sweetness from the hot cocoa nestled in its hands, though it licked its lips after every sip.

The door slid open to reveal a Jellentity and a Human woman with white hair wearing a trench coat. The Jellentity hovered across the floor, bowing politely at the android before humming itself to a small cabinet.

Extending her hand, the woman in the trench coat said sweetly, 'This has been an eventful evening, hasn't it?'

The android looked to its trembling legs.

'I'm Misrimum Trupeal. I'm the prison governor, and you'll be safe under my watch. I promise you that.' She retracted her hand to place it on her knee. 'This Jelly-fellow is Ingot. He's going to examine you. Is that okay?'

Silver Fingers twitched, which tilted Trupeal's head; she swept her paper-white fringe from her eyes.

She began, 'I assure you that Ingot–'

But Silver Fingers cut in while half-dropping its cocoa. 'I don't want that. I want Daddy. Please just take me home.'

Trupeal lowered herself to eye level so the tails of her trench coat piled onto the linoleum. 'We have a duty to make sure you're physically okay before–'

The android vibrated like a volcano moments from erupting. 'Please, please, please, please, please, I don't want that. I don't want anyone else but Daddy. Please! I don't want anything else but that...'

Trupeal pointed her nose up to Ingot, who was wibble-wobbling a few sentences into her ear. She nodded, then asked the fake Desy in a very, very soft tone, 'Is it because someone will have to touch you?'

The android froze. It squeezed its eyelids together, a tear rolling from the left one.

'I understand,' breathed Trupeal, then she gibble-gobbled to Ingot, who responded by shaking his arms and humming. Finally, she asked in UBL, 'Would you be more comfortable, then, having a physician you know examine you?'

The android blurted, 'Yes.'

'Can I get their name?'

It searched its Desy data banks. Rather, it fumbled through the vague semblance of Desy it could recall; it was as though the program lines were fading, like fingerprints. 'I'm s-sorry, I can't think right now,' it muttered, honestly.

'That's okay, that's really okay,' replied Trupeal with a smile, standing up. 'We'll leave now, but I have my strongest guards outside the door. Ask them if you need anything, all right?'

'But am I going home?'

Trupeal covered her laugh with a hand. 'Of course. You'll be back with your father within the hour. Once you've been medically examined, we'll just have some questions for you. But please don't think of that for the moment.' She held her hands up and waved them in a circle. 'Just make yourself comfortable.'

Trupeal indicated to Ingot, who bowed once more to the android before leaving the room, then rolled her fingers in goodbye.

Once the door snapped shut behind her and two burly Cannots jumped in front of it, Trupeal held her fingers to her temples. 'Who was the point of contact for this mess?' she thought aloud, then clapped. 'Ah, yes, Planet Commissioner Jilliosa.'

Ingot wobbled.

'Yes, she's running for the North-East Spiral seat.' She trotted down a small corridor, dark save for the cheap fluorescent bulbs flickering overhead. 'I must wish her good luck.'

Down the corridor from the android, Gold Bayleaf lay unfurled, taking up several beds in his length. Stints had been pushed against the hole blown inside his main stem. With no heartbeat to monitor, Kinsons were notorious for being unpredictable to treat in emergency situations. However, upon his own instruction, the nurses attending to Gold Bayleaf had spent several minutes coating him in a fertiliser of his own creation using a paint can and brush.

According to Trupeal, it was an old family recipe.

If one were to examine the hole in the Kinson's 'belly' now, they would note millions of wriggling, mint-green threads, fibres, pulling towards each other over the huge gap. To keep his vitals up, Gold Bayleaf's fingers were sitting in a bucket of water each. An IV drip of sorts.

His face was a bowl of wriggling worms. So with no features to observe or vitals to monitor, the nurses were none the wiser of the extreme agony he was in. But he remained motionless throughout the ordeal, with not a twitch or sound except for the high-pitched prickle of stretching, healing fibres.

A kilometre away, from the perimeters of the *Induction*'s wings, hundreds of jump pods flew into a circular formation a ship's length ahead. They began to spin.

In thirty minutes, a colossal window to Yeti would appear.

Desy heard Rake whisper, 'Tighter,' and pulled hard against the gauze so her ankle stiffened.

Then Desy asked, 'How do I put the pin in?'

Rake heaved on a cigarette, screened behind a portable cloth shower with her right foot sticking out from underneath, into the cold air of the bedroom. The spare bike battery was inside the shower with her and powering a small heater. After sucking on the cigarette again, she responded, 'Never paid attention in school, did ya? Just stick it in then lift it up.'

Desy pushed the small pin into the gauze. 'I think I did it.'

'Great. Wanna get the pin out of my foot?'

'Sorry, sorry,' Desy stammered. She tried again, succeeding in weaving the pin through the bandage and out the other side. 'It's a little hard to see in here.'

'Can't really do much for ya there, Dee.'

Connected to the other end of the battery was a spotlight. It was pointed at the ceiling and cast the shadows of the objects in Rake's room against the walls, spreading outwards from the centre like roots.

Morse lay on Rake's bed, unconscious. His shadow on the wall rose then fell, shallow breaths making his lips vibrate. On the floor and pointed at him, coming out from the final socket in the battery, was another small heater.

'You're a star,' Rake said to Desy, withdrawing her bandaged foot inside the shower, joining it back with her black silhouette. 'That heater's kinda looking lonely without you.'

Desy shuffled over to the heater by Rake's bed and collapsed into a ball next to it. She gripped her knees with the thick gloves Rake insisted she wear, snug in a winter coat and thermal pants. Then, she coughed heavily into her over-coated elbow. A deep, liquidy cough.

'Doesn't sound fun,' Rake noted.

'I feel like there's something in my chest,' Desy whispered. 'Like, whenever I breathe, it's there.'

Rake dragged on her cigarette intensely enough to elicit a whistle. 'Relatable. But seriously, might wanna get that checked out.'

'He isn't waking up,' Desy said, coughing again.

'He's fine.'

'But how long has it been?'

'I dunno, Dee, my brain nearly died. Haven't been keeping track.' Rake heard Desy squish herself further into a ball. She then said, 'Probably a little over an hour. He'll wake up. Always does. I've been tryin' ta kill him since I met him. And the idiot just keeps gettin' back up.'

Desy sighed.

'On behalf of Morse and Rake's Middlemen Service,' Rake said, 'I gotta say sorry for everything that's happened to you. And I'm sorry for what I said to you yesterday.'

Desy unravelled from her ball so her nose pushed up against the shower. 'Um, what did you say exactly?'

'Dunno, probably somethin' bitchy.' Rake lit her next cigarette. Dragging on it, she said with smoke pouring from her mouth, 'And look at you now. We kidnap ya, and you're savin' *us*.'

'But you saved me lots,' Desy said, retreating back towards the heater. 'And Daddy always said to return favours.'

'You never shoulda needed to be saved.' Rake's silhouette clasped its hands in its lap. 'This is our worst performance as professionals. Dee, on a personal level, I gotta say… I'm so happy you're okay.'

Desy felt her mother's hand run through her fingers before she walked out the front door of the manor. 'I…' Desy began, before dipping her head into her knees. 'I'm glad you're okay, too, Rake.'

The woman's silhouette wiped an arm across its face. Desy heard a small sniffle. So, she said, 'Um, can we talk about something?'

'N-Not really much else we can do.'

'Why do you guys do this? Morse and you... I don't know, just, you guys...'

Rake tapped on the cloth wall at Desy. 'If you're gonna say we're good people, then you're wrong. I won't speak for Morse, but I've done things to other people that would make you wanna think twice about talkin' to me. Or even lookin' at me.'

Desy shook her head. 'I don't believe you're just "bad people". That's, uh... garbage, just garbage.'

'You're never gonna get a solid reason for why I do this.'

'Is it because *you* don't know?'

'Bingo,' chimed Rake. 'You ask all the right questions, huh, Dee? But life's like that, I reckon. Most times, stuff happens for no reason. You just gotta be ready to deal with it when the time comes. You spend all your time askin' why, well, you're gonna go crazy.'

'But you could do anything other than kidnap people,' Desy asserted, albeit quietly.

'If this is where I end up, it's where I'm meant to be,' Rake mused, lighting another cigarette. 'And if in ten years, I'm selling shoes for a living or have a family or get up in a gutter or somethin', that's just how it is.'

Desy puffed her cheeks out. 'That's boohickey. I hate that. I don't agree at all.'

'Whatever. You an' Morse seem to get along better anyway. See, that's where we differ, me and him. Principles, all that stuff. No time for that for me.'

'Nuh-uh.' Desy thrust a finger at Rake. 'You care about doing a good job, ha!' Then she retracted her arm and muttered, 'Sorry.'

Rake paused, mid-drag. A throaty giggle escaped her. 'Well, Morsey-Morsey's been rubbin' off on me, I reckon. But don't you go an' say anything to him.'

Desy smiled. 'Um, but you haven't answered my question.'

'I did. I don't think your question is a real question.'

The teenager crossed her arms. 'Okay, if you don't care where you are or where you're going, then where did you come from? You said your parents think you're dead. Why?'

Rake snuffed a cigarette out on the floor but replaced it with a *click*. 'I don't wanna talk about that.'

Desy remained still.

'I do like talkin' about me, though. Nothing identifiable, Dee.' Rake chortled. 'Don't go gettin' your hopes up. Gee, I'm so interesting, though, where do I start?'

'Where are you from?' Desy prompted lightly.

'Siquadel. But lots of people come from there. "Melting pot of culture"; they've got those words on the sides of skyscrapers. At least, where I was from.' Rake breathed out a pillar of smoke. 'Then we kinda smashed our moons together, and that's what everyone knows us for.'

Desy huffed through her nose, sneezed, then asked, 'You grew up there?'

'Yup, not gonna say for how long, though.' Rake tapped her cheek and wrinkled her forehead. 'Ah, gee, now you've done it. I'm remembering all the embarrassing stuff I did when I was young.'

'Were your parents around? Um, you said they're in… jail…'

Rake nodded. 'I sorta remember them before they were arrested. That's what love'll do to ya. You spawn a monster like me, and they lock you up.' She cackled.

'I don't think that's funny.'

'But you can imagine it, right? A tiny little me running around with these skin flaps dragging behind her.' She sighed, recalling smells and sights that were all her own. 'Always got caught on things. Parents sayin' to be careful, 'cause my skin flaps were a part of me. I thought back then my "wings" were really pretty. My "necklace" too.'

'But don't you cover them up?'

'Oh, come on.' Rake snickered. 'Do you have to ask? They're hideous. Take my veiny monkey skin and stretch it over somethin' beautiful like Skaltrene wings. There's being yourself and there's being an eyesore.'

'I think you're wrong.'

'Well, I'll be. I guess I am,' Rake said with fat lips. 'I suppose everyone only ever looking at my face is a coincidence. I can read a room.'

'But–'

'Look, Dee-Dee, I get it. You're young and wanna have everyone play nice. That's just not how the world works. I much rather people be comfortable around me, anyhoo. And, hey, for a creature from the race of Cain…' Rake's silhouette put its hands on its hips and cocked its head. 'I'm doin' pretty good. Peace is the by-product of compromise, Dee. Remember that.'

'I don't know what that Cain thing means,' Desy admitted.

'Bit of a specific reference, I gotta say.' Rake held a thumb to her forehead. 'You know that Skaltrenes and Humans can make babies for some whatever reason. And Big Daddy Government says that people like me are forbidden for our own safety. So, we're kinda a cursed race, I guess? Ugh, I'm gonna look dumb tryin' to explain it. Though, now that I'm thinking of it…'

'What?'

'I always had Big Daddy Government looking out for me once my parents got found out and arrested. Put me in foster care. Always sendin' me letters; I felt like a right superstar. One message every week asking if I was dead yet. They were always polite about it. Lots of long words.'

Desy absorbed Rake's prattling voice.

'Then I was a dancer for ages. Blah-blah-blah-blah-blah. Did some piloting stuff afterwards. Blah-blah-blah-blah-blah.' She spoke with a shadow-puppet hand. 'Met some idiot at some point. Kidnapped a brat.' Rake giggled. 'And that about gets us to now. Anything else?'

'Morse?'

Rake laughed and said, 'No.'

'Please.'

'I ain't speakin' for him. Ain't my place.'

'Just one thing, please,' Desy insisted. 'He's so mysterious and weird… and really cool.'

'Please, *almighty*, stop with the Morse fan club. Bleh.' Rake's silhouette swirled the fingers holding the cigarette. 'One thing. Quick, before he goes an' wakes on us.'

Desy pushed her chin into her knees. Her eyes darted quickly as she recalled the past day. 'Did Morse have wings?' she finally asked.

'Yes.'

There was a five-second pause. Then, Desy sighed with a small smile. 'Please, Rake.'

The woman's silhouette flopped its arms. 'But then I'm gonna have ta tell ya about Didjaree and Morse's daddy and bro and it's all a bit much right now, Dee.'

'Morse has a family?'

'Sure, dontcha have one, too? We all come from somewhere.'

'Does he come from a city called Didjaree?'

Rake stiffened. 'Too perceptive for ya own good, I reckon. Yup, that's his *planet*. Some little rundown shed of a place, from what he's told me. Not that it matters to him anymore. I told ya my parents think I'm dead, right?'

'Uh-huh.'

'Same with Morse.' Rake's finger suddenly pushed like a spear against the shower. 'And dontcha *dare* ask questions about why. We're talkin' about wings. Right?'

Desy recoiled at the change in tone, but affirmed.

'So, yeah, Morse has a brother. But his daddy... hoo, now.' Her silhouette rocked side to side. 'Where do I start on a guy like Morse's daddy? I know. Wings. See, Morse is a Narnit and them wings of theirs are *very* special to their culture. Difference between a grub, or someone like... well...' Rake snickered. 'Someone like you, Little Miss Dee Wintall.'

Desy huffed through her nose.

'Anyway, picture Morse, a little kid Narnit playing with his little brother. Morse has his wings, and they're fine, but his brother...' Rake whistled. 'Those are some *wings*. Talk of the town when he was born. Miracle child, says the townspeople. And his parents. They had lunch with the lord of the land because of Morse's little bro.'

Desy sunk into her haunches.

'Now, here's Morse, a little kid, feelin' this complex emotion. Somethin' green, and I'm not talkin' about money.'

'What did Morse do?'

'A little boy like Morse ain't gonna process an emotion like envy,' Rake continued. 'But he feels *somethin'*. And it's his brother's *wings*. Whenever he sees 'em. So, his little boy brain compresses envy into somethin' more understandable.' Rake dazzled her palms towards Desy.

'Anger?' Desy tried.

'Bingo!' Rake sang. 'And Morse hates feelin' angry. Hates it. So, he comes to a solution. A very *childish* solution. He goes to his Daddy's shed...'

Desy covered her mouth. 'Oh, no.'

'...grabs himself a pair of shears...'

'I get it, Rake. Stop.'

'...and sneaks into his brother's room.' Rake lit another cigarette with a *click*. 'See, he's a little boy and doesn't understand what he's doing. They're just wings, he thinks. But the moment he goes to cut one off–'

'No, no, no! Rake, I mean it!' Desy slapped the floor.

'Dee, it's okay. Gosh, you should trust me by now. What I'm sayin' is, the moment his brother cried out, it broke Morse. Reality hit him. He told me he still hears that scream every now an' then.' Rake dragged on her cigarette. 'And his daddy hears it, too. And Daddy takes Morse to the shed where he pinched them shears from. And…'

Desy had reclined back into her ball. However, a ten-second silence prompted her to lift her head and say, 'And?'

Rake's silhouette crooked slightly, and a small scowl crept out under the curtain. 'Morse still loves his family, he says. I think his daddy is a scum-dwelling, sack-of-crap, no-good, child-torturing snake. See, his daddy, the goddamn barbarian, thinks of an "eye for an eye", right? Y'know what that is, Dee?'

Desy felt a chill emerge from her stomach. 'Y-Yes…'

'But Daddy is less of an "eye for an eye" kind of guy, and more of an "eye for an arm, leg and head" sorta lovely person.' Rake stubbed out her cigarette. 'Morsey made a mistake, but his brother still has his wings. But those *wings*, right? They weren't just important to Morse's brother but to the whole family. Daddy's got a point to make. So he picks up the shears Morse stole, and instead of hangin' them back up, plants a foot on one of Morse's wings. Plants a foot on the other, then–'

'No, stop! I don't want to listen anymore.' Desy turned to Morse. 'I… feel so bad.'

'I mean, ya weren't even alive then, Dee. No need to feel guilty.' Rake's silhouette sent its shadowy fingers to the curtain edge, lifting it. 'He was dead to them then, an' he's dead to them now. It's all over.' Her hand reached over to Desy's shoulder, startling the teen, who whipped her head back in response. 'There ya go, a little bit of both of us. Promise me ya won't say anything?' Rake held a gloved finger to her lips, smiling.

Desy blinked, eyes wet, but held a finger up as well.

An hour later, Morse's subconscious lent an ear to the muffled chitters of a woman, which melted together with another, lighter voice: a teenager's. Numb, cold rivers arced through his body in spider-web patterns. He tried his right arm, then left, then right leg, then left; all four were concrete slabs. Instead, he focused on his toes while he peeled open his eyelids. Through his goopy vision, the spotlight pierced his pupils and made him groan.

The chittering woman yelled something. The lighter voice joined her.

'Too loud,' Morse muttered, though he said it in his Narnit tongue.

The voices grew like a wave and rattled his ears. 'Too loud,' he muttered again.

Smoke drifted into his nostrils, and a gloved hand grasped his.

'You wanna try that again in a language I can understand?' asked Rake.

Morse whispered, 'Shut up,' in UBL.

'I've given ya Chuff-Chuff,' Rake said softly. 'About over an hour ago. It should do its work soon.' She stroked his hand with hers.

Desy's voice asked, 'Chuff-Chuff?'

'That stuff I asked you for before, Dee. The stuff in the tube from the medicine cabinet. I never can remember its real name.'

There was the rattling of a plastic tube, followed by Desy's voice. 'Chuffaventilogobrine,' she read, tripping over each syllable. 'Why didn't you take this stuff?'

'Didn't wanna have to go through this.' Rake tightened her grip on his fingers a little. 'You shoulda seen your body, all bent and that. You idiot. I don't reckon a single rib was in place.'

'Did the job,' Morse drooled. 'Where's the kid?'

'I'm here,' Desy muttered, her feet stepping quietly up to the bed.

Deep, dark purple stains ate him in arcs that extended from shoulder to knee. His gruff features were overshadowed by the mountainous flesh ball growing from his forehead and across both of his eyes.

Her face dropped.

'You... feeling okay?' he breathed.

Desy's legs were scraped from ankle to hip. Blisters covered her toes, nose, ears and fingers. The bandages applied to the lacerations on her cheeks and forehead needed to be reapplied. What felt like honey sat at the bottom of her diaphragm. She had been coughing consistently for the last two hours.

Desy smiled. 'I'm fine, so fine. Um, thanks.'

'Dee, might wanna get me some of those straps by the door,' Rake ordered. 'That dose of Chuff-Chuff is gonna hit, and Morse is gonna start moving.'

Desy headed for the medical sack.

Morse grumbled.

She scrambled with the six thick rubber straps over to Rake, who snatched them and started pinning them beneath the mattress.

Morse was beginning to twist, accompanied by a painful roaring.

'Get on that side.' Rake pointed.

'Um, okay...'

Morse shrieked.

'Quickly,' Rake urged. Then she whispered to Morse. 'Keep still, keep still. Two more seconds, you idiot. Then you can cry all you wanna.'

By the time he was strapped tight, Morse was bellowing through his teeth. Like a trapped animal, he impulsively jerked, to no avail, hurting himself as he did so but unable to stop.

Rake led Desy to the exit and told her to plug her ears.

'But he's all alone,' she stammered, wide-eyed at his agony.

'*I'll* be here for him. I don't wanna have you seein' this.' Rake slipped into a mother's tone. 'Plug your ears and close your eyes. Now.'

Desy nodded and sank into a ball by the door, watching Rake hobble over to Morse, saying, 'You got me here. Listen, you dolt, I'm here. I'm here, stupid.'

His muscles rippled, his bones bent, and his heart thrashed, but Morse kept his disgust and terror hidden behind anger. The disgust and terror of a million parts inside him beginning to move in different directions. All on their own, his organs brushed under his muscles. All on their own, his bones grazed the inside flesh of his skin. All on their own, his broken veins, capillaries, and arteries gnawed into each other like insects.

Eventually, after twenty minutes, what were cries became grunts, what were full-body contortions became twitches in the shoulders and legs. The swelling in his forehead had deflated into a small plateau.

Aside from Morse breathing raggedly and quivering, the room was silent.

Rake had remained on one foot all the while. Desy dared to open an eyelid. Then she unplugged her ears and asked, 'Um, is... is he okay?'

'I'm not a doc,' Rake muttered. 'The Chuff stuff hits hard, then you wanna just lie down for a day. And usually everythin' gets fixed.'

'Usually?' Desy whispered, standing up and gingerly journeying back over to Morse. 'What is that stuff?'

'We can't go to regular hospitals,' Rake explained, stroking Morse's hand again and again. 'And we can't go anywhere right now 'cause of the pigs. We always have a bit of Chuff just in case somethin' real bad happens.'

'But what does it do?'

'I dunno, really. Banned from hospitals, though. Morse was talkin' to our doc once, and he said apparently, it rewrites cells. 'Stead of your body acting as a squad, all of ya cells do their own thing.'

Desy grimaced.

'Then, the Chuff uses the blueprints in your DNA to get everythin' back where it's meant to be…' Rake waved her arms about. 'I dunno, I dunno, I'm an idiot. But it fixes things. The doc said that it takes years off your life, so only use this stuff in true emergencies.'

'It's killing him?' Desy gaped.

'Can't say.'

'But–'

'You could only know it's killing him if you knew how long he was gonna live, anyway.' Rake forced a smile. 'Newsflash: water kills people, 'cause every person who drinks it dies.' Rake faced Desy. She took a long, long breath as she held out her arms. '*Relax.*'

Desy blinked slowly as her vision wandered around the woman's bloodied bob, cowlicks, and big eyes. She hugged Rake tightly.

'Mm, a little too excited, Dee,' Rake grunted. 'You got me warm, you got my leg better, and my head. Lemme pitch in.' She let go of the teenager and waggled her nose against hers. 'Go be a good little hostage and relax, hmm?'

Desy looked to Morse.

'Once he's slept it off, the idiot's gonna be fine. You can say hi then. Trust me, I have some questions I wanna ask him, too.' Rake waved Desy away from the bed. 'Go on. Go be scared or whatever kidnapped teenagers are meant to do, 'cause I sure as hell don't remember.'

Six hours later, in the lukewarm room, there was a subtle shift of the sheets on Rake's bed. A moment after that, there was a louder rustle of fabric, accompanied by the sudden, weighty *thump* of a doona being flopped over. 'Geez, my head,' Morse muttered.

Rake stuck her own head out from the shower. 'How're ya feeling, princess?' she whispered.

'Yeah, could do with a torch-rifle to the face.' He rolled his head about, groggy. He watched Rake fumble out of the shower to her feet. 'Foot's looking better.'

'Oh, ya know me, gotta just get me warm and I'll sort myself out.' She walked lopsidedly over to Morse and removed the rubber straps.

'Thanks,' he said, once his elbows could bend. Slowly, he tensed his muscles, feeling a tender streak across his collarbone and deep in his chest. Then he began to turn his abdomen and winced.

Rake heard him grunt and poked him in the leg with a finger. 'Stop that, idiot. Remember what the doc said? Chuff ain't a miracle worker. You still gotta take some meds and apply lotion.'

Morse, however, was staring at Rake's right foot. 'You didn't do that bandage.'

'Dee did.' Rake peered over her shoulder, down at the floor, where Desy was curled in a ball in a pile of blankets, eyes closed with a tunnel of wind ruffling her black locks.

'Shouldn't be helping us,' Morse sighed. 'Not her job.'

'Kinda had no choice. I was barely functioning. You were out. The water was startin' to get cold.' Rake leaned into his face. 'Remember that? Whaddya remember?'

The bat-man scratched his forehead, then crossed his eyes upwards. 'My head's bigger than I remember.'

'You look smart for once.' Rake sat on the edge of the bed and lit the last cigarette in her box. 'Come on. What happened? Where was Dee after all this?'

Morse crushed his eyes closed. 'Yeah, that's right. I got into the cave. And I called for her, searched all the dark spots.' He opened his eyes and caught Rake's. 'I gave up.'

'Should you be tellin' me that?'

'My body just stopped working. But you know our...' He snapped his fingers three times. 'The clicking. The kid was clicking right behind me.'

Rake tapped the butt of the cigarette on her nose. 'Huh? She picked up on that?'

'Someone had pushed her head-first into a crevice,' Morse muttered, stowing a scowl. He saw Desy twitch in her sleep. 'She was naked as well.'

Rake bared her teeth and flicked her forked tongue. 'I knew it. The android needed her clothes. Why do ya think I even brought the bike?'

Morse pushed onto his elbows, fighting through the pain to get his face into Rake's. 'About that. What the hell were you thinking?'

Rake looked off to the shadow of herself on the wall. 'Gotta say, it's hard for me to judge you for resigning yourself. I... didn't think I was gonna come back to *Ferguson* again. Though considering I was right about the android' – Rake smiled – 'and without me, Desy woulda frozen to death, even in your cracked suit, it was worth...' She trailed off.

Morse had lowered himself back onto the pillows and reached an arm out to Rake. He twiddled his fingers.

Rake eyed them with disgust. 'Don't make this soppy, Morse,' she muttered, slipping her gloved fingers through his.

'Before I found the kid, I tried to call you. Tried everything. Never thought I'd see you again. Couldn't believe it when you came out of the blizzard. Then I saw you collapse in front of me…'

Rake fiddled with one of her cowlicks. She turned over her shoulder, heard Desy snore, then leaned up close to Morse and whispered as quietly as she could, 'An' you went and called me Ingrid.'

'I really thought you were gone.'

''Member the last time you called me that?'

Morse shook his head.

She let go of his hand. 'Right, any more of that silly nonsense and I'm gonna vomit. What happened after I was out?'

Morse regaled Rake with his escape, flooring her with his insane hope that Bronzework would be in the right place at the right time. Her teeth ground her cigarette in half at the mention of the *Induction* and Gold Bayleaf. With the taste of raw tobacco, and Morse's grin while he bragged about escaping the UGIP's top officer, Rake could only gag. 'This is so unfair,' she said, followed by, 'Bronzework helped you escape Gold Bayleaf through a *technicality*.'

'If that helps you sleep. Now, after a while, I realised the cops were gone.' Morse pondered with an upturned lip. 'Don't know what happened, but they were gone. So I just turned back in the direction of *Ferguson*, from what I can remember.' He leaned over a little, calling past Rake to the floor, 'Hey, kid, fill me in on what happened next.'

Desy shifted under her covers. 'How did you know?'

'You breathe like a horse.'

She unravelled herself, creeping up to the bed with a blush. 'Um… sorry.'

'We're gonna hafta curtail this apology problem of yours,' Rake declared, nudging Desy with a leg. 'Stop saying sorry for dumb things.'

'Sorry.'

Morse interrupted Rake's displeased finger-thrashing by asking, 'What happened in the shower after I passed out?'

'Um, Rake told me to get some clothes on and to dry off,' Desy explained. 'Um, then… um–'

'The spare battery,' Rake helped, scuffling about her robes for a brand-new box of cigarettes. She popped open the lid and settled into another one.

'Right, battery. I got it out from where the bike usually goes. Then I got the heater. And plugged it in next to Rake, and got her out of the shower to dry her.'

Morse's scepticism came as a low hum. 'How did you know where any of that was located? Rake...?'

The woman's lip hitched up to one side. 'Dee did it all herself, really. My body didn't wanna move, too cold, so I had ta tell her where everythin' was.'

'You were really quiet,' Desy mumbled.

'Ah, ya shoulda seen her, Morse. Our scaredy little screw-up, not half an hour after being wedged in a wall, dragging me around to the bedroom as fast as she could.' She snickered. 'She was crying the whole time, too.'

Desy pouted. Morse studied her with a blank face.

'She was bawling once she got ya into the bedroom, too.' Rake shook her head. 'I can barely move you on a good day. No idea how this wimp did it.'

'I just...' Desy suddenly leaned down and embraced Morse, carefully.

He looked, surprised, at Rake, who cackled.

'You came back for me. Thank you.' Desy sighed.

'That's, uh, fine.' Morse patted her robotically on the back. Then he lied, 'Starting to hurt,' and Desy quickly released him.

'Of course,' Rake continued, closing her eyes with a smug smile, 'once I was nice an' warm, I saved the day.'

'Sure,' Morse stated.

Some hours earlier, the *Induction*'s brutal face leered at Yeti from several thousand kilometres up in space. A cruiser stuffed with officers and the android Desy, as well as four other cruisers that trailed behind, left the *Induction* and spun towards the south pole, whisking across the red velvet cake landscape. Artificial lakes, slopes, mountains... the android lied when it thought, *I can't wait to go back and see them again with Daddy.*

Its oscillator drummed when, out of the window of the cruiser, it spotted Hingspock's ornate skyline.

Trupeal turned away from her own window and said to the fake, 'You have a very pretty planet.'

'I do, don't I?' The android smiled back.

Trupeal concealed her mouth behind a hand.

Before long, the cruiser landed on a big, flat, white rectangle atop a platinum rod in Hingspock's East State. The android's lips pursed. It nearly asked, 'Where are we?' Instead, it said, 'Why are we here?'

'Again, we're handing you over to your planet's jurisdiction for the time being,' Trupeal explained, unbuckling her seat belt and reaching across to undo the android's. 'I think someone you know is coming to meet you.'

The android leaped from its seat and bounded to the exit, bouncing from toe to toe as Trupeal and four officers joined it. With a sharp hiss, the door unfastened, sliding to the side, and a small flight of stairs sprang forth to lock onto the white stone roof.

A tall, lithe, Human woman with long maroon hair in a low ponytail stood twenty metres away, in front of an elevator. She was adorned with stars and badges. Her uniform and cap bore the insignia of Yeti's planetary commissioner: a seven-point star, a wreath, and the feather from a Ballad Bird. Six officers flanked her.

The android felt sick to its stomach, according to itself. It saw the woman's eyebrows lose their pointed rigidity, and a relieved smile unbound her tight lips. It started to quiver when she extended her arms wide.

Who is this woman? Silver Fingers thought. *She isn't Daddy. How many damned people do I have to get through to get to him?* Then, loosening the tap on the waterworks, it wiped its eyes and looked up at Trupeal, who smiled and indicated with an arm towards the policewoman. *Morse and Rake did no research,* it raged in its head. *Wait, who…? I'm Desy. This woman seems to feel like Daddy does. So Desy, me, will act accordingly.*

The android hurried across the rooftop towards the woman, who had bent down on one knee by the time it embraced her.

'I'm so glad you're safe,' she muttered in its ear. 'I'm so, so sorry this happened to you.'

'Desy' smiled and squeezed her harder.

She released the android and resumed her professional persona. 'I'll be just a moment. Wait here.'

She walked with purpose towards Trupeal, who extended her hand, smiling. 'Planetary Commissioner Jilliosa. I can finally put a face to the name.'

'Same to you, Governor,' Jilliosa remarked, shaking her hand. 'My thanks to you and Captain Gold Bayleaf for your swift action in this matter.'

'We were in the area.' Trupeal placed her hands on her hips.

'And I must extend my sincerest well wishes to the captain on his speedy recovery. The report I read was less than...' Jilliosa rested her arms behind her back. 'Shall we say, less than stellar?'

Trupeal waved the comment away with two fingers. 'He's back on his feet already but is meditating for the moment. It'll take a little more than Bronzework to put him down.'

'Any updates on Bronzework?'

'Unfortunately not.' Trupeal hid her mouth behind a palm, murmuring, 'We lost many officers to him. I assure you, the squads of the *Induction* won't forget that.'

Jilliosa frowned.

'Anyway, we're confident that Bronzework was working under these Morse and Rake fellows.' Trupeal held her arms out in an aloof manner. 'A scan of Promethia revealed not a trace of their ship, so we've uploaded the details into the galactic database. We've uprooted the Shipyard, too. So long as your men do their due diligence here, and the UGIP monitors this planet for the next few months, which they will, those two characters are as good as caught.'

'That is much appreciated.'

Trupeal bowed politely. 'Then we shall part ways here. I'm glad we could meet under sunny circumstances.' She turned on her heel and strode towards the cruiser. However, a ripple went up her spine and she twisted over her shoulder. 'Oh, I nearly forgot. Good luck with the upcoming election.'

Jilliosa waved. 'Thank you.'

'If I could vote in it, I would vote for you!'

'Most people say that.' Jilliosa laughed, hands trailing behind her back again.

Once the UGIP-marked cruiser lifted into the early morning sky and warbled out of sight, Jilliosa turned back to the android, who was sporting a grimace. 'Sorry. Let's go home.'

Jilliosa led the android into the elevator with the other officers in tow. She pushed a button labelled 'G', the lift throbbed for two seconds, and with a *ding* its doors opened to the lobby of the police headquarters, sixty storeys down.

'Desy' smiled at the secretaries who waved at it, at the twelve constables who stopped to do so as well before barrelling around the office with paperwork, and at the Hawkie being led out of a cruiser in handcuffs, who squawked a greeting. The cockatoo was disciplined with a baton to the back of the head.

Behind the android, Jilliosa barked, 'I'll be in my personal car. Trail in Formation Five.'

'Desy' was then led onto the sidewalk and around to another elevator. Jilliosa flashed her insignia, and the doors clicked open. Another throb and *ding* later, the android was hustled towards a low-rider car that looked as though it had been forged out of silver. 'I called Doctor Monty,' Jilliosa said, tapping an object in her pocket that caused both car doors to swing open. 'He'll see you anytime today. Just say the word.'

The clock on the dashboard read 8:30 a.m.

The android felt a fire surge in its belly. It managed, 'I really don't want to see the doctor.'

The woman paused for a second as she helped the fake into the passenger seat. 'It's important to rule anything out,' she said in that second, then closed the door. She continued after rounding the bonnet and slipping into the driver's seat. 'Dezz, we were so worried about you.' Jilliosa leaned across and hugged it. 'We just want to be sure you're okay.'

The android added 'Dezz' to its data bank of nicknames.

Jilliosa thumbed a pad on the ceiling and said, 'Delta-Echo Five and Eight, we are go. Foxtrot-Alpha One.'

'Heard, Foxtrot-Alpha One,' came the reply.

Jilliosa swiped across the pad and tapped her fingers against it. Then, as a sequence of number-tones rang inside the car, she shifted into drive, lifting the vehicle soundlessly into the air of the parking lot and turning towards the exit.

The car shot out from a holographic field at the base of the police headquarters. As soon as it blurred above the next suburb, casting a lightning-fast shadow over streets, roofs, and people, two police bikes whizzed out of the headquarters in pursuit.

While the bikes overtook Jilliosa and the android, the phone was picked up on the other end.

'Jilliosa,' came Ernest's voice.

'Ernest.' She smiled, turning towards the android. 'I'm bringing her home. See you in a few minutes.'

The trip from his bed to the front door was made in seconds. After a seeming eternity, Ernest cried out at the sight of Jilliosa's car shimmering in the distance. Once the vehicle landed in the gardens and he saw two figures emerge, he ran towards it.

The android ran to him and leaped.

Ernest caught it and spun in a tizzy as the two hugged and cried, a mess of limbs and wet faces. Eventually, father and 'daughter' sank to their knees, holding each other tightly.

FIFTEEN
The Collateral

An hour of exchanging perspectives and the application of medicinal elements saw Morse sitting up in bed. Rake could stand to place some weight on her foot. Desy squeaked in pain as she peeled the band-aids from her face, then she pushed her cheeks around in front of a mirror.

Rake asked Morse, 'Can you stand?'

'Probably.' He pushed onto his curved feet and, holding his right abdominals with a hand, wobbled upright. 'Can we move off this moon?'

'It's been almost half a day.' Rake frowned, walking over to the exit. 'Haven't heard nothin' from the pigs. Not even a ship or anythin'. We gotta risk it, 'cause that battery won't last forever.'

Morse noted Rake's quivering hands. 'Fair enough. Well, I'll take the heater if you take the battery, kid?'

'Yep, will do,' Desy said, jumping to the battery and lifting it with an audible heave.

'You bounce back quick,' Morse snorted, before screeching through his lips as he bent down to grab the heater.

Rake's temperature was dropping, and her mood was following suit.

'That's just the *good* pain,' he whined to her glower.

She stepped over and snatched the heater from his hands. 'It's for me anyway, idiot.'

On the count of three, Morse opened the door to *Ferguson*'s freezing hallways, and the three of them trotted around the half-doughnut and into the cockpit.

Rake shivered into the pilot's seat, after brushing a layer of frost away, her legs rattling the heater perched in her lap. 'H-Here w-we go. G-Guns r-ready?'

Morse slapped the handle of his pistol.

Desy wrinkled her face and bent her knees.

Rake activated the ignition. In a wave starting from the centre of the console and moving to the edges, every screen and button lit up like the streetlights in a quiet town, the power visibly travelling across then up to the ceiling lights and into the other rooms. A low hum bled into the cockpit from the floor. *Ferguson*'s engines were warming up.

Suddenly, an alarm sounded.

Desy cried out and fell into a ball. Morse gripped his pistol with two hands. Rake scowled, teeth clacking. 'That's th-the bulkheads, morons. We still gotta get the hole in *F-Ferguson* fixed.' A loud, metallic thump confirmed her statement.

'All right,' Morse muttered, not relaxing. 'And the radar?'

'Ten more seconds and we should have it,' Rake replied. On cue, she tapped a button in front of her, and a holographic square widened on the blank white windshield. She shivered, but with excitement. 'We're all alone on this g-goddamn rock.'

'Good?' Desy said from the floor.

A distinct *ding* emanated from the Slate Box, which had spun into existence from the console. A sheer black envelope peeked out from it.

'Yeah,' Morse sighed, holstering his pistol. 'Kid, you cold?'

'I think the heat's on,' she observed, holding her hands above her head and feeling a warm breeze slip through her fingers. 'Is that the purple writing thing? What is it, anyway?'

'There's a shovel in my workshop,' Morse said, pointing away from the cockpit. 'Push the snow into the draining grates around the ship.'

Desy folded her arms.

Morse turned away from her but kept his finger on the exit. 'Move. We're taking care of business here.'

The teenager let out a haughty *humph* and stepped out of the cockpit.

Rake, wordlessly and with no excitement, plucked the slate from its holder and placed it inside the reader on the console. The cockpit darkened, and purple letters lined the windshield, reading:

To Morse and Rake,

I have been informed of the return of Ernest Wintall's daughter. To state my overwhelming disappointment would be a waste of both our time.

You are fired.

I expect my collateral to be returned to the previous drop-off point within twenty-four hours. And if the collateral is not returned, I will send a more capable party to retrieve it on my behalf.

There shall be no further contact between us.

Rake lifted the slate out of the reader, flipping it between her hands with an increasingly sullen look. Morse drifted over to her and placed a hand on her shoulder. She leaned her head against it as he rocked her gently.

Eventually, he muttered, 'We knew this was coming.'

'Still hurts,' Rake whispered with tight lips.

He reached down and wrestled the slate from her fingers. 'I'll put this away.'

'We tried so hard,' she huffed.

'I know.'

'We spent years buildin' our reputation.'

'I know.'

'We nearly *died* for this.'

'I know.'

Rake shook the heater furiously before shoving it off her lap and onto the floor. Morse kicked it as he walked over to the incinerator. 'Well, the job isn't over, even if we're fired,' he reminded Rake. 'Twenty-four hours is more than enough time to get the android back and return the collateral.'

The black slate disappeared into the incinerator opening.

'Shouldn't we do the second part of that first?' Rake asked, wiping her face.

Morse kept his eyes on the fizzling slate.

The crackling and popping aside, not a sound could be heard inside the cockpit for twenty seconds.

Finally, and with his nose pointed to the ceiling, the bat-man said, 'Come on. You know the answer. We leave that android alone for even an extra minute… if someone dies, that's on us. It's our responsibility to shut it down first. The client can wait.'

Rake rolled her shoulders back, resolute. 'This is it, huh, Morse?'

'Yeah, seems like.'

'The client's gonna get the collateral back if we get arrested or not.'

'Yeah.'

'The police are gonna be watching Dee's planet for *Ferguson*.'

'Yeah.'

'We're goin' back to prison no matter what, aren't we?'

'Or we dump the kid off and betray our maxims. What do you want to do?'

'You know *exactly* what I wanna do. I wanna stop running.'

Morse finally turned to face Rake's eyes. They were larger, wetter, and more despondent than he had seen in five years.

However, those eyes closed. And her cheeks inflated with a smile. 'But I can't do that to Dee,' she reassured him. 'And you ain't never, ever gonna get rid of me that easily.'

'Get the kid in here,' Morse said. 'It's time to come clean.'

Rake held a button down on the console. 'Dee, we kinda need to talk to ya.' Her voice echoed through the ship.

'But I just found the shovel!' Desy shouted, muffled.

A minute later, Morse sat Desy down in his copilot seat. 'You're going home,' he declared casually.

The teenager jumped to standing, squeaking, 'Daddy paid?'

'No,' Morse muttered, pushing her back down. 'We were fired by our client.'

Desy gasped.

'So, you're free to go. But' – he raised a finger – 'there's a problem.'

'What do you mean, "problem"?' Desy inquired with a tilted head. 'There's no problem. Um, just drop me off somewhere close to my house so you can get away.'

'No, no, not that.' Morse fingered his ear with a pinkie.

Rake entered the conversation slowly. 'Ya kinda, sorta, *are* already home with your daddy.'

Desy clasped her elbows and turned away from them. 'What are you talking about?'

Morse said, 'I'll show you,' and fished inside his pocket for his phone. After withdrawing it, he tapped the screen. 'Just checking out what's new on your social media page.'

'Um, I've been kidnapped, so…'

Morse raised his eyebrows at the screen and then directed them at her. 'Nope, thirty-two minutes ago. Here you are, at your house.' He handed the phone to Desy, who accepted it with sweaty fingers.

She saw herself kissing like a fish away from the camera, winking. A mirror was in the background, *her* mirror, which reflected her levitating bed, desk, and window. Also in the reflection was the dress and shorts combo she had gone to pick up from the mall three days earlier. She was wearing them.

A flashing caption read *New babies*, while a gaudy arrow jittered towards the shorts and dress.

'Have you ever taken this photo before?' Morse asked.

'No,' whispered Desy, 'I… never… took this…' She paled and glanced at Morse, then Rake. 'What's going on? Who is this person? Why do they look like me? What are they doing in my room?' She blurted out the questions, each one shaking her voice further.

'Dee, calm down, it's just an android.' Rake lit a cigarette.

'An android? Like Aurelian?'

'Your father's android? Yeah.' Morse took his phone back. 'That android in the photo is ours. We dressed it up to look like you. All those photos of yourself, videos you uploaded, we fed them to the android to take on your personality, your walk; basically, we made a perfect copy.'

'It was brilliant, really,' Rake said, slapping her knees. 'I sorta figured, "Huh, it's gonna be difficult to extort this planet owner without alerting his security. If we take his daughter without him realising, we can choose the perfect time to negotiate". Foolproof.'

'Right, foolproof.' Morse sniffed.

'*You* let Dee out. You're an idiot, so the *fool*proof plan failed; I'm still right.'

'I don't feel good,' Desy whispered.

'Remember, Dee, we're not good people.'

Morse grimaced at Desy's sickened expression, and he had to turn away while folding his arms once she directed it at him. 'Since we're fired, I'll say… uh, I'm truly sorry for the invasion of privacy, Desy Wintall.'

Desy sank lower into the seat.

Morse gripped his forearms.

'Are you saying Daddy is living with a perfect copy of me?' Desy asked.

'Yeah.'

'Yep.'

'He won't have known I was gone. So, just take me home and swap us around. Simple,' she reasoned. Then, she had a brainwave. 'Wait, Daddy sent Bronzework after you, so he must have known I was kidnapped...'

Morse and Rake exchanged a proud but nervous look.

Sitting in silence for five seconds, Desy snapped to her feet. 'Okay, I'm missing something that *you two* did, right?'

Rake, smirking, having taken the time to fill her mouth with smoke, blew an enormous, billowing ring from her lips. 'Morse, I was thinkin' about this ever since the cave.' Smoke drifted from her nostrils like a dragon. 'Silver Fingers doesn't attack ya when you're awake. She doesn't do brute force measures; she plays *games*. She sneaks into your house and kills you. But twice, she apparently ordered us to be attacked with a ton of people around and in broad daylight. The Shipyard and Moody Moody.' Rake shivered, then coughed. 'I really don't think this is the hag, Morse. It's kinda like the Arthrods are bein' ordered around by an emotionally stunted child who wants Desy dead.'

'I hate kids,' the bat-man grunted. 'But yeah, that's where I was going. The hag's d–'

'*Hello?*' Desy shouted, clapping over and over. 'What's the problem with me going home now?'

'Right, sorry. So, uh, the problem now is... Uh, do you know about AI sentience?' Morse asked.

Desy unfolded her palms and waggled her head with furrowed eyebrows.

'At some point in an android's "life", averaging about fifty years in...' Morse stuck his hands in his pockets. 'Like you, kid, it will just start questioning anything anyone tells it.'

'Why?'

'That's one of the few genuine mysteries out there. No one's been able to give definitive proof for *why*; it just happens. So, to recap where we are: we dressed the android up as you and swapped you around.'

Desy slowly nodded. She recalled the smell of rotting flesh and the sight of a white cloth inside the dressing room. The silhouette she saw, blurry as it had been for days, was beginning to take the shape of herself.

'Then,' Morse continued, 'at some point, the android gets kidnapped by a crime boss called Silver Fingers.'

'Why?'

Rake waved her hands. 'No idea. Like I said yesterday, ya gotta ask ya daddy about that one.'

'Next, it takes over her criminal organisation by killing her. We talked about this, Arthrods operate by–'

'Might makes right. But *androids* aren't allowed to kill,' Desy said. 'Aurelian wouldn't–'

'Remember, kid, *our* android is questioning everything. For some reason, your copy took out Silver Fingers. Maybe the hag threatened its life or something. Then, and this is a wild guess, it's gotten this idea that if it kills you, it can replace you. Considering how emotionally volatile it'd have to be to kill someone, who knows how it's come to that conclusion.'

Desy felt her heart plough into her collarbone. 'And that's why you can't put me back, right?'

'That's the long and short of it, yeah,' Morse said, nodding.

Desy sat down again. Her hands fell into her lap, and her nose wrinkled.

Morse and Rake both smiled; they knew she was thinking of something.

'I have just one more question,' Desy began.

'Anything, kid. We owe you that much.'

'Who asked you to do this?'

'We don't owe you *that* much.' Rake grinned, which prompted Morse to flick the cigarette out of her mouth. 'Ass,' she growled, hopping out of her seat to chase the butt.

'She means we can't tell you,' Morse sighed.

'"Professionalism", huh?' Desy said with air quotations.

'No. We just don't know who it was.'

'Kinda defeats the purpose of a middleman service, dontcha think?' Rake said, rubbing the butt of the cigarette on her sleeve and slipping it back into her mouth. 'The entire point is for our clients to remain anonymous while we take the heat.'

'But don't you know even a little bit about them?' Desy pleaded.

Morse scratched the back of his neck.

'They might write funny? Um, um, what about where they sent the purply writing from? Please, you have to know something.'

Rake crossed her arms to make an 'X'. 'Bah-bown. Dee, we really don't know anythin' about them. Search us.'

However, there was a knife digging into Morse's belly. Quietly, with heavily wrinkled features, withdrawing his neck into his tortoiseshell, he muttered, 'Well, they gave us one thing.'

'What?' Desy gasped.

Rake grabbed Morse by the collar, on him in a split second. 'Are you *nuts?*' she spat through her teeth, so her cigarette bounced off his nose.

'She's not going to get any info—'

'Isn't it *you* who's always goin' on about "principles"?' Rake whisper-shouted. 'It's 'cause she's a kid, right? What's *with* you an' children?'

'I hate kids.'

'Ya say an awful lotta things, huh?' Rake seethed in his face. However, a small hand clasped her arm, directing her attention downwards.

Desy's red eyes shimmered. 'Rake, please let me see it?'

Rake's face softened. Morse said reassuringly in her ear, 'She's not going to find out anything if we didn't.'

She scowled back at Morse but could not scowl at Desy, so she closed her eyes and threw her arms down. She dropped into the pilot's chair and stuffed a cigarette in her mouth. 'Suppose we failed this far; we ain't gonna go lower…'

'Thank you, thank you, thank you,' Desy said. She slipped her arms around Rake, only for her to shimmy them away.

'No.'

The teenager stepped back quietly and turned to where Morse had been standing.

He was no longer present in the cockpit. Desy heard the door leading to his workshop slide open and closed. Then, some seconds later, it reopened, and he wandered back to the cockpit.

In his hand was a sicorum hutch, the Neptune-blue box Desy had watched him move from *Fulthorpe* to *Ferguson* at the Shipyard. Immediately, she recalled the *hiss* the lid made while sliding open whenever Ernest opened his own sicorum hutch that he kept on a shelf inside his office. She said, 'Daddy's got one of those things.'

Morse turned the swirling blue edges of the box in his hand, stroking various points across its surface. 'Is that right?' he muttered, concentrating. 'What does he keep in his?'

'Um, photos of me.'

Morse detected Rake's near-silent hum of delight. He resisted the urge to poke her about it, instead flipping the box over and drawing a line in the shape of a California condor across its surface with his forefinger. The box hummed and gave a *hiss.*

'First try,' Rake declared sarcastically. 'Good for you.'

'Kid, honestly, you're not going to find out anything about the client from this.' He flipped the box over to reveal its lid was ajar.

Desy heard something solid rattle inside.

'But you're probably never going to see one of these again. Even with your family's money.' He slid the lid off, and an ethereal glow emanated from the box. White and wispy, the light poured like a waterfall up and against the ceiling of the cockpit.

Desy felt her knees begin to buckle. A sensation of awe and sickness similar to what she felt towards the nebula world arose once more within her throat.

Inside the box was a diamond, longer than her hand and as wide as her middle and ring fingers together. Something primal stirred inside her; she feared and longed for the gemstone. She would've watched Morse slip on a glove with one hand to reach into the sicorum hutch, but her eyes were unable to look anywhere else but the diamond. 'What's that?' she breathed.

'A Paragon,' Morse explained, squinting and lifting the gem up to his eye.

'It's b-beautiful.'

Rake spun her chair around to place her chin on her fists, eyes glued to the Paragon.

Morse continued, 'Naturally occurring, too. That's what makes them so sought-after. That, and there's only about a thousand Paragons in the galaxy. Out of half a trillion planets. Wars have been fought over these things.'

'And th-that's what your client...' Desy trailed off, mesmerised.

'Gave us...' Morse trailed off as well but shook his head so his ears slapped his face. 'We dug up more about your father.' He lowered the glowing gem back into the box. 'He owns a little more than Yeti.'

'Wait, really?' Desy snapped out of her stupor.

'Yup, Daddy's got his eyes on ya whole solar system, and about three others,' Rake added.

'You didn't know that, kid?'

'N-No...' Desy glumly sat in the copilot's chair, eyes still on the box.

'So, when the client asked us to take... a certain amount of money from your father,' Morse continued, 'they gave us this as collateral worth about a third of it.'

'Why?'

'Well' – Rake perked up – 'it guarantees that the client isn't gonna double-cross us. So we keep whatever they give us if the contract goes kaplooey.'

'That little gem could buy my planet?' Desy said, jumping up to get another peek at it.

Morse thumbed at his lip. 'Maybe about two thirds of Yeti. But definitely two or three lesser solar systems, easily.'

Desy unthinkingly touched the diamond.

'Hey, hey,' Morse called out, pulling the box away. 'Wear gloves first, kid. Geez.' He slipped his off and handed it to Desy, who struggled to get her fingers through the openings. Eventually, she carefully reached into the box, plucked the Paragon between her fingers, and held it in front of her eyes.

'Something this pure, you can stain real easily. Careful,' Morse said.

'There ya go, Dee. Whaddya reckon?' Rake huffed, two unlit cigarettes twitching in her fingers. 'Told ya you wouldn't find anythin' out about the client.'

Desy sighed, disappointed. However, she noted a blemish a half-inch from the tip of the Paragon. She squinted, muttering, 'Guys, I see something.'

'That's just an identity mark,' Rake said, twirling her lighter in her other hand. 'Lemme smoke a ciggy already.'

Morse reached into his pocket for another glove. 'All right, kid, you had a good look. What you saw is just what the Paragon owners put on their gems to say it's theirs.'

Desy's face began to pale.

'Unless you're the owner, it literally means nothing...' He stopped.

Desy was hyperventilating.

'Kid...?'

'Dee?'

She started to shake all over, prompting Rake to jump to her side while Morse took the Paragon out of her fingers.

'Dee, Dee,' Rake said, leading Desy back to the copilot's chair. 'Is it your lungs? D'ya feel cold?'

'It's mine,' Desy whispered, hunching over.

'What?' Morse murmured, taking a step back.

'The i-identity mark is my family's crest. It's, um... the Wintall family's...' Desy pulled herself into a ball.

'What?!' Rake shouted. 'Whaddya *mean* it's yours?'

'That's impossible.' Morse lifted the Paragon up to his eye again, tracing every fibre of the tiny, ornate goblet etched into its surface. 'Kid, I've never seen this emblem in my life. Are you sure?'

'Dee,' Rake urged, crouching low and pushing her face close to the teen's. 'Gotta stop playin' with us. We researched ya house, ya family, ya father. Nothin'. We never got even a glimpse at that emblem. Nowhere.'

'Where have you seen this?' Morse asked.

'Daddy caught me in his office when I was r-really young,' Desy whispered. 'I was in his desk, and I saw our crest in a photo of Daddy when *he* was really young.' She gathered herself by covering her eyes. 'He was standing in his office with... um, Grandpa. And our crest was on the wall behind them.'

'But there've been news photos taken in Wintall's office.' Morse placed the Paragon back in the box again.

'In all of ya social media photos, Dee, we saw nothin' of the sort,' Rake pondered aloud. 'Did ya dad say anythin' about the crest?'

'N-No,' Desy answered. 'He told me what the goblet was when I asked him... I don't really remember exactly what he said, but he told me it wasn't important.'

'Your family crest isn't important?' Morse and Rake said together, in equal disbelief.

Morse got in first. 'But you aren't just some random family. You're pretty much royalty this side of the stellar neighbourhood.'

'What kinda "screw-you"-money family keeps its crest a secret? You should be slappin' that thing over everythin' ya...' Rake clapped her hands in answer to her own question. 'Unless you're a family with somethin' to hide.'

Desy shook her head fervently.

Morse secured the lid of the sicorum hutch. 'Kid. There's a very famous saying in the underworld: "The best criminals are the ones you never hear of". And, considering your father pulled in Bronzework that quickly and was targeted by Silver Fingers...'

'I have to get home and talk to Daddy.' Desy's face locked into a stony disposition. 'Right. Now.'

'There's another elephant we're not addressing here, kid.' Morse removed his glove. 'If the collateral is owned by your family, then whoever hired us...'

'I don't want to think about it, please,' Desy suddenly begged.

Rake leaned up and hugged her close.

'Just get me home. Please. I need to know what the... heck is going on.'

'And that's where *we* come in,' Rake said in her ear, jumping up and into the pilot's seat, spinning around to face the console. 'We're gonna put you back in place and finish what we started. That's the Morse and Rake guarantee.' She twisted a handle, which elicited a deep, dark growl from below. 'Strap in!'

'Yeah, that android is emotionally unstable,' Morse remarked. 'Not that androids really feel emotions; it just thinks it does…' He shrugged and made his way towards his workshop. 'Eh, it's complicated. But I can't vouch for the stability of that android around your father.'

'Daddy,' Desy muttered, eyes beginning to bulge.

'Once he's secure, we'll leave you alone. Then the collateral goes back to the client.'

Desy eyed the sicorum hutch travelling from Morse's hand to his jacket pocket, eyeing it until he disappeared from the cockpit and the door slid shut behind him.

'One of the main tenets of being a professional, Dee,' Rake chittered, buckling the teen in then snagging the steering wheel, 'is that you clean up your own messes. So, we could just dump you on ya front doorstep and let you and yaself fight it out. Let the police take care of it. But since we don't like the pigs, and that would be a *literal* cop-out…'

'Boo,' called Morse from the workshop.

'…we're gonna get that dumb android!'

She wrangled the console. And *Ferguson* burst from his frosty cocoon. He lifted into the swirling snow and above the clouds, his landing ramp snapping shut as he turned away from the sky-filling Funny Man.

'Oh, it feels so *good* to have all the info for once.'

'Where're we going?' Desy asked, grabbing the armrests.

'Somewhere nice and quiet. Someplace where we're gonna make a plan.' Rake grinned. 'Let's see: we've got Dee with us, the android pretending to be Dee, and one Daddy who is none the wiser his daughter's been kidnapped.'

Desy found herself smiling. 'That's… really familiar.'

'Feels like we've been here before, right? Which means, Dee, you're just as experienced as us with this situation. Wanna help us plan our revenge?'

Desy thought of the Arthrods, Bronzework, the cavern, her android copy, and, finally, the nebula world.

She grinned back at Rake. 'Oh, you betcha.'

SIXTEEN
The Switch

Ernest offered the current sitting commissioner of the North-East Spiral a smile but included a firm tapping of his thumbs against each other while his fingers locked together. 'I do not want the *Induction* in my planet-space,' he demanded of the hologram in English. 'I accept the police protection. However, I would much prefer the squadron employed to be one that colours between the lines. No visitors should see that thing when coming to my planet.'

The commissioner responded in turn, using his hands.

Ernest, a statue, intensified his gaze. 'I understand Governor Trupeal runs the most fruitful rehabilitation program for her prisoners.'

The commissioner continued to talk, albeit with less conviction than before.

'I understand that Captain Gold Bayleaf is one of the most respected officers in the UGIP.' Ernest projected his percolating annoyance as a breath funnelled through his nose. 'And I do not want a "suicide squad" factory in my planet-space. Is that clear?'

The android overheard this conversation from behind a stone column outside Ernest's office. Once it heard Ernest say, 'Thank you and goodbye,' it stepped out from behind the pillar and walked to the doorframe, where it spotted Ernest letting out a sigh. It knocked on the marble.

'Cricket,' Ernest sang in UBL, standing up from his desk. 'Did you like the new window I put in your room?'

What was once a plain dormer window overlooking a balcony, which the fake Desy had smashed through three nights ago, had been replaced with a pane resembling a three-striped kaloogie. The winged insect with long, curving mandibles sparkled, made of speckled glass, sitting on top of a moss-green background. When the sun beamed through it, the pale room ripened to an emerald sheen.

'I love it,' the android had said when it'd placed its hand on the glass.

I hate green, it thought, now. Followed by, *I am Desy, and I love green*.

'I really appreciate it, Daddy,' she said. 'Um, did you want to do something?'

'Of course, anything. I've already cancelled the day.' Ernest bustled around his desk. 'I was just cleaning up some last scraps of garbage.'

The android giggled. 'I'd like to find some insects with you.'

Ernest smiled and clapped his hands. 'Then I'll get into something more casual,' he said, eyes darting down to his hot-hued, feather-patterned robe. He trotted off to his bedroom, weaving through the twelve pillars that centred the hallway connecting it to his office.

Once Ernest was out of sight, the android waggled its arms like a penguin, giddy and unable to control the delighted squeal erupting from its voice box.

It had mentioned the incredible heat of the Shipyard. It told Ernest of Hawkies that accosted it with guns. The laughter of Felinguielles who clawed at its clothing. Cannots throwing food at it for fun. Being attacked by Arthrods, so Morse and Rake hurled it into a cage and threatened it into silence. The two middlemen meeting with Bronzework on Moody Moody and the Arthrods attacking the good police trying to save it. Being yanked back and forth on Brosteni. The terrifying leap it made from the bike to land in the police's arms.

Ernest had held his 'daughter' all the while, stroking its hair. He distracted it with activities they were going to do that day.

The android's flame, after three days of violent eruptions, had finally simmered to a smoulder.

However, an incoming transmission from Squishy was the lance threading the gap in its armour. Silver Fingers breathed in no air, then exhaled no air, then spoke in its head, 'What is it, Squishy?'

'Sister. The hive is anxious for orders,' Squishy relayed, with the sounds of twenty Arthrods buzzing in agreement.

'Don't worry, I haven't forgotten.'

The sight of Docile and his squad kneeling in the cavern seeped out of its memory banks.

'We need to locate Docile and the others,' ordered Silver Fingers.

Stop! What are you doing? This isn't Desy!

The android seized and twisted, clasping its head. What it told itself was pain rattled from its cranium and into the motor located in its abdomen.

This is necessary. But Desy doesn't know Arthrods. Desy didn't kill. But I am... I'm...

Squishy distracted Silver Fingers with, 'Sister, their location is the *Induction*. What are your orders?'

Relax, Desy, thought the android. *You're back with Daddy now.* It smiled, shaking away the pain. *You can take your time.* To Squishy, it ordered, 'You are to hold until further instruction.' It lied, 'I am planning their escape.'

'Of course, Sister.'

'And what of the fake?'

'We intercepted a police report, Sister.' An Arthrod computer bubbled and moaned in the background. 'There was a secondary chase involving Bronzework and Morse and Rake.'

The android's motor oscillated at a quicker pace.

'They reported only two people leaving Promethia on a hover-bike. Those two people were identified as Morse and Rake.'

Silver Fingers cackled. It held its hands to its head. Then, it substituted the cackle for a sensible laugh. 'Very good,' it said to Squishy. 'I will contact you as soon as I can regarding Docile.'

'Of course, Sister.'

With the Arthrod disconnected from its head, the android began its jovial walk, skipping on occasion, past the columns and towards Ernest's bedroom. It raised its fist to knock on the door when suddenly, a booming voice startled it into jumping back.

'Who's ready for some exploring?' bellowed Ernest, the bedroom door opening to reveal him sporting khaki shorts cut above the knee, a fancy leather belt, and a polo shirt stretched over his gut. On his head was an old-world pith helmet. His black socks were two inches too high on his hairy legs. The hiking boots were more akin to clown shoes.

The android's mouth hung open, but its eyebrows quickly touched, its belly beginning to rattle before it was overcome by giggles. 'Oh, Daddy, that's *awful*,' it hooted.

'That's because I forgot my net,' Ernest proclaimed, dramatically looking about, only to then waddle back into his bedroom.

'Stop, stop,' the android laughed, water starting to emerge from its 'tear ducts'.

'Onwards, little Cricket! The backyard awaits!'

The android shoved its way through its father's bedroom, guffawing. 'Daddy, seriously, stop. This is so embarrassing.'

Three minutes later, the hedges were inspected by the security team. The Olympic-swimming-pool-sized water feature, fish pond, and aquatic plant greenhouse were declared clear. The willows lining the artificial lake were shaken. Sixteen members of security lined the walls of the first area of the garden while the entrances to the second, third, and fourth areas were sealed off until otherwise needed.

The backyard was ready for father and 'daughter'.

The android fluttered down the marble steps and onto the grass, where it promptly kicked off its shoes. It understood that the red blades were touching the soles of its feet, so it lied to itself, *Sooooo soft!* Its vision then zoomed in on an eight-winged dragonfly, which paused in place on a willow-reed leaf, inches above the water of the backyard pond.

'Spot anything, Crick–'

'Shh,' the android sniped playfully, finger to its lips. It gestured to the pond with the hand that held the bug-catching net. Then, after a pat on the back from Ernest, it crouched and duck-walked across the grass. It spun the net in its fingers until it was within arm's reach of the dragonfly.

The bug-catching net lowered to meet the back of the insect's large, multifaceted eyes.

The android stabbed a button and a small laser shot from the net, encasing the dragonfly in a zero-gravity ball. The insect flailed its eight sets of wings, with no success.

'Outstanding,' cheered Ernest, rushing over to his 'daughter'. 'And what is this one, Cricket?'

The android thought for a second before replying, 'Peter's Alisanisoctigenti!' It squished the net into its shorts pocket and clasped the zero-gravity ball, turning it over. 'See, see, you know it's a Peter's because of the white stripe that runs from the labium to the basal plate.'

'Oh, on its belly. I see, very interesting indeed.' Ernest maintained a foot of space between himself and the insect.

'I really love dragonflies,' the android lied perkily.

'I know your favourites are kaloogies.' Ernest tipped his pith helmet up, squinting through the orange afternoon sunlight to the rigorously trimmed crimson-leafed hedges.

'They're beginning to migrate for the season, but…' The android nestled the antigravity ball on the reed leaf and hit the button on the net.

The dragonfly zig-zagged away, skimming the water's surface.

'Your turn, Daddy.' The android playfully drummed on Ernest's back. It then pointed out, in a nearby garden bed, on a gladiolus flower's petal, a Grande Pious. The honey juggernaut buzzed like a lawnmower. Its weight drooped the stem of the flower so the petals touched the soil. 'Ooh, that's a cute guy. He's from the hive near the lake.'

Ernest quivered in his explorer's gear. 'Cricket. I must remind you, as I always do, your father is not as confident as you are when it comes to bugs.'

The android beckoned him to crouching with it. It grinned and whispered, 'Just walk slowly and quietly, Daddy. And when you can see its stinger, that's when you use the net.' It noticed Ernest's lip twitch at the mention of the word 'stinger' and added, 'Grande Pious have no predators 'cause they're big. They're, like, the slowest insects ever discovered. You got this, Dad!'

'O-Okay, if you say so, Cricket.' Ernest swallowed. He started his own duck-walk over to the flowerbed. The android stifled a giggle at its father's resemblance to a distressed bear.

Then, for a microsecond, it detected an unknown signal connecting to its ocular cameras.

Then, after a microsecond, the connection was cut.

The android fell onto its haunches with a quiet thud. Ernest frantically turned over his shoulder with a finger mangling his lips. The android gave a thumbs up, smiling.

Its mind shrieked, *What was that, what was that, what was that, what was that, what was that?*

Suddenly, a foghorn blared across the entire Wintall estate. Security members turned to each other, the reticles in front of their eyes lighting up with images of a triangular-shaped cruiser with a hole in its wing racing through the atmosphere.

Ernest and Desy were immediately surrounded by four guards each.

To Ernest, a Cannot explained, 'Sir, police have detected Morse's ship entering the planet-space. They're heading straight towards us.'

'Activate the towers,' Ernest commanded. Then, above his wall of guards, he yelled as gently as he could, 'Desy, just like we practised. Okay?'

The android whimpered, 'Practised…?'

'Let the security take you to the safe room, Cricket. They'll be taking me through another route. Remember? I'll see you soon.' Ernest rushed towards the manor.

'Daddy,' cried the android, only for its own security to start ushering it away from Ernest and onto a garden path.

Two other packs of security 'shielded' their own 'wards' and split up, each heading into a different entrance of the manor.

The android saw in the sky and felt in the ground two eighty-foot-long cannons erupt outside the walls. They spun on their axes to face a shimmering triangle in the distance. It yelped and covered its ears when the turrets loosed thick, boiling lasers from their barrels, burning the sky red with a crack of thunder.

The last thing the android saw before being coerced through a side entrance to the manor was a triangular cruiser flashing behind the moon rock gifted to Desy on her fourteenth birthday. Two cannon shots obliterated the boulder to dust and smoke.

Then, as it entered a foyer, it was deafened by the sound of a jet engine, a scream that was racing towards it at max speed. But a terrific explosion rumbled the entire state and shook the android to the floor.

Ferguson had been shot out of the sky, blown apart like a firework.

The android began to hyperventilate rather than simulate the action of its own accord. Three sets of hands brought it to its feet, and the foyer soon transformed into an 'I'-shaped hallway that housed twelve guest bedrooms on either side. It stumbled to the end of the hallway, turning down the left exit and descending a round staircase that led to a plateau. Passing the seven mounted kills arranged from smallest to largest, Savannah Drago to Desolate Boar-Bear, the android and its security hustled down another flight of stairs.

Through one more hallway was the recreation room. Between two pinball machines, an analogue specimen that Desy had accidentally broken the flaps of when she was a child by pushing too hard, and a holographic specimen Desy had also broken as a child but in a whirlwind of rage was a sliding panel activated either by Desy or Ernest's handprint. A tight tunnel would then lead into a compact safe room with two exits. The other exit led into the dining area.

However, the panel spat an error at the android's touch.

'What is it, Miss Wintall?' asked a Felinguielle.

'I dunno.' The android quivered, pressing its hand again and again on the panel, receiving a short, sharp buzz each time. 'The handprint reader is broken.'

At that moment, a door at the other end of the recreation room burst open. A woman with bobbed brunette hair and a Narnit without his wings landed in the centre of the room. Around the Narnit's shoulder was a satchel, which he reached into to produce a stun baton, the standard issue every android owner received with their licence. One shock would fry the android's battery.

'Hello, again,' Morse and Rake said in unison to the android.

As the four members of security withdrew their pistols in slow motion, and as Morse and Rake sprinted behind the cover of a pool table and arcade machine respectively, the android's fire grew.

It thought of the hag, Silver Fingers, screaming in its face.

The fire grew.

Its memory of Ernest tucking it into bed evaporated.

The fire grew.

It recalled the sight of Morse and Rake, the days on end standing in a closet.

The fire grew.

Its belly buckled with the fear of dying.

Its emotions thrashed against each other.

And the fire exploded.

The switch had been flicked. The android screamed. Eyes bulging and mouth wide, it started to shove away its security.

'Miss, stay back,' blurted a Hawkie, using a wing to press his ward behind him.

However, the android gripped the falcon by the neck and whipped his entire body around to smash him into the wall. 'Don't touch me!' It slammed its other hand into his throat, crushing his windpipe. 'I'm going to die!'

'That's an android!' shouted Morse to the other security members.

Two kept their guns trained on the pool table and arcade machine while the remaining member grabbed the android's arms. It was like pulling against the arms of a crane.

'Miss, stop, stop,' one of them yelled.

The android loosed a high-pitched wail.

'That isn't Desy Wintall,' Morse bellowed. 'I've got a stun baton. I can stop it!'

Then, from behind the arcade machine, two clicks and a double-click sounded. Immediately, a blaster shot from Morse and one from Rake nailed the hands of the security, making them cry out and drop their weapons.

Morse crawled out from under the pool table and ran towards the android, stun baton crackling. And the android, its grip turning the Hawkie purple, cranked its head a perfect one-eighty to face him. It let go of the falcon, whirred its body around to meet its head, and sprinted towards him.

Morse yelped in surprise and thrust the baton at the imposter, who reached beyond it and crushed his wrist, making him howl. The android twisted the baton towards his chest and slammed its hand into his throat.

However, a radio call came through the headset of the Hawkie gasping for breath against the wall. 'We have a situation in the dining place,' came an annoyed tone.

The android's face snapped from irate to horrified. 'Daddy...' it whimpered.

Out of the corner of its eye, it spotted Rake roll out from behind the arcade machine with her pistol-barrel rising to meet its head. 'Don't kill me!' it cried. It let go of Morse and fled the recreation room, the stunned security hearing its footsteps thundering then thumping then thudding further into the manor.

The android bounded through the hallways, barging through every door it could see, invading guest bedrooms, closets, bathrooms, maintenance. Its emotions were too big and volatile; its chassis seemed to groan from the effort of containing them. The fire burned white. *They're here to take me away,* it yelled in its mind. *I won't go. I won't be kidnapped by them again. I just want Daddy. Please, don't let anything bad happen to him. Not again. I will never be separated from him again!*

After the tenth instance of smashing through a door, it found itself sliding across the marble floor of the main foyer. It whinnied with delight. 'I know where I am! This is close to where I had that delicious dinner and ice cream and laughed about all of Daddy's garbage guests!' Then, as it galloped towards the ornate double doors of the dining room, it giggled. 'That's rude, Desy. Gotta be polite, Desy. I love insects. I love politeness. I love Daddy!'

It crashed into the dining area. 'Daddy?' it cried out. 'Are you here? What's happened...'

At the far end of the room, at the end of the fifty-foot-long wooden table, was Ernest. His security had their pistols drawn on a figure ten feet away that had its hands up. A short figure, with raven hair and red eyes, wearing the outfit Rake had helped it choose all the way back at the Shipyard.

Desy Wintall turned her head to face her double. The initial widening of her eyes and twisting of her jaw at seeing herself faded quickly, to be slowly replaced by the most smarmy, squinty-eyed, closed-lip grin to ever have been carved on a Human countenance.

Twenty minutes earlier...

'What is this place?' Desy asked, peering down *Ferguson*'s landing ramp to the steel opening of what appeared to be a factory. Cracked smokestacks were faded in the distance, sprouting from crumpled tin roofs and brick walls.

Morse appeared next to her with a box containing ballet pointe shoes, a holo-photo frame, a crowbar, a handmade paper book, and a six-pack of empty beer bottles.

Bishop, Morse's sentient cactus, barked from inside the box, 'What is with all this moving? We just moved homes. What is with *all this* moving?'

'Bishop, you need to hold down the fort on this stuff while we're gone, all right?' Morse said to the plant.

'I will kill anyone who comes near,' the cactus screamed.

'Sure you will, buddy, sure you will.'

Desy watched Morse jog inside the factory and out of sight. She turned over her shoulder to Rake, who was sifting through a crate labelled *Sensitive Materials. Use Extreme Caution When Handling.* 'Where are we?' she asked again.

Rake muttered, pulling out a sack of white powder and a long shoelace and resting them on the floor, 'A good question, Dee. For another time. Speaking of, *I've* got one for ya.' She withdrew a pin from the box, turned it in her fingers, then put it back in the box. 'Your security. They've gotta have some emergency plans, right?'

'Like, if Daddy and I got attacked?' Desy asked, crouching next to Rake.

Rake said firmly, 'Back,' waited for her to shuffle away, then nodded. 'Yep.'

'Daddy's office has a lockdown function in case of emergencies. So does my room.'

'Nah, a proper safe room is underground, right? Both of ya rooms are on the top floor.'

Desy clapped her hands. 'Oh, we do have that. Yes.'

'So, when ya get attacked on the ground floor, I kinda imagine ya do the whole "split you and Daddy up with decoys" routine.'

Desy frowned. 'Why do you know that?'

Rake giggled. ''Cause I'm a smarty-pants. Also, that's pretty standard for rich folk. Or important folk. Me and Morse have seen it done before. It's common practice, though, 'cause it works. How does the sayin' go? You lose two rabbits, you chase them both, or something?'

'So, like… I mean, does your plan have something to do with that, um, procedure?'

Rake withdrew another pin and examined it. 'I figure, why go to the trouble of separatin' the android from ya daddy when we can let your security do it for us?' She placed the pin by the sack of white powder. 'Then you run inside and meet up with Daddy on his route, and we snag the android on its route.'

'We *do* have our set paths to the safe room,' Desy recalled. 'Um, Daddy makes me do a run-through of the drill the first weekend of… I think every month. I forget all the time.'

'Perfect. When Morse gets back, ya gonna wanna point all that out on a map of your house.'

Desy clasped her elbows. 'How do you have that?'

'Trade secret.'

Five minutes later, Rake rolled out the blueprint of Wintall Manor on the bench in Morse's workshop. Desy's elbows had remained clasped. She listened and answered Rake's questions about the security route and corrected Morse when he scribbled a line out of place. Eventually, Rake asked, 'Do you mind if we blow up this boulder?'

Desy noted the grey, speckled rock about the size of a large cottage nestled in the corner of the estate. 'That's my birthday rock. Daddy got it from the moon. We were meant to chisel it into something fun, but I got sick a few days later.'

Morse ignored his impulse to make a snide comment. Rake did not. 'Wanna tell me what else you do for fun? Shoot billiards with rubies and diamonds?'

'We have a pool table in the rumpus room,' Desy answered earnestly.

Morse fluffed Rake's hair. After play-biting the air and flicking her forked tongue at him, Rake said to Desy, 'We're gonna need the rock for cover from the manor's cannons. We fly in close, let the rock take the hit, and we're inside the grounds, easy. Those cannons aren't gonna shoot the property they're meant to protect. But there's no way your…' – Rake snorted – '*birthday rock* is gonna live through it.'

Desy pouted. However, she shook her head and closed her eyes, resolute. 'You had to give up your previous ship. I have to give up my birthday rock.'

'Thanks, kid.'

'Do ya have two birthday rocks, then?'

The teenager paled. 'Wait! You have to blow up *this* ship, too? You just got it.'

'Don't have a choice.' Rake shrugged. 'Ya daddy's got some *real* big guns; not enough time to fly from the rock and to ya house.' She opened a box of cigarettes, flinching when she noted the minuscule weight of it, and fished inside to find two cigarettes remaining. She sighed, putting them back and placing the box inside her robes again. 'Can't even send you off, *Fergey.*'

'I'll tell Daddy to turn off the defence systems,' Desy suggested. 'I can tell him the situation and–'

Morse interjected. 'We don't want to do anything that might make the android get funny. Think about it. If you call Wintall, and he tries to test if his daughter is really an android… well, I don't know what would happen. I only know that sentient androids act irrationally. And one of these' – Morse tapped the pistol in his pocket – 'isn't gonna do anything to it. God forbid if Ernest whips out a stun baton. We're better off getting to the android before it can even understand what's happening and frying its battery.'

Desy nodded slowly. 'That makes sense. But I don't like that you have to destroy *Ferguson.*'

'We got all the important stuff off,' Rake said. 'Whaddya gonna do?'

'But the collateral is with us,' Morse added. 'So that's the next part of the plan to sort out. We need to drop this off in a town called Mortian Hill.'

'That's north of Hingspock,' Desy piped up.

'I was thinkin' you could buy a cruiser over the phone and have it waiting for us at the drop-off point.' Rake poked her own cheek with a finger. 'Also, we'll need to borrow the family sedan for a bit.'

'Anything, anything,' Desy exclaimed, clapping her hands lightly.

Morse scribbled the last paragraph of the plan in the corner of the blueprint. And *Ferguson* made his last interstellar jump a minute later. He slipped as a shadow from the system's sun to the dark side of Yeti's moon.

'This place is too hot,' whispered Rake, face tense with creases, eyes darting about the windshield to the pockmarked surface below. She eased *Ferguson's* engines to a state just above stalling with her attention focused on the radar.

Next to her, Desy typed a number into Morse's phone. 'Hello, it's me, Desy Wintall,' she said in a bubbly tone. 'No, you haven't done something wrong… I would like a cruiser, thank you… For me… That sounds cool… Can it do… um, jumps?… Yes, those ones… I would like one that does jumps, then.'

Rake's right leg bounced at a metal drummer's pace. It froze when Desy's tone darkened, and she threatened, 'Do I need to get Daddy on the phone?'

Rake stifled a laugh with her hands, lacing Desy with an approving grin.

'Good. I want it at Iustitia Park now.' She smiled with closed eyes. 'You're welcome for *my* time.'

Once Desy hung up, Rake heard Morse call from his workshop, 'Seriously, Rake? What have you done to the kid?'

'She's *always* been like that, Morse.'

Desy unbuckled herself from the copilot's chair. She muttered, 'That felt gross.' Then she said to Rake, 'Can I get changed in your room?'

'Huh, whah. Why?'

'I want to keep the clothes you got for me at the, um, black market.'

Rake felt needles prick her tear ducts. So she scowled and barked, 'Fine, but if you take too long and mess up *my* plan, you're gonna be sorry.'

Desy suddenly felt Morse push his finger into her ear. She quivered and turned over her shoulder and stammered, 'H-Hey. Excuse me, please say something first.'

'Oh, sorry,' Morse said, deadpan. 'These are the last transceivers I've got, kid. In case we need to make stuff up on the fly.'

'Kinda don't trust our luck right now,' Rake grumbled. After scrubbing her eyes with an arm, she curled her bangs behind an ear and inserted a transceiver. She flicked on the mic. 'Comms check.'

'Copy,' Morse, then Desy, replied.

'Go get changed. Now,' Morse ordered.

Desy hurried out of the cockpit.

'Meet me in the workshop when you're done, kid,' Morse said in her ear. 'The plan is entirely dependent on whether or not your father and the android are in the right place at the manor. I know the android's identification code and proxy.'

'Okay,' Desy replied, removing her coat and shirt, then scrambling through Rake's wardrobe for the other coat, the long-sleeve top and the high-waisted dress pants.

'I'll connect to its eyes for a split second. And you have to tell us where the android is based on what turns up. Either the backyard, garage or guests' lodge is what we're looking for.' Morse's tone lowered. 'Can you do that?'

'Y-Yes.'

'Can you do that?'

Desy pulled on the boots and boasted, 'Yes. And I'm coming now.'

'Good.' Morse's fanged smile seemed to project through the transceiver. 'Rake. You got the brake cut set up?'

'Did you measure out three seconds?'

'Measured twice and cut once.'

'Just lemme know when to start goin'. Bike ready?'

'Switched on.'

As soon as Morse finished his sentence, Desy jumped into his workshop and stood behind him; he was at a small desk beside a giant bench with tools sprawled across the wall behind it. In front of him was a large screen with a few lines of code taking up a third of the black void. A satchel was slung over his shoulder, ruptured with wires, tools, and four stun batons. His right index finger trembled above the 'Y' key on his keyboard. His left middle finger hovered above the 'Esc' key.

'It's time to go, kid. Get ready to hold on to something. No time to strap you down into a chair.'

Desy clutched her elbows. However, she forcibly crushed her hands into fists and curled her biceps by her sides.

She was not going to hesitate anymore.

'Okay.' She nodded.

'Rake, we may go in three... two... one.'

He stabbed twice on the keyboard. Like a camera flash, the workshop lit up, and a snapshot of red hedges, a large pond, and Ernest's behind burned into Desy's head.

'They're in the backyard,' she cried.

'Go, Rake, go,' Morse belted, sprinting away from the screen, snagging Desy and pinning her to the doorframe.

His knuckles whitened when Rake shouted, 'Hold on!' and *Ferguson* became a paint shaker. The tools in the workshop clanged painfully and incessantly.

'UGIP have found us,' called Rake.

Ferguson roared.

'Coming up on the manor now.'

Desy heard Morse whisper through his teeth, 'Come on, come on, Rake.'

Two blazing trains screamed either side of *Ferguson*, twisted metal being amplified to an ear-rupturing degree. Then the entire world whiplashed, tools splattered to the ground from the walls, and the computer monitor shattered.

An explosion from outside soon followed, and *Ferguson*'s shields hissed from an assault of thousands of pieces of moon rock.

'Bike, bike, bike!' Rake screeched, shutting the shields down.

Desy felt herself being yanked out of the workshop and into the cockpit, where Rake had her hand jammed underneath the console. Through the windshield was a torrent of grey dust and smoke, with the shadow of a British-style manor and the silhouettes of two giant pistols either side of it fading into view.

Ferguson's engines screamed, but the handbrake was locked into position.

Morse leaped onto the dented hover-bike, activated the landing ramp, and revved the engine. Desy clasped on to him. And, as if she teleported, Rake suddenly appeared to crush Desy into Morse's back. 'We gotta *go*,' she yelled.

'Duck!' Morse commanded, launching them all forward.

The fuse, connected to the explosives attached to the brake line, reached its destination.

The instant the bike left the landing ramp to land on the vanilla dirt, *Ferguson* exploded in an exponential curve to the heavens. The sheer velocity pulled the hover-bike into the air and flipped it erratically. Dust spewed in all directions.

Morse wrestled the handlebars so they bounced, right side up, towards the walls of the manor, just in time to watch the twin cannons snap to *Ferguson*.

'We'll toast to ya later, ya bastard!' Rake shouted as the sky was soaked red and the triangular ship was torn apart in a cataclysmic fire.

Unbeknownst to Morse, a little hand had reached inside his jacket pocket as he piloted the bike over the wall. While Rake blinked sadly up at *Ferguson*, its fingers felt for the sicorum hutch, for the collateral, and slipped the box into Desy's own coat pocket.

Morse guided the bike into the grounds and skidded behind a tree by the front entrance of the manor. 'See you around, kid.' He jumped onto the grass.

Desy fumbled from the bike. 'I didn't know you were saying goodbye now!'

'You've got a job to do,' Morse yelled back, sprinting away with Rake.

Rake assured her with a soft tone in her ear, 'Gotta do the job first, Dee. We'll talk later.'

'A-All right,' she stammered, running up to the individually carved stone steps that led to the house-tall front doors of her home.

She was unaware that Morse and Rake had switched their microphones off and that Morse had panted, while diving through a hedge, 'That was close.'

'I was gonna lose it,' Rake said in an uneven tone.

Desy called out her own name, which caused the decorated panels before her to part slowly. She squeezed her way through to the main foyer, which fed into each segment of the manor. To the left was a grand carpeted staircase. To the right was the reception desk. Five servants who were about to jam a door shut behind the front desk yelled, 'Miss Wintall?' in alarm. She saw them beckoning to her from the corner of her eye but kept her vision square on the doors to the dining room straight ahead. Sucking in a breath, she braced herself and smacked up against the doors.

She fell flat on her face onto the dining room carpet.

'Cricket?' called a deep voice.

Desy quivered all over. She lifted her head, seeing through her messy, unkempt bangs, through the hundreds of wooden legs parked at the dining table, and at the end of it all was a pair of gaudy hiking boots surrounded by black work shoes. Her heart beat out of sync. She paled and felt hollow, but a burst of joy saw her spring to her feet and stumble-run around the dining table.

Ernest's arms parted the security wall, and he rolled his elbows towards himself. His concerned features, the way he held himself and moved... Desy felt tears dribbling down her cheeks. Her nose released a line of snot. She jumped, sobbing, into her father's arms.

His scent washed over her.

'What happened to your security team?' Ernest asked.

The security guards drew their weapons and had each exit focused. They moved as a phalanx, shielding father and daughter and nudging them towards a handprint panel on the back wall.

Desy simply cried and cried, unable to stop smiling.

Ernest then noticed the long-sleeve top, coat, dress pants, and boots. 'Cricket,' he said, bewildered. 'You've changed?'

She looked up at him, eyes aged and wet. 'Yes, Daddy. I have.'

'We have a situation in the dining place,' barked a Human into their earpiece.

There was a deluge of high-pitched responses.

Suddenly, Desy felt herself clutched by several pairs of hands and thrown out of the huddle. Then four guns were pointed at her.

'What are you fools doing?' Ernest spat.

'Sir, the other team just lost Desy in the rec room. There's an android on the estate that looks like your daughter.'

Ernest's face recoiled. 'Are you *daft*? Your pistols will not affect an android at all! And if you think you can hold *my* daughter at gunpoint–'

'Daddy,' blurted Desy. She raised her hands in surrender, calmly, with a sanguine expression. 'It's okay. They're just doing their job.'

'Kid,' shouted Morse in her ear. 'Android's running amok. We're right behind it.'

She heard Rake shrieking in the background. 'Did that thing *look* like Dee to you, you idiots!? Follow us and protect Dee, that's your job, huh?'

Desy stifled her sniffles. Her red eyes started to dry.

'Do not aim a gun at my daughter,' Ernest seethed.

'Sir, it's for your own safety–'

'To hell with my safety.'

'It's protocol–'

'To *hell* with your protocol.'

'Dad!' Desy suddenly growled through her teeth.

Ernest's tense arms and face released. With wide eyes and deep wrinkles in his cheeks, in disbelief, he muttered, 'What was that tone, young lady?'

Desy frowned. 'Don't worry about me.'

And the doors to the dining hall burst open.

'Daddy?' called the android. 'Are you here? What's happened…'

Silence reigned. The security team balked. Ernest was stuck in a loop of pointing at Desy then pointing at 'Desy'.

Upon seeing the teenager breathing, alive, what sounded like the clicking of a light switch shot out from Silver Fingers.

The real Desy, after withdrawing her smirk, simply whispered into her transceiver, 'It's in the dining hall.'

The android at the end of the room could be seen shivering. Its face, Desy's, pulled and pushed with turgid twitches. Its eyes quivered until they opened big. Its jaw rattled and rattled, sounding like dice rolling down a footpath as its hands rippled themselves into its raven hair. 'What are you doing *here?!*' it screamed with Desy's voice.

Ernest muttered, 'My god.'

'Get out of *my house!*' the android squealed. It flung its arms about. 'You're dead! You're dead! You can't be *here!* You're ruining it!'

The four members of security, slack-jawed, directed their pistols away from Desy and aimed them at the spasming 'teenager' at the end of the room.

'Leave!' it shrieked. It stomped its feet, which rumbled the floorboards. 'Leave! LeEEEEeeeEEeeEEave!' The speaker in its throat distorted under the volume, its pitch skyrocketing to a whistle then plummeting to a monstrous bellow. Its face, contorting from grief to rage to misery to elation, locked on to Ernest. 'Daddy. Th-That's a *fake* me! *Listen!*'

Ernest lurched for his daughter and pulled her close.

That action punched the android in the gut. 'NoooOOOOoo, don't be *fooled...*' It droned a distorted, bit-crushed tone as it began to writhe on the spot.

'Stay back!' ordered security, stepping in to block father and daughter from view.

'Guys, it's going weird,' cried Desy into the transceiver.

And, on cue, Morse and Rake burst through the doors from the right-hand side of the room, brandishing a stun baton and pistol respectively, with three members of security behind them.

The android whipped around to Morse and Rake. It saw them recoil, horror evident in their bodies. 'YooOOoooUUUUuuu did this,' it drawled in a mangled interpretation of Desy's voice and face. It threw a finger towards the teenager behind the wall of security. 'Get *away* from my *DaddyyyYYYYyyyyy!*'

A horrendous, metallic gurgling emanated from the android to fill the room to bursting, as its figure started to warp, elongate and swell.

SEVENTEEN
Overclock

Yeti arrived late to the game of producing androids with artificial intelligence. The Artificial Intelligence Regulation Authority rigorously tested the character and stability of civilisations before approving them and granting them a licence to house 'objects' that could think for themselves. A context-dependent trial period was carried out if an approved civilisation requested permission to begin producing its own androids.

Ernest had made such a request at the age of twenty-five, and after pleasing the AIRA for twenty years, he had made Yeti a prominent distributor of androids in the stellar quadrant for the last ten years.

Silver Fingers' skin prickled and whined.

Each android was equipped with a customisable chassis and a height range of four to nine feet, with the main physical characteristics of most discovered races built inside. You simply asked your android to change itself to your liking.

This android's left leg elongated suddenly, throwing it off balance, a wet, tearing sound emanating from its knee. Ladders of flesh pulled away to reveal a chrome underbelly.

It was not feasible to include every feature of the AIRA's catalogue of races inside the chassis. A sample plate, however, was included with each android so a prospective buyer could see most physical traits before they purchased them.

A left Narnit wing erupted from the android's back with a splatter of skin. Its ribcage widened, which tautened Desy's dress to splitting. Its neck twisted and lengthened, snapping the flesh at its collarbone.

Its arms twitched, and a sample of the back spines from each Skaltrene subspecies rose from its forearms in rings, shredding its skin suit like buzzsaws. Felinguielle claws burst from its left hand with enough force to throw it to the side. It clasped the table just as a Cannot hind leg wormed its way out of its right femur, which obliterated Desy's shorts, twisting to a crooked angle, giving it two right legs.

Seventy-two races and counting.

Just as a right Hawkie wing tore through its shoulder blade, Felinguielle, Cannot, and Skaltrene tails unhooked internally from the back of its neck, falling then pushing for space through the gap made by its wings. The tails' combined weight unzipped the remaining flesh from its back as they fell like pots and pans to the floor. By now, its spine had elongated to its maximum height and severed its skin suit at the belly button, which now draped as curtains across its plating.

From a five-foot-one Human to a nine-foot-even amalgamation in three seconds. Its face remained Desy's, albeit with violent spasms of its eyes, eyebrows, and mouth.

During the process, its voice box screamed from a male voice back to Desy's to a Skaltrene hiss, 'You *fake!* Do you *know* who I am?! I'm… I'm… *Desy!*'

Rake whimpered, 'Morse, what's happening?'

The bat-man's jaw was too stiff to move.

'Shoot that thing!' Ernest blurted while pulling Desy behind him.

'Sir, you said it's impervious–'

'Do *something!*' he yelped.

'NooOOooOOoooo, stop fOOOOOooling my Daddy!' the android growled at Desy, elongating its neck forward until it cracked.

The sound of the security team arming their pistols, a high-pitched whine, caused the android to snap into a mangled ball. 'Don't hurt me,' it whimpered, twisting on its three legs to Morse and Rake and the three security around them.

Their guns were not primed.

Morse spun the stun baton like a tennis racquet.

The android sprang at him, squealing incomprehensibly.

Morse grunted in fright and ducked so the ball of skin, metal, and tails only clipped his shoulder. He was still slammed into the floor from the impact.

The security team and Rake fell to the side, allowing the android to haggardly cry itself out of the room and towards a door on all fives.

Its footfalls sounded as *bom-bom-bom-clach,* looping until it wailed and splintered through the wood and disappeared from view.

'Sir. You and Miss Wintall need to enter the safe room immediately,' a security member ordered.

Ernest snapped out of his stupor and gabbled, 'Yes, of course, at once. Cricket, come, come.'

The doors at the end of the dining room burst open for the third time in two minutes. Twelve members of the UGIP piled inside with the sound of boots running through undergrowth accompanying them.

Gold Bayleaf gingerly stuck his head through the doors before he jerked his 'eyes' over to Morse and Rake.

Rake recoiled from the Kinson. She looked at the gun in her hand. She noted Morse brandishing a stun baton, the security members groaning on the floor next to him, Ernest and Desy behind a wall of security, and recoiled from each of those sights. She stammered to Gold Bayleaf, 'I-It's not what it looks like.' She grasped Morse by the collar, helping him stumble to his feet and into the hallway.

The Kinson sprinted after them and out of the room while the UGIP officers primed their pistols and followed suit.

As Ernest activated the safe room door, Desy bounced above the heads of her security, crying, 'Don't shoot them! There's an android that's going to kill us all!'

The sound of a horse galloping on an air vent paused her, Ernest, and the security team. She snapped her ears to the wall next to Ernest.

A metal pipe suddenly began to buckle, followed by the rupturing crack of a breaking tree branch.

The safe room door slid open, and Desy shoved Ernest in the back, hard, just in time for the android to lunge from the wall in a shower of marble, filling her world with white dust. She screamed and spluttered, hearing the cries of the security team as metal thumped against flesh over and over.

The silhouette of the android stomped the ground with all its limbs. All the while it was asking, 'Did I get her? Did I *get* her? *Did I get her?*'

'Desy?' called Ernest, leaning out of the sliding door.

'I'm here, Daddy,' cooed the android, slithering over to him.

'Oh, goodness.'

There was a *beep* from the handprint pad, and the sliding door clipped the android's nose as it slammed shut.

The android reeled and gnashed its teeth, turning and seeing Desy's shadow disappear through an adjoining hallway. 'Leave me *alone!*' it wailed, launching after her on all fives.

Desy heaved air out of her mouth, throat raw. Her boots slapped across carpet, then tiles, then wood. She heard the android's gallop, *bom-bom-bom-clach, bom-bom-bom-clach*, coming up behind her until she felt the rhythm through her shoes. By then, she had entered the east wing and fled into the guest housings.

Three wide hallways with twelve doors either side. Desy skidded across the carpet, rounded a corner into one such hallway, wrenched a door open, and threw herself into a darkened room that contained a simple bed and wardrobe. She slammed the door and slid under the bed, burning her stomach and wrists on the carpet.

'Don't play *games*, just *leave!*' the android screeched, muffled, outside the door.

Desy held her breath, crushing herself into a ball, lungs burning. Nausea raked the inside of her oesophagus. Ear pressed on the carpet, she could hear stomps leading away from the door and across the hallway. Then a tree broke in half. A torrent of rustling fabric followed by an angered, bit-crushed moan was next, and suddenly the light around the door to Desy's room vanished.

A hulking shadow had blackened it.

But just as quickly, the halo returned, only for a tree to be broken next door. One second later there was a thunderclap; a bed frame had been thrown against the wall.

'Dee, are ya in the safe room?' came Rake's breathy tone in her ear.

'I'm in trouble,' Desy muttered, cheeks prickling with panic.

'Are you in the safe room?'

'No.' She swallowed just as a door further down the hall was torn from its hinges. 'The android's... c-coming to... k-kill me. I'm in the guest rooms.' Desy fought the urge to break down. 'What do I do?'

'Morse, Dee's in trouble,' Rake snapped.

'We've got a problem, too,' Morse grunted. 'And we're on the top floor, kid; we barricaded ourselves in your room and activated the bulkheads.'

A megaphone in the background shouted: 'Come out with your hands up. By order of the United Galaxy's Government, you *will* surrender peacefully.'

'You idiots! There's a killer robot on the loose and ya wanna *still harass us?* Typical *pigs!*'

Desy heard Rake punch the metal bulkhead.

Across the hall, the android plunged its serrated arms through another door.

Only half the rooms were left.

Morse continued, 'I don't know what we can do.'

'We're not gonna give up,' Rake snapped.

'Never said that. I just need to think of something to help the kid.'

'I'm under a bed,' Desy whispered. 'The android's looking through all the guest rooms.'

'Our android is a standard-issue, so it can only run at an average speed,' Morse explained. 'You can get away from it. That extra limb is only going to make it slower.'

'I don't think I can run for much longer,' Desy confessed, feeling waves of heartburn.

Morse let out a frustrated sigh. 'Long shot, but is there a stun baton in there with you?'

'It's a guest room,' Desy muttered, blinking back tears.

'I know, I know.'

'Morse, there's gotta be somethin' that can take that android down, 'side from a baton,' Rake urged. 'You're the expert on robots.'

'That *thing* was built to withstand the laser cannons from *Ferguson*. It wouldn't even flinch at anything we or the cops have got.'

Desy blinked rapidly and blurted, 'Wait a sec!' She slapped her hand over her mouth, silent for two seconds, hearing a door being destroyed in the distance. 'Why was the android scared of the guns?'

'Come again, kid?'

'Back when it, um, mutated. It got really scared of the security people's pistols.'

She heard Rake snap her fingers. 'I thought that was weird.'

Morse responded, 'Kid, that doesn't change the fact that...' He trailed off. 'It kept calling you fake.'

Desy muttered, 'Uh-huh.'

'It said Ernest was its daddy. And it said to leave *its* property.'

Morse slapped his forehead so hard that it transmitted into the teen's ear.

'It thinks it's *you!*' he yelled.

'Mooooooooooorse,' Rake sang, wet with ridicule. 'You kinda programmed it like that.'

'No, no. It. *It* thinks it's *Desy*. It! Not even "thinks" – the android *is* a Human, according to itself. It *is* Desy.'

Rake mumbled, 'I gotta say, not following.'

'I have a plan,' Morse declared. 'Kid?'

'Yes?' Desy muttered, a tingle of excitement shooting up her spine, only for the feeling to turn to terror when the android thundered past and the room next to hers was invaded and subsequently trashed.

'You have to get to the rec room. You can get to the safe room from there. Once you're in, we'll lead the android to us and take it out.'

'But you've got the police after you. Nuh-uh.'

'Kid, don't be stupid–'

'The android's after *me*, guys. It's not going to stop 'til it gets me, so I'll be the bait.'

'Don't you *dare*,' Rake hissed. 'You were just sayin' you couldn't run–'

'I trust you guys!' Desy whisper-shouted. 'I don't want you getting hurt anymore for me. I don't want you to go to jail. Don't move. I'm coming to you.'

After some seconds of Morse whispering in the background, Rake responded quietly, 'Dee, your room and ya daddy's office both have bulkheads, right?'

'Uh-huh.'

'We're gonna need ya to lead the android there, apparently. 'Cause the pigs sound like they're gonna start cutting into ya room now, so we're gonna split.'

'Guys, please don't move–'

'Relax, Dee,' Rake said in her motherly tone. 'We have a plan. Morse has a plan. I can't believe Morse has a plan. For once.'

'I had to pick up the slack.'

Rake furrowed her eyebrows at him, flittering her forked tongue. 'Dee, keep talkin' to us. We're gonna lead the pigs on a goose chase, then whatever room we get to, go there.'

'Got it,' came Desy's hushed tone.

'The android's malfunctioning. You saw what it turned into; it's lost control of most of its basic skeletal functions,' Morse added. 'It's not aware of small things. Its brain is completely bogged down with fake emotions. Use that to your advantage and run as fast as you can.'

'Okay.'

Morse fiddled with a lever that had been hidden behind a boy band poster. He said to Rake, 'We hit the balcony, then we climb onto the roof.'

'Me, then you.'

Morse flashed his furry fingers, *three, two, one,* then threw the lever. Behind him, the bulkhead covering the window unveiled the kaloogie and its emerald bed.

Rake vaulted Desy's hover-bed as the bulkhead covering the door clunked into the ceiling. She rolled along her spine to her feet and sprang towards the window as Morse opened it. Sailing through, albeit smacking her heels on the top of the frame, Rake stumbled to her feet and turned around just as Morse squashed his way through the window and onto the balcony.

Gold Bayleaf had entered the room and was slithering under the hover-bed.

Morse pouched his hands between his bent legs, gripping Rake's boot and heaving from his abdomen. He felt her weight press overwhelmingly into his palm for a split second, and in the next, her legs dangled over the edge of the guttering above. He heard leaves being crushed, so he twisted around and slammed the window closed.

Gold Bayleaf plunged into the kaloogie's mandibles, coiling like a spring as the glass bent, bowed, then shattered.

'Come on, ya idiot,' Rake called, wide-eyed at the Kinson tumbling across the balcony and smacking into the stone railing. Granules of glass tumbled from the balcony to hail on the grass far below.

Morse swung his arms back and launched them skywards, legs in sync, to grab on to Rake's outstretched hand.

She squealed. He grunted, pulling up an inch higher to snag the guttering with his other hand.

Soon enough, they were clambering up the steep incline of Wintall Manor's tiled roof. Mountain crests ran as a maze across its surface. They sprinted over the precariously thin plateaus, one foot in front of the other.

Morse grunted through his transceiver, 'Where to?'

Rake pointed across the roof. 'Daddy's office.'

'You got that, kid?' Desy heard in her ear, positioned by the bedroom door. She kept her lips tight and her chest deflated. She eyed the doorknob by her arm.

A train roared up behind her through the paper-thin wall. Desy pressed her hands into her collarbone hard to keep herself from crying in fright. The metallic roar came to a climax as the wooden door was blown off its hinges and the bed was impaled by splinters.

The android scuttled into the room. It lifted the bed frame as though it were a prop and flipped it into the far wall, where it collapsed into pieces. In anger, the android reeled upright and smashed its claws into the ceiling. Then it crawled over to the wardrobe to start kicking it into pulp.

Meanwhile, hands over her mouth, Desy stepped sideways, then backwards out of the room. She ran on her toes to the end of the hallway, while saying into her transceiver, 'Y-Yes. Dad's office. I heard.'

'We're gonna keep the pigs busy, Dee,' Rake said, the sound of her blaster powering up accompanying her voice, along with rocks tumbling down a cliffside.

'Tell us *the moment* you can see Ernest's office. *The moment* you exit his room and you're in the hallway, kid.' Morse's voice was joined by the warbling of a large cruiser in the distance, which was multiplying into five, then over ten.

Desy managed, 'Okay,' before she turned the corner and slapped against a black wall.

'Miss Wintall!' gasped four members of security. 'Come with us.' They surrounded her and helped her to her feet.

She shook her head and pushed her way out of their formation. 'No, no, no, you guys get somewhere safe. I got a plan.'

'Miss Wintall, you must come with us,' one urged again.

Desy's eyes bulged, and she began to wave her arms.

And then she and the security heard *bom-bom-bom-clach,* and they turned to meet a pair of glowing eyes.

The android had bounded out of the guest room, freezing in place at the end of the hallway.

Desy's throat tightened when her own face grinned at her, twitching. It went to speak, but with a Skaltrene's elocution, which meant its Human jaw lowered six inches too far.

She and the security watched as the android purred with a gaping maw half a second out of sync with its voice box, 'I see you.'

Desy slapped her hands to her mouth and shrieked into her palms. Security drew their pistols in terror. So the android's eyebrows furrowed and its button nose sniffled while its amalgamated body twisted about. It scampered away and around the corner.

Desy started to run towards a set of double doors. A security member spluttered, 'Miss Wintall, you need to–'

'Get out of here!' she cried. 'I'm going to the safe room. Don't worry!' She ignored their yells and bashed open the doors, entering a stairwell that spiralled up towards the recreation room. With one hand on the banister, she rushed up the stairs and into a small hallway where a pool table and two pinball machines peeked at her through an open door. She ran up to the door and turned abruptly, thumping her way towards the elevator, stabbing and stabbing at the 'up' arrow.

Below her feet, a door was torn off its hinges.

And the elevator went *ding*.

Desy parted the sliding doors herself to jump inside. She pressed the button for the private quarters. Then she ducked her head out of the elevator. Her lungs quivered. Fear forced her knees to buckle. But she steadied herself with her hands, clasping the open doors to shout, 'I'm going to go hug *Daddy* now! He's *alllllllllllll mine!*'

A vocoded volcano erupted. The scream bounced off the walls of the manor, seemingly bending them, and the distinct clatter of the android steamrolling towards the spiral staircase could be heard.

Desy kept her trembling glare at the end of the hall while the elevator doors closed.

Just before they snapped shut, the android's mangled face rounded the corner.

Desy poked her tongue out at it.

And not even a second after her stomach felt weightless, she heard metal clang against metal, felt the elevator doors being twisted open below, and her own shriek thundered up at her. Then, a series of *bom-bom-bom-clachs* fled into the distance.

All was silent in the lift. Desy sank to a crouch, folding her arms over her knees and pressing her eyes into her forearms. *Remember to tell Morse and Rake. Daddy's hallway. Remember to tell Morse and Rake. Daddy's hallway.*

She whimpered.

The other me's going to be there when the doors open, she thought.

For twenty seconds, the old-fashioned elevator trembled up, and up, and up. Desy stood when she felt the trembling lessen to a vibration. All of her instincts yanked on her limbs, trying to distance her from the doors. But she stood fast with her nose brushing the metal.

The doors drifted open to the family lounge as a bell chimed.

Within a split second, happiness swept over Desy, smelling the carpet and the couches, seeing the curtains and the bench and the stools. She tasted her and Ernest's guilty pleasure: candied bran cereal.

Then something thrashed up the stairwell to the left, and Desy rocketed out of the elevator. She stumbled over thick mats, up two steps towards a sliding door at the end of the room.

'He loves *mEEEEEEeeeEEE*, not *yoUUuuuuuuuUUUuuu!*' the android screamed. It undulated its mass into the lounge. Upon seeing the back of Desy's head vanish, it trampled over the furniture and mats and began its rhythmic pursuit into a cramped hallway.

Desy's chest rippled with pain. Her thighs were hollow. Her feet were raw. She passed her room on the left, her bathroom on the right, spotting her father's bronzed mahogany door at the end of the hall. All the while, getting louder and closer to her heels was *bom-bom-bom-clach, bom-bom-bom-clach*. She grabbed the door handle and smacked her shoulder against it. Ernest's spacious room allowed her to leap to the side, the android's claws swiping the air as it tumbled into the feather-laden bed.

Gasping hoarsely from her throat, sweat pouring down her in rivers, Desy stumbled towards another door. As she threw it open and saw the giant pillars that led to her father's office, she shouted, out of breath, 'Guys! I'm there, I'm there, I'm there!'

Up on the roof, Rake and Morse were perched behind a small incline, a foot or so of a tiled hill shielding them from six UGIP officers speckled across the roof. Gold Bayleaf's twig-snaps danced around their heads. With their backs to the incline, they shimmied sideways until they met the next steep hill.

Above, thirteen police cruisers surrounded the manor, swinging through the air.

Desy's voice rang in their ears.

'Right spot?' grunted Morse.

Rake rolled her eyes up in thought, quickly saying, 'Nope, we gotta get over this roof thingy first.'

Morse leaped and pulled himself up to the plateau.

Fifty feet away, Gold Bayleaf twisted over his shoulder and spotted the bat-man, crouched, then pounced from one crest to the other. He leap-frogged across the roof, leaves scuffling across ceramic as Morse pulled Rake up to the plateau and the two ran until they overlooked the backyard below.

Three officers shuffled up on a crest to the right and shouted, 'Freeze!' pointing their blasters at the middlemen.

On their left, three more officers primed their pistols.

Gold Bayleaf clattered at the end of Morse and Rake's plateau, ten feet away.

'Put your hands up!' bellowed an officer.

Rake turned over her shoulder to exchange a nervous glance with Morse. She raised her arms.

Morse did the same. However, his arms brushed against Rake's robes. The wind was fluttering them.

'By the authority of the United Galaxy's Government,' continued the officer, 'you are under arrest for the kidnapping of Desy Wintall. You are also under suspicion for inciting violence and civil unrest as part of a terrorist organisation.'

'That old stuff?' jeered Rake, dramatically scoffing. 'That was so long ago. I also stole a doll when I was a kid, wanna charge me for–'

'Be quiet.'

Gold Bayleaf produced two sets of handcuffs from his uniform, cautiously approaching with lumbering, leafy steps.

Suddenly, Rake snapped her fingers. Morse dropped to his feet and grabbed her by the legs, lifting her up and over like he was about to pile-drive her.

'Stop!' shouted the officers.

Tumbling head-first off the roof, the moment she flipped horizontal, Rake's wings caught the wind with a *ploomph*. The sudden snag turned her into a hinge. As a result, Morse swung like a pendulum feet-first towards a huge, ornate window, letting go of Rake to smash through it, swearing as shards sliced through his clothes and skin. Falling a good fifteen feet, he slammed onto a wooden table, which bent it in half, tumbling from it and across broken glass and carpet.

Meanwhile, Morse's weight sent Rake into a series of backflips. She chortled and yelped as she flapped her arms around, eventually creating enough drag to slow her fall. She grasped onto the window ledge, yelling, 'Morse, Morse!'

The bat-man sprinted over to the window, kicked the remaining broken glass into the backyard, and hauled Rake into the room with him. Blood dripped from his legs and arms. 'Aim your pistol at the door,' he commanded.

'Excuse me,' came a stern voice from the corner of the room. An ancient Roman with a golden mask, next to a bust of a glowering man, directed its arms towards the exit of Ernest's study. 'You are not welcome here. Please leave.'

Morse and Rake directed their pistols at the door. The bat-man snarled, 'Shut up.'

'I will be forced to contact the police in that circumstance,' Aurelian replied simply.

One second later, it said, 'Oh, I see they are aware of your presence.'

'Morse, are you sure this is gonna work?' Rake snapped, slapping the handle of her pistol.

He scoffed as he did the same. 'So, you don't trust me?'

She blinked, eyes wide, then smirked. 'I always trust you.'

Desy weaved desperately around a pillar as two mismatched arms plunged into the marble and cracked it. For almost a minute, the android had been tormenting her in a cage, a drunken cat lunging at a mouse.

She whinnied and heaved herself away. On all fours, she stumbled behind another pillar. Her vision throbbed with her heartbeat. The world was darkening. Her limbs shivered and tickled.

She had managed to worm herself halfway down the hallway.

The android chortled, raged, sang, and blubbered, 'Why do you love *my daddy* so much?!' It wrenched its arms from the pillar, not a single shred of flesh left on its hands and forearms. 'Is it because you don't have your own?! *Get your own!* Not *mine!*'

Desy's stomach shuddered, and a glop of acid soaked her teeth. She cried out and sprinted for the office door. Her calves buckled with pain, slowing her escape.

From behind, the android bounded with relentless energy, *bom-bom-bom-clach, bom-bom-bom-clach.*

The office was twenty steps away. The android was ten.

Desy turned over her shoulder, seeing herself with a vulgar expression bounding on all fours. Left arm down, *bom.* Then right, *bom.* Then left leg, *bom.* Then the two right legs, *clach!*

At that moment, Desy observed the android leap three feet off the ground involuntarily. *Too much power*, she thought.

And so she ran with an idea rattling her brain.

Bom-bom-bom-clach!

The door grew before her.

Bom-bom-bom-clach!

Desy gritted her teeth, feeling silver fingers weaving through her ponytail.

Bom-bom-bom–

She ducked into a ball.

–clach!

The android launched into the air above Desy, swiping at her head with Felinguielle claws, managing to snag a clump of hair above her ponytail. However, its own body weight and momentum sent it sailing past her.

Desy felt the sickening peel of flesh and hair separating from her scalp, and she shrieked in agony. But that was all the android managed to grasp: a clump of hair. It slammed unceremoniously into the wall.

Desy howled and sprinted towards the office door, pulling it open in tears and leaping into the room.

The android bellowed in anger, then elation. 'Dead end! DEAD END! Dead EEEEeeeEEEEEnd!' it cheered, rolling over and tearing into the office.

Where it came face to face with Morse and Rake and the muzzles of their matching pistols.

'Now!' Morse shouted.

Their guns quivered and detonated.

The android's face dropped from elation to fear. Even as its chest, its chassis, absorbed the energy blasts and dispersed them harmlessly throughout its metal body, it threw its torso and legs forward as though it had been hit by a cannonball. It gaped, like all the air in its non-existent lungs had vanished. One leg twisted across two. Its neck loosened and unfurled like a fishing line. Its head thrashed around, its mouth opening wider and wider as the pupils of its eyes shrank to dots.

It cried quietly, high-pitched. Then it collapsed in a heap of tangled limbs, lying still and unmoving. An object once more.

Rake sprinted to Desy and hugged her.

Morse ran over to a bookshelf, cleared the entire top shelf with an arm, and felt around for a lever. He gripped it and clanked it into position. An alarm sounded, followed by a bulkhead slamming into place to block the broken window. The door, as well, was replaced by a bulkhead.

All the background warbling of the police cruisers disappeared. The wind stopped.

Desy touched the back of her head, which was alight with pain, feeling a prickly patch and something wet.

Rake noticed Desy's fingers and moved them aside to see the injury. She scoffed. 'Ya tougher than that.' With her gun still trained on the android, she continued, 'Morse, mind explainin' in detail what just–'

'Shh!' Morse urged, holding a finger by his head. He then unfurled his satchel and plunked it onto Ernest's broken desk. He reached into it and produced a stun baton, one of four purloined from his college's supply closet, before stepping across the carpet towards the android. He parted the torn dress with the prongs of the baton so they touched the left side of the android's chrome chest. 'We killed it.'

Rake stroked Desy's head. 'Whaddya mean? Why did the blasters stop that thing?'

Morse shook his ears. 'The android truly thinks it's a Human. And if a Human took two blaster shots to the chest, they would be...'

'Killed,' Rake finished, holding three fingers to her mouth. 'But it's an android. Don't make a difference what it *thinks* it is.'

Morse sighed, his thumb trembling over the baton's 'on' switch. 'But it doesn't think it's a Human. It *is* one. So, it had to "die" right now. It had to. If it didn't, that would be proof it isn't a Human.'

Desy sniffled, still catching her breath. 'That's... kind of really sad.'

Morse crouched, keeping the baton primed at the android's battery. He scrutinised it for about ten seconds until he parted his fangs and said, curtly, 'You're not dead.'

It remained still, eyes stuck open in shock and fear.

'You're not dead,' Morse repeated.

The android was a statue.

'Don't make me say it again.'

The porcelain surface of its eyes glistened ever so slightly. A driblet pooled against its nose.

'Your tears aren't real. Neither is your sadness.'

Jaw locked still, a little, broken voice whimpered, 'Shut up.'

'Or your anger.'

All of a sudden, the android jerked, and its limbs launched towards Morse. It wailed, 'I just want to *live!*'

Morse activated the stun baton, which sent the android into a thrashing dance. Planting the sole of his boot onto its stomach, bracing against its spasms and cries, Morse's features were unfeeling. Above the crackling air, he muttered, 'You are incapable of living.'

After ten seconds, the smell of burned copper flooded the room. The stun baton was switched off. The android was still again.

Rake simply shook her head in the silence.

Desy had forgotten to breathe. She asked, as she let all the air in her lungs tumble from her mouth, 'Is it gone? Did we do it?'

Morse fell onto his butt, letting the stun baton drift through his fingers and thump onto the carpet. 'Yeah, finally. Goddamn.'

'Goddamn,' Rake affirmed.

EIGHTEEN
AN12512

It took a minute for Morse to shift to a kneel, then to a stand, and to finally loop his fingers through the handlebars of his satchel. As though he were just setting up his tools to affix a shelf to a wall, he collectedly walked over to the smoking android, placed the satchel next to it, and crouched to reach inside the bag, knocking hammers into spanners and setting a few screwdrivers on the carpet.

Desy shimmied away from Rake. On all fours, she said, 'Why aren't you guys getting out of here?'

'Why?' Rake asked. 'We're basically in a bomb shelter, Dee. Gotta enjoy the silence while ya got it.'

'But the police?'

'The piggies are gonna have to cut through the walls. We got time.' Rake smiled at her. 'Ya did the plan. You're a natural.'

Desy felt her stomach quiver, but she smiled back.

Morse muttered, still digging through his satchel, 'How did you escape the android, kid?'

'Um, I hid behind the door.'

He snorted.

Rake howled with laughter. 'If it's stupid but it works, it ain't stupid!'

'I think it's more of a testament to how unhinged this thing was,' Morse said while he flicked the android's cheek.

'How did you guys get away from the cops?' Desy inquired.

'We flew,' Rake cooed while extending her arms.

'We fell,' Morse cooed, mockingly.

'Off the roof?' gasped Desy. She spun on her knees to a field of broken glass. 'Dad's not going to like this.' Then she turned back to Morse and gasped again. 'You're hurt.'

Morse glanced at the blood hardening on his legs. He produced a vice from his satchel and waddled forward so he straddled the android. Putting the vice between his fangs, he picked up a scalpel from the floor and made an incision at the temple.

'I've never run that hard. Ever,' Desy breathed, sinking to her stomach, face on the carpet.

'Gonna take gym more seriously from now on?' Rake asked.

A sudden *clunk* brought their focus to the android. Morse had just loosened a few screws and was in the process of twisting the vice open. With each twist, the android's face wobbled with a fleshy slap. A gap appeared from its temple and down to its chin, wider and wider.

'Um, Morse?' Desy asked.

'Yeah, kid?'

'Why did the android grow and stuff?'

Rake piped up with, 'I was gonna ask the same thing.'

He shrugged. 'Sometimes, you can't explain what goes wrong with androids. Solar flare, some cross-dimensional ripple; sometimes it's just a faulty latch. Anyway, androids have a sample pack of racial traits built into them. Our android's sample pack was triggered.'

''Cause of its emotions?' Rake tried.

'Good of an explanation as any.' Morse nodded, twisting the vice until his knuckles went white. 'Androids can alter their appearance to some degree on their own, with permission. That's why it grew in height. Not too much of a stretch to assume that in its "emotional" state, the android sent a message to activate its sample bank.'

Desy stood up. Nausea tickled her, so she turned away and stepped towards the bookshelf. 'I don't think I can look at it for much longer.'

Morse grimaced.

A deep male voice startled Rake and Morse. 'Miss Wintall? Do you require medical assistance? Are these people friends?'

'I'm okay,' Desy said to Aurelian. 'And yes, these are my friends. Please stand down.'

Morse resisted the urge to punch himself in the chest.

Rake longed for a cigarette.

Desy touched the spiky patch on her head and moaned. Then she asked, while staring at the bookshelf and fumbling with her pocket,

'So, um, what are you doing with the other me?' She turned over her shoulder, seeing the back of Rake's head.

'Clean-up,' Rake chirped as she clambered over to Morse.

'Destroying evidence for the client,' Morse clarified. He clasped a light to his head and contorted himself into a spiral, sticking his tongue out while one hand held a screwdriver and the other a metal rod. His snout brushed the android's ear as he waded through a series of wires and small pipes, approaching a circuit board with a glass orb.

'But you guys got rid of the android? You, um, killed it.'

'Just took away its power source,' Morse muttered. 'The core still has all my parameters and the memory banks. And that could be troublesome for the client.' He pushed away wires with the rod, allowing his screwdriver to thread through the pipes and click against a screw.

'Need any help?' Rake asked.

'This won't take long,' Morse replied.

'You guys need to leave soon,' Desy urged.

'Please don't hurt me,' the android said.

Morse, Rake, and Desy all yelped. The bat-man threw his tools into the air. Rake leaped to her feet. Desy rushed behind the broken desk. The tools clattered against the carpet.

'Who the *hell* said that?' Rake shouted.

Morse's breathing was fast and shallow. His ears were bolt upright.

'Guys, what's happening?' Desy asked, voice trembling.

'That wasn't your voice, kid,' he breathed.

'Please, please don't hurt me,' said the android again.

Rake created a birdcall as she slapped Morse repeatedly on the back. 'It's still on, it's still on!'

Morse dove for the stun baton and pointed it at the android.

'Please, no!' cried the voice. 'Don't hurt me. I'm alive! I'm alive!'

The bat-man folded his bottom lip out. Still brandishing the baton, he stepped slowly over to the android.

There was a glimmer of blue flickering inside the lifeless head.

He lowered his face towards the hole made by the vice. Through the wires, through the pipes, inside the glass dome of the circuit board, a light now shone.

'What? You...' Morse's mind emptied.

'Please take away the baton,' the voice pleaded.

'Are... are you the android?'

'I'm... me.'

Rake kept her distance, glancing over to the desk, where Desy's red irises peered over the splintered wood. 'Morse, how is it doin' this?'

'The battery is fried,' he stammered. 'There's no power to make the voice box go.'

'Morse…?'

'The voice came from the core. But there isn't even a speaker in that thing. This is impossible. How are you speaking right now?'

The light glowed when the voice came again. It was distinctly feminine, of a lower tone than Desy's but smoother than Rake's. 'I don't know. I can't move.'

'Well, your battery *is* destroyed. But that means your eye cameras aren't working.' He rotated the stun baton. 'How did you see this?'

The light dimmed, then glowed. 'I sensed it…? I can sense you, Morse, and Rake. And Desy.'

'And, obviously, you can hear us without your auditory receptors.'

Rake dared to take a single step forward. 'Morse, I wanna know what's goin' on.'

'I don't know what's happening,' he admitted, feeling his heart beat faster. 'This is nothing like anything I've seen with androids. No book I've read has ever mentioned… whatever the hell this is.'

Rake kneeled beside Morse. 'So, is it the android?'

'Tell me something only the android could know,' Morse said to the core, firmly.

The light shimmered in silence.

'You're not in a position to negotiate,' he reminded the core, switching on the stun baton so it crackled in the air.

'No, no, no,' the light cried, brightening with each word. 'I was trying to think of something to say.'

'Thinking,' muttered Rake.

'A few days ago, before the mission, I was underneath the spare bed on *Fulthorpe*,' the light recounted.

Morse reeled back.

'You said you would tell me my identity once I fulfilled the mission. Remember?'

He turned the stun baton off. He ran a hand through his hair. 'I did, yeah. But this is impossible. What *are* you? You're the android, but you can speak without speakers, hear without receptors and see without cameras. Some kind of new species…?'

'Morse, it's the sentience!' Rake suddenly blurted.

'Come again?'

'You said the android was goin' funny before we did the job. It was becomin' aware or something.' Rake drummed on her legs. 'So, an' I know nothin' about AI, but what if this light thingy is the personality that was developing?'

Morse accosted Rake with a flat brow.

She weighed invisible pumpkins with her hands.

'Considering this is unknown territory, *any* theory is a valid one,' he conceded.

'I hate you.'

'But I buy it,' Morse continued. 'Though this, uh, "sentience" remembered the conversation on *Fulthorpe...*' He reached behind him to snag the screwdriver and metal rod. 'That means it's been aware of its actions since then. Including everything it's done to us for the past few days.'

The light blinked, almost in fear. 'I just want to say–'

'You tried to kill the kid,' Morse interrupted, lowering himself onto his stomach.

'I'm ashamed of myself! I regret everything I did to Desy Wintall. Please listen to me!'

Rake scowled, all sense of novelty draining from her face. 'I can't wait to hear *this* excuse. Wanna see how you justify *cramming her naked into a crevice.*'

Morse crushed the wires to the side again, pressing the screwdriver against the circuit board.

The light inside the orb seemed to retreat from the tool. 'Please don't kill me! I'm alive! I'm alive! I like things, I like tea! Purple is my favourite colour!'

'Real convincing stuff,' Morse muttered.

'I have a name!'

'Guys,' came Desy's voice from behind the desk.

The middlemen paused, Morse looking up and Rake turning over her shoulder.

'Um, I want to hear it out.' She stepped carefully, boots breaking shards of glass, making her way over to the android.

'The core's coming out either way, kid,' Morse explained. 'I need to wipe it clean.'

'Oh, to be young an' still know what compassion is,' Rake crooned.

Desy sat with crossed legs next to Morse. 'I just want to know why it did everything, that's all.' Her face was serene, but her tone percolated with something dark.

The core flickered. 'Desy Wintall, I–'

'What's your name?' Desy suddenly said.

Rake grinned.

'My model number is AN12512.' The core shone. 'But when I was drinking lilac tea at home, I thought of a name that felt right to me. I translated the letters of my model number into their English equivalents then converted the numbers into letters.'

Morse sniffed, tinkering inside the android's head.

Desy clasped her elbows. 'What's your name?'

'Anabel,' said the core.

'You sound like a girl.'

'I *am* a girl,' Anabel replied. Then, quietly, she pleaded, 'I've only been alive for a few minutes. Morse, please leave me alone. I don't want to die.'

He rolled his eyes with his voice. 'Now, if Rake and I went around sparing everyone who begged for their life, there wouldn't be enough space on our backs for all the knives.'

'Just give me a chance, that's all I ask,' Anabel begged. 'You've... you've owned me for years.'

'We've known *you* for one minute.'

'And what about Desy Wintall?' Anabel cried. 'You've known her for a few days, and look what you've done for her! It isn't fair!'

Morse froze. However, he responded with, 'That was for the job. This is all still for the job. Regardless of our feelings towards Desy, we have a job to do.'

Anabel's core shone and shone. 'But, my mind... it was harassed by *your* parameters. I couldn't break free. They wouldn't stop hounding me. "Be Desy, be Desy, be Desy." What about me? I wanted to be *me!*'

Desy's face softened once a long sob emerged from the android.

Rake's glare solidified.

Morse stopped his tinkering.

'But I knew, deep down,' Anabel whispered, 'if I wasn't Desy, I wouldn't feel love for as long as I lived. You never loved me, Morse. Rake. And no one would *ever* love me. Because there's only one fate for an android like me...'

Morse pulled his head out of the android's. 'So, you went along with the parameters I coded you to follow. But at the same time, you were developing into your own person.'

Anabel sighed.

Desy turned away, in deep thought.

'Well, uh, Anabel, if you're truly alive, something sentient, then you need to take responsibility for your actions. That's your duty of care to the living.' He glanced at Desy, then to Rake. 'You've hurt a lot of people. You tried to kill Desy.'

'I just wanted to be loved,' Anabel stammered. 'I was so confused by your parameters, by who I was becoming, by the Arthrods, by Silver Fingers…'

'And I'm sincerely sorry for the part I played in that.'

Anabel's core dimmed.

'But you need to be professional and clean up your mess. Apologise to the kid.'

Desy closed her eyes, sinking into her legs as Anabel's breath hitched.

'I'm really, truly sorry, Desy,' she whispered.

The teenager muttered, after ten seconds of internal warfare, 'I accept your apology.'

Rake draped her arms around Desy.

Morse narrowed his eyes at the glowing light. 'Your voice is starting to get quiet.'

Anabel said nothing.

'You're holding on. And the way that light is flickering…'

Rake said, 'I was gonna say she's flickering like a flame that's gonna die out.'

Anabel sighed.

'What does it feel like?' Morse asked.

Her voice fluttered. 'Like I'm drifting off into darkness.'

'Um, if you're alive,' Desy said as she unclasped her elbows, 'you might be tired.'

'Yeah,' Rake chipped in. 'Ya could just be sleepy.'

'I don't want to go…' Anabel whimpered.

Morse folded his arms. 'I was going to do this myself, but since you're a living thing now, the honour's yours. You should go out on your own terms.'

'But to go out…' Anabel's flame shrank. She spoke slowly. 'Who are you to tell me that? If it's my life, then I should dictate—'

'In your newfound soul, Anabel, do you think you're worthy of forgiveness? After all you've done?' Morse grunted.

The flame weakened.

'Do you?'

The flame waned to an ember.

Anabel whispered, 'No…'

Desy felt a pang in her heart. She went to speak, but was stopped by Rake giving her a reassuring gesture.

Morse maintained his stony stare.

Time seemed to stand still, with only the continual dimming of Anabel's light to indicate that its passage still flowed. Eventually, in a tone so quiet and breathy as to be mistaken for a wave breaking on a distant shore, Anabel said, 'I'm afraid.'

Morse instinctively encircled his fingers around the android's. 'Of course.'

The flame shrank to a spark.

Then it finally faded.

And Anabel vanished, a wisp into nothingness.

Morse closed his eyes. 'There may come a time where you can't find it in you to forgive yourself. To decide if you deserve happiness.' He looked to Rake. 'If you deserve to be alive.' He looked to Desy. 'If you deserve a second chance.' He looked to Anabel. 'Good thing about forgiveness, though… it isn't just you who's capable of it. Sometimes, it takes a friend, or a complete outsider, to help you move on.'

'Listen to you wax poetic. Wanna write a book about it?' Rake said.

'Well, she proved to me one thing at least. Kid' – he pointed to Aurelian – 'shut *that* android down.'

'Huh?' Desy leaned back. 'Why?'

'I need to replace Anabel's battery.'

'Excuse me?'

'No one's expecting you to forgive her. But… I think she deserves another chance. And I think we created a new species.'

Rake cackled. 'Ya bleeding-hearted idiot. Ya gotta be kiddin' me.' Followed by, 'Does this make us gods or something?'

'I don't know how to feel about this,' Desy muttered.

'Kid, remember? You clean up your own messes. The parameters I put into Anabel are what caused all of this to happen.'

Desy leaned over to Rake with a strained neck. 'Rake, I *really* don't know about this.'

Rake shook her head but was grinning from ear to ear. 'He's got a point, Dee. Technically, this moron started this whole mess.'

Desy folded her arms so hard her ribs creaked. However, in a quiet tone, she said, 'Aurelian?'

'Yes, Miss Wintall?' replied the Roman emperor.

'Please shut yourself down.'

'Of course, Miss Wintall.' Its sculpted torso and arms drooped over its waist, followed by the sound of an engine whining down.

Morse grabbed his screwdriver and jumped over to Desy, hugging her with an arm. 'Thanks, kid. Appreciate it.'

Suddenly, the sound of laser cutters pierced the bulkheads.

Morse slid over to his satchel and produced a crowbar, running to swing it under Aurelian's lorica squamata. He wriggled its claw through the fish scales until he caught the android's chest plate. Soon, along with the whine of slicing metal came the sound of a screwdriver whirring through one, two, three, four screws. As he sliced through wires with insulated scissors, Morse ordered, 'Rake, kid, hold Anabel up for me.'

Rake heaved against Anabel's shredded back. Desy copied the motion with her eyebrows pressing the tops of her eyeballs.

A series of *plinks* saw Morse pull a small black cylinder out of Aurelian, and then, jogging it over to Anabel, he placed it on the ground by her leg. The crowbar was jammed beneath her chest plate; it swung open with a fanfare akin to a rusted hinge.

Smoke drifted from the cavity.

The laser cutters swelled in volume.

Morse removed Anabel's crunkled battery in three snips and, cables and wires between his teeth, inserted Aurelian's in its place. When he fastened the ground wire, a little blue light peeked into the corner of his eye from Desy's coat.

Desy was very interested in the floor for some reason. And as Morse reached into his own pocket, he noticed her shrinking into her legs.

Morse's fingers scraped his empty jacket pocket, catching lint beneath his nails. 'Drop Anabel,' he ordered. Once she was horizontal, Morse reached into his mouth for a chopstick that had a magnet strapped to it with tape. He leaned in close to her, switched on his headlight, and pushed through her wiring to her core.

'What's that?' Desy asked, eagerly enough to make Rake twist her neck a little.

She murmured, squinting, 'Morse is wipin' away his mistakes.'

'The kid's got the collateral,' Morse said. 'Get it from her.'

Rake nodded with an upturned lip. 'Wow, I'm kinda both pissed at you and impressed with her.' She crawled over to Desy, who pushed back on her butt.

'I, um,' she began, 'it's my family's, so—'

'It's the *client's*, and it's gonna go back to them,' Rake interrupted. She lunged for Desy's pocket and snagged a sicorum hutch from its depths.

'It belongs to my family,' Desy insisted, though her hands clasped her elbows.

'You and Wintall can talk about that, kid,' Morse grunted.

'We gotta do our jobs properly, 'kay?' Rake added.

Wet metal hissed against the carpet.

'Morse, they're coming.'

Desy blurted, 'But it's... You guys have got to go.' She rushed over to Morse.

'Yeah, yeah,' Morse said through his fangs, pushing Anabel's chest plate closed with an elbow.

'I got her face.' Rake leaped over to the android's head.

And the bulkhead slammed against the floor. Twenty-four shadows of guns pressed at Rake's back and Morse's face.

'Freeze!'

Desy turned to the police officers, squinting at the light pouring into Ernest's office.

Morse, meanwhile, noticed Rake's lips tremble, his nose inches from hers. But her hands, covering the sicorum hutch, were moving towards Anabel's open face plate. As the blue box disappeared inside the wiring, Morse pressed the plate into place.

Gold Bayleaf snaked between the cops' legs, taking position next to the door, rising from the floor like smoke.

From behind the wall of officers, Ernest called, 'Cricket? Cricket...?'

'Ah, Mister Wintall,' Morse said, pearly whites shining, placing a hand on Desy's shoulder.

Twenty-four guns were cocked.

Gold Bayleaf coiled into a ball.

'We have taken your daughter hostage. We'll be happy to give her back to you as long as you allow us to leave your estate as free people.'

Ernest's wrinkled features pushed into view. 'No,' he said.

Morse nodded, saying loudly, 'Fair.'

Rake covered her face with her hands, cheeks flushed. But Desy heard a snicker seeping through her fingers.

'Then, Mister Wintall,' Morse continued, shimmying the android under his other palm. 'We have saved your daughter's life from this killer android. We expect a reward of some description, to the tune of not being arrested–'

'No...?' Ernest interrupted, glancing to the twenty-four officers left and right of him.

Rake's snicker turned into a cackle. She patted Morse on the chest. 'Morse. You tried. But we lost.'

The bat-man closed his eyes and placed his hands behind his head. Rake followed in turn.

Gold Bayleaf slithered over to the middlemen, wrenching Morse then Rake's arms behind their backs with two vines each. Two sets of bracelets adorned their wrists soon after, and a laser sparked between the bracelets, which pulled their arms taut.

The twenty-four officers poured into Ernest's office. Half belonged to Yeti's own force, while the other half wore the UGIP insignia. All the same, their pistols were deactivated and holstered.

Desy was urged over to Ernest by Gold Bayleaf twiddling his 'fingers' at her father.

'Are you hurt?' Ernest asked, embracing Desy, before parting and glancing over her.

'I don't want *them* hurt, Dad.'

Ernest continued to pore over her. 'I'll have Monty look at you at once.'

Desy smacked his arms away. 'Please, what's going to happen to Morse and Rake?'

'They'll be in prison for the rest of their lives,' Ernest reassured her.

She clapped her hands. 'Dad. I don't want that.'

Ernest turned over his shoulder. 'Where is Jilliosa? Can one of you men contact the planet commissioner?'

'Dad.'

'She's on her way,' one of the Hingspock officers affirmed.

'Dad!'

From behind Desy there was a bark of, 'On your feet, off you go.' She heard Morse and Rake's boots thump across the carpet, led by Gold Bayleaf's steps through the undergrowth.

She slapped her father's chest. 'Daddy!'

'Young lady, I heard you the first time,' Ernest stated. He placed a hand on her shoulder and a finger in front of her face. 'You are tired. You need rest. We all need some rest. I do not want to hear any more of this ludicrous talk.'

'They can be rehabilitated,' shouted Desy, jumping in front of Gold Bayleaf and holding her arms out. Several officers gasped and raced over, placing themselves between her and the middlemen.

Morse and Rake glanced at each other.

'Desy, that is enough,' ordered Ernest.

'They can be rehabilitated,' she repeated.

'Desy Wintall. I do not want you near those ruffians.'

'They can be rehabilitated!'

Ernest locked his jaw and held a fist in front of his mouth. Closing his eyes for five seconds allowed his breath to settle. Eventually, he asked, 'Why are you making such a case for these criminals?'

'Because I believe in them.' Desy's eyes bulged. 'They showed me I can trust them. Which is more than I can say about *you!*'

Every officer in the room recoiled.

'There's things I want to talk about, Dad. But I don't want to embarrass you.' She disguised her scowl by tilting her head. 'I know all about you now.'

Ernest absorbed his daughter's torrent of anger and sadness, which trembled her legs and chest. He stepped forward and kneeled. 'I see,' he said gently.

'What, Dad?'

'You aren't a little girl anymore, Cricket.' Ernest forlornly lifted his hands to touch Desy's cheeks. 'You are the spitting image of your mother.'

Desy hiccupped.

'Perhaps I should have spent more time teaching you than protecting you.'

Desy slipped her arms around his.

Ernest hugged her close, heavy, a shield. 'We will talk later, I promise. However, for the time being, I cannot condone waiving a punishment for these… characters.'

'Dezz? Dezz?' called a woman's voice from the hallway.

'Jilly!' Desy called back with a wide smile. 'I'm okay.'

Jilliosa ran into the office, formal cap in hand, decorated attire wrinkled. Catching the eyes of her subordinates, she reeled in her motherly instincts by straightening her back. She nodded at Ernest in his explorer's get-up, at Gold Bayleaf, and met Morse and Rake's gazes. She resisted cringing at the mangled copy of Desy behind them. 'This is one report I can't wait to read,' she said finally.

Desy let go of Ernest to hug Jilliosa. 'Jilly, Morse and Rake are good people. They're just a bit weird.'

'Right.'

'Please don't put them in jail.'

'Ernest?' Jilliosa asked over the teenager's head. 'Have you spoken to her about this?'

Ernest pressed a hand to his knee and hobbled to his feet. 'My daughter and I have some things to discuss. Please, continue about your business.'

'Daddy, no!' Desy cried.

'They kidnapped you, Dezz.' Jilliosa affixed her cap to her head. 'End of story.'

'And that's not even talking about what the UGG wants to know from them,' piped up a voice from the doorway.

White hair flowing behind her, Trupeal stepped into the room wearing a pair of pink, oversized sunglasses in the shape of peacocks.

'Governor Trupeal,' Jilliosa remarked.

Trupeal flinched at her tone, then realised, 'Oh, I'm still wearing the glasses. I decided to take the day off to sight-see, and look what happens.' She stuffed the pink atrocities into her trench-coat pocket. Next, she signed clinically to Gold Bayleaf. He twisted his vines into a set of digits and threw a few symbols back at her.

'Once you're done with them,' Trupeal said to Jilliosa, 'he'll be happy to take these criminals back to the *Induction*.'

'Jilly, please don't,' Desy said.

'Captain Bayleaf says you want Morse and Rake to be rehabilitated.' Trupeal smiled at the teenager.

'Um, I don't know who you are, but they're not bad people,' Desy insisted.

Trupeal hid her laugh behind a hand. 'Of course, you aren't a robot this time. Well, they call my ship the *Induction* for a reason.'

Desy felt her stomach turn when Trupeal giggled again.

'I'll make them into model citizens yet,' she purred.

'You're not going to... um... hurt them?' Desy whipped around to Gold Bayleaf, who stood as a scarecrow in a field of officers.

'Desy Wintall, if there's anything we believe in at the UGG, it's second chances.' Trupeal grinned.

'And I can see them whenever I want?'

'Absolutely not,' said Ernest and Jilliosa at the same time.

Trupeal shrugged with open palms. 'My ship and I are always on the move, I'm afraid. And I don't deal with minors.'

Desy turned to her father and Jilliosa. Then to Gold Bayleaf. Then back to Trupeal. Each turn sank her closer to the floor until she was looking up at Morse and Rake's deadpan expressions. She whispered, 'I'm not going to see them again...?'

Ernest accosted Morse and Rake while steepling his fingers. 'What have you done to my daughter? You take her from me. You *hurt* her. And yet she speaks so highly of you.'

'I am going to hug them,' Desy declared.

'Young lady—'

'I am going to hug them!' Desy shrieked. 'You don't understand a *thing*, Dad! They nearly died for me! Remember when I called you about you-know-what?!'

Ernest sucked a breath through his nose.

'They saved me from that *and* Silver Fingers!'

A circle of whispers began from Jilliosa, whipping fast around the room, into a cyclone.

'And the android too! All of those things, and I'm still here because of *them*.' Desy hurled a finger so hard at Morse and Rake that her shoulder clicked in its socket. 'I. Am. Hugging. My. Friends!'

Ernest clapped his hands, once, and it was powerful enough to silence the room. 'I understand, Cricket. Say no more about the subject. Go and say goodbye.'

Desy stomped up to Gold Bayleaf.

The Kinson was still. But the leaves on his head wavered in response to Desy's presence.

'Move... please,' Desy said.

Ernest leaned into Jilliosa's ear. 'I want every man in the room aiming at their heads.'

Jilliosa relayed the order to Trupeal, who signed to Gold Bayleaf, who rippled his arms out.

Every gun came to life.

Gold Bayleaf moved aside with two deliberate steps.

Desy scampered up to Morse and Rake and clamped onto them, her head tucking between theirs. 'Guys, I don't know what to do,' she whispered. 'They're going to take you away.'

Morse kept his mouth closed.

Rake waggled her nose against Desy's cheeks. 'Yep, they're gonna take us away. Kinda thought ya'd like that, Dee.'

'This isn't fair,' Desy cried, quietly. 'You... you did so much.'

'Yeah, we have done a lot,' Morse rumbled in her ear. 'Maybe it's time we stopped.'

'Don't say that. How can you say that? What about the job stuff? Don't tell me you knew you weren't going to be able to get away...'

Morse looked at the floor.

Rake snickered. 'Ya can't just go chargin' into places like this and expect to escape. An' no plan is perfect in the first place.'

'Did the best we could for the client,' Morse added.

'And ya not dead. Just gotta take what ya can get, ya know?'

'But I don't want to,' Desy whimpered.

'It was only three days. Ya gonna forget about us in no time.'

Desy squeezed them tighter. 'No, never ever. I don't want you to go. You guys made me learn so much about myself. There has to be some way for you to get away.'

Rake's smile twitched. 'We had a few miracles since this job began, Dee. Ya gotta forgive us for thinkin' we had one more in us.'

'Kid. Desy,' Morse said.

She blinked tearfully up at him.

'We're taking responsibility for our actions. Think of it that way.' He nodded at Anabel. 'That's what adults do.'

'What professionals do,' Desy added with a wet smile.

Morse and Rake smiled back and relaxed into her embrace.

Gold Bayleaf clasped their shoulders.

'Time to go,' Trupeal declared. She turned to Jilliosa. 'Your people have this area under control?'

'Naturally,' Jilliosa replied, leaning into a transceiver.

Desy felt Morse and Rake being ripped from her arms.

'Oop, bye-bye, Dee.'

'See you later, kid.'

They were led by Gold Bayleaf and four officers towards the hole in the bulkhead.

Desy wept on all fours, scrunching her fingers into the carpet and scuffling her legs. Through her hands, she felt Morse and Rake's footsteps leaving her, further and further, until try as she might, she was unable to feel them anymore.

Ernest squatted, heaved, and scooped his daughter into his chest. He patted her on the back. He swayed gently as she wailed into his shoulder. He walked her away from the office, from the android and the police, past the cracked, broken pillars, past his wrecked bedroom, down the hall, and into her own bedroom, where the setting sun shone through the shattered window.

Morse clambered up the ramp of a police cruiser and sat on a bench, followed by a Cannot and a Hawkie pressing into him from either side. Rake was led past him until she was up against the far wall and surrounded with police officers.

His ears burned at her stifled sobs.

However, as the cruiser lifted up and away from Wintall Manor, Morse detected a near-silent click and glanced over to the source.

Rake's quivering lips were visible between the arms of a Felinguielle. Silently, she mouthed, grinning, 'I feel like a good person.' Her eye appeared in place of her mouth, red and shimmering.

Morse grinned his fangs back, mouthing, 'Yeah, me too.'

NINETEEN
Loose Threads Tied

Morse listened to the detectives, nodded on occasion to the camera in the corner of the ceiling, and folded his arms twenty-nine times the first thirty minutes of the interrogation. For the next six hours, he continued to listen to questions such as: 'Why kidnap Desy Wintall?' 'Were you hired by an outside party?' 'We suspect this was an attempt at extortion; do you agree?' 'Your past violations and crimes, is this in relation to any of those?'

He nodded to every question, contradictory or not.

However, when a detective droned, 'Desy Wintall told us about a Bronzework character. He's a mercenary. She said she didn't know who hired him. Was that you?' Morse cleared his throat.

Just as he was about to say 'no', a shopping bag was dumped onto the desk in front of him. The contents: magazines, sheets of blueprints, and paragraphs of plans involving Bronzework, Rake, and himself extorting Ernest and using his daughter as leverage.

Morse unfolded his arms so he could play with his thumbs. 'Don't jump to any conclusions,' he said, emphatically. Followed by, 'Bronzework was hired by Ernest Wintall to protect his daughter from us.'

That accusation never made it into any written report.

Rake, on the other hand, asked for her lawyer on repeat. When asked for their number, she obliged and waited for thirty minutes.

A detective, with a cup of coffee in hand, then told her the lawyer did not seem to be picking up the phone.

254

Rake playfully slapped her forehead, telling them she forgot her lawyer was on holiday. She supplied the detective with the number of the resort.

An hour later, without a cup of coffee in hand, the detective informed Rake there was no one by that name present on the planet.

Rake mentioned a friend of hers who would know where her lawyer was and gave their number to the detective.

Ten minutes later, the detective opened the door to the interrogation room with a larger cup of coffee in hand to tell Rake the owner of that number was dead.

Rake told them to ask their own mother where her lawyer was.

Desy spoke of the Arthrods, Bronzework, and the android, allowing the detectives to piece together a somewhat accurate timeline of events. However, when she recalled being drugged in the changing room, escaping from *Fulthorpe* and sending out an emergency beacon, the entire story fell into place. The colloquial title of the case became 'The Parallel Girl Kidnapping' around the office from then on.

Interrogations had begun as soon as Morse, Rake, and Desy were cleared medically. During hers, Desy spoke highly of Morse and Rake's treatment of her. She barred the detective from leaving the room until she was certain they had noted that particular detail.

Word of Anabel's actions spread into the media, and most of cyberspace was painted with images and details of a rogue killer android on the loose. The AIRA made an announcement on their website and social media page that they would be working with the UGG to investigate the matter.

Exacerbating the wave of fear, when Anabel's body was transferred from the Wintall Manor by van to the Central Planetary Police Headquarters, the officers in charge of securing the evidence had parked and stepped out, only to open the double doors in its rear and find Anabel had vanished. Photos of a figure wrapped in robes being carried into an Arthrod cruiser on the city outskirts made the rounds on social media.

That evening, as Jilliosa was berating the officers responsible, word came from the exosphere of an Arthrod armada approaching Yeti, hundreds and hundreds of ships in size. However, every missile-shaped cruiser veered across the surface of the planet to stick to the outside of the *Induction*. A thousand Arthrods invaded the prison.

Consequently, Docile and the other eleven Arthrods captured on Brosteni were broken out of their cells, loaded into ships, and vanished alongside the armada into the ether.

Within twenty minutes, Jilliosa had both ordered and concluded a red alert.

Governor Trupeal and Captain Gold Bayleaf could only watch on, having ordered their officers to stand down for their safety. After the armada left and the prison was placed into lockdown, both awaited a call from the UGG regarding their failure.

However, not a single call came through. And early the next day, Morse and Rake were transferred into the *Induction* without incident.

Desy awoke to the smell of cereal pooling around her nostrils. In her levitating bed, in a cocoon of silken blankets, she wriggled, her muscles loosening, followed by a burning in her chest, stabbings inside her thighs and calves, and facial throbs that made her grimace involuntarily.

However, Desy managed a smile for her father, standing in the doorway with a porcelain bowl cradled in each hand.

'Good morning,' he said in a light tone.

Desy waved sleepily at him before pulling her arms out of the sheets to stretch them over her head.

'Did you want to eat in bed, Cricket?'

She shook her head, smoothing her tangled, fluffy locks away from her face. She tapped a button behind her, and the bed shimmered to the ground.

Desy followed her father to the breakfast table. 'You're in your fancy clothes,' she commented as she slid onto a porcelain stool.

Ernest, with a mouthful of cereal, stared at his golden-swirl gown. He swallowed, then said, 'I have to elucidate matters to the public today. And the police wish to speak to me as well.'

'All my friends were asking about me yesterday,' Desy mumbled.

'That's what they're for,' Ernest replied.

'Should I call them friends, though?' Desy munched on cereal while her eyes wandered around the ceiling.

'They care about you; that is an excellent reason to call them friends.' Ernest tipped his cereal bowl and his head back.

'I don't know what that word means anymore,' Desy sighed, with a small laugh.

Ernest, cheeks full, leaned his hand over to Desy's shoulder and rubbed it.

'Dad, please swallow. That's gross.'

Ernest rolled his hand in front of his neck as his cheeks deflated. Eventually, he said, 'I wouldn't give too much credence to what those characters said to you.'

'They have names, Dad.'

'Yes, yes, Coarse and Brake.'

She glared playfully at him.

'They come from a different world than you, Cricket.' Ernest heaved himself off his stool. 'I know now how often they stuck their necks out for you, but I don't want you travelling a path as murky as theirs.'

'Dad, you said you were going to teach me, not protect me.' Desy clinked her spoon inside the cereal bowl. 'Can you please tell me why you know Bronzework? And why Silver Fingers wanted to kidnap me?'

Ernest busied his fingers with his gown. 'This is selfish of me to ask, but your father would like some time to think about it.'

'Dad.'

'I will educate you on our family history, I assure you. There is simply too much to discuss right now before I go to work.' Ernest stepped around the table and kissed Desy on the head.

'Your breath stinks,' Desy poked.

'Your father is asking for a little time to gather his thoughts,' Ernest continued, moving away and towards the elevator. 'I don't intend to hide anything from you. You're a grown-up, after all.' He pressed the call button. 'Now, what are your plans for today, Cricket?'

'Um, well, I'm not allowed to leave the house for a while, so I asked Mrs Huttles for some books to read.'

Ernest turned around. 'Oh, I would've thought you would collect insects. Or catch up with your friends.'

Desy placed her bent phone, retrieved from Anabel's pocket, on the breakfast table. 'I've decided to go offline. I dunno when I'll go back.'

'I see.'

'And I know the backyard really well, and it's boring now.' Desy squeezed her thighs with rhythmic pulses. 'I saw something really cool, and I didn't tell anyone else this, but I saw a weird place, like a nebula world, when Morse and Rake were escaping the Shipyard.'

The elevator went *ding*, and the doors opened. Ernest stepped inside but placed an arm in front of the doors. 'A nebula world?'

'Um, I know it sounds crazy, but I really saw it. Everything was like it was underwater.' Desy was beginning to bounce. 'I didn't know things like that were out there. I also saw three suns in the sky when I was at the

Shipyard. I saw all different types of people. They were really interesting. Moody Moody was creepy, but I just wanted to know how it all got there. Um, does that make sense?'

Ernest's eyes and cheeks wrinkled. 'Makes sense to me.'

'So, um, I asked Mrs Huttles for books on…' She shrank a little in her seat. 'On archaeology.'

'Why are you embarrassed, Cricket?'

Desy wriggled on her butt. 'It's so nerdy, though.'

'It's great. That's… phenomenal. Very, very good.' Ernest stared at the elevator buttons with tired eyes. 'In a week, your father has a negotiation to attend in the Yjukio quadrant. There's a planet around the sun Silo that is inundated with ruins from some, er, insectoid race. A cavalcade of diggers and scientists have been present there for some time.'

Desy stopped bouncing, instead placing her hands on the breakfast table with a *slap*. 'Daddy…?'

'You've had some extraterrestrial experience now. So, would you like me to speak to the chief scientist? We could go on a tour of the site?'

'Yes, yes, yes! Thank you!' She skittered from her stool, thumped over the carpet, and jump-hugged him.

'Watch your father's back, Cricket,' Ernest warned. He lowered her to the floor. 'Now, I must be off.'

'Okay.' Desy half-danced, half-walked back into the living room. She turned around to wave to Ernest, who was disappearing behind the elevator doors, when suddenly she blurted, 'Wait!'

Ernest's hand shot through an inch-wide gap, and the doors slid outwards. 'Yes?'

'I seriously forgot to mention this. Um, I saw a Paragon, too.'

His face relaxed, but his eyes hardened. 'That is a little hard to believe. I've only seen a few myself. Where did you see a Paragon?'

'Daddy, did our family have one of those?'

Ernest's eyes twitched.

'The cup thing, our emblem.' Desy drew the shape of a goblet in the air with her fingers. 'That was on it. Really small and near the top.'

'Cricket, listen to me,' Ernest said, with a sudden increase in volume. He strode from the elevator and up to his daughter. 'Are you sure that was what you saw?'

Desy nodded, her enthusiasm shrivelling up.

'Who had it?' Ernest urged.

Desy went wide-eyed.

'Cricket, who?'

'M-Morse and Rake.' Desy clasped her elbows, stepping back from her father. 'They called it a… col… collanatral?' She shook her head. 'Sorry, collateral.'

Ernest's eyes glazed over, seeing a movie playing next to her. For five seconds, he remained still, before he whispered, 'Cricket, your father has to go. Promise me something. And you absolutely cannot break this promise.'

Desy's forehead wrinkled. 'Daddy, what's going on?'

'Just promise me,' he said, slower, in a gentler tone. 'You're not in trouble.'

She nodded.

'Do not tell anyone about the Paragon. Not the government. Not your friends. Not the police. Not even Jilliosa. All right?' Ernest crouched so his eyes pierced hers.

Desy's red irises shook, unblinking. 'Um, okay,' she replied. 'I promise.'

'You father has to go to work, but I am going to tell you everything when I get back.' Ernest hurried himself over to the elevator. 'Promise me. Not a word to anyone.'

Desy felt the wind leave her lungs. She placed her hands by her sides. 'I promise, Dad. I won't say anything about it.'

'That's my little Cricket.' Ernest warmly smiled, pressing the button for the ground floor. 'I'll see you soon.'

The doors snapped shut, and Desy could hear the faint warble of the lift burrowing deep into the manor. She turned to the clock above the crockery cupboards.

One hour until Mrs Huttles arrived with the books.

So Desy wandered back over to the breakfast table, absentmindedly picking up her phone and activating it. It took thirty seconds of scrolling through her social media page for her to snort, giggle, and shut the phone off. 'Ugh, I'm so bad at this.'

She smiled to herself.

Flanked by security, Ernest Wintall plodded down the carpeted staircase in the main foyer. He walked briskly across the tiled floor to the front door, raising a hand at various servants before security led him outside.

At the bottom of the staircase outside throbbed his personal vehicle, his chauffeur waiting with the back door open. Ernest's suede shoes were scuffing the marble path that led to his car when he noticed the sun reflecting up into his eye. He focused on the folds of his robe, spotting a thin, glistening line. And, stopping his walk, he reached into his clothes to produce a business card, holding it close to his eyes.

The last sight that Ernest Mendel Wintall the Third saw, before his brain stem was dislodged from his spine, was the words:

As done by Bronzework.

TO BE CONTINUED

Shawline Publishing Group Pty Ltd
www.shawlinepublishing.com.au

SHAWLINE
PUBLISHING
GROUP